USS Hamilton
Broadsides

Mark Wayne McGinnis

Other Books By MWM

Copyright

Published by:
Avenstar Productions

ISBN: 978-1-7350108-6-1

To join Mark's mailing list, jump to:
http://eepurl.com/bs7M9r

Visit Mark Wayne McGinnis at:
http://www.markwaynemcginnis.com

Prologue

Pleidian Weonan Frontier Territory
Brillianne Bridge

Fleet Commander Twinwon

Fleet Commander Twinwon was not one to panic. To panic was not the way of the Pleidian Weonan. He took a moment to breathe . . . to find his center and still his racing mind. With a Bridge crew of thirty, the compartment was relatively quiet considering the circumstances. For a third time, he considered simply turning about and making a stand. To fight with honor – even against such overwhelming odds. How had he been caught so off guard?

Simple . . . the Grish had been cunning. Cunning and patient. And now, this enemy fleet of eighteen powerful warships had boxed them in. No, escape would be their only hope.

But how? His ship, the Brillianne, was battle-damaged with drives incapable of reaching FTL output; manufacturing a jump wormhole was out of the question.

Twinwon turned away from the high mounted logistical display and brought his full attention onto Haite Caheil. Trusting the Varapin pilot had always been a risk. The frightening-looking alien was a ruthless killer – he'd proven as much onboard Hamilton four months prior. But, thus far, he had kept to his word. He had delivered on his promise to assist the Alliance – while siding against his own kind.

The destruction of the supposedly indestructible Varapin fleet, months earlier, had yielded both adulation and criticism for the humans; the latter for bringing the Alliance (Humans, Thine, and Pleidian Weonan) into a war with an enemy that had already conquered one galaxy, Andromeda, and had their sights on another: the Milky Way.

Recently, there had been reports and sightings of strange-looking spacecraft within the far outskirts of Pleidian Weonan territory. Sightings of bird-like crafts, dark, with swooping wings and extended nose-like prows. Because of his stellar battle record and good standing with Empress Shawlee Tee, Fleet Commander Twinwon had been the easy choice to command the small fleet of five warships – to venture out into that distant and often contested frontier Pleidian territory. Thus far, no Varapin warships had been encountered, only the Grish, and in just three days, they had decimated his fleet. It was by sheer chance they'd managed to evade the same fate as the four other Pleidian assets within his small battle group.

"It was almost as if the Grish had had prior knowledge of our arrival here within frontier space," Twinwon said.

Haite's voice was high-pitched and grating, "Is that an accusation, Fleet Commander? That I set all this up just so I too would die at the hands of these foul piglets?"

Twinwon suspected the derogatory term had first been coined by Captain Quintos . . . or maybe his ridiculous ChronoBot, Hardy. Both had a strange sense of humor. Although, after a quick database search of Earth's swine species, Twinwon found the Grish to indeed look quite similar to pigs or piglets. He now thought about Quintos, currently on Earth behind bars awaiting his court-martial trial. The human was nothing less than a hero. There was much that Twinwon didn't understand about Humans.

Twinwon said, "These piglets, the Grish, are closing in on our coordinates as we speak. For the Pleidian Weonan to allow your presence onboard the Brillianne was no simple feat. So, tell me, Varapin pilot . . . how would you escape this predicament?"

"I would not have fallen into the Grish's trap in the first place . . . there were early indications . . . subtle telltale signs, that you missed. For one, the total lack of interstellar traffic within an area typically bustling with commerce. Then there were those destroyed communications hubs, four of them. Comms hubs that are used by all, no? And finally, you should have abandoned this mission the moment you encountered that far larger Grish fleet; instead, you chose to make a stand and fight. Your reliance on higher advanced technology than that of your enemy clouded good judgment. Five against eighteen . . . you were a fool not to run when you had the chance."

Twinwon resisted the temptation to have the insolent alien killed where he stood. But Haite was right. The Pleidian Weonans were indeed arrogant when it came to their technological prowess, and now, most probably, he would pay the price with his life – and that of his crew's. "You still haven't answered my question, pilot . . . how would you get out of this mess?"

"I have only one ludicrous idea to offer you. I assure you; the odds of survival will not be good. But . . . there is a way.""

Chapter 1

And so, here I sat. After three months, day by day, my jail cell seemingly growing smaller and smaller, while my frustration with the situation growing in magnitude. Having been brought up on formal charges, my counsel had assured me this court-martial would never actually go to trial. Not so much because I was innocent (*I wasn't*), but because public opinion was so heavily weighted in my favor. With the destruction of the advancing Varapin fleet there within that vast expanse between the Andromeda and Milky Way Galaxy's, at saving Earth from unimaginable terror, I had become somewhat of a celebrity.

My charged crime? I'd fired a flurry of smart missiles toward the *USS Brave*, a Corvette warship literally crawling with Varapin Warriors sucking the life force from a crew of close to five hundred. A desperate, pleading communique from the vessel's skipper had beckoned me to destroy the ship – and to do so before those few remaining on the Bridge were also abhorrently, torturously, dishonored. It was a foregone conclusion that what remained of the crew was already lost. Above and beyond the loss of life, there was advanced technology onboard that vessel the Alliance could ill afford to hand over to the enemy. So, it wasn't so much that I had given the order to destroy the *Brave*; it was destroying her while able-bodied men and women were still inhabiting her – that was the issue.

What was most surprising to me – in a kind of déjà vu moment – was recently receiving my second U.S. Space-Navy Silver Star accommodation from none other than EUNF U.S. Space-Navy's Executive Five Star Fleet Admiral, Cyprian Block. My first Silver Star had been awarded just as unceremoniously while recuperating from near-fatal battle injuries at Walter Reed National Military Medical Center several months ago.

This latest ceremony took place right here within my cell, and again, it was a small Senior Office contingent led by Admiral Block doing the honors. Again, it is my belief that public pressure had influenced the decision. Except for my mentor and friend, Admiral Block, I'm pretty much unanimously disliked amongst most military hierarchy. According to most higher-ranking officers, my leadership style is overtly casual, my adherence to proper Space-Navy protocol is near non-existent, and my propensity for showboating – taking dangerous risks – are becoming unacceptable. Block had let me read my own ever-growing personnel file, probably in hopes I'd change my contemptible ways.

What I did notice was most of the negative reporting had

come from none other than Captain Eli Tannock. He, while acting as my XO upon *Hamilton's* Bridge, had filed the formal charges against me.

This was no surprise. On our first mission together, he'd suffered a head injury, and I replaced him as Captain. His style was old-school - cross every T, dot every I - and mine was . . . well, *not*. Aside from taking his seat at Captain's Mount, I'd been successful, despite my somewhat cowboy approach. Last mission, he was assigned as my XO, which was likely humiliation enough without my having embarrassed his best friend, Chaplain Trent, by having him thrown in the Brig. Just temporarily, but still . . . Tannock wasn't a big fan. The man couldn't stand me, and I couldn't stand him; it was no surprise that he was the one who threw me under the proverbial bus. How we had been posted on the same warship - twice now - was beyond me.

While in custody (at least early on), I've had several visitors, most of whom were fellow crewmembers from *Hamilton*. And speaking of *USS Hamilton* – which I supposedly owned, another story altogether – she purportedly was back within Pleidian Weonan space undergoing repairs from her numerous battle wounds incurred at the hands of the Varapin.

My friend, Hardy – a 300-year-old, seven-foot tall ChronoBot robot - had apparently taken up residency some 800 feet from where I sat, perhaps keeping vigil under a nearby wharf or huddling within the shadows of an abandoned warehouse. I wasn't sure. Hardy, for several disjointed reasons, continues to be my protector. More than once, he has pleaded with me to allow him to storm the walls of this brig and free me. I'm fairly confident he could do so, and do so easily. But no, I would stay and let the powers that be decide my ultimate fate. I'd made my proverbial bed and was willing to pay the consequences. If I was found guilty of supposed US Space-Navy misconduct, so be it.

I heard the distant sound of a metal door *clanging* open and then slamming shut. Multiple hard-soled footsteps echoed within concrete hallways, getting louder. I looked up to the wall where a calendar was taped somewhat off-kilter. Lieutenant Gail Pristy, one of my more frequent early visitors, had hung it there and had penciled in all military tribunal court dates I'd be attending during my court-martial proceedings. Today was Monday, the 5th of September. Pristy had written in a meeting with my defense team, Judge Advocate General's Corps, better known as JAG's. I stood and mentally prepared myself for another tedious and seemingly pointless day of legal strategizing and wrangling. Typically, I would be moved to an interview room here within Norfolk's Brig Complex, where at least I'd be looking at a different set of four walls for a while. Standing at my cell's bars now, I watched as four Naval Officers – three Lieutenants and one Captain – came my way. Oh . . . and there was another prisoner in an orange jumper like mine, being escorted. I shook my head. *No way . . ., if they think they're going to double-occupancy my already too small a cell – wait . . . what the fuck?*

The Captain said, "We don't have much time." He gestured to the high-mounted camera on the wall, "Security feeds into this corridor will come back on in seven minutes. With a quick glance, I saw that the typically *ON* little red camera light was indeed off. But my attention was quickly brought back to the other prisoner. A prisoner who was about my same height, same build, same color hair, and eyes. *Holy shit* – the prisoner *was* me. Not someone who simply looked like me; he *was* me!

"What's going on here?" I said, directing the question to the captain.

For the first time, the man smiled. "Simple . . . we're breaking you out of here." He held up a hand to ward off my next question, "And before you get your panties all in a twist, we'll get you back here well before your formal proceedings."

"And who's he?" I asked.

"I think he's more like a *what* than a *he*. By the way, Empress Shawlee Tee sends her regards. She wishes she could be here herself but is dealing with other priorities right now."

"So, this is a Symbio-Poth? One made to look like me?"

"She said you were a quick study," the Captain said sarcastically. "As far as anyone will know, he *is* you."

With the jail cell door now rolling open, the Galvin Quintos Symbio-Poth hurried past me, taking a seat on my bunk.

I said, "Does he talk?"

"Of course, he talks. I think."

The Symbio-Poth rifled through the stack of books I had on my side table. "You like history, I see," he said.

"I guess . . . it's what LaSalle keeps bringing me."

The Quintos Symbio-Poth nodded, "I like mysteries, myself."

"Good to know," I said, turning my attention back to the awaiting officers. "I'm assuming this is important enough to jeopardize my ever hoping to be found not-guilty and gaining my freedom legally?"

This time, it was one of the Lieutenants that spoke up, "You have the opportunity to repay a debt. Fleet Commander Twinwon is in trouble . . . big trouble."

"Then say no more. I owe him my life several times over. Let's go."

While the five of us were winding our way through the myriad of prison passageways, I realized that these men were not *men* at all. They, too, were Symbio-Poths. One certainly couldn't tell by looking at them (or even talking to them), but they put off a certain kind of distinct *vibe* – a vibe I'd picked up on months earlier while visiting with my Symbio-Poth family onboard *Hamilton*. We made a left and then a quick right. *What had happened to my Symbio-Poth parents and older brother? Were their AI minds scrubbed and their bodies tossed onto a heap somewhere – maybe to be reconstituted as someone else? Or were they simply shoved into a plasma incinerator, atomized, as if they had never existed?*

We passed through one last metal gate, and then we were outside. The bright mid-day sunlight hurt my eyes, and I had to squint to see. Miraculously, no prison security guards had been in the vicinity as we exited the building. It occurred to me that this jailbreak had been organized and planned with nothing less than AI tech assistance. And there he was, thirty yards away from us – Hardy, leaning against a military hover-transport craft. His arms were crossed over his massive metal chest, as he was doing his best to look casual and human. But he looked ridiculous, and I couldn't have been happier to see anyone.

His face display showed that of his original looks, the somewhat pudgy, balding, and friendly-looking, John Hardy face from decades ago when Hardy was a man and not a robot.

"Welcome, Cap . . . you're looking fit as a fiddle."

"The wonders of doing 200 push-ups and 200 sit-ups each morning . . . not much else to do in a 10 x 10 cell."

A hatch opened at the side of the hover-transport, and Hardy gestured for me to climb on in. I turned around to look at my contingent of Symbio-Poth officers, stunned to see they were little more than deflated uniforms now splayed out on the ground. Bubbling puddles of pinkish-red goo oozed out from vacant sleeves and neck collars. The sight of these once talking, walking, seemingly breathing organisms . . . now turned into little more than melted Jell-O pops . . . struck me hard. The question of what had happened to my Symbio-Poth family was answered in the most frank and forthright manner possible. "I'm sorry, Captain . . . that was . . ." Hardy seemed to search for the right word, then said, "Insensitive." As if reading my mind, he shook his head, "No, I assure you, this is not what happened to –"

I held up a hand to stop him, "How about you just give me a sit report . . . bring me up to speed on what this is all about?"

I followed Hardy into the hovercraft, sending one last glance back toward the dissolving Poths. Now, even their uniforms were disintegrating – soon, there would be nothing left of them. The hatch closed, and I followed Hardy through the no-nonsense barebones military craft into a small cockpit with seating for five. Hardy positioned his bulk into the pilot's seat, and I sat down beside him.

Hardy quickly and efficiently went through a verbal pre-flight checklist. It was almost as if he was avoiding just getting to the point. Then the hover craft's lift thrusters engaged, and the vessel lifted off.

"Hardy . . ."

"Two weeks ago, there were multiple sightings . . . along with relayed sensor readings, possibly a Varapin warcraft."

"Where?"

"On the outskirts of Pleidian Weonan territory. An area considered by most to be frontier space."

There was never any doubt the Varapin would return to this galaxy. The defeat of their *Rage of the Gonjun Ract* fleet would have been both an embarrassment and inspiration for further vengeance.

"The Pleidians weren't going to take any chances . . . they quickly dispatched a small battle group, one under the command of Fleet Commander Twinwon."

"So, what happened? Did he confirm the presence of the Varapin?"

"That's still undetermined. What *was* determined was that it was a trap . . . by the Grish. The last communique from Twinwon had his five warships surprise- attacked by eighteen Grish warships. All Pleidian vessels were taking fire and were heavily battle damaged. According to Twinwon, the situation was dire. There were no further communications from the battle group after that."

That sounded ominous. "So . . . Fleet Command, they're responding? Or better yet, the Pleidians are sending another battle group out –"

"Neither, Cap. War has taken its toll on the Pleidians. And with the Grish having a war pact with the Varapin, all Alliance warships are spread particularly thin these days. But what it really comes down to is the Thine, Pleidian Weonan, and Humans are each going overboard in terms of protecting their own home-worlds."

"Understandable . . . but, you're saying the Pleidians aren't sending anyone after their own battle group?"

Hardy shrugged, a gesture that looked absurd on a ChronoBot. "Apparently, the Grish have been hitting the Weonans especially hard," he said.

Weonan was the Pleidian's homeworld, and since the Pleidian Weonan's military was the most powerful and capable of the Alliance, it made sense they would be the Grish's primary target. "Okay, I get it . . . everyone's protecting their own turf."

"Yup, circling the wagons," Hardy said.

"So, why am I here? Where the hell are you taking me?"

With a chrome finger, Hardy gestured toward the forward window, "*There.*"

We had ascended well out of Earth's exosphere minutes earlier and were moving deeper into the solar system in the opposite direction of the Moon. I saw nothing before us but the twinkling of a million stars. "Hardy, my patience is growing thin. This whole thing – telling me the absolute minimum amount of information –"

Hardy cut me off, "*Hamilton* . . . she's there, about eight thousand miles off our bow. She's cloaked . . . but she's there just the same."

I focused harder, knowing intellectually that the three-mile-long vessel would be impossible to see, even with a telescope. The dreadnought's cloaking capabilities were incredibly advanced, part of the reason she'd survived against a fleet of Varapin warships. "I wasn't aware she'd come out of space dock so soon . . . that all her repairs had been made. So, what? She's here stealthily protecting Earth?"

"You would have been notified. Remember, the *USS Hamilton* is not a US Space-Navy-owned asset . . . but one that is merely on loan."

On loan by me. I owned the ship outright, thanks to one Pleidian Weonan Empress, Shawlee Tee. *Hamilton* was a gift for rescuing her from Ironhold Station and that deplorable Pylor pirate, Cardinal Thunderballs, less than a year earlier.

The pieces were starting to fit. "Fleet Command has no idea *Hamilton's* here. And I'd venture to say, nor do the Thine or the Pleidians."

"Bingo!"

"And let me guess, Shawlee Tee . . . this was her idea. Hell, she's onboard, isn't she?"

"Bingo! Bingo! You win the stuffed purple teddy bear."

I let my head fall back against the headrest. "This is really a bad idea, Hardy. Off- book missions are not only unsanctioned by the US Space-Navy, but they're also probably illegal. I've already been brought up on one set of charges that could keep me in the brig for years!"

Hardy's face-display came alive with a bright yellow happy face. "And you'll have the most excellent alibi ever . . . right now, you're sitting next to Earl Capshaw within the CCU Norfolk Brig's mess. Earl's the idiot mastermind behind stealing a pallet of food replicator units from a Halibart Station's parts depot. His intent was to sell them on the black market. You just took your first bite of a freeze-dried waffle as Earl explains how he had been framed . . .how he's totally innocent."

I briefly wondered if Hardy's AI capabilities actually allowed for him to tap into CCU Norfolk Brig's security feeds to that level. Thinking about it, I was fairly certain he could. I had a growing list of questions, but they would have to wait. Hardy was slowing the transport and had slightly altered our course. Had I blinked, I would have missed it. We'd just passed through *Hamilton's* flight bay energy barrier.

Chapter 2

Having landed, we exited the hover transport. *Hamilton's* flight bay was deserted and seemed even more immense than usual. And without the typical constant commotion of bay personnel hard at work doing Arrow Fighters maintenance or repairs, or pilots comings and goings, not to mention the chorus of high-decibel revving spacecraft engines; it was *beyond* strange – as if I'd stepped into a ghost ship.

"Crew? Who's here?" I asked.

"Of course, there's a crew, but it's minimal. The good news . . . *Hamilton's* been battle repaired for the most part while back within Pleidian space. She was being tested with some kind of new technology gizmo. . . I was kept out of the loop since I wasn't around. Those tests are continuing now."

"You missed a lot of things while keeping vigil, I imagine." Hardy did one of his weird shrugs again.

"So, on whose authority were these alterations and tests

being made to my ship?" I said. And yeah, it was *my* ship, but still, it felt funny saying things like that.

"I have no idea. I'm basically your taxicab driver, Cap. I was told to deliver you here safely and on time."

We'd progressed three-quarters of the way across the flight bay expanse when another vessel suddenly crossed through the atmospheric barrier. Then another.

Tempted to wait and see who was arriving, I said, "Who is running things? Who's been the skipper?"

Hardy actually missed a step but recovered quickly. "About that . . ."

"No!"

Hardy's face display changed into a grumpy face icon. "Please, don't shoot the messenger here, Cap. I'm not particularly happy about it either."

So, Captain Eli Tannock would continue to be that same annoying burr under my saddle. The bane of my existence. I had a sense that things were only starting to unravel – to spin out of control. Months earlier, I'd been diagnosed with something called Late-Onset PTSD. It had reared its ugly head like an unwelcome serpent at the most inopportune times – such as when *Hamilton* was being attacked or any time instantaneous life and death decisions needed to be made. Sure, it was better now; my therapy sessions with an assigned psychiatrist had continued – even while incarcerated. I'd been given mental coping tools to use when I felt anxiety symptoms coming on. Deep breathing, distraction techniques, mindfulness, social interactions with designated proctors . . . *could Hardy be a proctor for me?* I took in several deep breaths and did my best to clear my mind.

I said, "Take me to Tannock. Let's get this over with."

Hurrying out of the flight bay, in the distance behind, I heard another transport coming through the atmosphere barrier.

Standing within the GravLift, Hardy said, "We have a quick stop to make on Deck 10."

"HealthBay?"

"Doc Viv has your TAC-Band."

Funny how just hearing her name caused my heart to skip a beat. "She's here."

"Yes. She's been a big part of the experiments going on."

By the time we entered HealthBay, my mood had taken a detour downward. I had been subjugated to a 10-x-10 cell for months all because of one man – fucking Eli Tannock. And now I find out he's taken my job? He's the skipper on my warship?

"You okay, Cap?" Hardy asked.

I took another deep breath, realizing my anger was becoming a kind of living thing. "Yeah, just mentally picturing the heel of my boot on Tannock's throat."

"That's the spirit. Positive imaging . . . maybe try picturing his throat under my heel instead. . . I weigh more."

I couldn't help but laugh at that. "Thanks, Buddy, I'll try that next time I fall into a mental rabbit hole."

HealthBay, as expected, was deserted. In fact, the place was dark. Only the light cast from various bedside diagnostic monitors offered any kind of dim illumination. A sudden shadowy movement off to our right caused me to jump; Hardy simply held out a hand. It was one of HealthBay's creepy, metal skeleton-like MediBots. The robot handed Hardy a TAC-Band and, as quietly as it had arrived, turned and disappeared back into the shadows.

"Here you go. My sensors tell me Doc's up on Deck 13."

"But you would have already known that, Hardy," I said, giving him a sideways glance. I looked at the TAC-Band. There was a blinking message icon. "Give me a second." I took a few steps away – as if that would make a difference. Hardy's hearing was nothing less than supernatural. I played the message – Doc Viv's face was one of concern and something else. Perhaps it was fear. "Quintos . . . I wanted to get this message to you somewhere in private. Things are . . .well, *off,* is the best way to put it. I'm not sure if it's politics . . . or something else completely. I learned a long time ago to listen to my gut . . . and my gut is telling me to watch my back. And for you to watch your back, as well. Be careful who you trust, Quintos. There are high-level decisions being made that don't make any sense. At this very moment, Hardy is blocking MATHR's prying eyes and ears from hearing this message. That was the reason you were brought here first. Someone close to you has turned against you, and don't assume it's the obvious choice of Tannock. Yeah, he helped to put you in the brig, but that was more about his bloated sense of a right and wrong – a kind of duty more than any kind of malevolence. Chances are, I'm just being overly suspicious. It's in my nature not to trust people . . . men, mostly. I'll see you when you get here." The message ended, and the TAC-Band went black. I secured it to my wrist and turned to face Hardy.

"Well . . . what's your take on all that?"

The ChronoBot' s face display was back to the digitized John Hardy. I'd come to realize this was the face he displayed when he was being more my friend than a subordinate. "You know I always have your back, Captain . . . but with all the technological advantages this mechanical body affords me, I have no more sense of a man's – or woman's – true intentions than you do. But I'll stay vigilant."

I thought about Viv's message. Who would be out to get me? Hell, I wasn't even supposed to be here. As far as the rest of the world was concerned, I was still sitting in my cell back in Norfolk. My TAC-Band began to vibrate, and I wondered if it was Doc Viv again, wanting to add to her previous cheery tidings. But no, it was none other than Admiral Cyprian Block.

"Admiral . . ."

"Before you start making excuses, yes, I know all about the escape and that look-alike Symbio-Poth sitting in your cell."

"Good to know, sir." I momentarily recounted Viv's words, *be careful who you trust, Quintos.*

"What's going on, Admiral? What's with all this clandestine bullsh –"

"Shut up and listen . . . I only have a minute to myself here." I watched as the admiral glanced about suspiciously. "You're to take command of the *Hamilton.* Assist the Empress

Shawlee Tee with her mission. You must find what remains of that Pleidian fleet and make a rescue if possible. But hear me out, Galvin . . . you are not to go up against the Grish. I know you take direct orders with a grain of salt, but the *Hamilton* cannot be detected there, let alone be witnessed having any kind of space battle. As far as Fleet Command is concerned, the *Hamilton* is still within Pleidian space, undergoing top-secret, experimental upgrades, and you're still doing push-ups and sit-ups in your cell."

He knew about my workout routines?

"Galvin . . . this new technology, if it can be made to work, not unlike US Space-Navy's FTL travel or Spring Jump Drives, can alter the course of this war. It's a total game-changer. You will protect this technology with your life and that of your crew. I'm serious, Galvin . . . if the time comes when the Grish, or any other adversary force, is capable of taking this tech . . . blow the ship. Destroy the *Hamilton*. Do it without hesitation."

"Aye, sir."

"Look, we owe the Pleidians more than we can ever repay. And I know you have a special relationship with the Empress. She had requested assistance from Space-Navy Fleet Command, and they refused. I'm putting my neck on the line here, Captain . . . while yours was *already in a noose*." He offered up a wry smile. "Don't fuck this up, son, or we're both royally screwed."

"You can count on me, Admiral."

"Good, because if you get into trouble, guess what?"

"There's no one coming to help?"

"That's right."

The connection terminated.

Stepping out of the GravLift onto Deck 13, I now realized where everyone had gone to. Whale's Alley, *Hamilton's* primary (and largest) passageway, was bustling with crewmembers. Like myself, still wearing my orange prison jumper, most here were dressed in their civvies, and even though this was a US Space-Navy warship, the atmosphere here was far more akin to a neighborhood block party than a military assignment. I shot Hardy a quizzical look.

There must have been close to one-hundred crewmembers here, segmented into two groups. One group, close to the lifts, and another several hundred feet away, closer to the entrance to the Bridge. No, not groups . . . more like *teams*. And there was yelling – taunting calls coming across the open divide. From the nearby team came the yell, "Red rover, red rover, send Gail's lipstick over!"

I looked to the far team and saw Lieutenant Gail Pristy there, dressed in snug jeans and an oversized blue sweater, holding up something small and shiny. Undoubtedly, it was a lipstick tube. Over-dramatically, she strode over to . . . *what the hell is that thing?* The contraption was taller than Hardy, but not like anything I'd ever seen before. Clearly, it was some kind of pieced together high-tech prototype – one that reminded me of H.G. Wells' infamous time machine. But this device didn't have a seat . . . more like a glass-enclosed pedestal.

Lieutenant Pristy proceeded to open a clear panel on the device, placing her lipstick on the pedestal. With dramatic flair, she closed the panel, stepped aside, and curtseyed. Everyone on both teams clapped as they hooted and hollered. It was then that I saw Derrota. Science Officer Stephan Derrota was one of the few crewmembers here wearing their uniform. And it looked as though he was the de facto master of ceremonies here – if that was by choice was still to be determined. Derrota took up a position behind the oversized gizmo and began tapping at a touchscreen. He now looked over to the other team's area while manually aiming *something*, which looked an awful lot like some kind of weapon. I tried to see (between the clusters of nearby bodies milling about) exactly what Derrota was directing his attention to. Then, I saw it. There was another big, identical-looking, eight-foot-tall gizmo.

Whale's Alley suddenly went quiet. No one moved. Hell, as far as I could tell, everyone was holding their breath. I could feel the anticipation. Something big was about to happen. Then it did happen. A flash – an incredibly bright flash, which had to have been some kind of laser pulse. Again, the cheers started . . . more hoots and hollering. I'd had enough of standing on the sidelines and was now pushing my way through the crowd; there was some balking and complaints until who I was became evident.

"Sorry, Captain . . . apologies, Captain . . . hey, watch out man . . . oh, sorry, Sir . . ."

I arrived at gizmo number two, surprised to see both Security Chief Alistair Mattis along with Major Vivian Leigh, together manning the device. Mattis was the first to notice me;

I stood before them with my hands on my hips, looking less than thrilled at what was going on.

Wide-eyed, Doc Viv saw me, too. Now, noticing one of her more familiar unconscious tells – that of her bottom lip being sucked between her front teeth, she looked like a young school-girl caught doing something she shouldn't. I almost laughed but maintained my stern expression. "What the hell is going on here?"

Once more, Whale's Alley went dead-quiet. All eyes were upon me. My voice had come out angrier and more author-itarian than I'd intended. I'd vowed to never be *that* kind of commander. So, I smiled.

After a brief hesitation, again, the passageway erupted into a frenzy of hollering and cheers. There were pats on my back and too many *welcome backs* to count. But all I could do was stare at the machine – the H.G. Wells-looking thingamajig and what was now situated upon its own enclosed pedestal. Gail's lipstick.

Chapter 3

"Perfect. You're just in time! The device is called a Port Entangler, Galvin," Derrota said, his eyes glimmering and chock-full of excitement.

I was well aware that when Derrota got like this, his Mumbai-accented words tended to tumble out so fast that he was hard to understand. But not wanting to douse his enthusiasm, I simply nodded – encouraging him to go on.

He placed a raised hand upon the Port Entangler as one would affectionally place a hand upon the flank of a prized horse. "With the exception of the science fiction realm, there's been many depictions of such a device. But there's never been anything even close to this . . . at least not in real-life. Galvin . . . this changes everything."

The crowd had dissipated to the point that even the few that still lingered nearby were now heading off to their respective quarters. Apparently, the ship had been pretty much empty until about three hours earlier – when crewmembers started arriving. This had been an impromptu gathering, as the interested crew came upon the in-process experiments taking place here on Deck 13.

I saw both Mattis and Doc Viv had finished up with the other Port Entangler, and were making their way over to us.

Derrota's eyes lowered to my jumpsuit. "Captain . . . so it's true? Hardy broke you out of the brig?"

I nodded. "But it's fine. Honest. I won't be missed and will be back there in time for my court-martial."

"How is that –"

"Let's just say there's a Symbio-Poth that looks a hell of a lot like me, sitting in my cell right now. Both Admiral Block and Empress Shawlee Tee felt my time could be far better served commanding *Hamilton*. At least for the mission at hand."

Derrota looked irritated. "Nobody's talking to us. Yes, we're aware of a mission, but no specifics. In any event, I'm supposed to continue on with my tests."

I felt a tap on my shoulder, turned, and saw Lieutenant Pristy standing there with an ear-to-ear grin. Before I could say a word, she lunged – hugging me so tight I was surprised she had that kind of strength, "So good to have you back on board, sir."

No matter how casual things get upon a military vessel, hugging your commanding officer takes things a bit too far – even according to my own casual command style. And, by her expression, I could see she realized as much now. "Um, oh crap . . . sorry, sir."

"Good to see you, too, Lieutenant," I said with an appropriate serious expression.

Doc Viv and Mattis, now joined us at the nearby Port Entangler. Putting my attention back onto Derrota, I said, "I'll let you all know what few facts I have on our mission if you'll – in turn – tell me about this . . . this *thing* here," gesturing to the nearby device. "Like what exactly is it, and how on Earth did it do what I think I just saw it do? Some kind of transporter, is it?"

Pristy said, "Um, I'm going to go change, Captain. Can you catch me up on the mission later?" Her face was still flushed with embarrassment as she scooted off down the passageway.

I caught Viv rolling her eyes.

"Sorry, I've got to go, too – get back to Security," Mattis said. "Seems there's a personnel fracas taking place there." Mattis hurried off after Pristy, leaving me with Doc Viv and Derrota.

Viv said, "Well, I'm not going anywhere. I want to hear why we're being deployed on a mission when the testing of our two Port Entanglers should trump anything else."

"First, tell me about your experiments and how this thing, what did you say, Stephan, changes everything?" It was then that an errant thought popped into my head. *Where was my old Captain nemeses?* According to Hardy, he was here onboard *Hamilton*, in some capacity. I said, "Where is Captain Tannock?"

Both Viv and Derrota exchanged a quick look. Doc Viv said, "You don't know? About Tannock?"

"Know what?"

Derrota let out a breath, "That it was Eli Tannock that had brought us this technological wonder in the first place."

I shook my head, "I'm confused. I thought this was Pleidian, Thine, or some other alien tech we had acquired . . . or absconded with, somehow."

Derrota's excitement returned, "No, Galvin . . . this is one-hundred percent human, actually made in France. And tech that is hundreds of years old."

My earlier thoughts about the Port Entanglers looking like something from an old H. G. Wells story returned. Looking at it now with more scrutiny, seeing its elaborate gold metal millwork and decorative Fleur de Lis adornments here and there, not to mention the large pull levers and old-fashioned meters and dials . . . yes, this thing really was an old relic. Someone had interfaced a modern touch-display to it – which looked totally out of place. And I was now more confused than ever. If I hadn't seen the experiment with Gail's lipstick myself, I would have thought Derrota was off his rocker.

Interrupting my musings, Derrota continued, "Eli bought the two of them at an auction, both Entanglers, some eight weeks ago. You'll be happy to know that Eli had taken a leave of duty from the US Space-Navy. Anyway, he was traveling with his, um, friend, Chaplain Trent, in Europe. It was there they came across these items which had just come up for auction. Eli spent a small fortune purchasing the two of them. Apparently, he had acquired inside information that these devices were more than just unique-looking nineteenth-century novelties.

In fact, they were actually developmental prototypes manufactured by none other than Louis de Broglie."

"Am I supposed to know who that is?" I asked.

"Don't feel bad; I didn't know who he was, either," Doc Viv said.

Derrota looked momentarily astonished that Viv nor I knew who this Louis de Broglie guy was.

"Look, quantum physics was basically established by Max Planck and Albert Einstein, which everyone knows, right? But after his own in-depth study, taking several years, Broglie presented a new thesis in the early nineteen hundreds . . . a study that revealed an important theoretical discovery . . . that electrons can behave as if waves, and, not only that, all particles and objects are associated with *matter waves*. This led to other later experiments . . . not to mention the infamous wave-particle duality test, which demonstrated the ability of photons to be both a wave and a particle. We're talking about the origins of Quantum Mechanics!" Derrota looked at me, then to Viv, as if any third-grader should know this.

Apparently, Doc Viv was far smarter than I was; after all, she was a doctor. She said, "That experiment is commonly referred to as *Young's Experiment* . . . another of the early quantum physicists back then, although they didn't call them *physicists* back then."

"Fine," I said. "So, Tannock and Trent purchased these devices at an auction. And from the looks of things, with a little work, you've actually gotten them functional."

Derrota gestured to a black canister - about the size of a

shoebox – secured to the side of the nearby Port Entangler. "I doubt Broglie ever got his devices to effectively work since they required immense amounts of electrical energy to operate. Back then, these entanglers would have been attached with cables to very high, steeple-mounted lightning rods. Our fusion power packs here are much more efficient," Derrota said with a crooked smile.

As much as I was enjoying Derrota's historical and scientific accounting, I needed answers. "Stephan! Where the hell is Tannock now?"

My good friend and *Hamilton's* Science Officer grimaced. "You have to understand . . . Tannock brought these devices to us, to me. Had them delivered to *Hamilton,* there in Pleidian space – while in space dock."

"Stephan?" I said, now losing my temper.

Viv interjected, "He's fucking in that machine there, Galvin!"

I stared at her.

She nodded. "In . . . the . . . machine."

I looked at Derrota. He nodded and then shrugged. "He insisted that he be a part of the experiments. It was an accident. A miscommunication."

I moved closer to the machine. "How would something like that even happen? There's a glass enclosure –"

Doc Viv said, "Yeah, that's diamond glass . . . we added that . . . later on. So, the same thing couldn't happen again. To someone else."

Okay. To be honest, I have to admit I wasn't entirely all that upset that the good Captain Eli Tannock had somehow been sucked up into that machine. I couldn't stand the guy. He was the reason I was court-martialed. But I didn't let that show. "How do we get him out of there? And are you sure he's not . . . well, irretrievable?"

That struck Doc Viv's funny bone for some reason, and she started to laugh. Covering her mouth, she said, "This is no time for jokes, Galvin."

"Who's joking? I'm totally serious. Maybe he's gone . . . his energy, his molecules, are, like, scattered to the four winds."

Even Derrota found that funny. Pointing to the touch screen, he said, "Galvin . . . Captain, he *is* in there. We can see him, at least his dynamic impression, still there within MATHR's storage buffer – a file created just days ago."

I turned my attention to Whale's Alley and scanned the passageway. I saw Hardy had taken up a position at the far bulkhead. Knowing he'd be listening to our conversation, I furrowed my brows questioningly as if to say, *is what they're saying true? Is Tannock in there? Stuck in that buffer?* Hardy nodded his big head.

"Who else knows about this? Admiral Block?" I asked Derrota.

Neither Derrota nor Viv answered.

"Wait, come on . . . no one knows?"

Derrota looked at his boots, while Doc Viv was suddenly preoccupied with one of her fingernails.

"Fuck. Does his boyfriend know? Chaplain Trent?"

"God, no!" Viv said. "Hey . . . we're figuring it out . . .

upsetting the chaplain, or anyone else at this stage, would be . . . premature."

"How about the Empress?"

"Oh, yeah, she knows . . . she's here onboard, you know," Derrota said.

Ignoring that, I said, "You do realize we're expected to head out on a mission, like, right away. Right?" I said.

They both nodded.

I thought about our situation. "Hmm, we'll have to make a stop at Morno."

"Homeworld of the Thine," Viv said.

"Good idea," Derrota said. "If anyone can figure this out, it's Coogong Sohp."

It was then that I saw them hurrying in our direction – Empress Shawlee Tee, along with Ensign Plorinne, both Pleidian Weonan, with their anatomically strange anomalies – heads with elongated openings at their centers. There was no person, anywhere, that has done more for me personally, had cared for me, as Shawlee had. She was the sister I never had. She was as close to me having *family* as possible.

"Galvin, so good to see you." She pulled me into an embrace – my second hug of the day – but one that was far more welcome.

I quietly said, "Thank you for getting me out of that brig. Once again, I am in your debt."

"It is I who will always be in your debt. Saving me, us, from Captain Thunderballs . . . I will never forget it."

Separating, she acknowledged Derrota and Doc Viv with a shy smile. "Progress finding your elusive Captain Tannock?"

I answered for them, "No. He's still in there. But I assure you, it's a top priority . . . right behind me sorting my sock drawer."

Shawlee laughed the hardest, which was surprising since I wasn't even sure Pleidians even wore socks. "I'm sorry, that was inappropriate. Science Officer Derrota assures me Captain Tannock is no worse for wear . . . in there. I'll be making a quick detour to Morno to find –"

Shawlee finished my sentence, "Coogong Sohp . . . yes. Who better than him to figure things out?"

I was now pretty good at reading her alien expressions and knew something was up. She tilted her head in a very human manner as if to say, *can we talk in private?* We stepped away from the group and spoke in hushed tones.

"What is it?" I asked.

"Galvin, getting to Pleidian frontier space sooner rather than later is of top priority."

"I understand. But the odds of finding Fleet Commander Twinwon, his crew, warship . . ."

"I know, I know. Most likely, they've all been . . . killed. And this is little more than a fool's errand . . . is that the right expression?"

"Yeah, that's the expression," I said sympathetically.

"Galvin . . ." she looked to be searching for her next words. "Twinwon. He's more than a Fleet Commander to me. We're . . ."

I smiled, "In a relationship?"

She nodded, looking somewhat embarrassed.

"I'm happy for you. Nobody deserves to have someone special in their life more than you do, Shawlee."

"I must return to Weonan . . . matters of state call me home." She looked at me with sad eyes.

"I promise, stopping off at Morno won't take much time. And I'll do everything in my power to find your Commander Twinwon. If he's out there, we'll get him back."

Chapter 4

USS Hamilton — En Route to Morno
0000 hours (Midnight)

Captain Galvin Quintos

I sat at my desk within *Hamilton's* expansive Captain's ready room, trying to concentrate. I was familiarizing myself with the most recent star charts of Pleidian Weonan's Frontier space – reviewing planetary systems and known inhabited worlds situated there within that distant quadrant of the galaxy. If Fleet Commander Twinwon had, *somehow*, evaded destruction or capture by the Grish, I needed a starting point where to begin my search.

Feeling a magnet-like pull, my eyes were drawn to a section off to the left within the compartment. When I had asked Hardy to move the two Port Entanglers to somewhere out of the way, I hadn't meant my ready room. *Damn robot has an odd sense of humor.* But just knowing Captain Tannock was right there, in some kind of buffer suspended animation, was creeping me out. Yeah, sure, on an intellectual level, I knew he wasn't watching me, but I couldn't ignore that I felt that he *kinda* was. I'd have the devices moved up to the Technology Sciences department first thing in the morning. Derrota and his team were already chafing at the bit to continue their experiments.

Leaning back in my chair, I looked from one Port Entangler to the other. They looked nearly identical – *nearly*. There were differences. Small things, mostly. Like pull levers and analog dials positioned differently upon brushed gold-metal dashboards. I said aloud, knowing he'd be able to hear me, "Hardy . . . you out there?"

A moment later, the door to the ready room swooshed open, and the big ChronoBot sauntered in. "You should call it a night, get some sleep, Cap."

Earlier, I'd asked Hardy to do some research on this Sir Louis de Broglie fellow and the science behind these devices.

"Have you had time to get the information I asked for?"

The robot's face display was still that of his retro John Hardy appearance. "I had that information within a zeptosecond of you asking for it, Cap."

"A zeptosecond –"

"That's a trillionth of a billionth of a second."

I was too tired to ask why he hadn't just relayed the information to me at that time. "Fine. Tell me." I gestured toward the two Port Entanglers. "Start with the technological aspects

. . . and please keep things at a level my human pea brain can comprehend."

Hardy moved closer to one of the Port Entanglers. He stopped and took on a *human* pose with one arm crossed over his chest, with the other arm propped on the other, his hand cupping what would be his chin – *if he had a chin*. He slowly nodded a few times, as if mentally deliberating on something – which I knew wasn't how Hardy's thought processes worked. His thought processes spanned little more than nanoseconds, or, as he most recently exclaimed, within zeptoseconds.

He reached over and touched the heavy, pivoting, glass gun-like portion of the Port Entangler with a metal finger. His reflection, distorted by the curved cylindrical shape, was looking back at him. "This prototype could not have been developed with the science technology that would have been available to Louis de Broglie in Earth's mid-nineteen hundreds."

I stood and came around my desk. "But . . . here the two machines stand. They are well documented to have been fabricated within Broglie's laboratory."

"I didn't say they weren't made, fabricated, as you put it, I'm saying they weren't made entirely by humans."

Pfft, I scoffed. "I think Sir Broglie would have mentioned something about little green men assisting him in his experiment notes and annotations –"

I stopped mid-sentence seeing that Hardy was attempting to pry open a section of the unit's housing. "Hey! Best you don't mess with that –"

But a panel was already swinging open. Hardy said, "Up

until now, sure, we've gotten these two units to operate, transport small objects from one unit to the other, but that doesn't mean we figured out *how* they operate. This . . . explains a lot."

What was now visible inside that small compartment, to my astonishment, wasn't any kind of technology derived from early in the twentieth century. Tiny purple, green and blue, lights twinkled on and off. Sparkling gold, liquid-like but not liquid, more like energetics, flowed within a series of clear tubes, or arteries, like that of some kind of advanced-technology circulatory system. I was fairly certain Derrota and his team had not discovered this hidden aspect of the two entanglers.

"What am I looking at?" I asked.

"Technology well beyond anything available within this galaxy . . . even now. What you're looking at is an AI, of sorts," Hardy said. He closed the panel and turned to face me. "Yeah, I'm sure Sir Louis de Broglie was an astute scientist for his time . . . but he had help. Let's just say friends of an interstellar nature."

"It doesn't add up. If these things have this level of advanced technology . . . why would Broglie need a lightning storm as a power source?"

"Well, it could mean the more advanced aliens had left, taking the two Entangler's power supplies with them . . . not trusting old Sir Broglie with advanced tech such as this. There's really no way to tell. In any event, may I make a suggestion, Cap?"

"Sure."

"Don't mess with these contraptions. Keep Derrota and

Doc Viv at arm's length. At least until Coogong Sohp's onboard to take a look. That is . . . unless you want more of your crew to join Captain Tannock stuck within that memory buffer."

* * *

It was two days later before we'd reached Morno's upper orbit and another full day before we had Coogong Sohp onboard *Hamilton*. To Derrota's chagrin, I'd taken Hardy's advice and kept the two Port Entanglers in my ready room – keeping Louis de Broglie's devices off-limits to everyone.

Coogong Sohp, a genius Thine scientist and friend, arrived onboard without his customary environment suit. Typically, he would be wearing a bulky, heavy-looking affair that contained a combination of internal robotics and Ambiogell, a mud-like substance that was akin to breathable air to humans. The Thine were basically highly intelligent maggots, to put things bluntly. They possessed little mobility, having mere nubs for arms and legs, thus the need for the internal robotics suits providing him a minimal kind of locomotion. But what Coogong lacked in attractiveness and agility, he more than made up for with atti-tude – and I found his sheer joy at being alive to be contagious.

Standing with Derrota, who was growing more impatient by the moment to get back to the entanglers, we waited to greet the Thine scientist within Whale's Alley. Now, seeing him emerging from a GravLift, along with two other Thine Scientists wearing their bulky suits – we were taken aback by his current state of being. In fact, with the exception of an environment helmet, he wore no suit at all. His head, if you could call it a head, was indeed visible pressed up to a faceplate and surrounded by Ambiogell. His two friendly, oversized eyes were unmistakably his. His plump worm-like body was gone. He had two arms, two legs, and a torso, but were now that of a skinny stick figure. In every way, identical to that of a first grader's drawing of a person. Black and maybe an inch or two in diameter, I found myself gawking at the mere sight of him.

Coming to a stop in front of me, and seeing my expression, Coogong Sohp's wide smile didn't falter. "So very nice to see you again, Captain Quintos. I apologize if my altered appearance has caused you any distress."

"Coogong . . . no, it's me who needs to apologize . . . for staring."

Derrota leaned in closer, still examining the stick figure before us. "Interesting, not robotics . . . and not organic . . ." Derrota straightened up and, still looking baffled, said, "What —"

Coogong said, "Tendril Albicon. Let's be honest; a Thine's birth body has little functionality. More hindrance than useful, yes? But unlike humans and other beings within the universe, we place little importance on our physical appearance. I have chosen to be a scientific test-subject for a new procedure. My lower body, as you would put it, has been discarded, while my brain's neural junctures have been reassigned connection to this Tendril Albicon formulated construct." He raised one of his stick-figure arms where thin twig-like fingers waggled with an abundance of dexterity. Coogong said, "Think of this form as a kind of smart silicon made up of trillions of micro-tendrils braided together. I am stronger and more agile than you are, Science Officer Derrota. But there are . . . aspects of this construct that will take time for me to fully get used to."

"You are always welcome here, Coogong, in any form you choose to take," I said.

"Well . . . I am most excited to observe your new transport device. Please, take me to it now."

"Hold on!" came a familiar female voice. Doc Viv emerged from a newly arrived GravLift; her hair was down and a little tousled. Obviously in a hurry getting here, and now wearing her officer's casual attire, I got a quick glimpse of cleavage before she finished zipping up the front of her jumper. My heart rate elevated into overdrive at just seeing her like this – *untamed disarray. Damn it! I really need to get over this schoolboy crush thing.* I must have over-compensated because, seeing my grumpy face, she said, "Hey, if you don't want me here –"

"Oh, sorry, no I'm just . . . um –" conscious I was stammering and acting like an idiot, I tried it again, "Don't be silly. Of course, I want you here."

But her attention was already on Coogong. "Tell me, my friend, how are you doing with your . . ." She hesitated, glancing around.

"It is fine, Doctor Leigh, you may speak freely of my . . . what did you call it? Depersonalization-derealization disorder. Is that the term you used?"

I shouldn't have been surprised that the doctor had been

involved in some capacity with Coogong's medical procedure. I knew the two of them were close.

Seeing the bewilderment on my face, she said, "Coogong's just taking a bit more time adjusting. As you can imagine, fully embracing a new body such as this at a cognitive level . . . well, it may take a while longer." She held out a fist, whereby Coogong, in turn, gave her a fist bump.

We headed as a group toward the entrance of the Bridge. I said, "I've invited Hardy to join us. He's made a new discovery."

"What kind of discovery?" Derrota asked.

"One, you're going to kick yourself for not finding yourself."

Chapter 5

Sitting on the Captain's Mount, I gave the order for Helmsman Chen to take us out of Morno's upper orbit.

"Aye, sir. End-point course is set for star Pleidian system CV-928. Initiating manufacture of a wormhole."

"Thank you, Helm. XO Pristy, we'll be maintaining stealth-running for the entirety of the passage."

"Yes, sir. Just know . . . I estimate doing so will add a full day to our voyage," she said.

"XO, we're in a ship that's supposed to be in space dock, on a mission that does not exist, all with a mostly unauthorized crew."

"Copy that, Captain . . . we're on a ghost mission."

Eyes on the Halo-Display, I leaned back in my seat and watched as a confluence of brightly colored prismatic spatial distortions took form into the mouth of a great, yawning wormhole. Our final destination: Pleidian Weonan Frontier space, which was hundreds of light-years distance from Morno. *Hamilton* would need to make three additional jumps, and with the added *JDTR's* – Jump Down-Time Requisites (those necessary wait times between jumps), the journey was estimated to take approximately nine days.

As the bow of our three-mile-long dreadnought entered into the wormhole, I braced myself for the bright flash, momentary wave of nausea, and feelings of disorientation that accompany this kind of bending of space-time spacial anomaly transitions. Because of our relatively new spring drives technology, our jumps had been getting progressively longer – which, in turn, only exasperated those previously mentioned physical effects.

When it came; the flash, the need to vomit, the dizziness – my minimal Bridge crew of seven took in a collective breath. It was a few moments before anyone spoke.

"Captain . . . all systems operating nominally . . . jump successful. We have arrived just outside of the Maug-Laon star system."

"Thank you, XO." I took in the dim red dwarf star and her four ultra-close-proximity rocky and mountainous planets. On a dissecting course beyond *Hamilton*, an old, but still operational, pea-green US Space-Navy communications hub was being highlighted by MATHR – a glowing red circle and a meta-tag description made prominent on the Halo-Display. We were still relatively close to Earth, some eight light-years distance, but it wouldn't be long before these kinds of recognizable human influences would no longer be encountered.

I got to my feet, stretched my back, and said, "XO, you have the Captain's Mount."

Lieutenant Pristy stood and said, "I have the Captain's Mount. Um, sir?"

"XO?"

Looking somewhat uncomfortable, she looked about the Bridge, "Um, maybe later . . . I can get a few minutes of your time?"

"Of course. Talk to MATHR to set something up."

I left the Bridge, not giving Gail Pristy another thought – something I would come to regret in the days to come.

Entering the Captain's ready room, I found what was typically my quiet refuge away from the hustle and bustle of command – anything but that. The two Port Entanglers were right where they'd been placed two days earlier, and there were nine individuals milling about, doing one thing or another. Even Hardy was here, hearing his bossy Bostonian accented voice above everyone else's.

"Don't be an *igit!*"

Igit, I knew, was a Bostonian term for the word *idiot*. Hardy had used it on me more than once when he thought I was being dim-witted. In this case, he was chastening both Derrota and one of Coogong's two scientists.

Derrota, who had a number of interface connections attached within that hidden, alien-tech compartment, was arguing with Hardy over something I would have zero capacity to understand. I caught Derrota's eye and gestured him over to me.

"What are the chances we can have all this moved up to Science and Technology . . . like soon?"

"Not good, Galvin. As much as it seems like a clusterfuck in here, we've made remarkable progress."

"Okay. And what exactly is the endgame? I already saw you had the thing working."

Derrota looked irritated, "The US Space-Navy has little use for a glorified lipstick tube transporter."

It was then that I saw the small cage full of white mice. My head was already shaking, "Absolutely not! The days of animal testing in the name of science are long past." I must have made the declaration louder than I'd thought, because everyone stopped what they were doing and looked at me. I put my hands on my hips while making a stern *I'm in charge here* expression.

Doc Viv emerged out of the group, looking annoyed, "And you think I'd be okay with that? The torturing of small rodents?"

"Well . . . it certainly looks like –"

She smiled, "I'm just busting your balls, Quintos. Yeah, we kinda *are* breaking a number of animal rights rules here . . . sorry."

Derrota chimed in with a positive inflection, "They've all come through the experience with flying colors . . . so far."

"Physically, at least," Hardy added.

My eyes lingered on one particular mouse currently running

in circles within the confines of one of the glass-enclosed entangler pedestals. I put up a hand, "Can I get everyone's attention for a moment?"

The Captain's ready room came to a standstill. Even the revolving mouse stopped its continuous circuit behind the glass. "How about everyone taking a short break - maybe grab a cup of coffee." My eyes settled upon the three helmet-wearing Thine scientists who wouldn't be drinking coffee or anything else any time soon. "Just take a time out . . . for a few minutes."

I pointed to Hardy, Viv, Derrota, and Coogong. "The four of you, over here. I need a debriefing before you go any further." This was literally my ship, and I had the feeling things were quickly getting out of hand. And not only did I not know what the people in this compartment were doing, but what the endgame was. Admiral Block had given me my marching orders: find Fleet Commander Twinwon. This other business, the archaic-looking Port Entanglers had seemed to me to be little more than a nerd hobbyist's diversion. Clearly, I'd been wrong.

The five of us convened within the ready room's seating area – a leather couch and two overstuffed armchairs. "Sit . . . except you, Hardy." He was a thousand pounds of metal – no furniture would survive his heavy girth.

I looked at each of them individually, "Between the four of you, I need a down-and-dirty sit report on these port things. Like, ultimately, what do they do and *how* do they do it? And since this is, in fact, a warship, what are the military implications for this technology?"

"May I?" Coogong said, looking at his three collaborators.

Both Derrota and Doc Viv nodded, while Hardy did one of his weird shrugs.

"Captain, as advanced as our Thine – or even Pleidian – science has come in recent years, there has always been one area where substantive science breakthroughs have been sparse. That is the transmission of intact molecular systems from one location to another. Yes, I am well aware of your many science fiction depictions of such technology, but there has been no real-world working application of such technology . . . not ever. I would go as far as to say that there are no viable records of transporter-type apparatuses being present *anywhere* in the galaxy."

"So, I guess Louis de Broglie was a whole lot smarter and more important than anyone thought," I said.

The stick figure Coogong continued, "Perhaps. But what we suspect, though, was that the good scientist had somehow come into contact with the alien AI technology, tested it, and built his contraptions around it."

I let that sink in – that we may never know the true history of events, this being hundreds of years in the future. "So, how do these things work?" I looked at Hardy, who I'd already asked to explain this to me earlier without an adequate response.

"First, let's speak of Quantum Entanglement in and of itself. Quantum entanglement works in such a way that a group of particles, or let's say for simplicity, *two particles*, behave as a single system. Suppose that we sent one entangled particle from one Port Entangler over to the other . . . no matter the distance between them. Let's say the transmission was received, while the other entangled particle we kept within the originating Entangler. Then we measure simultaneously various parameters of the transmitted particle, as well as the other one within the originating device. This is where the *magic* happens, Captain. The particle at the receiving end *feels* that a measurement has been made. And that particle will change its state, accordingly."

Basic quantum mechanics is utilized for much of 22nd-century tech and was standard teaching in high school. So, none of what Coogong was saying was all that new to me. But I kept my trap shut and listened.

"Knowing the measurement result on the sender's side . . . which can be sent via a regular information channel, perhaps via a micro-laser link, you can get an exact copy of the sent particle – at the receiving end entangler unit. This is not that surprising if you think about the fact that reality, as we experience it, does not have a concrete *state* until we put it into perspective by measuring it, yes?"

Derrota, who was now sitting on the edge of his seat, added, "As for the whole entangling particles aspect . . . there is a standard procedure: hitting two separated electrons with photons. The two photons are then combined into a single wave and interpreted, revealing information about the states of the two electrons. If all goes according to plan, the electrons can be considered entangled. If not – there is an assembly line with some clever checks and balances; the whole process can be repeated quickly enough to promise entangled particles. So, in the end, we are guaranteed to have an entangled pair!"

His enthusiasm was almost contagious. "Okay, I got the basics of quantum entanglement. Which, in the case of our two test units, uses those big laser guns to transmit the molecular data." Even Viv looked impressed with my deduction. "How about you tell me how our application, here, applies?"

Hardy's face display now showed none other than that of Albert Einstein. He raised his mechanical hands, "Look, it's pretty simple, Cap. Considering transport of a molecule is possible, there should be a statistical correlation of particles of the molecular system in the endpoint which agrees with the initial correlation. The other day you saw Gail's lipstick get teleported successfully from one device to the other. But come on . . . that's too simple a test. There's not much to a tube of lipstick. Other tests included the sending of active technology and test devices, like timers and such. That all worked fine. But the real question everybody was asking was, *how would the transporting of organic material fare?*"

Can I interject?" Doc Viv asked but didn't wait for an answer. "It was not my fault that Captain Tannock got sucked into that machine."

I looked at her blank-faced. "No one said that it –"

"He was helping with the tests. Not sure why the fuck he had to be there anyway . . . it's not like he's a scientist. Just because he discovered these devices –"

"Just tell me what happened."

Viv was clearly upset now. "We had just started with the

teleporting of organic-type material. We'd given Tannock the menial job of placing various items on the transmitting side. But, apparently, the Entangler unit was still active . . . still switched on. Both Tannock and the tomato he was holding got zapped. Sucked right into the device's – actually MATHR's – memory banks."

I tried to picture what she'd described. "Wouldn't just his hand, and the tomato, get sucked in?"

All four of them smiled at that.

"What? What am missing?"

Coogong said, "As unfortunate as the *occurrence* was for poor Captain Tannock, this was an amazing and profound scientific discovery."

"Okay . . . go on," I said.

Doc Viv said, "As upset as we were about Eli, umm, Tannock, we decided to continue on. He'd want us to, right?"

I shrugged, not really caring what Tannock would have wanted.

"More vegetables were successfully sent. Soon, we had double of everything. Fruit coming out of our asses. Exact and perfect replicas," she said.

"And this all took place out in Whale's Alley . . . before I got here," I asked.

"Yeah, we stopped to take a break, to let some of the newly arriving crew have some fun," she said.

"Red rover?" I said.

Viv nodded. "Probably not our finest moment . . . considering Eli was –"

Derrota said, "That catches you up to speed prior to the two units being moved here to your ready room, Galvin. We knew we could not move much farther before confronting one major scientific and humane hurdle."

I knew what he was going to say, "Having two identical organic lifeforms," I said.

"That's right," Derrota said. "Two identical tomatoes, no big deal. Two identical mice?" he waggled his head back and forth. "We're starting to cross a line."

"So, what did you do next?" I asked.

Hardy said, "Turns out there's a lever control for that – was there the whole time. During the transport process, as soon as the successful transmission confirmation is sent back, the original object is . . . atomized."

I'd thought I'd smelt smoke when I'd entered the ready room.

Viv said, "We were making amazing progress, Quintos . . . we were transmitting actual living beings, mice, from one side of the room to the other. And from all indications, our testing, they were healthy . . . normal."

Derrota took over, "But the big question was, how much of the originating conscience was left in the new mouse?" She made a bewildered expression. "No way to tell."

Thinking about it . . . there *was*. "We can ask Tannock if and when we get him out of that memory buffer."

"So, that's where we're at, Cap," Hardy said.

"What's next? Hopefully, it'll be getting these devices out of my ready room."

"Soon, Captain Quintos," Coogong assured me. "We have decided that it is time to fabricate the next-generation, modernized Port Entangler."

"Just one?"

"Yes! That is where modern technological achievements will assist us. We will not need *two* port Entanglers; in fact, *that* would be a hindrance for any future functional applications. Operationally, the proposed entangler's only restraint will be its laser beam having an unimpeded line-of-sight connection."

Only now was I allowing myself to imagine the military applications of such a technology. The near-instantaneous transporting of troops onto an enemy ship, or the rescuing of crew from a doomed vessel – such as that of the *USS Brave*, which I'd given the order to destroy – with several crewmembers still alive.

I stood up and said, "Let me make myself perfectly clear. At no point will any of you even consider transporting a living person until Captain Tannock is successfully extricated from MATHR's memory. No one's quantum entangled molecules get zapped from one place to another without my say so."

Chapter 6

The next two days of the mission were quiet and, dare I say, wonderfully non-eventful. *Hamilton's* small crew of approximately 350, down from a standard detachment of multi-thousands, were all putting their proverbial noses to the grindstone – a smaller crew having to do multiple jobs to keep the ship operational. I'd reviewed the list of my fellow Spacers that Admiral Block had assigned to the mission. From past experience, Block apparently knew who I'd want – at a minimum – along for the ride. Well, with the exception of Captain Tannock. From my Bridge crew under the supervision of my XO, Lieutenant Gail Pristy, Science Officer Stephan Derrota and his team within the CIC, Ship-Wide Maintenance crew (now under the direction of Crewman Lasalle), Captain Wallace along with a squadron of hot-shot Arrow pilots, 55 Army soldiers (which was new), and 55 top-notch Marines. Of course, there was the Engineering and Propulsion crew under the charge of Chief Craig Porter, and Chief of Security Alistair

Mattis and his team of security people. Doc Viv had a minimal team of doctors and nurses under her purview. That still left several hundred of *Hamilton's* crew I was unfamiliar with. Time permitting, I'd introduce myself to each of them.

I'd promised to stay out of the Science and Technology department on Deck 29 – at least until the next phase of the transporter development was ready for demonstration. The thing is, I don't really like being kept in the dark. That's why I instructed Hardy to occasionally transmit live feeds from that area of the ship into my Captain's ready room. Yeah, at first, I felt like a creepy voyeur, but I got over it. I didn't need any surprises, and from what I was viewing, all was going well with the new Port Entangler's development.

It was soon after one of my late-night Science and Technology department viewing checks that I decided to head off to the ship's gym. I'd started a fairly rigorous exercise program while in the brig, and I didn't want to lose any of my positive results. By the time I'd changed into shorts and an old T-shirt and left my quarters, it was close to 0100 hours. The ship passageways were quiet and deserted. And since Hardy was amongst those up on Deck 29, I had the kind of alone-time I was craving.

Entering the gym, I heard the telltale noises of weight machines clanking and sounds of multiple men huffing and grunting. *Looks like others in the crew have the same idea for a late-night workout.* On my way over to the bank of tread-mills, I saw them; five beefy guys, all had sleeves torn away at the shoulders, all tall and beyond muscular and ripped.

That, and they were US CAPRI soldiers. I knew this because their drenched with perspiration sweatshirts had the CAPRI emblem displayed on their broad chests in big, bold letters. CAPRI forces had started out as a gun-for-hire kind of private contract military force some fifty years prior but eventually had been merged into the US Army as an ancillary support contingent. They quickly became known as the *ugly stepchild branch* of the armed forces, with an ultra-conservative, 98.5% male-dominated enlistment roster. Known for their arrogance, even if no one else thought of them that way, their perception of themselves was that of America's *baddest* of all bad-asses.

Passing by, I offered a cordial nod and decided on the treadmill farthest away from the muscleheads.

"Hey . . . you. Uh-uh . . . gym's off-limits right now. Beat it. Come back in the morning."

I didn't need to look to see which of them was talking to me. I already knew. It was the biggest and ugliest one that had made a snarly face as I'd passed by. And sure, I could inform the lot of them that I was the ship's skipper, but that just seemed, well, like a pussy move.

I said, "How about you mind your own business, I'll mind mine?"

I got myself situated onto the treadmill and told the machine, "Start level seven." I selected which wraparound nature track hologram I wanted – starting out at a Colorado wilderness trailhead, and soon was immersed in a different, natural world. Since the treadmill made no noise, I could hear the chirping of birds and the sounds of a babbling creek off in the distance. Hitting my stride, I said, "Level nine." My stride lengthened, and my breaths deepened. The path meandered left, and I saw there was a steep rise coming up ahead. It was then that I felt the yank at the back of my T-shirt. In a matter of two seconds, I'd gone from pure bliss to confusion and pain. I was sprawled out on the gym floor, trying to figure out what had happened. *Did I misstep? Did I do a cartwheel off the back of the treadmill?*

The abrupt laughter informed me that it wasn't my own clumsiness that had me lying on my back gasping for breath. Now, attempting to sit up, a sneakered foot pushed me hard and back down again.

"You have a hearing problem, boy?"

"You don't want to do this . . . get your damn foot off me," I said, feeling hot anger rising by the second. I looked at my wrist; it was time to call in the cavalry. *Fuck!* My TAC-Band was still back in my quarters. I never forget my TAC-Band. I looked to the ceiling; I knew that all I had to do was tell MATHR to send security. But really? I literally was going to call my mother for help? *Pussy move.*

Still on my back with that foot on my chest, the biggest and ugliest one knelt down next to me and sneered. He must have said something clever, but I missed it. He looked up to his cohorts, and they all laughed. All five of the boys had flat-top buzz cuts and looked nearly identical to each other. Their names were embroidered onto their sweatshirts in red hand-written lettering: *Bob, Cash, Alex, Troy,* and right here next to me, *Garrett.*

I punched Garrett hard in the mouth. Was it the best punch in the world? Maybe not. But it was enough to draw blood and make the guy's eyes stream tears. I took that moment of surprise to squirm to my feet and, with my fists clenched, was ready for what I knew would be coming – a beat-down of epic proportions. *Shit!* I feigned left and darted right, figured if I could just keep moving – then the first punch clocked me on my right ear, staggering me. Church bells continued to ring in my head when the second punch landed on the bridge of my nose. Strange, instead of going over like a toppled sycamore, my legs straightened, and my knees locked. The next punch wasn't a punch at all, but some kind of spinning back kick to my solar plexus. That doubled me over and had me spewing chunks. At least the boys were having a good time, I thought. The laughter was coming pretty much non-stop now.

On my knees, I croaked out the word, "mother," . . . but it came out more like "*moffer.*" MATHR does not respond to *moffer.*

One of the other CAPRI muscleheads (I think it was *Cash)* said, "Time to put this boy to bed for the night." He had a fistful of my hair in one hand, which was pulling my head back, making my chin extend out. I detected, more than actually saw, he was ratcheting his other arm back for another punch. Someone said, "Say goodnight, Gracie" – more laughter. I waited for the punch to come. It didn't come. I squinted open one swollen eye. *Huh, someone else has joined the party.* It was hard to hear what was being said above the ringing church bells, but I was pretty sure I was hearing a woman's voice in the mix. *Purple.* She had streaks of bright purple in her hair. And she, too, was big. And tall. And muscular. I knew someone who had purple streaks in her hair and is big and tall. *God, I wish she was here, now. Wanda. Wanda, Wanda, Wanda.*

I realized that no one was holding a fistful of my hair anymore. In fact, I wasn't being held at all. I winced, hearing the all too familiar sounds of hard fists hitting exposed flesh. Surprisingly, it wasn't *my* flesh. I managed to get both my swollen eyes open and saw that the tall, big, muscular woman was doing all the punching and kicking and a whole lot of kick-ass acrobatic shit to those five CAPRI fuckers – none of which were still laughing. *Oh Wanda, you crazy girl.* I smiled just before drifting off into unconsciousness.

* * *

I awoke sometime later, and it didn't take me long to realize I was lying in a bed. Above me, a little out of focus, was a slow rotating medical avatar – my avatar.

"Let me guess, Quintos; you didn't mention to those thugs you were the ship's captain?"

I didn't bother answering Doc Viv's question. I turned my head just enough so I could see her standing at the side of my bed, arms crossed and wearing a bemused smile.

"Will I live?"

"Don't be such a baby . . . you're fine. You had a nasal fracture; I repaired that. You also had a partial eardrum rupture that's been repaired, too. You'll have two black eyes and some swelling for a few days . . . other than that, you'll be fine.

The circumstances that had put me here were coming back to me. *Oh fuck, had I really been rescued by a girl?*

"Thanks to Wanda, you'll be cleared to get back to work tomorrow."

Guess that answers that question. "Is she still here?"

"No, she said she had better things to do than babysit you . . . I think she went back to the gym."

"How did I get here?"

"She carried you. Like a babe in a mother's arms."

"Fuck."

Viv laughed. "Here's the thing, she made me promise not to tell anyone what had happened. That she had stepped in to, um, save your *puny ass*, as she put it."

I pushed myself farther up in the bed and waited for the throbbing in my head to ease. The overhead lights were low, but I could just make out five other beds were occupied at the other end of HealthBay.

Viv said, "They didn't fare quite as well as you. One of them, Garrett, will require surgery to repair a crushed lower jawbone. And because he'd bitten completely through his tongue, he may forever talk with a lisp."

"Seriously?"

She shrugged, "Time will tell."

One of the CAPRI grunt's monitors had started to beep.

"I gotta' go. You're free to leave. Get a good night's sleep and take it easy over the next few days."

"Thanks," I said, but she had already turned and strode off.

Hardy was pacing back and forth outside the entrance to HealthBay, "You look like shit."

"I feel like shit."

"I should have been there. If you knew how much shit I'm still getting from LuMan –"

"I've told you a hundred times; I don't need a 24/7 bodyguard."

"Clearly, you do. Although . . . you seem to have come out of it well enough."

"Wanda came to my rescue. Although, I did get in one good punch."

"Yeah, wasn't a bad punch, Cap . . . I've reviewed MATHR's security feeds. As for Wanda saving your ass . . ." I watched as he pulled an animated zipper closed on the faux lips of his John Hardy face display. "My lips are sealed."

"Thanks, but I have no problem admitting the truth." Seeing that Hardy's face display had gone blank, I said, "What?"

"Nothing. Just that, maybe best if you go with the don't-ask-and-don't-tell philosophy. As far as most of the crew is concerned, you're bigger than life. They'd follow you into the gates of hell. They respect you that much. So. let's just keep this . . . incident, to ourselves."

"I told you, I'm not going to lie about it."

Approaching the GravLifts, Ensign Plorinne emerged. Seeing me, he gave me two enthusiastic thumbs up, "You sure showed those guys who the boss was." He threw a few punches into the air, "Wham! Bam! Five are down for the count!"

I stopped, "No . . . that wasn't . . ."

But Ensign Plorinne was already heading away, still shadow boxing fists into the air. I looked up to Hardy. "How would he have even heard about it? If Wanda's not talking, or the doctor?"

The ChronoBot' s John Hardy face display was now a bright color pink, as he faked embarrassment.

"No . . . you didn't. You lied about what happened? Then gossiped about it like a little schoolgirl?"

Entering the GravLift, he said, "No! I did not lie. I promise. I just didn't relay the entire truth . . . basically allowed people to come to their own conclusions."

"That's still lying. And you need to knock that shit off. I don't need you, or anyone else, trying to protect me. I don't care that I got my ass kicked . . . I was attacked from behind, you know . . . and it was five against one! And they were all a lot bigger than me!"

"Dost, thou protest too much, Captain?"

"Oh, screw you."

Emerging onto Deck 13, several crewmembers caught sight of us within Whale's Alley. Feeling their eyes upon me, I obverted their stares. "I can't believe you put me in this predicament," I said under my breath. With an angry wave, the hatch door to my quarters slid open. I let it close behind me without a goodnight (more like a *good morning*) to Hardy. Furious, I found my TAC-Band where I'd left it on the bathroom counter and messaged Wanda.

Capt. Quintos: Thank you for saving my ass last night, Wanda. Without your help, I'd be in worse shape.

Wanda: No idea what you're blabbering on about.

Capt. Quintos: Ok. Have one question for you . . .
Wanda: Shoot.

Capt. Quintos: Can you teach some of that Kung Fu shit to me?

Wanda: Would rather not. But Maybe.

Chapter 7

I allowed myself six hours of sleep. My first TAC-Band message was to my XO, letting Lieutenant Pristy know I wouldn't be on the Bridge today and maybe not tomorrow either – but if anything arose, I'd be there in a flash. My second TAC-Band message was to Wanda, letting her know I was on my way over to their barracks. I had to stand my ground, arguing with Hardy that I wanted him with Derrota and Coogong up in the Science and Technology department, ensuring that transporter thing didn't capture any more of my crew into the buffer memory.

Although there were a total of 55 Marines posted to *Hamilton* for this voyage, I knew a certain five of them, *this one misfit squad*, would be keeping mostly to themselves.

* * *

Arriving at the barracks, the five of them were waiting

for me. Gym mats were laid out on the deck, and several heavy bags hung from overhead metal rafters. Three virtual, projected, alien avatar combatants were having mock hand-to-hand fights on replaying loops. On a nearby bulkhead was a pegboard with an assortment of lethal-looking weapons; knives of various thicknesses and lengths, long spears, and fighting bamboo staffs that I later learned were called *Bōjutsu*. And, strangely enough, several lengths of rope, called *Nawa*. There was also a medieval-looking spiked ball-and-chain thing called a *flail*. Not only was I having second thoughts about this, but I was also already devising believable excuses as to why I had to leave in a hurry.

Wanda was stretching out her quads on one of the martial arts mats. She snickered . . . "Glutton for punishment, huh, Cap?" She stood and pushed several strands of aqua-purple streaked hair behind one ear. Her bicep bulged in the process, reminding me of an overfilled water balloon.

"You look like crap," Sergeant Max said, the squad leader of this band of Marines. He had short copper-colored hair, and his face had an abundance of tiny freckles, giving him a boyish look, although I knew from past experience that he was one tough Marine. To his right was Grip. Big, Black, and all muscle; even unarmed, he looked lethal – a tightly-coiled boa constrictor capable of striking at a moment's notice. Finally, there were the gargantuan twins, Ham and Hock. I'd like to say they only looked dumb, but they really were idiots without two wits between them. But nobody could slight them for any lack of any loyalty to their team, their ship – and to me, their Captain.

I looked from Wanda to the others. "Um, I thought it would just be you teaching –"

"Nope, you get all five of us," Max said. "We're a team, Captain. We fight as a team and we train as a team. You have a problem with that?"

"No, not at all." I tried to remember a few of my excuses for leaving early but nothing came to mind.

Wanda said, "Hey, unless you want to keep getting gang pounced in the gym –"

"Prison-bitched," Hock added with a laugh.

"Take it like the French," Max said.

"Asphalt head-bounced," Grip added.

"Ball-sack pinata party," Wanda finished.

I waited for them to stop laughing.

Grip stepped in close to me, looking me over like I was a deformed goat being presented at a small-town county fair. "Don't expect miracles, Captain. There's only so much we'll be able to do with you."

Wanda said, "I suggest we get him started with the stacked expedited course."

"Stacked expedited course?" I repeated.

Ham nodded enthusiastically. "It's my all-time favorite."

Hock rolled his eyes, "It's because there's not much you need to memorize. It's based on memory muscle training."

"That's muscle memory training, but close enough, Hock," Max corrected.

He continued, "We'll be teaching you from a wide variety of fighting disciplines; Muay Thai kickboxing from Thailand, Tang Soo Do from Northern Korea, Chinese Kung Fu, and Israeli Defense Force, Krav Maga techniques. And for your ground-based grappling techniques, nothing beats good ol' Brazilian Jiu-Jitsu. But you want to avoid getting laid out on the ground; on the ground, a skinny guy like you would get yourself ape-fucked before you know it."

"Good to know," I said.

Wanda fought back a chuckle, "Here's the thing, Captain. The stacked expedited training course extends beyond the walls of this makeshift dojo."

Blank-faced, I stared back at her. *Extends beyond the walls of this makeshift dojo, how is that possible? Surely, she's speaking metaphorically...*

All five of the Marines seemed to find humor in that. Max suddenly spun around to engage with one of the virtual alien avatars. I recognized the move as a spinning heel kick, and Max seemed to have accomplished the maneuver expertly – putting the alien, a lizard-man combatant, onto his back. What I hadn't expected was the sound made when his barefooted heel connected with the virtual alien's head. His foot didn't simply pass through the projected image, as one would expect, but had made physical contact. These avatars were far more than just virtual simulations. *Fuck!*

Unsteadily, the avatar lizard-man got to his feet – not looking happy with Max. Both Ham and Hock laughed, thinking it was enormously funny.

Max said, "For this to work, you'll need to commit to your training . . . see it through to the end. No commitment, we can end things right now."

Relief washed over me. *He's giving me a way out. Thank God!* But somehow, my mouth began operating on its own accord. "I have no problem committing to this. I finish what I start." *What the fuck?! Why did I just say that?*

"That's good. But you should know exactly what you're committing to. Four hours of dojo training each day."

Four hours! I have a ship to command, buddy. I said, "No problem."

"And of course, there will be the 24/7 avatar shadowing . . . for the entirety of the voyage. We call them Mo, Shred-Ma, and Chi."

The names sounded familiar, but I couldn't place them – probably some kind of elite fighting team.

"What is this 24/7 avatar shadowing you're talking about?" I asked.

"Just that. When you leave here, Mo, Shred-Ma, and Chi will go with you. You won't see them, of course. They'll stay in cloaked mode until they strike."

On cue, three small black objects descended from high above. These, I figured out, were the individual projectors for the fighting avatars. I watched as they silently hovered around us and then, in unison, went invisible.

"Forget about those things for the time being," Wanda said. "Let's get an understanding of what you do and *do not* know when it comes to combat training."

The US Space-Navy's boot camp is twice as long as that of

the regular Navy's on Earth. And there's a standardized hand-to-hand combat course that's thorough enough to keep green Spacers from getting their asses handed to them in a pub fight, but not much more than that. I said, "Best you pretend I don't know anything and start with self-defense basics."

"Yeah . . . that would have been my suggestion anyway, Captain," Wanda said. "And just so you know . . . drop that self-defense bullshit. If you're not playing offense, you're already toast. Let's call it *self-offense*. And by the way, if you hadn't been the one to throw that first punch in the gym, you wouldn't be here now. We have no time for sniveling cowards."

"Sniveling cowards. Got it."

"Or rule-following goody-two-shoes . . . we fight dirty."

"Okay . . . that shouldn't be too tough for me; I'm not much for rules."

And so, it began. For the next four hours, the five Marines took turns kicking my ass. By the time I'd reached the GravLifts, I was both limping and cradling a sprained elbow. Stepping inside the lift and instructing MATHR to get me back to Deck 13, I leaned against the back wall and closed my eyes – grateful for the respite. That's when I heard them – Drole, Shred-Ma, and Chi. I moved just in time to avoid a punch to the face from Shred-Ma, only to find myself kicked in the gut by Drole. Still bent over, I managed to block the overhead hammer blow from Chi. I dove headfirst onto the floor, rolled, and came up with my fists up and tightly clenched – but the three avatars were gone. The lift door expanded open, and there stood my XO.

Her expression went from one of being startled to one of concern. "Captain?"

"XO Pristy," I said, lowering my hands and straightening up.

She looked about the lift's interior and then back to me. "Are you . . . um, alone in here?"

"Yup. All alone." I looked to the glowing GravLift menu and saw that we were currently on Deck 11. I remembered her new XO quarters were on 11.

"You're starting your morning shift."

"That's right." She gave me a once over, "Did you get any sleep at all last night?"

"Sure . . . just hit the Gym –"

"Captain, everyone knows you're training with the squad."

"The squad?"

"That's what the Bridge crew call them. The squad . . . those badass Marines that don't play well with others."

I shook my head. *Is Hardy totally incapable of keeping a damn secret?*

It's okay, Captain . . . we know it's because you got your ass handed to you in the gym. I don't blame you a bit."

A little embarrassed, I simply shrugged. Saying nothing is better than making up lame excuses.

She smiled and leaned past me to tap on the GravLift menu. As close as she was, I could smell the fruity sweetness of her fragrance, or perhaps it was just her shampoo. She could have just as easily spoken the command for Deck 13.

Motion.

Standing two feet behind Pristy was none other than fucking Shred-Ma, and he was making faces at me – taunting me.

"Oh no . . . not now," I said under my breath.

"Not now?" My XO said, her attention back, full on me. The beginnings of a smile on her lips.

"No, I didn't mean you . . . I was talking to you. Never mind."

She looked about the compartment, mystified. The lift door expanded open, and she strode out into Whale's Alley. She looked back over her shoulder, "You getting off here, Captain?" unable to keep a full grin forming on her lips.

I nodded and followed her out into the passageway.

She said, "Don't worry about it. I saw his reflection . . . that combat avatar of yours." She was now laughing without restraint as she headed off toward the Bridge. "Get some sleep, should be another non-eventful day on the Bridge."

Chapter 8

What I hadn't expected was being awakened three times while I tried to get some much-needed sleep. The first time, bleary-eyed, I awoke to screaming, or maybe it was yelling. Chi was at the foot of my bed, going through the motions of a Japanese karate kata. When I put my pillow over my head, he jumped up on the bed and stomped down on my balls. Furious, I reached for his legs only to grasp empty air – he was gone. Two more times I was awakened, but those times I managed to get myself up and out of bed while doing my best to repel a brutal onslaught of punches, kicks, and the sweeping of my legs from out beneath me. God, I was really starting to hate these fucking avatar warriors.

By mid-day, I was up and out of bed feeling no less tired than when my head had hit the pillow hours earlier. *This is ridiculous.* I had to tell Wanda that we needed to set a few boundaries when it came to my combat training.

I'd gone so far as raising my TAC-Band to leave her a stern message. But no, I knew what she'd say. *Your enemies will not adhere to a schedule. You're either prepared for battle, or you're not.*

Instead, I contacted XO Pristy. "Status on the Bridge, XO?" I said.

"Non-eventful. We're preparing for our next jump. All systems are operating nominally, and long-range sensors have picked up zero enemy vessels in the area thus far. Seems this really is a cakewalk of a mission, Captain."

"You didn't really just say that, did you?"

"Nope . . . I wouldn't be dumb enough to jinx things like that. You coming in –"

"In a while," I said, cutting her off. "I want to drop by Science and Technology, and then –"

"The barracks?" She said, now cutting *me* off with a smile.

"That reminds me, you mentioned you needed to talk to me the other day."

Seeing her there on my TAC-Band, I saw her smile fall away, "It's no big deal. Probably best to forget about it."

She was looking uncomfortable. "Up to you," I said, "feel free to schedule something with MATHR."

She shook her head, "I'll see you when you get here."

"Hold off on manufacturing that next wormhole 'til I'm back on the Bridge," I said, unnecessarily. It was policy that a warship's Captain is present when jumping into unfamiliar territory.

After stopping off at the Bridge – where I presided over the next intergalactic jump – I headed off to Deck 29. I was still feeling jittery from several more surprise attacks encountered along the way here. My left cheekbone throbbed, as did my right wrist, from where I'd been grabbed by Drole, and flipped in some kind of Aikido throw-hold. I found Derrota, Hardy, Coogong, and a cluster of other scientists within one of the larger labs. The two Port Entanglers were there in the compartment, as well as two other items that I hadn't seen before. Hardy was bent over, the upper half of his body obscured within the thing's console.

So involved with what he was doing, Derrota didn't notice my approach until I was standing right next to him. It wasn't unusual for him to be disheveled, but today he looked downright raunchy.

"Oh, Galvin . . . just in time."

"When was the last time you slept, Stephan? Or showered?"

Derrota took a whiff at one of his own armpits. "Oh, my. I've been meaning to take some time . . . but this is just too exciting. The progress we're making –"

"Stephan . . . you need to pace yourself. And ensure those around you do the same."

He nodded, now looking contrite.

"Where's Doc Viv? Thought she was as excited as you, being a part of this."

Momentarily perplexed, he said, "Oh, that's right. She had a surgery . . ." he looked at his TAC-Band, "this afternoon, actually *now*. Something about a reattaching a severed tongue."

"How about you bring me up to speed on your progress," I said, gesturing to the device.

"Yes, our Port Entangler, version *deux*. Come! Let me show you."

Derrota led the way over to the new Entangler, leaving a wake of sour body odor behind him. Hardy extricated himself from the console's innards and stood while retracting chop-stick-looking probes back into his mechanical hands.

"Cap, we have much to show you." Hardy stopped talking while he assessed what I imagine was the purple bruise forming on my cheek. He reached for my right wrist and did an assessment of that as well. "You have been injured, again. I cannot allow this to continue."

I couldn't help smiling at his concern. "I'm dealing with it. Talk to me about these things."

From behind me, Coogong said, "We have taken circuitry from the original devices, analyzed it, and, humbly, I dare say, improved upon it."

It was still a shock to see Coogong standing there as a skinny stick-figure. "Okay, what more can this thing do beyond those two over there."

"For one thing, Cap," Hardy said, "We now only need one device."

Excited, Derrota chimed in, "Galvin . . . we've been trans-porting items all over the ship. Then bringing them back again in one piece."

"I thought there was a line-of-sight issue – that the laser couldn't be obstructed for it to work."

"Once we conjured up superior optical communications tech, we abandoned that methodology. We're now using a specific type of optics and a photonics class of lasers to transport our entangled mass-energy. Beams that contain something called *spacetime wave packets.* They follow alternative rules of physics when they refract, that is, when they pass through various materials."

I looked skeptical.

Hardy said, "Look, standard laser light slows down and usually stops as it travels into denser material, yes? In contrast, spacetime wave packets behave in a manner where they don't need to change speed; in fact, they *speed up* within denser materials. Cap . . . these pulses of light can arrive at different points in space . . . and do so at the same time. So, no matter what the properties of the medium are, it'll continue on as if it's not there."

"So, there's no limitations as to where our entangled energy mass can be sent or retrieved?

"We don't know for sure yet, Galvin," Derrota said. "We're seeing distortion . . . interference, at the sixty-thousand-mile mark – probably radiation-induced. These spacetime wave packets start to get hot at such long distances."

"Wait, how do you know what happens at sixty-thousand-miles out?" I asked.

"Because we've been sending all kinds of shit out into space and bringing it right back again."

I looked at Hardy. "Really?"

"Yeah, Cap . . . really."

I turned and gave the Entangler unit a closer look. It was nothing like the other two. Shiny chrome, like Hardy, its circular profile rose a foot off the deck, its diameter about six or seven feet. That and the floor of the thing was glowing. Heavy black, snake-like conduit cables were attached to the separate touch screen console Hardy had been working beneath just minutes earlier. I looked at the new entangler and then back to the other two Port Entanglers.

"I don't see the laser gun like those two have."

Hardy said, "Uses that different kind of laser . . . which I've just explained to you. Laser energy that is not transmitted via those kinds of archaic distorted glass optics."

Derrota, looking proud of himself, said, "We're using one of *Hamilton's* aft Phazon Pulsar cannons."

My heart skipped a beat. "Wait, you're actually firing one of our Phazon Pulsar weapons . . . one capable of immense destruction, into our own damn ship?!"

Hardy held up two mechanical hands in mock surrender, "Hey-hey, there's no danger. Honest. The gun's been totally repurposed. In fact, it physically cannot cause any damage at all."

"And nobody thought, just maybe, the ship's Captain should have been consulted with some of this?"

"It's my fault, Galvin," Derrota said. "I'm sorry. We, *I*, got so consumed with our progress, I guess all perspective went right out the window."

Truth was, I couldn't help but be impressed by their progress and having accomplished this one-of-a-kind scientific achievement. Theoretical or not, if this thing worked as described, this was beyond any of my expectations.

I said, "This is interfaced to MATHR?"

"Of course, . . . the mathematics are beyond complex, not to mention, the memory requirements are substantial," Derrota said.

"And it's working well . . . no hiccups?"

All three – Derrota, Coogong, and Hardy, smiled. All three said, "No hiccups" simultaneously.

"Then I have just one more question for you . . . why in hell haven't you attempted to bring Captain Tannock back from MATHR's seemingly now-accessible memory banks?"

Looking spellbound, the three of them looked to each other and then to me. Derrota said, "Um, we forgot about Captain Tannock."

Hardy said, "I didn't forget. I'm incapable of forgetting. I don't like the guy . . . and I know you don't like him either. Why don't we just let him stay where he is for the time being?"

With the wave of a hand, I signaled for the ChronoBot to put a cork in it. "Enough! We need to at least *attempt* to retrieve Tannock. Like before you get working on anything else. Understand?"

Hardy stomped over to the entangler's console while letting out a loud breath. And considering the robot didn't actually breathe, it was all for dramatics.

Hardy's face display morphed into a cartoonish, confused-looking face. "This is interesting . . . actually, more *odd* than interesting –"

"What?" I said, losing patience.

"Well, it's just . . . I see Tannock's file sitting there in memory storage."

"So?"

"Well, there's another . . . um . . . physical mass, another item in there, as well. Has an older file creation date. Funny . . . never noticed it before. MATHR must have done some virtual house cleaning, rearranging, of the files," Hardy said.

"How much older?"

"Like . . . hundreds of years older."

I had a really bad feeling about this. About to tell Hardy to NOT access that file, I realized I was too late; his metal fingers were already tap-tap-tapping on the console's touch screen.

The illuminated pedestal suddenly went from being just softly lit to being blindingly bright. Sucking sounds emanated as there was an upward building of ten-inch or so block segments being added one after another. Clearly, something was forming and taking shape before our eyes. So far, something that had two legs and wore outdated 20th Century baggy black trousers. *Shit!*

Chapter 9

Pleidian Weonan Frontier Territory
Brillianne Bridge

Fleet Commander Twinwon

Having made several *creative* escapes while the *Brillianne's* cloaking capabilities had miraculously come back online, Fleet Command Twinwon had to face reality. They had evaded this Grish fleet for the last time. No longer cloaked, propulsion off-line, they had run out of options. Twinwon slammed a clenched fist down onto the armrest of his seat. Not only had this powerful Grish fleet caught up with them, but they were also now positioning to finish them off.

"Fleet Commander, thirteen of the enemy warships have established weapons-lock on the *Brillianne.*"

Twinwon already knew as much but said nothing. *So, what are you waiting for, swine?*

His second looked resolute, "Commander . . . it is time. We have no other recourse other than to . . . surrender."

Twinwon did not respond to his second's spineless plea, as he continued to stare up at the logistical display. *How had things gotten to this point?* His fleet – gone. His ship – incapable of putting up any real defense. Primary propulsion reactor – on the verge of going critical – and last, but not least – breathable atmosphere spewing out to space on multiple decks. Everything, including hope, was lost.

Only now, defeated, did Twinwon turn to Haite Caheil. "Very well, we try things your way . . . if it is not too late." Twinwon had negated his idea when Haite had first suggested it. Any plan that included the destruction of the *Brillianne* was ludicrous. But now that the vessel was all-but-lost anyway, his concern was for those few still alive – a measly 85 crewmembers.

The Varapin pilot's raspy voice, as unpleasant as it was, held no malice. "If we move now . . . yes, there may be time."

"The three shuttles . . . you have prepared them?" Twinwon asked, knowing Haite Caheil had spent the better part of seven hours within the flight bay of the *Brillianne.*

Twinwon said, "Helmsman, the self-destruct apparatus?"

The Pleidian junior officer held up one of his light blue faintly glowing arms. There, a matt black device was strapped to his wrist. "It has been armed, Fleet Commander . . ." He gestured with his other hand toward a series of three blinking on and off buttons.

"Make a shipwide announcement . . . anyone who isn't within the flight bay boarding a shuttlecraft in five minutes . . . will be destroyed, along with the ship."

* * *

Minutes earlier, Twinwon had ordered everyone off the Bridge. In a mass-exodus down a dimly lit corridor, he couldn't help himself feeling a growing resentment towards the Varapin pilot. Sure, intellectually, he knew none of this was his fault. But this ridiculous last-ditch effort for survival was, in fact, that hideous alien's suggestion, right? They made a quick right turn and were now running at full speed through one more wreckage-strewn passageway. Twinwon inwardly cursed; he and the rest of his out-of-breath Bridge crew had already exceeded the mandated five-minute deadline by at least twice that. Having to make detours around breached, closed-off decks had slowed their progress to nearly a crawl at times. He glowered at the black-cloaked Haite Caheil gliding along up ahead. *How is it his feet never touch the deck?* Twinwon, aware of his negatively spiraling thoughts, cleared his mind and centered his consciousness. Only then did he allow himself to think of the Empress. She was his sole reason to continue in spite of what seemed to be insurmountable odds. He would so love to look into those amazing, beautiful eyes once more.

They arrived at the flight bay as other crewmembers emerged from different entrances. The battle damage here was no different than the rest of the ship. Multiple fires raged throughout the expansive compartment. Near the open bay doors off in the distance, Twinwon noticed there was an enemy missile, still intact, protruding halfway out from a bulkhead. Why it hadn't detonated, he couldn't even surmise.

All were converging toward the center of the bay, where the three shuttles awaited. Each vessel had a max crew capacity of 30. Approaching them now, Twinwon was amazed at their transformation. Looking at any of the three, you would not believe they were anything but large segments of scorched ship wreckage. Ragged-edged girders and shredded hull segments had been positioned onto the now shapeless shuttles so perfectly, Twinwon now felt a glimmer of hope.

Along with his Bridge crew, the fleet commander entered through the aft hatchway of the closest shuttle, where crewmembers were quickly ushered to open seats. Every moment counted. So consumed with his thoughts, Twinwon hadn't noticed Haite Caheil was seated next to him.

Twinwon said, "I don't get it . . . why haven't they fired on us? Why spare *this ship* and not the others? Is it that they want to capture me . . . make an example of me?"

The Varapin pilot looked to be considering that. "No, Fleet Commander, I think you have it wrong. It is not you that they want to take alive; it is me."

"You?"

"The Grish have similar long-range bio-sensors to the Pleidian Weonan. My unique bio-signature undoubtedly has been detected. I am a traitor to my people. As the Grish and the Varapin have made a war pact . . . my intuition tells me that I am the one that will be made an example of. Varapin high command would want to make a spectacle of my capture and public execution. Now, please, I must concentrate on this next component of the plan to work."

Haite Caheil rose upward as if being lifted by invisible strings. Effortlessly, he glided between still standing crewmembers, coming to a stop where the shuttle's pilot and co-pilot were seated. Twinwon stood and gestured to a nearby standing crewmember to take his seat. By the time he reached the cockpit, which was open and unobstructed to the rest of the shuttle, he listened as the Varapin pilot conveyed –in explicit detail – what steps needed to be taken.

On a viewscreen, feeds from the other two shuttles showed the nervous faces of the other two shuttle's pilots.

As instructed, all three shuttles initiated their lift thrusters. Once the three vessels had climbed to fifteen feet off the deck, Haite Caheil said to the other two pilots, "Now, you will transfer all navigation control over to this shuttle, do so now." The pilots looked hesitant to do so. "Going forward, we must maneuver as one unit. Even a millisecond of lag time by any one shuttle would be catastrophic." Both pilots did as instructed.

Haite placed a coal-black, boney claw on the shoulder of the pilot before him. "Now, bring all three shuttles right to those open bay doors, to the very precipice of open space."

Without looking at the helmsman, Haite Caheil said, "Give me the device."

Interrupting, the shuttle pilot looked to Fleet Commander Twinwon while bringing a hand up to the side of his head, touching the auditory membrane there. "Sir, the Grish are making contact." Listening to a voice only he could hear, he nodded once then twice in silent confirmation. "It is an ultimatum. We are to lower what is left of our shields and prepare to be boarded. We have two minutes to reply before being fired upon."

Twinwon's mind raced. Haite's plan was surely suicide. Perhaps he should negotiate. Why not make an offer to the Grish? This Varapin traitor in exchange for safe passage out of this sector of space? He felt Haite's beady eyes upon him. No doubt, the Varapin was surmising what must be going through his thoughts. Twinwon let out a breath and said, "Do as Haite Caheil has asked . . . we cannot trust the Grish . . . we have no other viable options."

With shaking hands, the helmsman unstrapped the device from his own wrist and handed it to Haite.

"What exactly happens next?" Twinwon asked.

"Note that I have already diverted maximum power to each of the shuttle's aft shields. The timing of the following three steps must be perfect. Pressing the first button will engage a unique energetic field, one that will surround, encompass, all three shuttles."

"What does that accomplish?" The helmsman asked.

"It will block the Grish's sensors from detecting lifeforms. Now be quiet . . . we have very little time. The second button will initiate *Brillianne's* self-destruct sequence. Understand . . . that is not an instantaneous process. It will take 2.3 seconds before the ship explodes."

"And the third button?" Twinwon asked.

"The third button has been configured specifically to interface with this shuttle's propulsion system. By perfectly timing the press of the button, this shuttle, as well as the other two linked shuttles, will blast out of here a millisecond prior to the ship's destruction. At nearly instantaneous maximum thrust, we can expect G-forces of no less than nine, maybe ten." Haite glanced aft. "Those of you who are not seated and strapped in, will die . . . and, subsequently, become a projectile unto yourselves . . . killing others in the process."

Twinwon turned to face his crew. Terrified eyes stared back at him. "Everyone sit-down! If there are no available seats, sit on the deck. There's plenty of harness strapping along both bulkheads. Everyone . . . secure yourselves!" Turning his attention to the two pilot video feeds, he said, "If you haven't already done so, pass on those orders!"

Taking his own advice, Twinwon scrambled to the portside bulkhead and began to strap himself in.

It was a full minute before crew personnel on all three shuttles had settled down and appeared to be secured and ready for whatever was to come next.

Twinwon watched as the Varapin donned a bulkhead harness, secured it tightly around his body. Only then did he lift the small black device and then position one of his black fingers over the first button. "On your orders, Fleet Commander."

Twinwon thought about the cataclysmic fate of the *Brillianne*, the probability that he, along with those left of her crew, would be little more than space dust within mere seconds. Finally, he thought of Empress Shawlee Tee. *I'm sorry, my love . . .*

Twinwon said, "Press the button."

Twinwon had a fleeting sense of the shuttle being rocketed out of the *Brillianne's* flight bay – but that was it. The immediate destruction of the warship, certainly, must have occurred. But Twinwon, nor any of the crew, would have been conscious to witness that. The effect of nine G's on the Pleidian Weonan anatomy proved to be severe. Severe enough that not all onboard the three shuttles had survived. Twinwon would later learn that eleven crewmembers on shuttle #1 had been lost.

Now, coming fully awake, every millimeter of his body ached. Even so, he was astounded by the total lack of ambient sound – the absence of vibrations – and the lack of gravity within the shuttle compartment. *Have we accomplished nothing? Are we now little more than* actual *space debris?*

Painful as it was to turn his head, Twinwon looked toward the shuttle's bow – out through the forward window. He saw the blur of a passing star. This offered him some hope – hope that just maybe, not all was lost. Blinking to confirm what he was now seeing, Twinwon realized he might have been unconscious longer than he first thought. Haite Caheil was now seated within the pilot's seat. *That* and the co-pilot's seat was empty. He spotted seemingly lifeless bodies floating, unrestrained, behind the cockpit.

Others were now coming awake. Groans and a few painful

wails filled the compartment. Fleet Commander Twinwon scanned the shuttle's interior and found his helmsman, as well as the ship's surgeon, both awake and looking about the shuttle. Making eye contact with the surgeon, Twinwon said, "Attend to those needing your help."

Once he'd unfastened his harness, Twinwon, weightless, pulled himself forward until he was within the cockpit area. He took the co-pilot's seat and strapped himself in.

"I need an update, Haite. What's the status of the two other shuttles? Loss of life, the Grish . . . all of it."

"All three shuttles endured the explosion. Surprising, since I had expected one or even two shuttles not to have made it. Loss of life has been consistent with that of this vessel. Eleven here, ten on shuttle #2, and twelve on shuttle #3."

"We've lost almost half our numbers?"

"Thirty-three dead, fifty-two still alive . . . although, there are numerous injuries," the Varapin pilot said, offering a hand gesture toward the noisy compartment behind.

"You've been in contact with the other pilots?"

"Affirmative . . . they fared better than those of this shuttle."

"And the Grish fleet?"

Haite Caheil took several moments to answer. "Uncertain. Although this shuttle's primitive long-range sensors have not detected other vessels in the vicinity, we cannot be certain our escape went completely unnoticed. We can only hope that the Grish simply witnessed the outward trajectory of exploded space debris and not three intact shuttle-crafts."

"And if they had noticed?"

"I have purposely held off powering up our propulsion systems. That would be like transmitting a beacon signal."

"Well, we can't just glide along in space indefinitely. There's limited fuel, rations, and water will soon become a concern."

Haite pointed a black clawed finger forward, "There is any number of remote planetary systems close enough for us to reach within several days. But only one, called *Unero*, is inhabited with individuals that will register adequate similar bio-readings as that of the Pleidian. A world that has indigenous Pleidian, Mantarian, aSplee, but mostly an indigenous species – similar to humans - called Juvian. This is a unique multi-genome, only partially-integrated exoplanet comprised of numerous, mostly combative, colonies."

"And . . . what, you're suggesting we hide in plain view, something like that?"

Haite didn't bother to answer.

"What about you? You didn't mention there were any Varapin floating around on this planet. You already mentioned their sensors could differentiate your particular bio-readings."

"I will keep the bio-shielding device with me . . . on my person. Do so for as long as it remains charged."

Twinwon was already hating this plan and made no attempt to hide his feelings. "What's to keep *Unero* – its inhabitants – from blowing our three shuttles out of the sky as we try to land?"

"That will not be a problem. The inhabitants are technologically primitive. What would be considered a pre-industrial age."

Twinwon looked at the ghoulish looking alien. *He will most definitely need to stay out of sight.* He scanned the readouts on the control board. "Pleidian shuttles are short-range vessels. Landing on *Unero* will consume most, if not all, our fuel. We will be stranded there, perhaps indefinitely."

"So, you tell me, will your people look beyond the wreckage of the *Brillianne* to come looking for survivors?"

Twinwon wanted to believe the Empress would never stop looking for him, but in truth, he did not know for sure. "Only time will tell. We'll need to scan local space for both the enemy and our salvation."

Chapter 10

USS Hamilton – Science and Technology Lab

Captain Galvin Quintos

T he Port Entangler version *deux* continued making those almost comical sounding sucking sounds, as more and more of the individual's form progressively took shape on the unit's raised platform.

No one spoke once the last block of bio-mass *thunked* into position at the top of the man's head.

The man looked to be in his late 40s, perhaps early 50s, as tufts of grey dominated much of his unruly hair. A small Hitleresque mustache was perched above his upper lip. Very much alive, his eyes sparkled with intelligence and curiosity.

Wearing a mid-20th- century business suit, he looked out of place here in this 22nd-century laboratory.

"Impossible," Derrota said.

"You think?" I said.

"If I am not mistaken, we are looking at none other than Sir Louis de Broglie, himself. The brilliant French quantum physicist. The very same physicist who created our original entanglers."

"Well, that would make some kind of sense . . . right? That he got himself . . . somehow trapped in his port entangler?" I said.

The nearly 280-year-old man had yet to speak.

"Louis de Broglie went on to live a prestigious long life . . . died at the ripe old age for the time; 94 in 1987. Does he look 94 to you?"

"No. So, maybe this isn't Louis de Broglie –"

"Oh, but I *am* Louis de Broglie," said the man in heavily French-accented English. He looked about the compartment in bewilderment. Then, noticing both the ChronoBot, (Hardy) and the stick-figure Thine (Coogong), his mouth gaped, and he made an indistinguishable drawn-out sound– not so much of a groan as a questioning *uhhhhhh*, sound.

Derrota said, "You speak English, Sir Broglie . . ."

"Other than French, of course, I speak five languages – all badly," he said, his head still swiveling around taking in *Hamilton's* interior. "May I ask . . . where on Earth am I?"

Derrota and I exchanged a quick look. I said, "Sir Broglie, I am Captain Galvin Quintos, and you are currently *not* on

Earth." I let that sink in before continuing. "You are on board a ship, *USS Hamilton* . . . what you would call a 'spaceship.' And if that's not overwhelming enough for you, the current year is 2171."

The small man took in the information with surprising restraint. "You are American, no?"

"That's his question?" Hardy exclaimed. "Not that it's 220-some-odd years in the future? Or that we're on a flippin' spaceship? He wants to know if you're American?"

Sir Broglie eyed the ChronoBot looking as though he'd gotten a whiff of something bad. "I do not like this . . . this . . . what are you? Some kind of rude robot?"

"That's exactly what he is," I said. "You'll have to excuse Hardy. He has no manners."

Derrota took a step forward, "Sir Broglie . . . I cannot tell you how honored I am to meet you. I am the ship's Senior Science Officer." He held out a hand for the physicist to shake.

Looking reluctant to do so, Sir Broglie took Derrota's hand in a kind of limp three-fingered shake that was uncomfortable to watch.

Sir Broglie shot Hardy a sideways glance before saying, "I have many questions. But I am an intelligent man. Deducing much of what must have happened, I suspect I have been, inadvertently . . . um . . . captured by my port entangler device into Galion memory, no? I wasn't so much as *captured,* as copied . . . yes, that makes far more sense. The . . . what is the word? Ah, the entangler *setting* must not have been configured for the destruction of the original transmitted mass."

"Galion memory?" Derrota asked.

"Yes . . . the alien technology. Galion."

"So, you knew the technology was alien . . . was from another planet?"

"Of course, I did. I knew the alien that provided it. The lizard-man from Galion."

Derrota said, "Sir . . . none of your writings mention anything about an alien —"

"You think I'm a fool?" Broglie spat. "A Nobel Prize-winning quantum physicist who claims he has been visited by an alien being? You say you are the science officer; I say you are an idiot!"

Crestfallen, Derrota stared back at the French man, unable to speak.

I said, "You must be tired; perhaps you'd like to freshen up. Spend some time in one of our cabins."

"Apparently, I have been asleep, more or less, for over two hundred years. So, no. You will now send me back to the year 1948. Perhaps I will return here later . . . after I check on my laboratory . . . spend time with my family."

"Look, Frenchy, for someone who claims to be intelligent, you haven't quite connected all the dots yet," Hardy said.

I inwardly cringed at the ChronoBot' s comment. Not that it wasn't true, but even if he didn't like the man, Hardy could at least try to be sympathetic to the guy's plight. This situation must be more than a little overwhelming for him.

"Yeah," I said, "You were never actually gone . . . you lived out the rest of your life."

"Went on to provide incredible scientific breakthroughs in the field of quantum –"

"Shut up! All of you . . . just shut up! I must return to my own time . . ." then stymied, Sir Broglie's eyes were now darting back and forth between them. "Oh my . . . you are correct . . . I cannot return. I would disrupt everything. It would be, unexplainable . . . there being two Louis de Broglie's."

Hardy's face display showed a big yellow happy face. "You don't need to worry about that, Frenchie . . . we wouldn't know how to get you back to 1948, any more than any other time in history. No new-fangled time machines, just lying about the ship . . . sorry."

Looking unsteady on his feet, the physicist looked as if he might pass out.

"Derrota, would you mind escorting our guest to HealthBay. Be a good idea if he gets a full examination. He's been through a lot."

Derrota, looking concerned, took Broglie by the arm and gently guided him out of the compartment.

Coogong said, "He will need time to adjust. This must be quite unsettling for him."

"Whatever," Hardy said. "Cap . . . shall we bring Captain Tannock back as well? Get that over with?"

Ugh. Just the thought of dealing with one more unpleasant personality.

"Or . . . I can do a re-check of this entangler's connections. Run some more tests . . . that sort of thing." Hardy offered.

I looked to Coogong and then back to Hardy. "Yeah, why rush things, right?"

* * *

It was wishful thinking my combat avatars would stay hidden once I'd left Deck 29. This time it was Drole and Shred-Ma who attacked as I stepped out from the GravLift. I blocked Shred-Ma's roundhouse kick to my head but took a front kick to my groin from Drole. Luckily, I'd thought ahead. Prior to leaving my quarters today, I put on an athletic cup. The kick to my balls had no effect, and I was able to step in and deliver an uppercut to Drole's chin that put him on his ass. I flashed the menacing avatar a victorious smile, "Not this time, shithead."

Who would have thought two virtual combatants could be so vindictive? By the time I arrived within the Marine's barracks, I was covered with blossoming head-to-toe bruises.

The five of them were waiting for me. While Max looked to be officiating, they'd paired off and were taking turns with attacking and defensive moves. As far as I could tell, no one was holding back.

"You're late," Max said.

"Sorry, there were unexpected . . . interruptions."

"Nah, that's unacceptable, man," Grip said. "We're here. We're investing our valuable time for your benefit. The least you could do is show up on time."

"I apologize."

Wanda, who had just thrown Ham's oversized bulk onto

the mat, came over to me – her eyes taking in my most recent battle bruises, evoking a satisfied looking smile. "You obviously haven't learned much."

"Hey, it's three against one. Not to mention, they have the element of surprise."

Wanda stuck out her lower lip and feigned sobbing. "Does mommy need to cuddle poor little Captain Galvin?"

"Screw you," I said, trying not to smile.

"Okay!" Max said, clapping his hands together once. "Let's get down to it. Today, we'll be working on your MED-FT's."

"MED-FT's?" I repeated.

Hock bellowed out a hearty Jethro kind of laugh, "It stands for, most effective dirty fighting techniques."

Max continued, "We'll be working on the long-knee, the short-knee, the throat-chop, and if we have time, several elbow-strikes. While each of these is highly effective, taking out an opponent quickly. Done effectively, they're difficult to fend off. So, we'll be working on the best defensive tactics as well." Max looked about his crew.

"How about I start off with him?" Wanda said.

"All right," Max said. "We'll switch things up in fifteen minutes. We have a lot to go through, so everyone, make the best of your time with the Captain."

While I paired off with Wanda, the others paired off and began to spar.

Wanda said, "We'll start with the long-knee. We'll be using the Muay Thai version technique."

"Got it. Muay Thai version," I said.

Hands relaxed and her shoulders slightly hunched forward, Wanda began to move left and then right – as if looking for an opening to strike. "I love Muay Thai. It's one discipline that is always evolving . . . transforming. Known as the *Art of Eight Limbs* –"

Before I had time to react, she'd darted forward. As if reaching in to hug me, I felt both her hands come around and take hold of the back of my head. As she yanked my body forward, she propelled her own weight forward while ramming a knee up and toward my jerked-in lower face. It was only by chance that had turned my head, just enough, that my nose hadn't taken the brunt of the impact. Even so, I saw stars and my knees began to buckle.

"Man up, Captain," Max shouted from the other mat. "She put nothing behind that love tap. Now you try it. And Wanda . . . easy on the defense . . . let him complete the maneuver."

I blinked away my watery eyes and the throbbing pain in my cheek. *What was I thinking? Who in their right mind signs up for this kind of punishment?* Now, watching Wanda getting into her defensive stance, she taunted me with a mocking sneer. "If you were any more of a pussy –"

I lunged. But instead of reaching for the back of her head, I grabbed a fistful of hair on the left and right sides of her head. And while yanking her head down, I stepped in and drove my knee up into her face with all the pent-up anger and need for retribution I could draw upon. I'd love to tell you I put Wanda down on the mat with a bloody nose, but unfortunately, I can't. Just as my knee was about to impact her face, she rolled the two of us forward while sweeping my feet out from under me. It happened so fast that I lost all sense of what was up and what was down. Only when I was laid out on my back – her sitting on my heaving chest – did I comprehend the magnificence of her move.

"That was awesome! But Max said you were *not* to use a defensive move."

The others, including Max, laughed.

Wanda said, "What did *Hock* say? We're practicing MED-FT's" . . . most effective *dirty* fighting techniques. Rule number one, never believe an opponent will play fair."

"Got it," I said, wishing I'd crushed that little nose of hers.

"Get up, and I'll show you how I did that."

And so, it continued. For four-and-a-half more hours, I learned just how despicable these five Marines were. How ruthless and conniving they were, not to mention, amazing combatants – each having their own areas of pain-inflicting expertise.

* * *

I arrived on the Bridge, no longer caring who saw my battle wounds. In fact, I was somewhat proud of them because I wasn't the only one who had them; right now, Wanda was sitting on a table in HealthBay, having her recently broken nose attended to.

On the Halo display, I could see a manufactured wormhole

was starting to take shape. MATHR must have alerted the Bridge crew of my impending arrival.

Turning around from her Tactical station, XO Pristy said in a low, conspiratorial voice, "Captain . . . is it true?"

I asked, "Is what true?" using her same conspiratorial tone.

"That we brought back a 280-year-old scientist from the past. That, and he wants to go back to his own time period."

Seeing everyone on the Bridge was leaning in to hear my reply, I said loud enough for all of them to hear, "Yes, it's true. Sir Louis de Broglie, famed genius physicist from the 20th century, has been . . . um, successfully downloaded from MATHR's memory banks. And yes, let's just say he's not exactly thrilled to be here."

Pristy looked incredulous, "You'd think he'd be ecstatic to be here. To see the many scientific developments . . . see how his work has influenced the future."

She was right; his reaction had been odd, to say the least. "Well, he's been through a lot. Perhaps, in time he'll adjust and —"

"It shouldn't be a surprise . . . some people are just dicks," came Hardy's voice from behind. "Me? I think that the guy's in love with himself. Gets a boner every time he sees himself in the mirror."

I said, "Hardy, show some decorum. You're now on the Bridge."

"And if he's not the one making the *great* discovery, he's not all that interested . . . maybe he's even jealous." Hardy was now standing at the side of the Captain's Mount. He wore his retro John Hardy appearance on his face display. "Just saying."

"Captain, we're ready to jump," XO Pristy said.

Up on the Halo-display was an awaiting, yawning-wide wormhole that shimmered and glimmered with the typical full-spectrum of bright colors.

I knew we would be dropping deep into Pleidian space – what would be considered the *fringe* of Frontier Space. That, and we'd be arriving fairly close to the last known coordinates of the *Brillianne* and Commander Twinwon's destroyed fleet.

With a quick glance at my armrest readouts, I ensured *Hamilton* was indeed still cloaked, "Full shields enabled, and let's go to battle stations, XO. Helm, take us in."

Chapter 11

USS Hamilton

Pleidian's Fringe Frontier Space

Captain Galvin Quintos

At jump completion, the Bridge crew (including myself) took in a collective breath. No less than fifteen Grish warships were in the vicinity, and it was only by sheer luck we hadn't landed right on top of another vessel.

"Status Report!" I barked.

XO Pristy, busy tapping at her control board, responded, "No sign that we've been detected, Captain. But I wouldn't engage propulsion . . . even cloaked, being this close, our radiation signature would set off alarm bells."

The 3D contours of a Grish warship on the Halo display looked close enough to reach out and touch. Pristy said, "She's less than three miles off our starboard side."

"Cap . . . my sensors have picked up debris," Hardy said.

"What kind of debris."

"The kind you'd find from a destroyed Pleidian warship."

"He's right, Captain," Pristy said, "The Grish fleet looks to be searching the remnants."

A large and jagged hull section tumbled into and just as quickly out of view on the Halo display.

"I'm currently monitoring the piglet's comms . . . One of their vessels is transmitting on an unencrypted channel. They have just confirmed . . . this is indeed what is left of the *Brillianne,*" Hardy said.

I thought of Empress Shawlee's parting words . . . *Twinwon. He's more than a Fleet Commander to me.*

With so many of these piglet warships – along with the fact *Hamilton* had so few crew on board to man the weaponry – I wondered if we could prevail. Although most functions were automated, humans were still very much needed in times of battle.

Hardy said, "I calculate the odds of a *Hamilton* victory at close to 50/50."

"Even if she could, that's not our mission. I'd be breaking a direct order from Admiral Block."

A number of Bridge crew heads turned in my direction.

"Fine, I've broken orders before, but the repercussions of *Hamilton* being spotted here would put more than just us, *me*, in hot water. Block's going out on a limb for the Empress, and I'm not going to chance the resulting collateral damage."

"Captain, "XO Pristy said, "if this, here, is all that is left of the *Brillianne,* why such a detailed sensor search? No one could have survived such a cataclysmic explosion."

Good question. I looked to Hardy with brows raised.

His face display was a spinning pinwheel of moving dots – *his thinking face.* "I'm only getting bits and pieces of things. But it sounds like the badly damaged *Brillianne* had not been destroyed by the Grish. That the ship self-destructed upon receiving orders to surrender and prepare to be boarded. *That,* and . . . one or more Grish fleet vessels had detected outgoing rapid thrust signatures, just prior to the explosion."

I smiled, "An attempted escape . . . one they tried to hide with the blast."

"Perhaps they'd used a shuttle or two?" Pristy said. "So why hang around here? They'd be long gone by now?"

Hardy said, "Because they have no idea which direction they've gone. Open space is damn big . . . they're looking for clues. That perhaps those momentary thrust signatures could give them some kind of a directional read to go on."

XO Pristy sat back in her seat and then spun around to look at Hardy. "*Hamilton's* sensors are good, but not that good. And MATHR has no clue, either."

The spinning pinwheel dissolved back into Hardy's retro appearance. "Pleidian Weonan shuttles do not utilize the same propulsion fuel mixture as their far larger fleet vessels. In time, they'll come to that realization. But for now, I know which direction the two –no, *three* – Pleidian shuttle crafts went."

"Send the directional coordinates to the Helm," I said.

"Done," Hardy said.

I turned to John Chen sitting at the Helm console. "Can you get us out of here on tiptoes, crewmember Chen? The piglets are already searching for divergent propulsion signatures."

Chen pursed his lips while thinking. With a slow nod, he said, "An anti-matter flush could get us moving."

An anti-matter flush was actually a maintenance procedure conducted by the Engineering and Propulsion department. The buildup of anti-matter was typically not a big problem, but over time, it could cause anomalies. The good news, there was no radiation factors associated with the process. That was the entirety of what I knew about it.

"And where, exactly, does this anti-matter flush exhaust out from?" I asked.

A crease formed between Chen's brows, "Sorry, sir, I'm not sure.

Hardy's spinning pinwheel had returned.

I said, "MATHR, hail Chief Porter."

A moment later, Chief Craig Porter said, "Go for Chief Porter."

"I need a quick answer, Craig."

"Hello to you too, Galvin."

"Where, specifically, does an anti-matter flush exhaust out from?"

Several seconds passed before the Chief said, "Out the ass end of the ship. But we're not scheduled –"

I cut him off. "How long will it take you to implement the process?"

"Um . . . ten minutes, maybe."

"Okay, Craig, get that started, will you?"

"Sure, Porter out."

"There's one problem, sir," crewmember Chen said. "Currently, we're not facing in the correct direction. The anti-matter flush will propel us in the direction of that Grish Frigate over there." He pointed to the Halo display.

Sure enough, there was a stationary, mid-sized warship there.

"And we can't use propulsion to maneuver," Hardy added, stating the obvious.

"Port and Starboard docking thrusters don't use propulsion . . . I think they're basically blasts of steam," Pristy said.

"You're right!" I said. "Space station docks, shipyards, they all abhor the cumulating radiation from docking vessels. There's been a fleet law on the books for 75 years that non-radiation docking procedures must be utilized."

I looked at my TAC-Band. Nearly four minutes had passed since I'd given Chief Porter the go-ahead to flush the anti-matter. "The big question is, will the Grish pick up on *Hamilton's* steam thrusts?"

"They're actually pretty adjustable, Captain," Chen said. "Guiding a three-mile-long dreadnought into space dock takes a good bit of finesse. Sir."

"So . . . you can limit the expulsion?"

"Exactly . . . I'll take it slow. Pivot *Hamilton* around on her center axis."

"Okay, do it now. And let's just hope the Grish don't pick up on the moisture being sprayed into space."

Hardy waved away my comment. "Nah . . . it'll be like a fart in the wind, sure you can smell it, but it'll be fleeting, and you have no idea where it came from."

Chuckles erupted from around the Bridge.

"This is no laughing matter, people," I said. "We screw this up, and we could find ourselves fending off an entire Grish fleet. Which, again, is *not* our mission."

Hardy leaned down closer to me. "I don't like this."

"Like what?"

"That we're staying cloaked . . . having to hide from the piglets. We should be frying their asses . . . making bacon, extra-crispy style."

The ChronoBot's core, John Hardy's personality – perhaps a tad crude – was emerging. At some point, I'd have to remind the ChronoBot I was still the ship's captain above and beyond being his friend. Boundaries.

"No one likes this . . . why don't you just concentrate on the Grish comms chatter? Ensure our actions remain unobserved."

Taking in the Grish Frigate and the lack of any real movement thus far, I said, "Helm, need I remind you the anti-matter flush will commence in . . ." I looked at my TAC-Band, "three minutes and ten seconds?"

"No, sir," Chen said. "I'll increase the expulsion rate."

As the seconds slowly ticked by, my patience was starting to grow thin.

"We have movement, sir," XO Pristy said, looking up at the Halo display. "But will it be fast enough?"

Chen, sounding irritated, said, "If I increase the amount anymore, Gail, someone out there's going to see it."

She shot Chen a snide schoolgirl expression.

Hardy said, "We'll still need another 32 degrees axis spin to miss that frigate."

At that moment, *Hamilton* jostled. "What was that? I said.

Both Hardy and XO Pristy said, "The anti-matter flush," at the exact same time.

I looked at my TAC-Band. "But it's a full minute early!"

"The flush process is not an exact mechanism," Hardy said.

But I wasn't listening to Hardy. I stood, watching as events unfolded up on the Halo-Display.

"We're going to hit that frigate," Pristy said under her breath.

"No, we're not," Chen said.

Hamilton was picking up speed, fast. Yes, the dreadnought was changing direction, but not nearly fast enough. *Shit, we're going to hit that frigate.*

"It's like watching an approaching head-on train wreck in slow motion," Hardy said.

"Knock off the twaddle, Hardy," I ordered. "Chen . . . can you increase –"

"Not without overshooting our desired course. And not without sending us headlong into a different ship."

Pristy said, "Now approaching 1.5 clicks to impact, sir, and we're picking up speed."

"Maybe it's for the best we hit the son-of-a-bitch."

"Zip it, Hardy. I'm not going to tell you again!"

"Less than a mile and closing," Pristy said.

From above, MATHR's voice made everyone jump.

COLLISION IMMINENT. BRACE FOR IMPACT!
COLLISION IMMINENT. BRACE FOR IMPACT!

"Half mile!" Pristy said."

"Everyone, brace for impact!" I yelled while stepping back and taking a seat myself.

The Grish frigate now completely filled the Halo-Display. I closed my eyes and held my breath. No one dared speak.

Chapter 12

USS Hamilton - HealthBay

Major Vivian "Viv" Leigh - Ship's Primary Physician

Having completed the surgical procedure on reattaching the young Marine's tongue, Viv was looking forward to getting back to the Science and Technology Deck. As both a medical doctor and scientist, she was fascinated by quantum mechanics – more specifically, quantum entanglement. The prospect of physically transferring matter from one location to another – *well* – the implications of such technology were endless. And although it wasn't spoken of much, everyone knew the largest implications would be the transport of organic matter, namely, human beings.

Still in her scrubs, she exited the Surgery Center. She stopped upon hearing the near/by, unmistakable accented voice of Stephan Derrota. Striding down the HealthBay passageway, she found the ship's Science Officer standing within the hospital section. And he wasn't alone.

"Stephan?" she said.

"Ah! Doc Viv." He glanced to the short, oddly dressed man beside him. "This is Sir Louis de Broglie."

She gave the man a quick once-over. "That's impossible."

"Says the woman wearing a pink clown costume," Broglie said with a sneer.

She turned her attention to Derrota. "Stephan?"

"Apparently, Captain Tannock wasn't the only one *unwittingly* captured within a port entangler's memory. It was MATHR who yielded another copy file –"

"I am a real person! Am I not standing right here breathing the same air as you? Am I not flesh and blood, as you are?"

Listening to the little man's French-accented rant was proof enough for her that this was, indeed, the famous physicist from the early to mid-1900s. The man was a genius. She'd studied his works in college. In fact, his Ph.D. thesis first postulated the wave-particle duality theory – an early central component of quantum mechanics.

"Is he injured? Exhibiting ill effects from his time in stasis?" she asked Derrota.

"You are asking this imbecile if I am ill? Why not ask me directly? What kind of doctor are you?"

"Fine. Why don't you have a seat? A full examination will take only minutes." She gestured to a nearby bed. "I promise you won't feel a thing."

Sir Broglie's nostrils flared, "No, no, I prefer any examination be conducted by a male doctor." As he moved toward the bed, he began untying his necktie.

"You don't need to undress, Sir Broglie. And I assure you, women are every bit as competent as men at most things, maybe even better. Here you go, hop on up onto the bed."

Derrota stifled a grin.

Within moments of the little man being seated, a hovering medical avatar popped into view above him. As it slowly spun around, virtual metatags began to appear along the avatar's torso.

Viv said, "Oh boy . . . your lungs are in pretty bad shape . . . what, you smoke cigars, maybe a pipe?"

Broglie waved away the question with the flip of one hand.

"And your liver . . ." Viv said, letting out a breath. "It's in pretty bad shape. Open your mouth for me."

Reluctantly, her patient did as asked, exposing a mouth full of yellowed and brown-tinged choppers.

"You have tooth decay and severe gum disease, which explains issues with your heart health and other organs."

"Well, I live my life as I see fit."

She continued to study the avatar. "What I don't see are adverse complications from being transported." She smiled, "You're as about unhealthy a specimen as I've seen in my career, but that's not caused by any kind of port entangler."

"I could have told you that much."

Before she could continue, MATHR began broadcasting:

Collision Imminent. Brace for Impact!
Collision Imminent. Brace for Impact!

"What is this? Are we to crash into something?" The French physicist asked, looking around HealthBay.

Viv flagged down a passing med-tech, "Complete the exam, Carl . . . he'll need a few hours with the dental bot, and a NewGrow for his liver and heart. Infuse him with nanobots for cholesterol builds – his arteries are pretty gunked up. And most important, don't let him out of your sight."

Bringing her attention to Derrota, she said, "And you, Stephan, you're going straight to your quarters where you'll first shower and then get a few hours' sleep. I see you back on Deck 29 anytime soon, and I'll issue a *medically unfit for duty* order . . . got that?"

"Got it," the science officer said, looking properly chastised.

* * *

She arrived on the Bridge in time to witness five large warships in extremely close proximity to *Hamilton*. MATHR had ceased with her warnings – apparently, disaster had been avoided. With her eyes on the Halo display, she joined Hardy at the side of the Captain's mount. "What are we doing here?" She asked. She could tell they were moving, just not very quickly.

Hardy said, "Trying to go unnoticed."

"This is a Grish fleet . . . shouldn't we be firing smart missiles, deploying Arrows, that sort of thing?"

The Captain said, "Once again . . . those aren't our orders, Doc." He shot her a sideways glance, taking in her rumpled pink scrubs. "Not that you're ever unwelcome here, but we're a tad busy right now."

"Sorry. Two quick questions. One, when were you going to tell me about our new arrival? The Frenchman with the bad teeth?"

Hamilton was sliding in between two Grish warships now. She wondered how it was possible – even being cloaked – that they'd gone unnoticed thus far.

The Captain said, "Sorry. The Frenchie was a recent surprise. Didn't Stephan bring him to you in HealthBay?"

"Yes . . . he's there now."

The Captain barked, "Helm, heading change . . . five degrees port!"

"I'll try, sir," John Chen said.

Thinking that an odd response from a helmsman, she let it go. She had come here for one reason, and with the Captain this distracted, it was the perfect time to ask permission.

"Um, my second question . . . since Sir Broglie is relatively healthy," she lied, "and has zero negative effects from the port entangler –"

The Captain cut her short with a direct stare. "You better not be asking me what I think you're asking me. That's the real reason you're here . . . isn't it?"

She felt her face flush. She was caught, and they both knew

it. Angered, she spat back, "So, what? We just continue trans-porting mice for eternity? Or sending mindless drones out into space and back? Science demands we take this to the next level!" She had raised her voice a little louder than she had intended to.

"Did I not mention this wasn't the best time for a chit-chat, Vivian?"

She hated when he called her that. Or did she actually like it? She wasn't sure. She felt the others on the Bridge staring at her.

The Captain continued, "And do I need to remind you that there's still another crewmember trapped within MATHR's memory banks?"

"Hey, it was you that opted to keep him there, from what I hear."

Looking contrite, he said, "Well . . . we needed to see how the Frenchie had withstood the process. No sense in bringing him back if he's only going to die or have serious health issues."

"Yeah, I'm sure you were sitting here, wringing your hands with worry about Tannock's health," she said.

"Listen, I know you're chomping at the bit to move forward with human experiments . . . but we still don't have enough data. Talk to Stephan; he's not sure how the process can impact one's consciousness."

XO Pristy said, "Captain, we've cleared the Grish fleet. From all indications, our presence here has gone unnoticed."

Hardy said, "Not so fast, Lieutenant . . . chatter between

ships has picked up within the last few minutes. Anomalies have been detected."

Viv said, "Okay then . . . I'm going to the Lab."

No one was listening to her.

She continued, "I'll bring Captain Tannock out of memory stasis . . . do further physical examinations."

Still, no one was listening to her.

"And only then will we move on to human experiments."

The Captain was now standing with Gail Pristy at the Tactical station and deep in discussion – something about Grish sensor capabilities.

She took a step backward and then, slowly, turned away, striding toward the Bridge's exit. Once out into Whale's Alley, she both felt hand heard the ChronoBot coming up behind her. *Shit!* She turned around, now walking backward, "What is it, Hardy?"

"You may have pulled a fast one on the Captain back there, but come on, you really think I wouldn't notice? That I didn't hear what you said?"

"I don't know what you're talking about."

"Yeah, right. Doc, listen, I have a better idea than bringing old Captain Tannock back out of mothballs . . . at least for the time being."

Hardy had caught up with her now, and the two of them were walking side-by-side. She said, "Go on . . ."

"Let *me* be your next guineapig."

"Thanks' Hardy, but I'm sorry to say, you're a mechanical _"

"Hey, hey, thanks to my *Sheentah* creators, I have an organic-based AI . . . I have a real, functioning brain. That, and I have a consciousness, one as human as anyone else's on board this ship."

She heard the defensiveness in his voice and truly regretted that she'd minimized his humanity. The truth was, Hardy *was* a person, not a simple robot. "I'm so sorry, Hardy. And you're right." She stopped and looked up at the towering mechanical man. "In fact, you'd be the perfect next test specimen. Who better than a ChronoBot that can maintain perfect data records throughout the process? And between you and LuMan, you should be able to track any issues with consciousness. Would you really be willing to do this? You know the Captain would be against it."

"True . . . he had a problem with human experiments . . . but I am not human . . . not anymore."

"Why don't we talk to Coogong and Stephan when he wakes. And maybe we don't bring this up to the Captain just yet." Hardy did his faux zipping-his-lips thing on his face display. Viv had never been this excited about any one scientific discovery as those provided by the Port Entanglers – so she knew what her own motives were with these experiments – but not Hardy's. She wondered why he would jeopardize his relationship with the Captain by subverting his orders. But the truth was that this was too important to worry about any such trivialities.

Chapter 13

USS Hamilton

Pleidian Weonan Fringe Frontier Space

Captain Galvin Quintos

After the close call with the Grish fleet – and narrowly missing that frigate – I decided to spend some time catching up on mundane paperwork within my ready room. Then came the interruption from Drole, Shred-Ma, or Chi. Not sure which was the one who had snuck up behind me; he's even gotten his virtual hands wrapped around my neck. I managed a yelp, and that's when I heard several soft chimes coming at my door. The Avatar disappeared. After catching my breath, I said, "Come in."

XO Pristy entered, looking about the ready room. "Are you alone in here, Captain? Is everything okay?"

I rubbed my neck, "Yes. I'm fine. What can I do for you, Lieutenant?"

She suddenly looked nervous, like she regretted disturbing me. "It's nothing . . . forget I –"

"Why don't you sit down and tell me what's going on. Something's been gnawing at you for days, so spit it out. I promise you'll feel better if you get it off your chest."

She briefly looked up as if saying a silent prayer and then took a seat in front of my desk. While she gathered her thoughts, I stayed quiet.

"Okay . . . you know that my tour of duty contract is coming up, right?"

I nodded. It had actually slipped my mind, but I did remember she had yet to reenlist – had thought she just hadn't gotten around to it yet. I'd never even considered she'd want to do anything else with her life.

"Captain . . . I don't think *this* is the right place for me anymore."

I let that sink in. How could this not be the right place for her? She was young and far more competent than I was at her age. Her prospects within the U.S. Space-Navy were limitless.

"Do you mean . . . on this ship, on *Hamilton*?" I said, trying to tamper down my growing concern.

"Yes. Well, the military in general. I'm thinking I should pursue a life in the private sector."

"Private sector?"

"Well, yeah . . . you know, my dad has a successful law

practice. He wants me to join his firm. Do the whole Pristy and Pristy Attorneys at Law thing."

"But you're not an attorney."

"No . . . but I have a year and a half of law school under my belt. I received my undergrad degree at 21 . . .I'd started law school when things fell apart at home; then, I joined the service. I thought you knew all this."

"I did, I do!" I said defensively. "I guess I just don't understand what's changed. I thought you were happy here. Has something happened? Was it something I did or said?"

She looked back at me with a forced smile. There was a glint of moisture building in her eyes. Self-conscious, she sniffed and looked down. "Captain . . . it's just too hard."

Oh God . . . please don't say it. I knew Pristy had feelings for me. A kind of crush thing that I had been certain would fade in time. I'd thought she'd meet someone onboard; hell, when fully-manned, *Hamilton* had thousands of male prospects, any of whom would be ecstatic to start a relationship with her. And I certainly wasn't the kind of captain to give two hoots about who-dated-who onboard my ship, as long as it didn't interfere with their on-duty job performance.

"I know you have feelings for someone else onboard. Everyone knows it," she said, almost defiantly.

Fuck! "Lieutenant . . . Gail, there's always going to be gossip on board a ship like this. Rumors. Don't believe everything –"

Her eyes narrowed, "So it's not true. You and Doc Viv aren't . . . well, a thing."

"No! Of course not. We're just friends." I'd said it with

enough resolve that I almost believed it myself. But the truth was, I didn't know what my relationship was with Viv. What I *did* know was that she could be infuriating. Sure, she was beautiful, but also secretive – not to mention ridiculously intelligent – and always two or three steps ahead of everyone around her. My mind flashed back to Deck 49, to Cherry Park, to one specific night. The softly illuminated Japanese tōrō lanterns and the path that had eventually led to that intimate garden area called a Korakuen. There, a hot springs pond billowed with steam. And it was there, in the near pitch-darkness, that I'd had an encounter with a woman. She'd made love to me while never speaking a word. It was only later she had let it be known – yes, it had been her; it had been Vivian.

"Hello? Did you hear me?"

I nodded, "Yes, I heard you." I hadn't. I'd mentally left the conversation thinking about Viv. I tried to recall what Gail was saying. Something about . . . *us. What about us?*

She continued, "Well, do you? See something . . . anything, between us?" She waited, her eyes now boring into mine.

I said, "Come on, Gail. We work together, right? Like mere feet apart from one another on the Bridge."

"So?"

"You honestly would throw away what has the makings of a brilliant career . . . and for what?"

That had done it. Tears were now making wet tracks down the contours of her pretty cheeks. "After this deployment, this mission, I'm leaving the Service." She stood up, not bothering to wipe the tears from her face. "You need not worry; I won't make a scene. Be the very picture of indifference and professionalism while at my post."

"Gail . . . please. Sit down. Let's talk this through. You know I care about you and how important you are on this ship."

She stood up straight, her eyes fixed at some point above me. For a moment, I thought she might have noticed one of my combat avatars, but no, she was just standing at attention. "Am I dismissed, Sir?"

"Yes, Lieutenant. You're dismissed."

Minutes after she'd gone, I continued to stare at the closed door to my ready room. The truth was, I cared deeply for my XO. She was my right hand onboard *Hamilton,* and I honestly wondered how I would manage without her. *Shit!* Could I have handled that any worse?

The door chimed again, and I wondered if it was Lieutenant Pristy coming back, but what more was there to say?

"Enter," I said.

To my relief, it was Stephan Derrota. He looked somewhat more rested, in a fresh uniform, slightly less rumpled than the last time I saw him.

"Galvin . . . I think I know where they went."

Switching mental gears, I realized he must be referring to the fleeing Pleidian shuttles. "I thought you'd be up on Deck 29 . . . working with the Port Entangler."

"I'm taking a break from that. Viv's up there. Said she and Hardy had some rudimentary experiments they wanted to follow up on."

"Okay, so tell me your idea."

Derrota took the same seat Gail had occupied earlier.

"It was actually something Hardy had mentioned to me a while back. He said that LuMan had once traveled within this quadrant of space. There's an OIM world that may be the perfect hideout . . . if they had enough fuel to reach it."

The OIM tag Derrota referred to was one that had an *Occluded Interaction Mandate*. Most worlds within the cosmos do not support any kind of life. But those billions upon billions of those that *do* support life – specifically, those that have a burgeoning life form developing along a more advanced evolutionary progression – would be considered "intelligent life." These worlds that support civilizations that have not yet realized interstellar space travel were at issue. They were to be left alone, to be unaccosted – allowed the freedom to either join the throngs of other spacefaring beings or not. Even the most aggressive alien species tended to observe what most star charts tagged as having an OIM.

"Okay," I said. "Why this particular world?"

Derrota said, "MATHR, bring up the star chart I was most recently looking at. I think it's PL-59832."

The Halo display above my desk now showed a 3D depiction of an eight-world planetary system with what looked to be a yellow dwarf, similar to Earth's Sun, at its center.

Derrota grew the size of the virtual star system by expanding his hands outward and walking between the now, encircling basketball-sized worlds. "This is the Zoyam system. And this here, the fourth exoplanet from the star, is called *Unero*. It is inhabited. Recorded bio-readings suggest the natives include Pleidians, aSplee, Mantarians . . . and Juvians. Juvians closely resemble humans." He looked over to me with his hands on his hips. "Galvin . . . if you were fleeing that fleet of piglets, where would *you* go? To a relatively nearby world with an accommodating atmosphere and environment, but one where your Pleidian bio-readings could be easily scanned . . . or would you take the chance on reaching a faraway world? One where there are other Pleidians, perhaps millions of them, where you could attempt to meld into their indigenous society, and hopefully, stay undetected?"

"But you said yourself, it's tagged as an OIM exoplanet," I said.

"Yes . . . and that only means the Pleidian crew would have to keep their presence there a secret. Perhaps merge with locals while doing their best not to share any kind of advanced technology."

"Okay, let's say we reach this world . . ."

"Unero"

"Yes, Unero. What makes you think we'll be able to find those that escaped the *Brillianne,* hiding from the Grish? You said it yourself; they'll be blending into society."

"That, Galvin, I do not have an answer for. But surely, they would leave some indication, maybe hidden breadcrumbs to follow."

The door chimed, and in strode XO Pristy. Professional and all business, she said, "The Grish . . . they're hot on our trail. Not sure how they detected us, but they're in pursuit."

"How close?"

"Real close. They'll overtake us at our current speed in ten minutes. Suggest we transition to FTL or jump."

I looked at Derrota. "You have coordinates for this Unero world?"

"Yes. A half light-year's distance from our current location."

I stood and came around my desk. "XO, prepare for a rush-jump."

She hesitated, looking at me with an *are you sure we want to do that* expression.

There are basically two distinct manufactured wormhole jumping methodologies deployed by US Space-Navy starships. The preferred – and recommended – means was to manufacture a wormhole with its pre-prescribed jump-in and jump-out coordinates, then carefully maneuver the vessel, or a fleet of vessels, into that spacial anomaly's yawning mouth at slow, sub-light, velocity. The second means, called a *rush-jump*, is far more dangerous and currently forbidden for US Space-Navy vessels to even attempt – due to prior losses of ship assets and crew personnel. On the positive side, there is no lag time with a rush-jump; no slow-and-precise entry into a wormhole with relative safety. No, rush-jumps take place at FTL velocity; synchronized, ships are jumped in an instant.

"Do it, XO. We don't have the luxury of going by the book right now. Simply going to FTL won't guarantee our propulsion signature won't be tracked."

She nodded and hurried from the ready room.

I said, "Hope you're right about this, Stephan. If we stop

tracking those shuttles along their progression, we may never find them. You've told me yourself; lingering propulsion signatures are fleeting. So, if they're not on Unero —"

"I know Galvin, but I think we have to make this leap of faith."

Chapter 14

USS Hamilton

Science and Technology Department

Major Vivian "Viv" Leigh - Ship's Primary Physician

Viv had been pleasantly surprised to find the lab empty. Even Coogong and the other Thine scientist were absent.

Hardy was patiently standing upon the platform of the Port Entangler version *deux,* which everyone was now simply calling the *PE-2*.

Standing at the adjoining console, Viv reviewed the myriad of settings she and Hardy had come up with. Utilizing MATHR's internal PPGS, *Pulsar Positioning and Guidance System*, which all Space-Navy vessels employ for geo-locating coordinates down to within tenths of a centimeter anywhere within the Milky Way Galaxy. *Hamilton* was currently moving at sub-light velocity, so, of course, there was no wiggle room for getting the math wrong. They had come up with an arbitrary – but constant – location that would be 86 miles off *Hamilton's* port side. Over the past hour, the two of them had already transported a wrench, a food replicator, and a white mouse, they named Spot because of a black patch on its hindquarters, off to that same distant, spacial, location. All three transports had been successful in both directions. The mouse had survived. Placed within a temperature-controlled enclosure, with enough air to breathe for the few seconds needed for the test to complete, Spot, seemingly, had made the trek with no ill effects. But what about its consciousness? Were its memories still intact? Impossible to determine.

Viv looked up from the console. Hardy had chosen a new animated icon for his face display – a pair of bright red dice being rolled over and over again.

She said, "You're right, Hardy. This is a gamble. The more I think about it, the more I'm having second thoughts."

"Just push the button . . . Doc. This will make me famous . . . me being the first intelligent being to have his molecules transported out to space and back."

Viv positioned her forefinger over the blinking *ready* button. She thought about Galvin and how royally pissed he'd be if he knew she was doing this. She said, "You'll be out there for three minutes."

"Yeah . . . just like Spot."

She smiled and forced herself to let out a measured breath and pressed the button.

Hardy's face display went black. She felt it as much as she saw it. Hardy had just enough time to say, "Wait!" The ChronoBot froze, one mechanical arm starting to rise.

There was nothing she could do. What had Hardy detected in those final few seconds? Starting at his head, block segments of Hardy began to disappear, and then he was gone. She watched the count-down timer ticking down from 2:59, 2:58, 2:57 . . .

That's when she felt it. The ship shuttered. Then came the momentary wave of nausea, followed by feelings of disorientation. Breathless, she said, "Oh my God . . . we just jumped. Hardy!"

"Hardy?" Coogong said, entering the lab. His typically smiling face there within his sealed helmet was not smiling. "Doctor Leigh . . . what have you done?"

She shook her head and tried to swallow. "Please tell me *Hamilton* didn't just make a jump."

"I cannot do that, Doctor. We have, in fact, successfully initiated a rush-jump."

"No! MATHR's supposed to announce any immanent jumps!"

Coogong, his voice still calm, said, "Since rush-jumps are unsanctioned for Space-Navy vessels, I'm assuming it was an emergency tactic. But not to worry, the jump was a success. All is well with *Hamilton* and her crew."

Seeing the return of his friendly smile only deepened her growing despair.

"Um . . . Where is Hardy, Doctor?" Coogong asked, now looking about the lab.

Her eyes slid back to the digital counter. 1:45, 1:44, 1:43 . . . She realized she was chewing the inside of her cheek. A nervous habit she thought she'd broken back in college. She pointed to the empty PE-2 platform.

Stick figure Coogong moved fast, joining her at the console. He reached for the control board, but Viv caught his spindly hand before he could touch anything, "No! Don't!"

Viv and Coogong held each other's stare.

Finally, he said, "Hardy transported . . . prior to the jump?"

She nodded. Closing her eyes, she tried to mentally slow the rapid pounding in her chest. I've killed him . . . I've killed Hardy. And the Captain . . . Galvin, he's going to kill me. And he's going to hate me FOREVER! He's more than a robot . . . they're actual friends . . . no, more like buddies! And I killed him! My life, as I know it, is over. I'll probably go to prison for this . . . oh God . . ."

Doc Viv was not a crier, but she thought about, considered, crying now. No, she was too freaked out to cry. *Fuck, how do I fix this?*

Still calm, Coogong said, "First of all, my dear Vivian, do not underestimate how robust a machine a ChronoBot is."

She really didn't need or want, to be consoled right now. "Look, Coogong, I just transported that ChronoBot out into deep space. He's back there, and we're here . . . wherever that is. And, if we had a rush-jump situation, I imagine it was because we had to. Like the fucking Grish were firing on us or something like that. Hardy is still back there with them!"

Coogong looked to be pondering the situation.

"Maybe the original version of Hardy is still in memory," she said, now tapping on the control board – her fingers a frantic blur of motion.

Coogong shook his oversized looking, helmeted, head, "No . . . already destroyed, most likely."

She saw that the memory buffer was indeed empty, with the exception of Captain Tannock.

She said, "I need to tell the Captain. Shit! I really, really, really screwed up." Raising her TAC-Band, this time it was Coogong who stopped her, taking her wrist and lowering it back down.

"Not so fast, Vivian," he said. His eyes leveled on the countdown timer. "Why not see what happens?"

So, they waited.

At the 45 seconds mark, Viv said, "But ever second we wait . . ."

"Let's just see," Coogong said.

And so, they waited. Both stared at the empty pedestal until the timer wound down to the last few seconds: 6, 5, 4, 3, 2, 1.

The first block segment to reappear began forming from the bottom. Within seconds, the ChronoBot was indeed there in its entirety. Standing upright, it made no movement upon the pedestal.

Viv stared at Hardy's blank face display. Where was the annoying spinning pinwheel or irreverent cartoon caricature?

Where was any sign that this ChronoBot's consciousness, that Hardy, had survived the ordeal?

Viv and Coogong waited. Finally, getting annoyed, Viv said, "Oh, for shit's sake, are you in there or not, Hardy?"

It took several seconds before the ChronoBot turned his head in their direction. "That . . . was . . . crazy weird." He said, his face display flickering to life and resolving into his retro John Hardy appearance.

Viv wasn't sure if she wanted to punch the big robot or kiss it. The relief she was feeling was palpable. She said, "How? How are you standing here right now?"

"You know I've been pondering that same question," Hardy said. "But I would venture to say it's because, of course, my subatomic molecules, somehow, still maintained their entanglement at the quantum level."

"Mmm, yes, Hardy," Coogong said. "Certainly, the timing was right . . . perhaps your molecular construct was still present within the wormhole but still entangled just the same. I do not recommend that experiment be repeated."

"You think?" Viv said, now breathing easier. Now, taking a closer look at the ChronoBot, she said, "Any other observations? Any issues, malfunctions, even minor ones?"

"Nope . . . I'm good."

Viv glanced over to the mouse cage where Spot was running around, also looking healthy with no ill effects. It was then she noticed the small black spot on the mouse's left hindquarters. Hadn't the black patch been on its right hindquarters? She brushed off the thought – the stress was obviously getting to her.

Chapter 15

USS Hamilton – Fringe Frontier Space
Approaching the Zoyam System

Captain Galvin Quintos

With *Hamilton* having completed the rush-jump successfully some fifteen minutes earlier, I took in the approaching planetary system. Derrota, standing at my side, was busy on his tablet.

"Any sign of them?" I asked.

"No. But, there wouldn't be, would there? Not if their full intent was to evade being detected by the Grish."

"Yeah, but certainly they'd hope to be found, eventually. By keeping track of friendlies such as us." I stood while contemplating our next move.

The Halo-Display switched from a wide view of the Zoyam system to a zoomed-in view of the fourth exoplanet, Unero.

"Looks a lot like Earth," Pristy said.

I said, "Uh-huh, with one major difference."

She looked back at me, "That being local space is completely void of technology . . . no satellites, no high-orbit spacecraft, no intergalactic commerce. This is how it must have looked in our own solar system hundreds of years ago."

I must have made a strange face because she said, "What? What's wrong?"

Derrota was looking at me now too.

"I said, "The Grish fleet. Eventually, they'll arrive here."

"Probably," Derrota said. "I'm not sure what their motivations were, why finding those fleeing shuttles were of such importance to them, but clearly, they were not about to give up."

I nodded, "And they've probably figured out by now we're both looking for the same thing. Those Pleidian shuttles along with what crew remains inside them."

Pristy said, "Oh, crap. *Hamilton's* drives are fully operational . . . our propulsion signature . . . they'll be able to detect our presence here, perhaps for days. They'll know we're here even if we're cloaked. We'll have led then right to those fleeing Pleidians. And if we make any attempt to land a ship, we may as well transmit a big *here we are*, beacon."

"The big question, has MATHR detected Pleidian shuttle signatures in this vicinity?" I asked.

"No . . ." he said, working his tablet. "We'd need Hardy for –"

As if on cue, we all felt the familiar tremor vibrations

coming up from the deck. Hardy said, "Did I hear my name being tossed about?"

"Pleidian shuttle signatures . . . what do your sensors tell you?"

Joining Derrota and me, the ChronoBot hesitated before speaking. "Maybe, well, kind of."

"What does that mean?" I asked, in no mood for any of his antics.

"It means, yes, there are, and they're nearly imperceptible levels of radiation. But it's far too faint to be definitive. It could be little more than solar flare indications . . . there again, if what I am detecting is that of shuttle propulsion radiation, I'd guess a few days, maybe a week, has elapsed, dissipating the signatures."

Crewmember Grimes at the Comms Station said "Captain! We're being hailed."

XO Pristy said, "Coming from the exoplanet, from Unero. Whoever it is, they're using Pleidian communications protocols."

I stared at the blue, tan, and green world on the Halo-Display. "So, they can see us, but we can't see them . . ."

"Like with what they'd provided *Hamilton*, Pleidian's do have excellent cloaking technology," Derrota said.

Grimes said, "There's a video signal along with the audio."

"Open the channel," I said."

Three Pleidian Weonan's stood, huddled together, a campfire blazed in the background.

"That's Fleet Commander Twinwon!" came an excited

voice from behind us. I turned to see young Ensign Plorinne standing at his station, an outstretched finger pointing to the Halo-Display.

"Captain Quintos, I cannot tell you how happy I am to see you," the fleet commander said.

Ensign Plorinne joined Derrota, Hardy, and I at the Captain's Mount. "The Empress will be most pleased you are still alive, sir . . . most pleased indeed."

"Greetings, Plorinne. And Thank you." Twinwon held up a hand, "Our power reserves are limited. Not sure how long we'll be able to converse."

I noticed several things all at about the same time. One, Twinwon was injured, his head was bandaged, and he was leaning against another of his crew. Two, off in the background, I could just make out the remnants of a shuttlecraft. One that had obviously crashed landed – which no one could have survived. And there, a fourth figure had just entered the feed, none other than Varapin Cyclone Death Fighter pilot, Haite Caheil. The ghoulish-looking hooded alien was hovering less than a foot off the ground. His face, black as obsidian, was contrasted by his exposed white jaws.

"That is one ugly mother –" Hardy cut himself short, seeing my wary expression.

And at that moment, it all made sense to me. It was Haite Caheil that the Grish were so intent on finding. Never wanting to disappoint that evil empire, the Grish were doing the Varapin's bidding. I imagined the Varapin would pay handsomely for the capture of this now infamous traitor.

I said, "Fleet Commander, what is your situation? You're injured. What's the condition of the others?"

"We were three shuttles. One," he gestured behind, "crashed . . . no survivors. My shuttle is close by; ten of us survived. The third shuttle, we think, is relatively close, but we've not been able to make contact. We have been searching. I must tell you, a Grish fleet –"

"We know all about the fleet, Fleet Commander. We avoided being detected but think they will figure out where you are just as we have. We don't have much time to rescue you."

Twinwon looked confused by that. "How many are there in your battlegroup? Why not simply destroy the Grish fleet? Need I remind you they are your enemy as they are ours?"

"It's complicated. The *USS Hamilton* is here alone, and this is not a sanctioned US Space-Navy mission. Let's just say the Empress has a lot of sway with Admiral Block and with me. So, we're doing our best not to be discovered. And to make things even more complicated, I'm supposed to be sitting in a brig cell, awaiting a court-martial."

"Yes, Captain . . . I am well aware of your personal plight back on Earth. So, it seems you have come here at great risk and sacrifice on your own accord to rescue us. I thank you . . . we all thank you for that."

"You're welcome. But we need to move fast. As I said, the Grish could show up here at any moment. Provide your geo-coordinates, and we'll come and get you."

"We cannot leave this world without first finding the

survivors of the third shuttle. We believe they are alive since their shuttle is cloaked."

"They haven't attempted communications?" I asked.

"No. But there could be any number of reasons for that. As discussed, all three shuttles were running on minimum fuel . . . as with our own shuttle, power reserves are critical."

I looked at Hardy and then Derrota. Sending a rescue vessel down to Unero was out of the question, and having *Hamilton* staying put was equally out of the question. I was honestly stymied as to what to do next.

Hardy said, "I have an idea . . . but you're not going to like it."

"At this point, any idea will be welcome." I gestured to Twinwon. "Can we call you back in twenty minutes?"

"Yes . . . we'll power down comms until then." The feed flickered out.

"Talk to me, Hardy," I said. "And remember, Twinwon, understandably, won't leave his stranded people behind."

Hardy said, "How about we have that one operational shuttle of theirs take off from Unero, leave orbit, and intersect with *Hamilton* and land within our flight bay . . . ensure there are enough radiation breadcrumbs for the Grish to later connect the dots?"

I said, "The trick will be leaving just enough breadcrumbs that it doesn't seem too obvious a deception. But yeah, if the piglets could be able to puzzle that out, it could work. And when the Grish see *Hamilton's* left the system, they'll have little reason to do much more than a cursory sensor scan of Unero.

They'll want to go after *Hamilton* . . . continue their pursuit of the Varapin traitor."

XO Pristy had been listening without comment thus far, but I could see she didn't like the plan.

"Spit it out, XO . . . this is no time to be shy."

"So, while we take the Grish on a wild goose chase, we just leave Twinwon and what crew he stays with on that exoplanet? Leave them all behind?"

"That's right. After a jump or two, *Hamilton* will be impossible to follow. They'll give up and go home. Then, we'll make our way back to Unero. At that point, we can assist Twinwon with his search and rescue mission, collect everyone, and be gone."

Pristy's brows went up questioningly. Derrota had a similar expression, while Hardy's face display was blank.

"Shit," I said, realizing what they had already figured out. "Of course. The Grish will leave behind a number of recognizance drones for good measure. Piglets will want to maintain eyes on this system, on Unero, for good measure."

Hardy said, "So, can I finish telling you my original idea?"

"I thought you had," I said, conscious I needed to get back to Twinwon soon.

Hardy said, "We do all that, just as you've proposed . . . have Twinwon send up that shuttle of his to *Hamilton,* and then *Hamilton* skedaddles out of here leaving a barely detectable trail behind. But just prior to all that, we send down a well-equipped team . . . one that can assist with the search and rescue."

I looked at the ChronoBot shaking my head, "Are you not tracking the conversation? What's wrong with you, Hardy? We can't send a ship down to Unero! That would screw up the ruse!"

Hardy's now displayed stupid big yellow happy face did not bode well. "Who said anything about sending down a ship? We can transport the team down to the planet . . . one at a time."

It took me a few moments. "Wait. You mean, as in use a highly experimental Port Entangler for that? The same port entangler that hasn't been tested with human subjects? Are you out of your frickin' robot mind?"

But it wasn't Hardy who answered my question.

"Quintos, you need to relax and take a breath."

Only one person on board *Hamilton* calls me by my last name. I turned to see Doc Viv standing there with her arms crossed over her breasts. She was still wearing her wrinkled pink scrubs.

"I was hoping to tell you this under less stressful circumstances, but further tests have been made. Tests that verify that organics can be successfully transported out of the ship and back again."

I fought back the urge to roll my eyes. "Transporting mice into space is not the same thing, Viv . . . we have no idea what happens to an individual's consciousness."

She pursed her lips, glanced to Hardy then back to me. "Okay . . . well, I know we shouldn't have . . . but I tried a little experiment with Hardy."

Oh no. It took all of my willpower not to erupt. "What kind of experiment?"

Her face flushed, and she attempted an awkward smile. We sent Hardy out into deep space . . . eighty-six miles to be exact."

"While we were moving!" Hardy said.

She shot Hardy a stern look before saying, "The point is, Hardy has a very human-like consciousness . . . an organic AI brain. He's come through the ordeal perfectly fine. And don't forget we have Sir Louis de Broglie, who's another example of someone coming out of the entangler successfully."

She had a point there. I said, "Still . . . sending a ChronoBot into space is not the same as sending a human, no offense, Hardy."

"None taken."

"Well, I think it's a good idea," Pristy said.

"Seems like our only option, Derrota said. "Gives us time to find the missing Pleidians while getting the piglets out of here."

My mind raced as I played out various scenarios. I really didn't like any of this. Looking at my XO, I said, "The only way I can agree to this is if I'm the first one to attempt transport down to the exoplanet. If I survive, I'll lead the team on Unero. So, that means you'll be in command of *Hamilton*, XO. Granted, there shouldn't be any trouble; you'll be staying far ahead of the piglet's fleet, but not far enough they lose track of *Hamilton*. And you'll need to give us enough time to find the missing Pleidians."

All eyes were on Pristy. She raised her chin, "You can count on me, Captain. We'll do our part."

"Under no condition can *Hamilton* go up against that Grish fleet. That would be a no-win situation."

"I understand," she said but now looking slightly less confident.

Hardy said, "Hey, things get too out of hand . . . you can always bring Captain Tannock out of mothballs."

Chapter 16

After discussing the basics of the plan with Twinwon, he was relieved to hear that a team would soon be arriving on Unero to assist with the search for his missing shuttle and crewmembers. He let me know, the shuttle was somewhere deep within occupied territory. I didn't go into any detail on exactly how we'd be arriving, but he should get his piloted shuttle taking off and intersecting with *Hamilton* within the next hour.

Everyone had their marching orders; Derrota was to research Unero's geographic and wildlife characteristics. Hardy was to plot the most likely landing sites of the missing, not to mention, cloaked, shuttlecraft. Doc Viv, who was insisting she'd be coming along, was to gather medical supplies and equipment needed to support possible injuries, as well as research the biodiversity aspects of the world's inhabitants. I'd already informed Sergeant Max to ready his team; they'd be providing security for the mission.

So, I only had one last crewmember to talk to. I'd messaged

him that I would be coming by within the hour. Arriving at the Ship-Wide Maintenance depot, located far aft within *Hamilton*, it occurred to me I hadn't actually been in this part of the ship prior to today. Considering there were hundreds of SWM crew-members onboard, handling everything from making repairs to complex environmental filtration units to sleuthing out broken connections within the multi-strand laser-fiber braid that crisscrossed all through the ship's confined crawlspaces, to the more menial jobs of cleaning and disinfecting the hundreds of compartments, passageways, and heads. As with the rest of the ship, here too, there was but a skeleton crew meandering about. I passed by a long line of slumbering, upright, SWM-bots as I looked for the department's main office. I marveled at just how clean everything was here. Everything in its place. Pegboards lined the bulkheads with every kind of tool imagin-able. I spotted an open door up ahead with OFFICE stenciled above it.

Standing within the entrance, I knocked on the wooden threshold, something not typically found on a Space-Navy spacecraft. The department was now under the direction of Crewman Lasalle, who was black, in his fifties, was muscu-lar with broad shoulders, and spoke with a deep Southern Louisiana drawl. On his desk was a stack of at least eight old fashioned, hardback historical reference books. He turned in his chair to face me. Smiling, he stood, "Good to see you, Captain. Sorry, the place is such a mess . . . with limited per-sonnel we're – "

I waved him off, "Come on, your shop is immaculate,

which doesn't surprise me one bit. Look, we're under the gun here, so there's little time for chit chat. What did you find out?"

There were few people onboard *Hamilton* that knew more about US history than LaSalle. So, when I'd heard the pre-industrial Unero citizens were having colonial-type skirmishes, much like those of the revolutionary war skirmishes on Earth, I knew LaSalle could be a goldmine of perspective. I needed to know what we'd be walking into down there if we were forced to encounter any of the locals.

"MATHRs been helpful, to a degree," LaSalle said. "Of course, there's no computer technology on that world, no databases to breech. So, we've been doing things the old-fashioned way."

"And that is?" I asked.

"Spying, using *Hamilton's* high-resolution zoom telescopies. I think I have an idea of who is who. On Earth – in the early 1700s – it was the colonials, native Americans, and the British all in conflict with one another. Here on Unero, it's the colonial Pleidians along with the human-like Juvians striving for independence from the British equivalent, the Mantarians. Add to the mix; the primitive native Indian equivalent would be the aSplee race. It really is remarkable how similar a situation this is to our own early historical evolution. One big difference, though, we were all human back in the eighteenth century on Earth; here, we're dealing with altogether different genome alien species."

I took in what he said and nodded. "Doc Viv is delving into the biodiversity aspects." Looking at him now, I'd come to a decision. Unfortunately, he would be, at least physically, the least trained for such a dangerous mission.

"LaSalle, I want you to come along with us. Be a part of our away team."

He laughed and gestured to a mop and bucket holding vigil in the far corner, "Well, I've never fired a tagger or shredder, but I'm a true warrior with a mop handle."

"I don't need you for fighting the natives; I need you for your smarts, for your historical perspective."

"You're serious?"

"As a heart attack."

He pondered this. "You know, we'll need to fit in . . . have the right clothing and such."

"As I said, I'm hoping to avoid any interactions with the locals."

He shrugged.

"Okay, fine . . . you just got yourself another job to do with little time to do it. You'll be outfitting the team with appropriate garb. We have replicator and fabricator devices on board for just such a purpose."

"But I'm not . . ."

"Clock is ticking, LaSalle. And bring extra outfits for Twinwon's Pleidians already down on the surface."

I left the big SWM crewmember, looking both nervous and excited. He had orders to be ready to go within three hours and to meet at the Science and Technology department.

* * *

Arriving on Deck 29, I strode into pure pandemonium. Like backstage of a big Broadway show on opening night. Everyone was well aware of the tight time restraints and the need to get down to the exoplanet's surface on schedule. Max's team was there and dressed in the specific militia uniforms LaSalle had designated for them. Derrota and I were dressed as Militia officers, while Doc Viv was to be dressed in the clothes of a kind of handmaiden; apparently, female surgeons were uncommon on Unero.

I found LaSalle talking to Doc Viv over next to the port entangler, PE-2, device. They seemed to be hashing out something but looked up as I approached.

I asked, "How are we doing?"

Viv, not looking pleased, said, "We could use another week to prepare and still not be ready."

"What's the problem?"

"The problem is, we'll be walking into one minefield after another. Language and dialect issues, for one. Having never encountered actual Unero locals, our audio implants will not have corresponding translation data."

"So, we won't be able to talk to –"

"Shush! Let me finish," Viv chided. "It doesn't take long for our implants to learn new languages. The more a local speaks, the better it'll be for the rest of us. I've already networked all of our implants. The entire away team will be able to take advantage of the evolving translation data gathered by any one of us."

I thought about that. It wasn't ideal, but it would have to do.

The issue of us actually speaking any of the foreign languages was less of a problem since our latest tech implants provided Neural Interpretation and Causal Vocal Harmonization – basically, giving us the ability to speak, forming the right vocal cord, tongue, mouth, and lip movements corresponding to any translated language information being process by the brain. On a good day, it was only 95% effective – but it would have to do.

I looked about the noisy compartment. "Where's Hardy? We can't go without Hardy."

Derrota and Viv looked at each other. Eventually, Viv said, "Have you given any thought to how bringing along a seven-foot-tall ChronoBot may impact this mission?"

At that precise moment, a horrendous *ROAR* filled the compartment. Several people screamed; even more dove onto the deck for cover. And there it was, standing upright at the open hatchway into the lab. To say the beast was ugly would be an understatement. Easily eight feet tall and covered in dark brown matted fur, it looked to be a cross between a North American Grisly bear's body with an African Crocodile's massive head. The beast roared again while raising its two dinnerplate sized claws. With the exception of Derrota, Viv, and myself, everyone else was huddled together at the opposite bulkhead. I caught a glimpse of Wanda – no longer having purple and pink streaks in her hair – among the group of scaredy-cats.

I yelled, "Enough! Hardy . . . you're scaring the children!"

After a moment of dead silence, a few of the away team began to moan, and others laughed nervously. Eventually, some, and then all of them, approached what I later would find out was called a Craw Beast. Hardy's costume, if you will, had been fabricated from images provided by LaSalle's zoom spy telescopes, and it was amazingly realistic. And how they had duplicated the beast's foul smell was beyond me.

"Come on, Quintos, he scared you too . . . if even for a second," Viv said, appraising me.

"Nope. Not for a second," I lied. In actuality, instead of a fight or flight response, I'd had one of my mini DOPTSD paralysis attacks. I'd simply frozen up. My delayed-onset post-traumatic stress disorder was much better these days. I hardly ever had an attack. And working with Wanda (and dare I say, even the three combat avatars), I was mentally better equipped to deal with such high-stress situations. Still, suddenly seeing and hearing that towering hairy beast enter the compartment, it had scared the living shit out of me —no one needed to know the truth. I'd let them all think I was one cool customer.

"Okay people . . . if were done horsing around, we have a mission to complete. I moved over to the PE-2, where Coogong stood behind the console. He would be staying behind and be our transport engineer – delivering us down to the exoplanet, and later, bringing us back up.

I stepped up onto the PE-2's pedestal. Now, at least a foot higher than everyone else in the compartment except the Craw Beast, I got the high-up visual perspective that Hardy had all the time. Offering a crooked smile, they all looked more like guests at a costume party than an away team. All except one. She was making her way through the crowd.

"Captain, I just wanted to wish you, well, *everyone*, a successful mission."

I looked down into XO Pristy's emotional, somewhat glistening, eyes. "And a safe return to you, Captain . . . we'll need you back on *Hamilton* ASAP . . . so don't get yourself hurt or killed."

"I'll do my best, XO. Just take good care of the old gal while I'm gone. Keep your distance from the piglets, and remember, this dreadnought is supposed to be in space-port."

Someone yelled, ". . . and you're supposed to be behind bars, Cap!"

As laughter erupted, I gave Pristy a serious, assuring nod. "Just keep your cool and be the best commanding officer you can be."

"I'll try," she said. "Just come back in one piece."

I looked over to Coogong. "Guess I'm ready when you are."

Chapter 17

Exoplanet Unero

Pleidian Shuttle Encampment

It wasn't until I was down there, actually standing upon Unero's rich brown soil, that it occurred to me that I had . . . well, died. The original me had been destroyed up there on *Hamilton,* and this *me* was a replica. I did a personal self-assessment of the reassembled molecules standing here. I felt fine. I felt as much me as I ever had.

Moving several steps away from my current transport location, I raised my TAC-band, which was mostly concealed within a worn leather strap, and informed Coogong to go ahead and start sending down the rest of the team. There was something heavy and oppressive about this place; perhaps it was just the time of day, dusk.

While I waited, I took a look around. We'd purposely chosen a location a mile's distance from where Twinwon's shuttle and crew were located. I wasn't prepared to get into our new port entangler capabilities just yet. Yes, the Pleidians were Earth's allies; that doesn't mean we automatically hand over our most prized technical achievements. There was an abundance of trees, a forest, surrounding the clearing I was in. They were like thick pines, each maybe a hundred to hundred and fifty feet tall – but the color was off, more turquoise than an evergreen color. Sounds of night critters were all around me – similar to that on /earth, but there again, different too. Something, the silhouette of a winged creature, swooped down from above, and I ducked just in time to avoid outstretched claws. "Fuck!" *What kind of bird attacks like that?* I looked up and around into the darkening sky, not wanting to be caught off guard again. Unfortunate, walking along within unfamiliar surroundings while looking up was a recipe for disaster.

He attacked from my left side. In retrospect, I can thank Shred-Ma, Drole, and Chi for my survival. The attack was just the sort of thing I was getting used to, and I reflexively moved accordingly. Jabbed at my face, the six-foot-long wooden spear missed my nose by a fraction of an inch. Without thinking, I used my body's own shifting momentum and spun into a kind of cartwheel. Derived from Brazilian Capoeira martial arts, the Aú sem mao kick is a beautiful thing when attempted by a master – which I was not. But the heel of my left foot clobbered the native attacker on the chin, putting him down on the ground. With him still looking stunned, I followed up with an old-fashioned field-goal kick to the head.

I didn't have time to commend myself on subduing the native; three – no, four – more raised spears seemed to have come from nowhere, surrounding me. Keeping low, they moved, making side-stepping motions, while jabbing outward with their spears. I'd been lucky taking out one of these guys, but four more, no way. In the growing darkness, I could just barely make out their physical size but not so much their features. As big as a human man, they were hairless and muscular. Oddly, they wore a kind of wrapped leather skirt thing around their hips and were bare-chested. I remembered LaSalle telling me the natives here were called the aSplee race.

Keeping low, I moved with them, spinning around every so often while trying to anticipate who would be attacking next. The four were talking between each other in hushed tones. At first, it was all gibberish, but then, I started catching the odd word here and there – understanding some of it. My implants were working overtime to construct a translated vocabulary for me. In any event, it wasn't coming fast enough, and I wouldn't be talking my way out of this situation.

Two of the aSplee attacked at once, the one directly in front of me and the one directly behind me. I blocked the spear coming at my face, but not the one coming at my back. I'd managed a half-turn, so the razor-sharp point of the spear only grazed my flesh instead of piercing it. There was a delay before the pain hit, enough that I had time to dive to the ground and roll and then roll again. I knew, by this point, I was done, that I wouldn't be able to roll my way to safety. Gritting my teeth, I prepared myself for being skewered like a scared pig.

The horrendously loud sound that tore through the forest was both terrifying and welcome at the same time. I'd heard that very same sound, a gargantuan kind of roar, not much earlier on *Hamilton*. The Craw Beast jumped, from who knows where, to my right side. On all fours, the Craw roared once more while baring curved fangs a saber tooth tiger would have envied. Wide-eyed, the four aSplee natives, careful not to make any abrupt movements, took several slow steps backward.

I got to my feet and did my best to stand tall. I felt the warm wetness of blood saturating the back of my uniform. *Interesting.* I now knew a few of their words. "If you want to live . . . do not move!"

Memorized, the natives looked at me and then to the towering beast. One of them swallowed and then spoke, "You speak the language of the aSplee."

"Of course, I do."

"And the Craw Beast . . . he is . . . your pet?"

I could almost see Hardy looking indignant there beneath his oversized headpiece.

"Yes, this Craw Beast is my pet. He is named Jaws. Jaws is hungry; it is well past his supper time."

In concert, the four of them took another tentative step backward.

"Really?" came the unmistakable voice of Doc Viv. "This is how you've been entertaining yourself while waiting for us? Tormenting the locals? Scaring them half to death?"

I didn't have to see her there behind me to know she was already taking in that deep slice across my upper back.

"Does it hurt?"

"Yeah, it hurts." I pointed to the aSplee, "You there . . .

leave . . . run away. If I see you again, I'll offer you up to Jaws. He'd like to make a meal of the four of you. Do you understand what I'm saying?"

Interesting, I thought, seeing them nodding like that – it must be a universal gesture around the galaxy.

Hardy's muffled voice emanated from his crock headpiece, "What do you want to do with the other one?"

"Other one?"

"Laid out on the ground with a split lip."

Doc Viv, now using applying some kind of artificial flesh suave onto my injury, said, "I checked on him when I arrived. He'll have a nasty headache when he wakes up, maybe a mild concussion. What did you hit him with, anyway?":

"My heal."

I was still turned away from her, but even if I wasn't, it would be too dark to see her expression.

Others were coming through the trees now, Derrota, LaSalle, and Max's Marines.

"Looks like we missed all the fun," Wanda said, using the glow of her own TAC-Band to assess Doc Viv's handy work. "Bet that hurts."

"Tell me I don't have to wear this fur costume the whole time we're down here," Hardy said.

"He's own here for five minutes, and he's already whining?" Grip said, joining the conversation and shaking his head.

"How about we keep the chit chat to a minimum," I said. "Wanda, douse that TAC-band. We're clearly not alone here, and we're being watched. Hardy, how about you use that big AI brain of yours to lead us to the Pleidian encampment?"

Max said, "In the dark, someone's going to get hurt, break an ankle. If you give us a few minutes, we can make us several flame torches."

"Good idea," I said.

I heard the aSplee man groan. Viv, who had left at some point to see to his injuries, called over, "Quintos. If you're going to talk to him, this would be the time to do it. I've given him a mild tranquilizer . . . but he should stay coherent."

I found the two silhouettes, one seated, one kneeling, in the dark. I knelt down next to them. Attempting to speak in his language, I said, "My name is Galvin. What are you called?"

Max approached with a flame-lit torch, which cast the surroundings into a flickering amber light. He handed it to me and disappeared back into the darkness.

The native, looking nervous, said, "Raptor."

I noticed the tangled necklaces around his neck. Various sized bird talons were interspersed. "We are not here to harm you . . . to fight with you. Do you understand me?"

He rubbed at his still oozing, swollen lip.

"Well, you did try to poke me with your spear, first."

Raptor didn't say anything.

"We're going to let you go. But first, can you answer a few questions?"

He looked a little confused, and I wondered just how much of my translation's algorithm was working. For all I knew, I might have just asked him his shoe size or if his sister was as ugly as he was.

He said, "You are not Juvian . . . not like the others." His eyes left mine and found Viv's. "None of you are Juvian."

Viv leaned in, "How can you tell? How are we different?"

He looked at her hand and pointed, "Thoug nams."

She and I looked at each other, clueless to his meaning. Then Viv said, pointing to her own fingers, "You mean fingernails?"

"Yes . . . that is what I said, fingernails."

The translations were updating in real-time.

He continued, "Juvians I have seen . . . their fingernails are on inside of fingers." He gestured by running a finger along the fingertips on his opposite hand.

"Crap!" Viv said, looking annoyed with herself. "I missed that. It was my job to –"

"Don't worry about it, Viv," I said, looking at the native man. "Raptor, the others, the Juvians, are there any near here?"

He shook his head. "Only Dash Coot." He pointed to his own face and made an oval motion with a finger.

"Ah, Pleidians," I said.

"That is what I said, Pleidians," Raptor said. "You will tell me how . . . how you befriended the Craw Beast?"

"You saw the beast?"

He nodded. "Yes – when I pretended to be dead."

"Perhaps another time. So, there's no other Juvians or Pleidians around here? How about the Mantarians? Any of them about?"

His eyes widened at the mention of their name. "No . . .

those evil spirits are hiding . . . near the settlement. They will attack soon."

"Which settlement?"

"Pleidian . . . some Juvians are there, too."

I felt him coming, heavy impacts on the ground – from the direction of the tree line. When he appeared, the eight-foot-tall Craw Beast holding a flaming torch in one claw, the native man shrieked. Moving with incredible speed, Raptor was up on his feet and fleeing into the forest.

More equipment had been transported down to the surface during the few minutes we were speaking to Raptor. Each of the Marines hefted a pack onto their backs and synched up the straps. As authentic as their militia uniforms may have been, those packs were anything but regulation looking.

I counted heads, Derrota, Doc Viv, LaSalle, the five Marines, Max, Wanda, Grip, Ham, and Hock, our fur-covered ChronoBot, and me, ten in all. "Let's move out, people. We've already missed our arrival time with Twinwon's group."

I watched as the team got moving, some walking in pairs, others single file. I said, "Hardy, best if you shadow the team off in the forest . . . you look ridiculous walking along with the others like that."

"Roger that, boss," Hardy said, moving off into the trees and was enveloped into the darkness.

Bringing up the rear, I felt my TAC-Band vibrate. Checking the message, I saw that it was from XO Pristy.

XO Pristy: Pleidian Shuttle arrived and is secured within the flight bay. Hamilton currently making its way out of the system. Still no sign of Piglets. Will re-establish contact in a few days. Good Luck Cap.

I tapped back a short message.

Capt. Quintos: Copy that. Godspeed XO.

I looked up to the brilliant star-filled sky above, even though I knew there'd be no chance of seeing the big dreadnought as it made its way out of the system. I thought of Gail Pristy sitting upon the Captain's Mount and the heavy responsibility she must be feeling right now. "You got this, girl," I said under my breath.

Chapter 18

Exoplanet Unero

Approaching Pleidian Shuttle Encampment

On approach to the encampment, we found ourselves suddenly surrounded by armed Pleidians. As much as they'd tried to surprise us, they hadn't. They were starship crewmembers, not trained for on-world military service. A tad clumsy stepping on and snapping twigs, their uniforms rustling as they moved about, we heard their hushed voices announcing our approach.

Twinwon stepped into the torchlight ahead of our procession. I moved forward to the front of the line and returned the fleet commander's welcoming smile. *Why not?* I'd let him think he'd pulled a fast one on us. We shook hands, and his people began revealing themselves from behind the line of trees and a tall crop of nearby foliage.

"Thank you for coming, Captain Quintos. Interestingly,

we were not alerted to a vessel descending to the surface. Even cloaked, our sensors should have been triggered. Your Thine cloaking technology has its faults."

I made no attempt to explain how we'd gotten onto Unero undetected. Looking around, I noticed Haite Caheil was not among the Pleidians.

He continued, "Our shuttle has lifted off, along with our injured, and has intersected with *Hamilton*. As our other shuttle, close by, crash-landed and was heavily damaged, we will be at your mercy, Captain, getting off this world."

"Well, there's still your third shuttle," I said.

"Yes, fortunately, it remains cloaked . . . we are taking that as a good sign it is still operational. But not hearing from her crew, that does not bode well."

"You have any idea where it is?"

"We believe it is closer to the settlement . . . which lies thirty miles due west of here. We are currently within native aSplee territory."

Derrota chimed in, "Oh yes, we've already encountered the aSplee."

Twinwon assessed Derrota with a curious gaze. "They are a dangerous and ruthless people. I see you are dressed as local settlers – but are unarmed. How many losses have you suffered?"

I said, "None. We had an encounter but eventually came to an understanding."

Twinwon looked unsure what that meant. He said, "In addition to the aSplee, the wildlife here is a threat. Large carnivores prowl these forests. Nighttime is especially dangerous. I've lost two of my crew to something called a Craw Beast."

Behind Twinwon, along with his unaware crew, now loomed a gargantuan figure. With a stirring of a breeze, I got a whiff of its wretched, gamey smell.

I said, "Hardy . . . that's not funny."

Twinwon, along with his team, spun around to face the looming animal. What I hadn't expected was the Beast to lunge forward and bite the head off of one of the Pleidians. Screams erupted as the beast turned his attention to another and then another Pleidian – sweeping swipes of the Craw's giant claws cleaving them both nearly in half. Arterial blood arced into the air, spraying my face in the process.

Max and his Marines were, in fact, armed. Their tagger weapons, having been hidden from view, were now lighting up the night with bright bolts of energy. The Craw Beast roared – clumps of fur set afire by one bolt after another finding its mark. Undeterred, the beast attacked – its massive girth leaping high in the air – a trajectory that would put him on top of the still firing, unwavering group of Marines.

Suddenly, another Craw Beast was present – this one somewhat smaller than the other. Moving with incredible speed, it reached up with one outstretched arm and grabbed a fistful of the leaping Craw's belly fur. With a sufficient yank, down came the bigger of the two beasts. The ground shook with the impact. By now, I knew it was Hardy who had intervened. *It's about time.* Animalistic shrieks filled the air as Hardy positioned one of his feet onto the now squirming Craw Beast's exposed throat. With a quick downward stomping motion, there was a loud *Crack!* Silence returned to the forest.

Doc Viv was checking the Pleidian bodies for signs of life. The Marines had already dispersed and were moving out into the surrounding trees. Good, we didn't need any more surprises.

* * *

By the time we reached the Pleidian encampment, it was dawn, and the first rays of sunlight were streaming in through the surrounding trees. Several large tent-like structures – what I later learned were called *pop-up pods* – had been erected, and flames still blazed within a nearby rock encircled fire pit. A lone, armed, Pleidian crewmember came out to greet us. Had Twinwon left the security of this camp to him alone? And then I saw Haite. He was moving toward us in the distance. His dark hooded form swept through the accumulated mist and lingering smoke from the fire.

"Got to give it to him; he sure knows how to make an entrance," Viv said.

He slowed and drifted to a stop some six feet out. "Ah, Captain Quintos, Doctor . . ."

"Haite . . ." I said while Viv simply raised her chin in acknowledgment of the Varapin pilot.

Hardy, who had only now brought up the rear of the procession, now occupied all of Haite's attention. He made a sound, which I took to be a kind of laugh or chuckle. "Your silly robot . . . good you were able to find an adequate use for that machine."

It was common knowledge the two had little admiration for one another. I said, gesturing to a crumpled mass of metal at the far end of the encampment, "Tell me, that shuttle there, anything still work? Is it partially operational?"

I already knew it was, from what Twinwon had told me. To what extent, I didn't know.

"It will not fly again – if that is your question," Haite said. "Other than that, minimum power can be restored, allowing some communications and cloaking capabilities."

"Well, I see it . . . so maybe the cloaking isn't –"

Haite interjected, "As I said, power reserves are low. It is good you have brought your robot. I surmise his sensors are adequate to detect any Grish arrivals into the star system?"

Derrota was already shaking his head, "It may be too late, at that point. If the Grish detect the presence of that shuttle, we're all in trouble."

I said, "We need the Grish to think there's nothing here for them . . . and to follow *Hamilton's* propulsion signatures out of the system . . . give us time to locate your third shuttlecraft."

The Varapin opened his palms in deference, "It was a call we had to make, Science Officer Derrota."

"Guess it's a good thing we brought along several auxiliary power packs . . . should suffice to keep that shuttle's system's running, at least for a few days," Derrota said. "But it's more than just the Grish . . . it is imperative the locals be kept in the dark as to who we are, where we are from."

"Ah, you speak of your Space-Navy's ridiculous Occluded Interaction Mandate, yes?" Haite asked. "The Varapin make no such assertions . . . I believe you have a saying; *it's a dog eat dog universe* . . .or something to that effect."

No one spoke for a few moments. Then it was LaSalle's deep Southern baritone that broke the silence, "I suppose the difference is, we are not here to conquer or subjugate these people . . . no, they must be allowed to evolve technologically, unmolested."

Haite Caheil's expression was impossible to read, but guessing, he thought our efforts were naïve.

Moving on to a different subject, I asked Derrota, "Any new thoughts on how we're going to find that third shuttle and her crew?"

Out at the fringe of the campsite, I watched as a group of solemn-looking Pleidians began digging several graves. Twinwon stood nearby with his hands together, fingers steepled. Head bowed, he looked to be saying a silent prayer.

Bringing me back, Derrota blew out a breath and combed fingers through his black hair. Funny, his militia uniform was starting to look as rumpled as his uniforms up on *Hamilton*. "Yeah," he said. "En route to the camp, I spoke to Twinwon about the third shuttle. He says he has portable sensor equipment that is superior to ours. And he believes, if we can get close enough, like within a few miles, maybe they can get a lock on the shuttle."

Doc Viv said, "I'm exhausted. Need to find a place to bunk

for a few hours." We made brief eye contact before she strode away.

"I suggest we expect the worst," Haite said with finality. "There are but two reasons those crewmembers would not have made contact. One, they are dead, or two, they have been captured. Whereby they will soon be executed. Perhaps a waste of time to even search for them, no?"

"Of course, we will search for the crew," I said.

But even if they are dead, that third shuttle will need to be destroyed," LaSalle said in defiance to Haite.

I eyed Viv ducking into one of the encampment pop-up pods. "Let's all get some sleep. We'll move out tonight, less chance of being spotted by the locals."

"You mean like the aSplee," LaSalle said with a crooked smile.

I shrugged, "Maybe if we're lucky, word has spread about our trained Craw Beast."

Chapter 19

I awoke, groggy, to the sounds of excited hollering, some kind of commotion going on outside the pop-up pod. Sitting up, I saw Derrota, still asleep on the cot next to mine. Viv's cot, directly across from mine on the other side of the pod, was empty. Swinging my legs down, I found my boots and slipped them on. Checking my TAC-Band, I saw there were no new messages. Getting to my feet, I nudged Derrota's cot with the toe of my boot, "Rise and shine, Stephan . . . we're burning daylight."

He awoke, snorted, and wiped a bit of drool from his chin. "Okay . . . I'm up . . . I'm up."

I emerged into golden afternoon daylight. It was as if I was seeing the terrain for the first time. As much as the alien landscape was indeed similar to that of Earth's, it was also quite different. The sky above was a different hue of blue, less of an azure and more of a powder blue. The surrounding trees were a greenish turquoise, and the soil was dark and rich, a dark copper, like that of an old penny. The system's star above looked pretty much identical to that of Earth's Sun.

Derrota was now at my side and hopping up and down, trying to slip on his left boot. "What's all the racket about?"

Both humans and Pleidians within the encampment had stopped what they were doing to take in what was happening. It seemed as though everyone's attention was on Hardy. Standing next to him was Doc Viv, still dressed in her handmaiden dress, and bent over, hands on her knees, seemingly laughing uncontrollably. I exchanged a quick look with Derrota.

"Let's go see what's going on," I said.

The two of us headed off toward the far side of the clearing. We passed by Max and his team, who looked to have been in the process of stowing their now compressed pop-up pod components back into the hold of the wrecked shuttle. But they too were now looking at the goings-on at the edge of the camp. Twinwon and several other Pleidians were standing atop the crashed and ruined shuttle behind the propped-up tree trunks and camouflaging greenery and looked to have been adjusting a comms array there – now they too stood and watched in the direction of Viv and the costumed ChronoBot.

Reaching them, Viv, hands on hips, had taken few strides closer to the edge of the clearing.

"What's going on," I said.

"*Shhh,* keep your voice down," she scolded. "You'll scare them off."

Derrota said, "Oh! I see them." He pointed, "There between that crop of trees. See them?"

I scanned the trees and then, sure enough, saw them. Two – no, three – large Craw Beasts. These were the largest I'd seen thus far. "What are they doing?"

That got Viv laughing again.

Hardy said, "Just shoot me now . . . get it over with."

"All three are mature sows," Viv said. "And from their behavior, I'd say they are in heat."

One at a time, the large furry creatures moved forward, turned around, and bent over, exposing their ample backside. There, on all fours, the sow would shuffle its paws in a kind of peculiar dance. After a good minute or so, they would retreat to the others and let the next one repeat the same, for no better word, kind of *taunt*.

Derrota said, "They want to mate with Hardy . . . they're showing their sexy parts to him. . . hoping to entice him over."

I tried not to laugh – but keeping the smile from my face would be impossible. A quick glance to Hardy showed he was looking everywhere but those three courting sows.

"Ah, come on, Hardy. You should be flattered. You're like *the man* in these parts. All the chicks want a piece of you."

Hardy abruptly stood up straight. "Captain, according to my long-range sensors, the Grish just jumped into this system."

I turned to face the shuttle. Now running, I waved my hands over my head and yelled, "TWINWON . . . GET THAT SHUTTLE CLOAKED. . . NOW!" I pointed up to the sky.

He got the message and immediately climbed down from the shuttle's roof and went inside. Several moments later, the shuttle disappeared from view.

Hardy, Viv, and Derrota caught up to where I was standing, catching my breath.

"What?" Viv asked.

"Where's the Varapin? We already know he's who they're after."

"I am here," came the grating voice from behind. He hovered in closer. He held up one arm, and the sleeve of his robe fell away, revealing the device strapped to his thin black wrist. "My bio-form cannot be detected."

"Stephan, you're certain our human bio-forms can't be differentiated from the Juvian on this world . . . we're that much alike?"

Derrota looked to ChronoBot, "What do your sensors tell you, Hardy. Can you differentiate the difference?"

"Yes, of course, I can. But you're comparing brass tacks piglet technology to my original Sheentah tech . . . I would be surprised if the minor DNA deviations are picked up upon."

I said, "If you're wrong, they'll destroy this world with their plasma weapons and not give a second thought to it . . . any kind of OIM directive be damned."

From what I could tell, the encampment was pretty much packed up. I saw Ham and Hock using tree leafy branches to wipe away indications that any of us had been here. The rest of Max's crew were now hefting and shouldering their large packs. Twinwon's people were making their way toward us.

Viv handed Derrota and me each an energy bar, "Bon appétit, boys."

In addition to Twinwon himself, I counted a total of ten in

his crew. They were all dressed in similar colonial-style outfits to our own Juvian Militia outfits that LaSalle had fabricated. Supposedly these were the same as what local Pleidians would be wearing – slim-legged cream-colored pants, maroon, white, or dark blue shirts covered by various shades of leather vests. The footwear was moccasin-like and came to just below the knee. Each of them carried an odd-looking rifle, more accurately, a musket. A powder flask was worn from a long strap, along with an across-the-chest leather haversack.

"The muskets use a kind of flintlock mechanism quite similar to those used during our own revolutionary wartime period," LaSalle said. "But, by no means the same." I hadn't seen him arrive. I gave him an appreciative nod; he'd clearly put a lot of work into getting all of us properly attired for this mission.

He said, "Sargent, can you help me distribute the rest of these weapons?"

Seeing the surprise on my face, LaSalle said, "These were the last crates to be transported down to the surface, just prior to *Hamilton* leaving the system. I believe they are identical to those used by the Juvian and Pleidian militias. With one important distinction." He handed me the antique-looking musket.

I accepted the weapon and ran a hand along the worn-looking oiled wood stock. The blue/grey steel barrel was nicked and strife with what looked to be years of use. "What distinction?"

"I've already shown the others here while you were asleep," LaSalle said. He took hold of my weapon and turned the stock so it was upside down in my hands. "See that decorative iron-work item there? "I nodded, seeing the coins-sized disk that was notched at one end. "Well, it turns." He turned the disk, and I heard it make an audible *click*. "See, it's now pointing to the right."

LaSalle stepped away. "Now, find a distant target and take the shot."

Everyone was looking at me, most with bemused smiles. I raised the musket, took aim at a hanging branch some thirty yards away, and squeezed the trigger. The weapon fired off with a loud *Crack!* But there was no expected recoil into my shoulder – no puff of smoke from the triggered flintlock mechanism. But I'd hit my target – the hanging branch had been eviscerated. I said, "Wait . . . are you telling me you've integrated a tagger into this thing?"

"LaSalle smiled. "Not me personally, MATHR did the heavy lifting . . . but I'm pleased with the results. We all know how important it is to blend in . . . adhere to OIM directives. But this should provide us with a little added security. We all need to remember that those dials are on a timer. After ten minutes, they will automatically pop back to their original position . . . making the weapon nothing more than a basic flintlock musket again."

"Wow . . . you've really put some thought into this. Excellent job, LaSalle."

The man looked uncomfortable with the compliment and busied himself, handing out several more weapons. He said, "I suggest those of you carrying standard-issue taggers, leave them in the shuttle."

Wanda was the first to object, "How about we be extra careful not to leave our guns behind? As nice as these old-fashioned rifles are, they're no replacement –"

I cut her off, "Let's do as LaSalle suggests. There's always a chance one of us can be captured or killed. We can't risk contemporary weapons ending up in one of the local's possession. Even with these muskets, we'll be taking a big risk."

It took another thirty minutes before we were on the move. As well hidden as it was, I didn't like the idea of leaving the shuttle here unattended. It wasn't a difficult decision; Haite would stay behind – it's not as if he would ever have blended in with the locals, anyway. But I had to ask myself, do I trust this alien enough to leave him unattended? The answer was emphatically NO. But there wasn't much trouble he could get into with a heavily damaged shuttle and no one but aSplee natives running around.

We found a well-trodden dirt road to follow. Now at the front of the contingent, along with Twinwon, Derrota, and Doc Viv, we moved at a good clip. While Hardy was staying close, well hidden within the trees, he was staying in contact via my audio implants. Utilizing his unmatched sensor capabilities, there was little chance we'd be walking into a jeopardous situation. Looking back now and then over my shoulder, I noticed Max's Marines were always revolving positions – and like Hardy, mostly shadowing the procession from the cover of the forest. So, I wondered why were the hairs on the back of my neck standing up. Something was off – something was wrong.

At the ten-mile mark, Hardy said into my implants, "We're approaching a campsite."

"You're just telling me this now?" I asked.

"I'm not picking up ambulatory life forms."

"As in someone moving around?"

"No, like only one still beating, erratic, heartbeat. . . I'm just saying, prepare yourself for something . . . distressing."

"Go ahead and tell our crewmembers, Hardy, especially the Marines, via comms. I'll talk to Twinwon."

The Pleidian Fleet Commander was already looking at me, "What is it? What has happened?"

"Up ahead. Guess there's a campsite. Sounds like a grisly scene, from what Hardy tells me."

Twinwon turned to update his people, telling them to be on the ready – to pass it on down the line.

Even before we'd reached the campsite fifty feet ahead and off to the right of the road, the smell had wafted in our direction.

"I know that smell," Doc Viv said. "Burnt flesh."

Approaching the area, the lingering smoke was acrid and thick. We saw Hardy was already there, looking about the campsite, but not moving. I said to Twinwon, "Best you and your people hang back. No sense all of us –"

He nodded, "Fine. They'll hang back. But I'm going in with you."

"Suit yourself," I said.

As we entered the small clearing, I could hear Max's team setting up a perimeter around our position. There were bodies (more accurately, body *parts*) strewn all over the ground. Most were blackened and charred. "Talk to me, Hardy . . . what do we have here?"

"Pleidian militia . . . they had made camp and settled in for the night. A surprise attack by the Mantarians."

I watched as Doc Viv check several of the more intact bodies for any sign of life. As far as I could tell, the dead Pleidians didn't look all that different than Twinwon's crewmembers. I said, "How do you know it was the Mantarians who did this and not the aSplee natives?"

"Because they got one of them," Hardy said from the other side of the clearing. "Shot him in the noggin. Ugly mother-fuckers, these Mantarians."

We joined Hardy, and sure enough, the thing lying in the weeds *was indeed* one ugly motherfucker. He was big, maybe eight or nine feet tall. The only thing that was even a little similar to the rest of us was that it was a bipedal being. All other similarities stopped there. Its head was very large in comparison to the rest of him, and there was an abundance of skin—folds and folds of stretchy drooping skin everywhere. The mouth was practically lost in the folds, as were the tiny eyes. Oddly, the nose was large and bulbous with flaring nostrils. Hair at the top of the head grew out in white steel wool-like tufts. As for the rest of the body, it was more of the same – so much excess skin. The dead Mantarians clothes were not all that different from our own, with the exception that there were all kinds of leather thongs, like straps, which cinched the sleeve and pant cuffs - and at the neck opening. I imagined they were used to corral all that loose skin, keep it from flopping out.

"So, these are the beings that want to dominate the world?" I asked.

"LaSalle said, "More than that, Captain. They intend to exterminate all other intelligent lifeforms. They come from another, much larger continent. The Mantarians outnumber the Pleidian, Juvians, and aSplee, combined, three to one. For five years, they've been coming across the ocean by shipfuls."

"Hardy, any idea about these mutilations . . . the burnt body parts."

"I've, well LuMan, many years ago . . . came into contact with a genetically similar being. And in a not-too-distant star system. They were called the Mash. In addition to looking just like these assholes, they had a unique eating ritual. Somewhat like a game, they liked to char their quarry over an open fire and then toss the still-burning parts –limbs, heads – to another asshole, in between taking bites. Again, not sure if it's more of a ritual or a game."

Derrota said, "I like these Mantarians less and less."

Twinwon looked like he was going to be sick. He said, his voice barely audible, "Hardy, is there any way to determine if any of my crew are among the dead?"

"No, sorry, Fleet Commander. Not to be insensitive, but you all come across as looking the same to me. If you had bio-readings, a database, from that third shuttle, I'd have something to compare these bodies to."

Twinwon took a deep breath but said nothing.

"This one still has a heartbeat!" Doc Viv yelled.

It took me a moment to determine where she was calling from. We found her leaning into what remained of a torn and scorched lean-to tent. "Someone help me slide him out of here!"

I maneuvered myself into the tent alongside her and saw the body she was attending to – interestingly, it wasn't a Pleidian. He was badly burned on one side of his body, but the guy looked as human as me.

Viv said, "Get on the other side of him and take hold of an arm and his leg. Gently now. Okay, let's slide him on out."

Once out in the diminishing light of the day, I could see the man (actually, a Juvian) was in bad shape. Viv was already at work administering to his injuries, injecting him with a bright florescent green liquid, then spraying his burned areas with what I recognized as an active flesh regrowth compound.

She said, "I've injected him with healing MediBots, which are specifically suited for human anatomies, so I've either helped him . . . or just killed him."

Hardy, now looming nearby, said, "Yeah, I think it's the latter . . . sorry, doc."

"Shit!" Viv said, checking the Juvians pulse one last time before standing up. She said, "Shit!" and stormed off.

I, too, stood up.

"Cap . . . FYI . . . the Grish just left the system. In fact, they jumped out."

"Jumped out. We didn't anticipate them jumping."

"No . . . no we didn't."

Chapter 20

USS Hamilton
Pleidian Weonan Fringe Frontier Space

XO Gail Pristy

Pristy, sitting at the Captain's Mount, was lost in her own thoughts, only fractionally aware of any of the goings-on around her on the Bridge. She was thinking about Galvin. For the umpteenth time, she admonished herself. *You had to do it . . . you had to blabber on and on about your feelings. And then what did you do? You give him an ultimatum. Fuck!*

"XO . . . you're not going to believe this," Helmsman Grimes said, now working at the Tactical station.

"Report, Helmsman."

"It's the Grish." Grimes was tapping at his control board. "They've jumped in behind us."

"On display!" she yelled, louder than she'd meant to.

And there they were, a relatively tight grouping of eighteen warships. "Distance?"

"Ninety-three million miles . . . and closing."

"Please tell me they don't see us. Tell me it's just by chance they jumped in this close to us."

Five seconds, then ten seconds went by. "Visually, no. But I'm betting they see our propulsion signature. Normally, it would be impossible to distinguish, but they've done little else but analyzed propulsion signatures of late. I think they know it's us."

She stared at the Halo-Display and started to chew at the inside of her cheek. *Damn it!*

"We could rush-jump out of here," Grimes said.

"I already know that, Helmsman. But those aren't our orders, are they?" she knew she was being snippy but didn't care. "It's our job to keep the Grish occupied while the Captain and his team rescue Twinwon's crew. We jump, and there's a good chance the Grish will simply return to the Zoyam System and Unero."

"Copy that, XO," Grimes said.

She continued to stare at the display. *What would the Captain do?*

The Grish were closing on them.

"XO? Orders?"

"Helm . . . I want a full thrust burn of thirty-seconds. Everything *Hamilton's* got, but we keep it below FTL. After that, cut all drive output, shut them down completely. Then, use our docking thrusters like before to initiate a hard port turn."

"And then what?"

"And then we drift and hope our cloaking capability really is that good. Do it, Grimes."

"Yes, sir."

* * *

Sir Louis de Broglie had wandered much of the immense ship by now. The scientist was a curious soul by nature. Thus, he had made one marvelous new discovery after another. He felt he could spend years roaming the corridors and passageways, and only scratch the surface of what this great ship had to offer – which thus far was one incalculable scientific achievement after another.

Having come full circle, he had made his way back to Deck 29 and the Science and Technology Department. Here, he was most comfortable, having the most understanding of his beloved Port Entanglers – even the newer, modified version. He was fairly certain he was familiar enough with it; operating the device would not be a problem. Over the preceding days, he had had ample time to think. He had to come to terms with the fact that he could not return to his own time period. There could not be two Louis de Broglies. No, he would stay here. He would learn of the many technological advancements made and the science behind them. Surely, he would excel at doing so. No, he would become an essential member of this crew. In time, the captain would notice his superior intellect and make him the vessel's Science Officer. Certainly, Stephan Derrota would find something better suited for his limited intellect.

Upon entering the lab, Louis de Broglie was encouraged to find the compartment was empty. He worked best alone. Making his way over to the PE-2, he saw that the console was active. Little lights were strobing on and off, and someone had left the 3D display on. It was the **Transactions Menu**. And there it was, a listing of all the transport tests made over the last few days. De Broglie took notice of the transport of Hardy out into deep space and his subsequent return. And later, the crewmembers who had been transported down to the Unero's surface. After that, much equipment was sent down, as well. *Well, they certainly are making free use of my machine, aren't they?* He thought, with a growing sense of proprietorship. *They steal my invention, change it in ways God only knows how, and now pretend I don't exist.* He was getting more and more irritated by the second. He held out his forefinger and tapped at the virtual display. He wasn't sure what it was he was tapping at, but nothing ventured, nothing gained. A different listing, menu, came into view. There, he saw a new heading:

Port Entangler Memory Storage

Here again, he saw much the same listings from the **Transactions Menu;** everyone and everything that had, at one time, been brought into memory storage. He knew full well that these stored items were set to automatically delete once a successful transport was verified. All the listings, Hardy, the numerous crewmembers, the equipment, were faint and annotated with a **Deleted** designation. All but one. *Hmm.* De

Broglie let his forefinger linger over the name, waggling over it a few times. He tried to remember who this individual was. Had they forgotten him? Was he supposed to be among those down on the surface right now? Was the poor man now idling his life away in virtual memory much the same way he had? De Broglie would not wish that fate on anyone. So, he poked at the listing of one: **Captain Eli Tannock.**

Immediately, the PE-2 came alive. The dimly lit pedestal now glowed brightly. There was a ramping up of sounds – energy being increased. This machined was indeed different than his two port entanglers. De Broglie took a step backward, and then another. The first of the segments *thunked* into view on the floor of the pedestal. Shoes and trousers. Then another, more of the legs came into view . . . and within seconds, the man was standing there, completely reformulated.

He was an older man, his salt and pepper hair was cut very short, and he wore the uniform he recognized as one of the ship's officers.

De Broglie said, "Captain Eli Tannock, I presume?"

The man stood there upon the PE-2 pedestal, unmoving. Only his eyes moved from side to side. Then he found Sir Louis de Broglie. "Who the hell are you?"

At that very moment, *Hamilton* made an abrupt turn to the port. Both Tannock and Sir Louis de Broglie were thrown off their feet and onto the deck. MATHR announced:

Battle Stations . . . Battle Stations . . .

Chapter 21

Exoplanet Unero

Captain Galvin Quintos

It had changed everything – seeing that dying Juvian lying there on the ground – suffering. Yeah, sure, maybe he had juxtaposed fingernails, but the guy was human looking in every other regard. And that, justified or not, had elicited a kind of bond – a kind of kinship. Already no fan of the Mantarians, now I found I'd already picked sides, and it hadn't happened consciously. So be it.

We were back on the road again, having spent the previous two hours digging graves for all the dead. All except one, I ordered the fleshy giant to be left where he lay, for foraging animals or pecking birds. Fuck him.

We marched along, quiet for the most part, each of us lost in our own inner thoughts. My thoughts had turned dark.

Thinking about the dead, the body parts – they'd been torn, not cut. Were the Mantarians that strong, powerful, that those Pleidians had literally been torn limb from limb?

Viv said, "I hear water running . . . hear it? Maybe it's a creek or small river."

I listened and heard it too, the soft babbling of water flowing.

"I'm walking beside a creek, thirty feet to your left in the trees," Hardy said.

Viv said, "How about we take a little break?" And before I could say it would be better if we keep moving, she was already scurrying off and had disappeared into the treeline.

The rest of us left the road and followed the same narrow path Viv had found. By the time we arrived, she had already removed her boots and had rolled up her pant legs. She was wading along the shore of a creek that was about fifteen feet wide, and I'd guessed to be five to ten feet deep. She looked up, seeing the rest of us arrive, and laughed, "This feels amazing! Come on in, Quintos, why not let your hair down once in a while? Kick off those boots and join me . . . all of you, come on in!" She kicked at the water, splashing it toward us.

I saw Hardy emerge from a particularly dense thicket of trees on the other side. "I'm picking up life forms within that stream. That may not be such a good idea, Doc."

"Oh, come on. Don't be such a party pooper, Hardy . . . all streams have a few little fishies."

I wasn't the only one who was tempted to feel that cool water on my feet. Derrota had gone so far as to start pulling off one boot. That's when Hardy tossed a bowling ball-sized boulder into the middle of the creek.

The water erupted, coming alive with movement. The surface of the creek seemed to be boiling. And then I saw them. Creatures. By the hundreds, they were rushing out onto the shore. The size of a small dog, maybe a chihuahua, they were beyond disgusting looking. Purple, they were part fish, part multi-tentacled octopus, and part snapping *something*. I didn't have to look hard to see that their ever-snapping mouths were filled with tiny, sharp teeth.

Viv yelled, "Ouch! The thing bit me!"

Not only that, but the creature was still latched on, hanging limply onto her exposed calve. Only now had she looked down and saw it there. Momentarily paralyzed, as were the rest of us, she screamed.

I ran to her, while everyone else must have figured it was every man for himself. Those that didn't get back fast enough were kicking at the little beasts as if their lives depended on it – and perhaps that wasn't so far from the truth. I splashed my way into the water and swept Viv up into my arms. I could feel bumps and thumps against my boots and tugging at the fabric of my pants.

"Get that thing off of me, Quintos! Get it off me, now!"

I almost laughed. I think the corners of my mouth turned up, just a tad. "Okay . . . let's just get away from the water. You're going to be fine."

She screamed, "He's looking at me . . . he's fucking looking at me!"

And it was true; the creature had, in fact, swiveled its over-sized, strangely intelligent-looking eyes to look right at her. Hurrying up closer to the road, I put Viv down on the ground and knelt down next to her. For the moment, I wasn't sure what to do. Should I grab the thing and just yank at it? Or maybe, try to pry open those powerful little jaws, first?

Viv screamed again. And then again.

I saw there was a softball-sized rock half-buried in the dirt nearby and dug it free. "Hold still. I don't want to miss."

"Just kill it! Hurry up, kill it!"

Again, I almost laughed. I raised the rock up over my head and hesitated. *Now that's interesting*, the creature's eyes were now locked onto mine. And they had widened. It knew. It knew what was coming.

"Smart little fucker, aren't you?" I said aloud. Taking careful aim, I brought the rock down hard and fast. But within that brief half a second, maybe three-quarters of a second, the creature had let go and was gone – was scurrying back down toward the creek, making little squawking sounds.

* * *

Three hours had passed since the ordeal at the creek. Viv, as were several others, was limping. That, and muttering curses.

"What was that?" I asked.

Viv gave me a wary glance, "I said I'm starting to think I should have stayed onboard *Hamilton*. Hardy is programmed with enough medical proficiency."

I didn't respond. I hadn't twisted her arm to come along. Although, she certainly did liven things up.

"What?" she said.

"Nothing. Does it still hurt? Your bite?"

"What do you think? Do you think I'm limping along here to get sympathy?"

I shook my head. No . . . a stupid question."

I heard Hardy's voice in my implants, "A battle has commenced."

I heard the distant gunfire – a lot of gunfire. I said, "Any way we can get a view of it? See what's going on?"

"There's a hill that's not far," Hardy said. He showed himself from the trees. He waved his Craw Beast claw in the air. "Come this way; we'll take a shortcut up the rise."

I glanced back to Viv, "You okay doing a little off-road hiking? Or you stay can back . . . wait for us if you'd like?"

"Screw you, I'm not waiting here . . . alone."

"Can I see it?" I asked, looking at her bandaged calve.

"No . . . let's just go. You're really starting to piss me off." She headed off toward Hardy. I exchanged a quick glance with Derrota and Twinwon, who both offered up a noncommittal shrug.

The hill was more than a gentle upward slope, and we were all huffing and puffing by the time we'd reached the top. Viv, one arm slung around Derrota's shoulders, had needed help. Others who had gotten nips and bites at the creek were also struggling.

Joining Hardy, he gestured down into the valley below. But

I'd already locked onto the rise of blue-grey smoke and the still-active gunfire. The battle hadn't relented.

"What's the situation?"

"There, a mile or so beyond the skirmish, that's the settlement," Hardy said.

Twinwon said, "My crew . . . can you tell if they are there? There in the settlement?"

"Maybe. But like I said, Pleidians are Pleidians as far as my sensors can discern. What I can tell you is that a number, well, *twelve* to be exact, of your kind are being cloistered together in the middle of that settlement. A settlement that is being held by Mantarians. It could be your crewmembers that are prisoners, or it could be other Pleidians being held there. I can't tell."

"And the fighting?" I asked.

"Juvians are there, and over there," Hardy said, pointing a dinner plate claw. "And Pleidians are there, there, and there. But the Mantarians are holding their ground. That settlement won't be back in Pleidian or Juvian hands any time soon."

"We need to get down there. We need to rescue my crew," Twinwon said with growing irritation.

"We will. But we need to be smart about this. And we need to remember; this isn't our fight."

Twinwon was pacing now while not taking his eyes away from that distant settlement. "Look, I don't need a lecture on your Occluded Interaction Mandates, Captain. I'm getting my people out of there, your OIM bullshit, be dammed!"

The words he had spoken were in near-perfect English and, by his tone, was not open to discussion. The truth was,

Twinwon was a Fleet Commander and at a far superior rank than that of my Captain's rank. Thus far, he'd been content to let me lead this contingent, but he was putting his foot down, and I couldn't really blame him.

The rest of Twinwon's Pleidians had made their way up the hill by now, taking a knee or finding a boulder to lean up against. None of the marines were in sight – they were setting up a perimeter around our current location. Glancing back to Hardy, I saw that he wasn't looking down into the valley, but off to the left, over to an adjoining hill, one not quite as tall as the one we were standing on.

"What? What do you see?"

The fur-covered ChronoBot said, "I think . . . yes, it could be . . ."

I scanned the distant hillside, shaking my head, "I don't see anything –" Then I saw something. A glint. A quick flash of sunlight.

Viv was now looking through Derrota's portable PowerScope device, said, "Could that be the shuttle? Maybe the reflection off of the forward window."

Hardy said, "No, that is a foil juice pouch. Gadmian Rind, flavor . . . minty."

Several of the Pleidians stood and peered off to the distant rise. Twinwon said, "Included in our crew rations. Rations that can be found on any one of our three shuttles. We have to be close to shuttle number three!"

"There," Hardy pointed. "I'm detecting a three-degree heat

variant right there between the two hillsides. Has to be the shuttle, and she's perfectly cloaked."

Chapter 22

USS Hamilton

Pleidian Weonan Fringe Frontier Space

XO Gail Pristy

Ryder assessed the Halo-Display with a creased brow. "What a clusterfuck."

XO Pristy had summoned Captain Wallace Ryder to the Bridge some ten minutes earlier, and she wasn't so sure it had been a good decision. But already having a limited crew onboard *Hamilton*, and now everyone else she would normally count on to assist with critical decision-making – Captain Quintos, Hardy, Science Officer Derrota – all who were back on Unero. She'd figured the highly experienced Arrow Fighter pilot would provide the best situational assessment, acting as a sounding board for her own decision-making.

"I don't know what to tell you, Gail. All we can do is keep

to the Captain's instructions," he said. "It's your job to maintain this wild goose chase, right? Give the team back on Unero time to rescue those donut heads."

Her expression made it clear she hated that derogatory term for the Pleidians. "I already know that, Ryder," she said. *God, the man could not be any more arrogant.* "But this is a three-mile-long dreadnought. Maneuvering this big tub, at least within sub-FTL velocities . . . those smaller ships will overtake us and do so soon."

"Then just go to FTL. I don't know what else to tell you."

"We go to FTL, we lose the piglets in our dust . . . we're back to square one . . . and no longer keeping that fleet occupied."

He scratched at his stubbled face. She wondered when the last time was he'd shaved –or showered, for that matter.

MATHR announced:

Captain on Deck

Both Pristy and Ryder spun around.

She was surprised by the announcement – it was virtually impossible for the captain to be back on *Hamilton*, not that she wouldn't be ecstatic for his timely return. But it wasn't Captain Quintos making his way forward within the Bridge. It was Captain Eli Tannock. *Oh, God . . .*

"Sit Report, Lieutenant," Tannock said with unmasked hostility.

Pristy and Ryder exchanged a quick glance. She wondered how much or how little the man was aware of. Where was she supposed to begin? At the moment he'd been sucked into that machine, the Empress's off-books mission to Unero . . . where?

"It's good to have you back, sir," she said. "How –"

He cut her short, "How have I emerged back into the world of the living?" He spat accusingly. "Or maybe I should be the one asking the questions? Like how come it took a man from the mid-20th Century to figure out how to retrieve me from buffer memory when some of the keenest minds in the sector were right here on board this ship!"

She wanted to tell him that answers to those questions were above her pay grade. That, yes, there had been a conscious decision to leave him there within MATHR's memory banks, but only until things settled down a bit.

"I can't answer that, sir. I know little of the *situation* you speak of. I apologize. What I can do is bring you up to date on *Hamilton's* current situational predicament. And I could really use your help, sir."

Behind her left ear, she heard Ryder whisper, "Well played, Gail."

Watching Tannock's face, the back and forth shifting of his eyes, the myriad of micro-expressions mirroring his inner conflicting emotions, she wondered if the man was even sane. She knew Captain Tannock well, had served under him for several years – this person standing before her was not that same man.

He moved quickly, startling her. He waved a hand in the

air for her to move aside. She did so and watched as he took the Captain's Mount.

All eyes were on Captain Tannock. But with a quick glance around the Bridge, she realized that wasn't true. All eyes were on her. Eyes that spoke louder than words – *what the hell are you going to do about this? Certainly, he cannot command this dreadnought.*

"I'm still waiting, Lieutenant!" He said, staring straight ahead at the Halo-Display.

"Captain," she said louder than she'd intended, "*Hamilton* is currently being shadowed by a Grish battle group of no less than eighteen warships. My orders are to evade battle but keep the enemy close in pursuit."

Tannock's head tilted fractionally to one side – like a dog trying to make sense of his master's unintelligible human words. She continued, "I'm not sure how much you were aware of prior to your um . . . anyway, *Hamilton* was brought out of Pleidian spaceport at the request of Empress Shawlee Tee. A small Pleidian fleet under the command of Fleet Commander Twinwon was investigating possible sightings of Varapin vessels here in Pleidian Frontier Space. It is suspected it was a ruse. The Grish fleet, not unlike what they had done with the 2nd Fleet at Auriga Star System over a year ago, an ambush that destroyed all of the Pleidian vessels."

She waited for the Captain to comment or ask pertinent questions, but none came. So, she continued, "Three Pleidian shuttles had managed to escape the attack . . . had used their stealth capabilities, along with the distractions of battle, to escape. Those same shuttles were eventually tracked to the distant Zoyam star system, and specifically to the exoplanet, Unero. It is there that our team is attempting to locate and rescue any Pleidians still alive. Needless to say, *Hamilton*, is not supposed to be here. Again, this is an off-the-books operation." She let out a silent breath and caught Ryder's eye. He shrugged noncommittally.

"Captain . . . do you have any questions?" she asked. She saw that Grimes had spun around in his seat and was looking unsure about something.

She said, "Crewmember Grimes?"

"Sir . . . it's the Grish fleet. They're gaining on us. If we want to avoid weapons lock, we'll need to accelerate to FTL . . . at least for a while."

"And we'd lose them in the process," Ryder said, shaking his head.

Captain Tannock suddenly stood. "No more!"

Pristy waited, biting her tongue. *What is he doing now?*

"No more running! Battle stations!"

Immediately MATHR's voice was repeating the orders from overhead.

Tannock said, "Helm! Come about . . . we will not run from these bastards. Gunneries . . . man your weapons stations!"

That was automatic, Pristy thought. That's what going to Battle Stations means. What Tannock wasn't cognizant of was the fact that *Hamilton* was operating with a minimal crew. Yes, many of her guns could be utilized, sure, most were automated, and there were various bots that could be deployed, but all those would need to be conscripted into action. *What the hell is the man doing?*

Tannock turned to face Ryder, and as if noticing him for the first time, smiled and looked relieved. "Captain Ryder. You are just the man I was hoping to see. Get down to Flight Bay . . . ready your Arrows. . . ready your pilots. Soon, we attack!"

Now it was Ryder's turn to look aghast. Disobeying a direct order from the ship's Captain was a court-martial offense – one made even worse when at times of imminent battle.

No doubt now; Tannock was off his rocker, Pristy thought. As any Space-Navy Captain knows, he would be required to contact the Bay Chief Frank Mintz first; that was his realm. Deploying a squadron of Arrow Fighters was an immensely complicated undertaking. Ryder was in command of those pilots, sure, but nobody moved in or out of the bay without Mintz's direction.

John Chen, who had just come back on duty, took a seat at the Helm Station – taking back the mirrored control from Grimes at Tactical. Chen, apparently having heard the Captain's recent orders, said, "Reducing speed and coming about."

There was one alarming thought that kept cycling through Pristy's head. *We are not supposed to be here. We cannot be here . . . Hamilton cannot get drawn into this fight!*

"Captain! Three, no . . . now four, Grish vessels have established weapons lock on *Hamilton*."

"Distance, Tactical?"

"One hundred twenty million miles and closing, sir."

Pristy felt as if she was watching the cascade of one disastrous

event after another from outside of herself. *I can't let this happen
. . . I have to do something.* Slowly, starting with one backward
step, she put distance between herself and Captain Tannock.
By the second and then the third step, it was evident the man
was paying attention to those around him – and clearly, he
was unhinged. Turning around, she ran for the entrance to the
Bridge. Once outside and within Whale's Alley, Pristy spoke
into her TAC-Band, "MATHR, find Coogong . . . wherever he
is on this ship, connect me to him, fast!"

It seemed like minutes, but in actuality, it was mere seconds.

"Lieutenant Pristy, is there an issue? How may I assist you?"
came his soothing calm voice.

"Captain Tannock is the damn issue, Coogong. How the
hell is it that he's sitting at the Captain's Mount. Why would
you release him from –"

Coogong interrupted, "I would not have done so without
contacting you first. No, we can thank our visitor, Sir Louis
de Broglie, for that ill-timed complication. I apologize for not
monitoring the PE-2 device more closely."

She realized she'd just dumped all her frustration on poor
Thine scientist, who was not to blame in the least. "Listen to
me carefully, Coogong. The Captain . . . Tannock, he's not in
his right mind. I don't know if it's from him being kept so long
in virtual suspended memory or head injuries he'd sustained in
the past. It doesn't matter. He's about to put *Hamilton*, and her
crew, in grave danger. He needs to go."

"I understand the predicament, Lieutenant. But are you
not talking about a Space-Navy crime, mutiny? Your career

would be over, and I am afraid to say . . . you will be robbed of your freedom."

I'm not talking about dragging Tannock away in leg irons and throwing him in the brig, Coogong."

It took a few seconds for the scientist to catch up. "Oh, I see . . . you want to put him back into virtual memory."

"My question to you is, can that new Port Entangler device zero in on Tannock, right there on the Bridge? Can we . . ." she tried to think of a delicate way of saying it, *oh fuck it,* "Can we zap him where he is sitting? Like right now, before it's too late?"

"Lieutenant Pristy, although I do commiserate with your predicament, I cannot involve myself in your onboard politics. I am a guest here from an allied world."

"Can you show me how to do it?"

Chapter 23

Exoplanet Unero

Captain Galvin Qunitos

I didn't like this. Too many unanswered questions. Like why hadn't the crew of that third shuttle made contact after landing here? If the craft had crashed-landed, how is it none of the surrounding landscape had been affected? And most importantly, where were they all now? Hardy was not picking up lifeforms within the craft itself, although, it being cloaked as it was, it could be there was sufficient shielding from his sensors.

Max suggested we break our ranks up into four squads. If this was some kind of ambush, he wanted us to be well prepared. We would come at the shuttle with two flanking squads, while a third squad would stay atop the hill, keeping the higher ground. His Marines, the fourth squad, would do what they do best by staying hidden and interspersed within the surrounding trees. It made sense to me, and I gave the order for us all to get moving.

Gunfire crackled in the distance as my squad, which included Derrota, Doc Viv, and Hardy, made our way down the hill through course brush and ramble. It oddly brought back memories of my childhood in Clairmont, my brother Eric and I playing Army using broom handles for rifles. And here I was again, dressed in a kind of costume, carrying a makeshift musket.

As we approached where the shuttle sat cloaked between the two hills, Hardy, towering over us, was making too much noise. Each step he took crunched and ground the dry vegetation beneath his feet.

"Can you at least try to be stealthy," I scolded in a lowered voice.

"Yeah . . . that won't be suspicious at all . . . an eight-foot-tall Craw Beast tiptoeing through the bramble."

"Well, just walk quieter!" I said.

Viv said, "You guys should start a stand-up comedy routine."

Ignoring her, I saw the other team, Twinwon leading the way, approaching from the other side. LaSalle was there too; he offered up a little wave.

I said, "Can you disable the shuttle's cloaking device from out here?"

Hardy shook his Craw head, "No way, Jose . . . would need

to get inside. Remember, this is advanced Pleidian cloaking tech."

Seeing movement, I watched as Twinwon and another of his crew, keeping low, scampering to where the shuttle, supposedly, was. He straightened and looked to be feeling the open air in front of him – like a street mime performing at a make-believe window.

Twinwon's arm suddenly disappeared from view, and a moment later, the rest of him. Then, his crewmember also disappeared. Clearly, they'd accessed the vessel's hatch release. Thirty seconds later, Shuttle #3 popped into full view.

We approached the shuttle from both sides. The aft hatch was open, and, coming around the rear of the shuttle and looking in, it was evident that no one – other than Twinwon and his crewmember, was in there. Twinwon was forward, seated in the pilot's seat. By the time I'd joined him, he was already getting to his feet.

"The shuttle seems to be in perfect condition. No damage," Twinwon said.

"And her crew?"

"There are several log entries, like the initial landing here, then teams going out on information-gathering recognizance missions, but nothing that explains the entire crew of eighteen disappearing."

A shadow fell over them from behind. Hardy had entered the shuttle and was clumsily, using one of his Craw claws, to tap at the vessel's AI interface panel. Twinwon looked ready to chastise the ChronoBot.

"Let him . . . no offense, but, as rude as he can be, his AI can run circles around even Pleidian technology."

Hardy said, still tapping away, "Good . . . very good."

"What?"

"All of the previously-onboard crewmember's bio-readings have been scanned and stored into memory." He turned to look at us. "I can tell you unequivocally that those Pleidian bio-readings I detected in the settlement . . . they are an exact match."

"And what about the others?" Twinwon asked, looking from Hardy to me.

I already knew the answer. I knew Hardy would have no trouble detecting the bio-readings of someone who was alive or dead.

"I'm sorry, Fleet Commander . . . I can confirm they have been killed."

"Where are they? Where are their bodies?"

Hardy didn't answer right away. Again, I knew what he was going to say before he said it.

"They have been . . . dismembered, burned, and mostly consumed . . . eaten. Much like what we encountered at the previous encampment . . . the Mantarians, they are truly a monstrous race. I'm sorry."

Twinwon fell back into the pilot's seat. "I want them to pay for this." He looked up, stared into my eyes, and said, "You can either be with us or against us, Captain . . . but this act cannot go unanswered."

"How about we concentrate on rescuing those of your crew who are still alive . . . at least for now."

It took another few minutes to reengage the shuttle's cloaking system and secure the aft hatchway. We regrouped and headed up the next hill, where we could get a better vantage point viewing the settlement. I walked with Max; this would be his expertise.

He said, "Cap . . . rescuing those Pleidians, it's really not that difficult. We're dealing with primitives here. They have no real military organization; their weaponry is a joke . . ."

"And making a rescue without killing any Mantarians? Keeping to our mandate?" I asked.

His expression said, *are you sure we really care about that?*

"Look, Max, this world deserves an opportunity to evolve organically. Come on; Earth has had their ruthless, barbaric civilizations."

"I don't know; this seems different somehow. But you're the boss. You get to make the hard calls. You say we go by the book, and we go by the book."

If any one officer skirted going by the book more than me, I was unaware of who that was. No, I was not a rule-follower, and I'd paid the price for that numerous times in my career.

"Can you, can we, get those Pleidians out of that settlement or not?"

"Without killing anyone?"

My shrug was my answer.

"Maybe. We'll go in after dark. Our ocular implants will

give us a big advantage. I'll need to study the building construction used –"

A deep, Louisiana accented voice interrupted Max. I wasn't aware LaSalle had been tagging along right behind us.

He said, "Stacked horizontal logs with mud and other debris to fill the gaps. Nearly identical to that of early European and early American building practices."

Max let out a breath, "There'd be nothing easy about breaching that kind of construction. No cutting through outer walls . . . we'd need to go in through the front door. And there goes any opportunity to go unnoticed."

Both Max and LaSalle were looking at me because I was smiling.

"This does not have to be so difficult."

"Oh, really?" Max said with heavy cynicism.

"Yes, really. Look, from my standpoint, we should make every attempt to keep our presence here a secret. But that doesn't mean we can't push things to the limit. If our breaching that dwelling is anything but stealthy, yet is beyond screwball, that still won't imply extra-terrestrials were here causing trouble."

LaSalle gave me a sideways look. "Go on . . ."

I scanned the area around us and found what I was looking for. I pointed, "There."

Both Max and LaSalle didn't say anything for a moment.

Max said, "Oh . . . yeah, I guess I should have thought of that."

LaSalle said, "So, what? We just send Hardy in there to knock on the front door?"

I shook my head; Nah, I'd do more than that . . . I'd have him break down that door. I'd have him clamor and flail about like a crazed beast. You tell me, would you stay in that log cabin facility with a wild Craw stomping furniture into splinters and roaring like a lion, or would you make a mad dash out of there as fast as possible?

Max smiled and then laughed. "And what . . . then those Mantarians now hiding in the bushes would just watch as our Pleidian prisoners follow this wild Craw out of the settlement?"

LaSalle laughed too, "Like rats pursuing the pied piper. I guess it could work. There will be stories about this. Hell, it may become folklore . . . passed on for generations. But, yes, it won't go as far as involving alien intervention."

I felt pretty good about my idea. Little did I know, soon, I'd find out just how wrong I'd been.

* * *

It took another four hours before it was dark enough. We had assembled fifty yards outside the perimeter of the settlement. Earlier, Hardy received his marching orders without hesitation; in fact, he was excited to get started.

"Remember, Hardy; there'll be no deploying of those hidden plasma cannons of yours . . . none of your typical antics. You understand?" I said as sternly as I could manage while knowing just how silly my directives sounded.

"Roger that, no big guns, no antics."

Max said, "You'll need to get in there and get out pretty

quick. It won't be long before Mantarians from the other cabins come running. Me and my team will be close by . . . can provide limited cover from the trees, as you and the prisoners make your escape."

Doc Viv had been mostly quiet about the plan, but even in the quasi-darkness, I could tell she was unsure about things.

I moved closer to her. Keeping my voice low, I said, "What? Spill it."

"I don't think it's going to work, Quintos. Simple as that." She'd said it loud enough that LaSalle, Max, even Twinwon, had heard her.

"Why the hell not . . . it's a great plan," I said defensively.

"Really? Let me ask you a question then. If it were you that was one of those Pleidian prisoners in there, and an eight-foot-tall Craw Beast came storming in – would you follow it out into the night . . . like that little mouse following the pied piper?"

We all looked at each other, but no one had a quick retort.

She continued, "Maybe Hardy can offer up a handwritten note from Twinwon . . . oh wait, Craws don't have pockets to carry things like that . . . do they? Or maybe Hardy can remove his stupid Craw head to let them know he wasn't really a Craw . . . oh wait, he's a ChronoBot. A ChronoBot just as scary looking as a Craw."

"I hate you. I really, really hate you." I said.

But I wasn't about to give up on my idea; it still had merit. "Okay . . . one modification, and yes, I know it's not perfect, Hardy will pretend he's Twinwon."

She looked at me with skepticism.

I said, "Hardy, you can alter your voice, right? You can sound like someone else if you choose."

"You betcha." He placed his dinner plate claw upon LaSalle's shoulder and said, "I can talk in a deep southern drawl," sounding just like LaSalle – then placed his claw on Viv's shoulder, ". . . or I can talk like the good doctor. '*Quintos, you're in over your head.*'" He'd nailed her voice as well as unique speaking inflections perfectly.

"Good. Actually, really good. Now give Twinwon a try . . ."

Fifteen minutes later, watching Hardy lumbering along out from the tree line where the rest of us had gathered, he was doing a pretty good job acting all animal-like. Approaching the cabin where the prisoners were being held, I started having second thoughts. *This just might be the worst idea I've ever had.*

Candlelight flickered from several windows. Most of the other cabins within the settlement showed signs of activity as well—flickering candlelight from windows, abrupt laughing sounds, even a kind of chorus of singing.

"He's approaching the door," Viv said to my left. Shoulder to shoulder, I could feel the warmth of her body next to me. Looking bemused, she'd captured her bottom lip between her front teeth. She was enjoying this way too much.

BANG! WHACK! CRUNCH! Hardy had crashed through the cabin's front door and stomp over it. Five seconds later, hollers and screams emanated from inside. The first of the Mantarians – wearing pants but no shirt – came stumbling out. Then, at a full sprint, he headed off in the direction of the other cabins. Others followed suit – each waving their grotesque flapping-skin arms and yelling warnings into the night.

So far, so good, I thought – allowing myself a modicum of self-congratulation. There again, I was pretty sure all of the Mantarians had evacuated the cabin. *What's taking so long?*

As if reading my thoughts, Viv said under her breath, "Maybe it's the fact that Twinwon is five-foot-ten, while Hardy, the wild Craw Beast, is eight feet tall?"

"Shoosh!" I said, annoyed while mentally prompting Hardy to hurry up in there.

And that's when things started to go wrong – when the proverbial wheels, one by one, fell off the wagon.

Mantarians were coming out of the other cabins, a number of them holding lit torches overhead. The once dark settlement was being illuminated by flickering amber firelight.

"Fuck!" Max said from somewhere nearby. "They've got their muskets. What's taking Hardy so damn long!?"

Wanda, who had been keeping out of sight, said, "They'll pick off the prisoners like ducks in a pond."

I closed my eyes – *this can't get any worse.*

Suddenly, Hardy, the colossal Craw Beast, filled the door's opening. He roared and waved his claws – a tad too dramatically if you asked me. My ocular implants clicked, and I heard Hardy's voice in my ears, "Ah, boss? What do I do now?"

I said, "Did you get the prisoners? Are they with you?"

"Affirmative on that."

"Well, don't just stand there like an idiot . . . go! Head toward the trees!"

Hardy did as told and was now stomping forward, looking very much like a grizzly bear, well . . . except for that alligator-looking head of his. But all my attention was still on the cabin's dark door opening. I saw a uniquely Pleidian head peak out, then another and another. The prisoners were there but debating whether to follow the idiot Craw Beast.

First one, then another, then all the rest of the Pleidians were sprinting from out of the cabin in pursuit of Hardy. *Run, you sons of bitches, run!*

A handful of the Mantarians were readying their long flintlock weapons. Each had progressed to a different stage of the ridiculously slow loading process – whereby powder flasks were being used to pour gunpowder down into their musket muzzles. Tiny wads of cloth were being placed within the muzzle, followed by the projectile, probably a lead ball or bullet. Detachable ramrods were being used to tamp the lead ball down into the barrel until there's snug with the powder in the breech above the trigger mechanisms. And by this time, the Hardy, moving way too slow, was only halfway to the tree line.

"Move it, Hardy!" I said in a hushed voice. Fortunately, the ChronoBot heard me and picked up his pace a little. All of the Pleidian prisoners had caught up to him by now, and, as if he really were the pied piper, they were scampering along right after him.

Raising their weapons, I knew the Mantarians would start firing any second now, but would they hit anything from that distance – I doubted it. In a few more seconds, we'd have our escaped prisoners here with us, and we could get out of here.

The musket fire was loud – real loud – and I felt myself tense with each explosive pull of the trigger. The prisoners hunched lower and picked up their pace.

And that's when the totally unexpected happened. A lone flaming arrow struck Hardy at the side of his head. Then five more flaming shafts struck his torso one after another. The giant Craw Beast was literally set afire.

High-squealed yelps and battle screams emanated from all around the forest.

LaSalle said, "it's the natives . . . it's the aSplee. They're attacking!"

From high arching trajectories, flaming arrows were now raining down upon the Mantarians. The accuracy of the strikes was beyond amazing. Soon, no less than ten of the fleshy skinned Mantarians were on fire and screaming in agony.

Slacked-jawed, I watched the unfolding of events, totally memorized.

Twinwon, standing at the treeline, was welcoming his compatriots into the relative safety of the forest. Not one of them had been shot by musket ball or pierced by a flaming arrow.

Hardy, on the other hand, was still standing out there in the open, about thirty feet short of the tree line, and within view of, well . . . pretty much everyone. Many more flaming arrows were protruding from his Craw Beast hide by this time, and Hardy was flailing about with his large claws trying to pat the flames out. His incessant, loud cursing was being transmitted directly into my audio implants and no matter how I tried to talk to him, tell him to stop, he wasn't listening to me. Granted, anyone in this predicament, a walking talking bonfire, would be frantic. But Hardy wasn't just anyone. He was a ChronoBot, a battle-bot who was virtually indestructible. This tantrum was all in his head.

"Oh, no. No-no-no-no . . ." Viv said with trepidation.

We looked at each other, both of us thinking the same thing. *This changes everything.*

Hardy, standing there, a smoldering mess of burnt, hanging rags – was clearly not a ferocious Craw Beast. He was something else. He was all metal. A highly reflective, oh so mechanical-looking, robot thing. A *so very alien-looking* thing.

Chapter 24

USS Hamilton
Pleidian Weonan Fringe Frontier Space

XO Gail Pristy

She waited for Coogong's reply.

"Please, let me better understand your request. You want me to show you how to transport a member of your crew, a Captain nonetheless, into *Hamilton's* – MATHR's – virtual memory? Oh, I do not think I can do that, Lieutenant. I am sorry."

She looked back over her shoulder into the Bridge. Every second counted. Tannock was obviously mentally impaired and was hellbent on going to battle with a Grish fleet – one that outnumbered *Hamilton* eighteen to one. That, and she'd had explicit orders not to engage the enemy under any circumstances.

"Well, how about you just show me how the thing works

. . . what buttons to press? I'm already somewhat familiar with the original port entanglers."

"I will show you how to use the PE-2 device only as intended. To transfer inanimate, or animate, matter from one location to another here on the ship."

"Fine. And thank you, Coogong. I'm on my way up to Deck 29 now . . ."

She gave one last look back into the Bridge. The Halo-Display showed they were still a good distance from the enemy. She had a few minutes – a very few minutes. Now, sprinting down Whale's Alley, she suddenly stopped in her tracks. Out of breath, she said, "Idiot!" She called Coogong back on her TAC-Band.

"Lieutenant?"

"Coogong! Transport me to the Science and Technology Department. Please, do it now."

She wasn't all that sure it could actually be done; this was sort of like a one-way ticket to a place without having been transported there via the PE-2 beforehand. She recollected that it may be a prerequisite – *or was it?* But there again, she knew Coogong and Hardy had been making further modifications, enhancements, prior to the mission down to Unero.

"Prepare for transport, Lieutenant."

She felt off-kilter, sick like she was going to hurl. And in that instant, she knew the transport process had begun. Begun and, evidently, ended. She was now standing upon the PE-2 pedestal within the Science and Technology Department laboratory. She looked about the compartment and saw the stick figure Coogong as well as the strange-looking Sir Louis de Broglie. She wanted to reprimand the old scientist – tell him that his meddlesome actions had put the ship and the lives of everyone on board in jeopardy. But there was no time for that now. She stepped down from the pedestal and joined Coogong at the adjacent console.

"No theory, Coogong . . . just down and dirty nuts to bolts directions on using this interface."

Coogong bowed his helmeted head. He started by explaining each aspect of the control board – how to initialize the display and retrieve previous transport data. She saw all the crewmember names of those who had transported down to Unero, as well as Captain Tannock's retrieval from MATHR's virtual memory. She also saw her own transport listing from just moments before. It took another five minutes to go over the individual configuration settings and the actual transport process.

Coogong said, "All crewmembers onboard *Hamilton* have been added to the database, something I have been working on most recently. The PE-2 is also capable of transporting various items –"

"I'm sorry, Coogong," she said, cutting him off and shouldering herself in front of him. "I think I've got this." She used the locater interface to pinpoint Captain Tannock's bio-readings down on the Bridge.

Coogong said, "Now, you select his –"

"I got this," she said, rapidly tapping on the control board. She already knew where she was going to send him. And it wasn't back into virtual memory – but somewhere almost as inescapable. She went about tapping in the destination physical coordinates. A 3D wireframe interpellation of the intended compartment was now showing on the display.

"What . . . where, is that?" Coogong asked, leaning in.

"It's called the Pinion Reconcile Cabin . . . about as far aft onboard *Hamilton* as you can go."

She manipulated the 3D wireframe perspective around in order to view the center of the compartment. She smiled and let out a relieved breath. The dark, boxy-looking object was called a Grish Isolation Encase. The very same Encase one Ensign Hughes had ordered specifically off the Interstellar DarkNet and used to imprison his kidnapped quarries. Hugh's, the once murderous crewmember, was long dead and gone, but his creepy prison hold had yet to be removed from the ship. Pristy made a few more last second adjustments and, with her finger poised over the 'Transport' button, looked at Coogong to ensure she had not made a mistake.

"Are you sure you want to proceed, Lieutenant?"

She held his stare a moment and then that of Sir Louis de Broglie. He smiled and nodded appreciatively. She had the feeling he was whacko as Tannock – a reminder that long term stasis within virtual memory was a bad idea.

She tapped the button.

She said, "How do I know it worked?"

Coogong pointed to the 3D wireframe display. Where there was once an empty Encase box, there was now an Encase with the distinct shape of a person lying on his side within it. That and he was moving.

"Oh, okay, good." She was well aware of their scrutinizing stares. "It's not forever. I'm not a total monster."

Neither said anything.

"It's just until Captain Quintos is back onboard. Anyway . . . I'd appreciate it if," she waved her hands around over the console, "if we can keep all this to ourselves."

She didn't really expect an answer. Raising her TAC-Band, she hailed Grimes, who'd still be seated at Tactical.

"Go for Grimes . . ."

"Jump us . . . Rush Jump the ship!"

Chapter 25

Exoplanet Unero

Captain Galvin Quintos

I t was more than a lull, more than a brake or respite – it was a total reset. The gunfire ceased, the yelling – the war cries – it all stopped suddenly and definitively. All eyes were on the towering chrome ChronoBot. Now, standing there motionless, as if being still would make him, somehow, any less noticeable, Hardy's face display came alive exhibiting his original, authentic, face – and it was glowing a bright reddish-pink color. He said, "Oops."

Viv said, "You know . . . he truly is an idiot."

"Yup." I tried to think. How was I going to spin this? How was I going to turn this around from this total clusterfuck of a situation?

Suddenly, Hardy's face display went brilliant gold. So bright was the illumination coming out of his oversized head; it was nearly impossible to look at him. Like looking at the Sun, you had to turn your eyes away or risk blindness.

But squinting helped. I watched as the ChronoBot raised his hands high overhead. He looked up to the heavens and began to murmur, no, chant, a series of at first unintelligible phrases.

Viv said, "He's speaking each sentence in multiple languages, in Pleidian . . . now Mantarian . . . now Juvian . . . and now aSplee," Viv said, smiling.

It was then that I saw him. LaSalle had stepped out from the tree line and was just barely visible in the clearing. His words being heard a second before Hardy's. LaSalle was disseminating the speech for Hardy to voice.

"We the People of . . . Unero, in order to form a more perfect Union, establish Justice, insure domestic Tranquility, provide for the common defense, promote the general Welfare, and secure the Blessings of Liberty to ourselves and our Posterity, do ordain and establish this Constitution for . . . Unero."

Of course, I knew the words by heart – the U.S. Constitution's preamble. Clever, LaSalle had swapped out *the United States of America* for the word *Unero*.

Derrota stepped out from the trees to join LaSalle at his side. Max and his team also emerged, each of the Marines speaking the hallowed words of our early American independence. Viv and I stepped forth, suddenly bathed in the golden light. We repeated the iconic words in each of the alien languages.

aSplee natives emerged from the forest, some holding

bows, others holding wooden spears. Next came the all too human-looking Juvians and Pleidians, most clutching long guns. LaSalle walked forward, still dictating the preamble. He raised his hands over his head, mimicking Hardy, who was standing at the center of things. Fifteen feet from the god-like being, LaSalle lowered down to one knee and bowed his head.

I said, "Let's get on out there."

All of us from *Hamilton* and Twinwon's shuttle crews did what LaSalle had done – walked toward the deity with hands raised up to the heavens. Then, several paces out, we took a knee and lowered our heads in divine reverence.

But my eyes were tracking those all around us – the indigenous, combative peoples of Unero. The first to join us were the aSplee. Mere feet to my left was a young bare-chested warrior. His hands reaching high, his head lowered, he was repeating the preamble in his own language and was attempting to say the words in the other languages as well. I stole a glance around the settlement and saw that virtually all the inhabitants of this land were either kneeling or in the process of kneeling.

No, Hardy was not an alien interloper; he was a God. He was a descendant from heaven above. A messenger of peace. So, was this a perfect solution? Not really. But at least our mandate had not been completely breached.

I felt my TAC-Band start to vibrate. Obscuring the readout with my hand, I read the message written in all caps:

XO Pristy: HAMILTON BACK IN SYSTEM! GRISH HOT ON OUR TAIL!!!

I messaged back.

Capt. Quintos: Can you transport us out?

XO Pristy: Affirmative.

Capt. Quintos: Start with Hardy . . . now if possible.

XO Pristy: Stand by.

It took thirty seconds. Starting at his feet, segment-block by segment-block, Hardy began to disappear. Last to go was his still blazingly bright head and upward stretched arms. Pitch darkness befell upon the settlement, and I – everyone – was night-blinded.

While eyes began to adjust to the dark, the sense of heavenly providence still persisted. Someone nearby was sobbing – it was the young aSplee warrior. I was under no illusion; the fighting would probably resume. But those meaningful words, ones derived from a world many lightyears away, may just have a lasting effect. Who knows?

I tapped at my TAC-Band and spoke, "Get us out the hell out of here, XO. Twinwon's people first, then us."

"Copy that, Captain. Glad you're okay," she said.

Hearing her voice was a sweet reminder of how much I appreciated her – having her as my second onboard *Hamilton*. *Or was it something more than that?*

* * *

Back on board, my first order of business was to ensure Haite Caheil was transported up to *Hamilton* from his second shuttle location down on the surface – only to discover he was not there. Apparently, the Varapin pilot had double backed to that first, fully operational shuttle. According to Hardy, it was in the midst of him entering the settlement cabin that his sensors detected the shuttle's drive coming alive, and soon after, the vessel taking off from Unero. Because it was cloaked, Hardy was unable to make contact or to remotely take control of the craft. I'd never fully trusted that ghoulish alien, and now my suspicions about his motives had been justified.

It was a slow process bringing everyone onboard via the lone PE-2 device. But once all, both *Hamilton's* and Pleidian crewmembers, were safe onboard, I ordered both remaining shuttles destroyed. Two Phazon Pulsar blasts and there was nothing left of the advanced *alien* technology.

Entering the Bridge, I saw XO Pristy seated upon the Captain's Mount. MATHR announced:

Captain on the Bridge

She stood and relinquished the chair to me as I approached. "Sit Report, XO?"

Normally, I'd take her report within my ready room, but at

present, we were under battle station conditions, and I wanted to be here where I could make battle decisions at a moment's notice.

She kept her voice low enough so that only I could hear her over the battle stations klaxon alarm, "Captain, as directed, we had kept the Grish at bay. Staying just far enough ahead of them to keep them on our tail, but not going to FTL and losing them. It was working – it had been a good plan."

I was listening to her, but my eyes were locked onto the Halo-Display. The Grish fleet was here and in pursuit of us. Fortunately, thus far, they had not attacked.

She said, "That's when Captain Tannock strolled onto the Bridge."

That got my attention. "What? No way. He's in MATHR's virtual memory . . . until –"

"No, Captain. As it turns out, our *guest* from the past, the Louis de Broglie guy, had been tinkering around with the PE-2's console and noticed the file. Deciding that someone had been inadvertently forgotten that someone was languishing there in virtual memory, so he transported Captain Tannock out."

"Oh, no."

"Yeah, well, he showed up here asking for a situation report. I didn't know what to do. With you gone, he was the ranking officer onboard the ship."

I closed my eyes and rubbed my temples.

"He didn't like the fact we were running from the Grish. He had no interest in my reasoning . . . that *Hamilton* was not supposed to be here. That going into battle, especially against far superior forces, was not our mission."

I looked about the Bridge, "So . . . where is he now? Did you put him back into virtual memory?"

"No. I didn't know how to use the new PE-2, and Coogong would not support putting someone into long-term virtual memory . . .due to the fact that the device seems to have adverse effects on an individual's mental state. Both de Broglie and Tannock were proof of that."

"Again, XO, where is he?" I said, not really sure I wanted to know the answer.

She pursed her lips and made a face that almost made me laugh.

"Well, I didn't have much choice in the matter," she said indignantly. "And remember, Tannock was the ranking –"

"Yeah, I get it, the ranking officer."

"So . . . whatever I did, it couldn't be, like, an official act. That would be paramount to mutiny, right?"

"Um, yeah, I guess."

"So, I thought, what would you do? God knows you rarely do things by the book."

"Get to it, XO!"

She smiled while looking guilty. "Well, you remember that thing Ensign Hughes had ordered of the Interstellar DarkNet . . . you know, to imprison his victims."

"The Grish Isolation Encase?"

"That's it, he had hidden way aft, within the Pinion Reconcile Cabin."

"I thought we got rid of that thing."

She shook her head. "Oh, it's still there . . ."

"You didn't . . ."

She shrugged. "I didn't know what the hell to do with him. He was about to take us into battle. He was about to get us all killed!"

"And he's, still in there now?"

She sucked her lips in and widened her eyes, a cute, innocent child-like expression. "Yeah," she said, drawing out the word. "How much trouble am I in?"

"None. I think it's pretty much a brilliant idea."

"Really?"

"Really. But we can't leave him in there indefinitely."

She let out a breath, her relief exhibited by the dropping of her shoulders and the softening of her facial muscles.

"I think I may have an idea," I said.

Chapter 26

Without waiting for Pristy to comment, I said, "Get over to HealthBay. Find Doc Viv and relay the same story you just told me. Ask her to ready a bed, somewhere in isolation where it won't be observed by other crewmembers."

"Okay . . . then what?"

"Ask her to have a sedative IV ready."

Pristy slowly nodded and smiled. "You want Viv to put him under. Like for the rest of the mission."

"Hopefully, she'll go for it. After you speak with her, get on up to Deck 29, and transport Tannock from that Isolation Encase into the awaiting bed."

She was about to head off when I caught her arm. "You won't be done until this conversation, and all the video feed files taken from around ship or your actions, are excised from MATHR's memory. So, you'll need Derrota's help with that."

She looked at me with a crooked smile. "You've done this sort of thing before, I take it?"

"No comment."

She hurried off, and I hoped this wasn't going to come back and bite her, and me, in the ass. I was already supposedly sitting in a prison cell awaiting one court-martial.

I said, "Tactical, status of the Grish fleet?"

Grimes tapped at his control board, "Sir, they've moved fifty thousand miles closer over the last few minutes."

"How is it they tracked *Hamilton* back to the Zoyam star system?"

Grimes turned in his seat. "That's the thing I don't get, sir. After Captain Tannock, um . . . left the Bridge, we commenced a rush jump. Then two more rush jumps to ensure we couldn't be followed. But it seems that the Grish have gotten surprisingly good at bird-dogging jumping starships . . . tracking wormhole telemetry. Detecting propulsion radiation is an art unto itself . . . and they may be better at it than we are."

I knew *Hamilton* was currently cloaked. "Have they been pinging us?"

"Oh, yeah, definitely, sir. Grish stopped using passive scans a while back. I'm not sure how, but their sensors are now taking full measure of us."

Being able to bypass our cloaking capabilities was disastrous and would have long term strategic implications I didn't even want to think about right now. "So, they know Haite Caheil is no longer here onboard."

"I assume so, Captain."

I was about to hail Hardy when I felt his heavy footfalls approaching the Captain's mount. "You know it's creepy when you do that, right? You showing up right when I'm about to hail you," I asked.

"I am a God-like deity . . . or have you forgotten?"

"I suppose you'll be reminding all of us of that for the rest of our lives."

Before he could answer, I asked. "Haite Caheil . . . please tell me he's not onboard one of those Grish vessels trailing us."

It took a beat. "Actually, he *is* onboard one of those Grish vessels trailing us. Sorry, Cap . . . I should have noticed."

"It's okay . . . guess even deities make mistakes, huh? It doesn't make much sense, though. I figured the Grish fleet would be the last place he'd want to end up. It would be a fast ticket back into Varapin hands – or claws. He'd described the kind of public execution he'd be facing if ever apprehended."

"Unless . . . he had something of value to offer in trade."

I looked at Hardy, thinking about that. Then it hit me. I was tempted to rub my temples again; my head was hurting from lack of sleep. Hardy did not need to say another word. It was our newfound Port Entangler, *transporter*, technology. It would be a total gamechanger for any intergalactic power. And, as of right now, the U.S. Space-Navy was the sole proprietor of such technology.

I said, "How likely is it that Haite found a way to hack the PE-2's build schematics from within that absconded shuttle?"

"That Varapin pilot has proven to be well accomplished doing just that sort of thing in the past, Cap," Hardy said. "I am reviewing MATHR's remote access logs as we speak. Do you want the bad news or the not so bad news?"

I looked at Hardy with an expression that said I'm in no mood.

"Seems the Varapin pilot had indeed accessed *Hamilton's* AI . . . and yes, he now has all the necessary build schematics necessary to reproduce much of a PE-2 device. With that said, the Grish cannot communicate that information out of the system at the moment. There are no accessible communications hubs in the area . . . but that will change, soon."

My heart skipped a beat. "And our cloaking technology, frequencies and such forth, used by *Hamilton*, I suppose that too has been pilfered!?" I didn't wait for an answer. I swallowed and tried to stay calm. "Okay . . . Obviously, we cannot allow Haite to transmit any of that information back to his home-world of Devastin. And the piglets, they absolutely cannot be allowed to have it. How can we jam their comms signals?" I asked.

"More than that, Cap . . . Fleet Command be damned, we need to destroy that fleet. Think about it. That technical data has already been dispersed into their fleet-wide network nodes. Right now, there are eighteen individual sources that can disseminate that classified data the moment they are within range of a Hub Comm. Pleidian cloaking secrets, the port entangler transport designs . . ."

I stared at the Halo-Display. "So, why are they still following us? With their newly acquired treasures, they should be jumping away as fast as possible. Putting lightyears between us."

Something Hardy had said kept bouncing around in my

head. "You said the Varapin pilot now has the build schematics used to reproduce *much* of a PE-2 device. But not all?"

Hardy was apparently now thinking. His face display depicted an old 20th Century Pong video game being played – *pinging* noises sounded each time the little pong bounced from one side to the other. Considering Hardy didn't actually need time to think, this was just one more of his annoying antics.

"Hardy!"

His face display changed back to his more commonly used, and just as annoying, spinning pinwheel. "The build schematics are incomplete. Reviewing the data now, I can see that some of the original design, those originating from Sir Louis de Broglie's two units . . . which specifically dealt with quantum particle entanglement, had yet to be uploaded into MATHR's memory. Perhaps an oversight." He attempted a human-like shrug.

My mind raced. As one aspect of our mission had been completed, the rescuing of Twinwon and his surviving crew, we now had a far more important mission. One that, if not successful, could devastate the Alliances' war effort.

I saw Derrota had entered the Bridge and was headed toward the CIC – he was undoubtedly making a beeline to MATHR's interface intent of the deletion of certain security video feed files described by Pristy. She, too, had entered the Bridge.

I yelled over to Derrota, "Stephan!" I waved him over. By the time both Pristy and Derrota had reached the Captain's Mount, I had the workings of a barebones plan in mind.

But first, I said to my XO, "You spoke to Doc Viv?"

Pristy offered a two thumbs up response. ". . . and he's now fast asleep in HealthBay."

I knew that at some point, I'd have to deal with what to do with Tannock long-term, but not now. "Thank you, XO . . . good job."

Fleet Commander Twinwon, accompanied by Ensign Plorinne, were making their way toward us. *Shit!* He wasn't going to be happy about the theft of Pleidian cloaking technology.

I said, "Welcome, Fleet Commander." I quickly brought Pristy, Derrota, and the fleet commander up to speed on the issues with the Grish fleet and the breach of highly sensitive information – how that same information had been disseminated to all of the Grish ships currently following us.

Twinwon took the news with far more restraint than I would have. He closed his eyes and shook his head. "This is my fault. *Hamilton* is only here because of me. Because of my inability to deal with the Grish fleet in the first place."

"It *is* kind of his fault . . ." Hardy said, agreeing

"Why don't you put a cork in it until spoken to?" I snapped at Hardy. Turning to Derrota, I said, "Stephan, what can we do to bring our cloaking technology back online? The odds are already stacked against us; we can't go into battle with our big dreadnought as exposed as it is."

Derrota scratched at the back of his head. He looked at Twinwon, "Pleidian cloaking technology . . . how familiar are you with what was implemented here on *Hamilton*?"

Twinwon said, "I'm a fleet commander, not an engineer. But I suspect your robot here knows far more than the rest of us."

Hardy's face display depicted two eyes, a nose, and a closed zipper for a mouth. Why he was being even more aggravating than usual was beyond me. "Damn it! Just say what you have to say, Hardy," I ordered.

"Pleidian cloaking tech utilizes an ingenious algorithm of swapping multi-band spectral frequencies whereby the Varapin use only high MV-band spectral frequencies, and the Grish use an altogether far more antiquated methodology using refracted light mitigation."

"Hardy! Can you help Derrota bring our cloaking back online or not!"

"Yes . . . probably."

"Come on, Hardy," Derrota said, already heading away toward the CIC.

I said to their backs, "I want an update within five minutes or sooner!"

XO Pristy had taken her seat back at Tactical, while Grimes was seated back at the Helm station.

"I need the location of the nearest Comms Hub . . . how much time do we have before the Grish can transmit?"

Pristy tapped at her board. "Yeah, that would be within the NorPliet Sector. We're a ways out from there at our current pace, maybe two and a half hours. It's a Grish Hub . . . one that the U.S. Space-Navy, nor the Varapin, would have access to as far as I know." She spun around. "But it doesn't make sense. Any one of those Piglet ships can jump away right now. Accomplish a data transfer up close and personal to that in-system Hub."

She was right. It didn't make sense. Wait. *Or did it?* I had to smile. I knew Haite Caheil was as devious an individual as they come. But he was also very, very, smart. This newly acquired trove of information would be his ticket to redemption within the Varapin Empire. But it was information the Varapin Counsel of Nine would not want to share with their loosely allied with, Grish partners. I looked up at the Halo-Display. "If I'm right, and I think I am, Haite Caheil has taken command of that fleet. There's no way he's going to allow the piglets to acquire so crucial, so advanced, technology . . . Pleidian cloaking for one, nor the Port Entangler transport tech. Tech, he now knows is incomplete."

Pristy said, "I don't get it. It doesn't make sense."

"It does if you have a devious mind," I said under my breath. "I made eye contact with her. "Look, Haite is being faced with a dilemma. Sure, he's letting the piglets think they'll be sharing in all this newly acquired technology. But that's not going to happen. No way. In the end, he won't let *any* of their ships jump away. Nor will he allow them to get close to that Comms Hub. They'll attack long before then."

"Okay . . ." Pristy said, looking thoughtful.

"Only Haite will be transmitting that information . . . and only back to Devastin, certainly not to any other Grish assets."

Twinwon said, now looking excited, "So he'll command the Grish fleet to attack . . . to disable *Hamilton*, but not to destroy her outright. He wants what remains of the design for your Port Entangler transporter."

"Bingo. Only then will he have enough for the Counsel of Nine to accept him with open arms. Sure, the Pleidian cloaking technology would be nice, but it would not be enough. But the transporter technology, now . . . that would be something else."

Pristy said, "But that would mean he'd have to destroy the Grish fleet too."

I nodded, "He's walking a razor's edge. But one thing's for sure, after getting what he wants, it won't be a Grish Comms Hub, he'll be heading for . . . it'll be a Varapin Comms Hub."

No one spoke. Figuring out Haite's most probable intentions was one thing. Doing something about those intentions was another. We were greatly outnumbered, *Hamilton* was operating with a minimal crew, and worse, we were running with cloaking that was compromised.

I was thinking, strategizing, distracted while looking down at my boots.

XO Pristy said, "Captain . . ."

"Hmm?" I said, still looking down.

"Captain!"

I looked up, "What!" But there was no need for Pristy to explain herself. There, bigger than life, was none other than Haite Caheil himself.

Chapter 27

How the Varapin pilot had commandeered our Halo-Display, I had no clue, but I had a feeling I was about to find out.

"Captain Quintos . . . I am impressed."

It took me a moment to compose myself. To free my face of the utter surprise at seeing him looming there before us.

Haite had expanded his three-dimensional Halo-Display image to that of a towering twelve-foot-tall version of the ghoulish hellion.

"Listening to your exchange, you've figured out much, Captain. Not everything, but the fundamentals."

Christ! How long has he been listening in . . . How, has he been listening in?

As if reading my thoughts, Haite said, "Your vessel is now under my complete control."

I instinctively looked up.

"Yes, MATHR no longer answers to anyone but me. This dreadnought is no longer under your command."

My first thought was to get Derrota to disable all but the most essential MATHR subsystems. I tapped at my TAC-Band but was surprised to see Haite Caheil's animated icon staring back at me. I spun left to face the CIC. Derrota hurried into view, coming to a stop and looking out of breath; he shook his head, making a befuddled expression.

All I could do is smile. The Varapin pilot had played us all – played me. "What is it you want, Haite?"

"I am not without feelings, Captain." He tilted his head, and I suspected he was attempting a smile, but it was impossible to tell since his mouth was little more than exposed teeth and jawbones. "Well, there I go, lying to you right out of the gate. Let's just say, I appreciate you providing me with . . . what is the human term? Ah yes, safe harbor, while the right circumstances presented themselves to me. So, while I am unable to feel or even understand true compassion, I do understand honor. The asylum you and your crew provided me for all these months compels me to offer you a choice."

Derrota had disappeared back within the depths of the CIC. I could only hope he and Hardy were coming up with a means to disable MATHR so we could take back control of *Hamilton*.

"Your actions already prove you have little understanding of true honor, Haite," I said. "Why don't you just say what you came here to say and be done with it?"

"Alright. Your choice is quite simple. You can choose life for you and your crew or a merciless death. I am prepared to evacuate all but one of you back onto the surface of Unero."

"All but one of us? And who would it be that stays behind?"

"The Thine scientist, of course . . . Coogong."

That alone explained a lot. Haite's plan hinged entirely on presenting a fully operational PE-2 transporter device to the Counsel of Nine. Having scanned MATHR's records, he's already confirmed that the build schematics are indeed incomplete. Perhaps he feels Coogong could provide those missing design specifications. But I already knew, Coogong didn't possess those. Perhaps he would be able to fill in the blanks over time, but time was not something Haite would have. He'd have one shot at redemption.

I turned to scan the Bridge. Everyone was on their feet, looking up at the menacing being.

Twinwon said, "Who is it you seek?"

I gestured to Ensign Plorinne. Catching his eye, he hurried over to us. "Yes, Captain."

"Remove your TAC-Band." I looked about the Bridge and said, "Everyone, remove your TAC-Bands and stomp them into the deck." It had occurred to me that any TAC-Band communications could easily be changed or manipulated.

I followed my own instructions by removing my own TAC-Band, tossing it to the deck, and stomping it hard with the heel of my boot. Starting with XO Pristy and Twinwon, everyone else, including the Ensign, followed suit.

I placed a hand on the young Ensign's shoulder and drew him in close. Whispering into his ear, I said, "Listen to me carefully. You're to leave the Bridge and head directly to the Science and Technology department. Find Coogong and tell him to report to the Bridge at once. Then, head to the ship's barracks. Track down Colonel Drake Bonell . . . he's in charge down there. We have fifty-five Army / US CAPRI soldiers, along with another fifty-five top-notch Marines onboard. Explain to the Colonel what's going on. Also, explain he cannot use any comms devices typically under MATHR's influence." I gestured to the crushed pieces of my TAC-Band on the deck. I sent a glance up to Haite, who was still patiently waiting for me. "Ensign, my instructions to the Colonel are to ready and arm his troops for battle. That, and to be ready to assemble within Hold 7." I knew for a fact that the oversized Hold 7 had been previously battle damaged and had yet to be outfitted with communications conduits – the necessary multi-strand laser-fiber braid that crisscrossed most of the ship's hidden accessways and unction tubes. The hold lacked any connectivity to the rest of the ship other than overhead lighting and a lone operating hatch door.

The Ensign pulled away, anxious to get going. "Hold on, hold on! Next, you're to head up to Security, find Chief of Security Alistair Mattis. Explain the situation. Have his team destroy their TAC-Bands. Then instruct him to deploy his security teams throughout the ship. They're to check every compartment, every corridor, and passageway. There are several hundred people on board this ship. All personnel . . . everyone, is to destroy their TAC-Bands and then head over to Hold 7. Again, Ensign Plorinne was about to move off. "One more thing. Get word to Captain Ryder, send someone as a messenger; I want the flight bay entrance physically blocked off."

"Can I go now?" Plorinne said, looking exasperated.

"Everyone onboard meets in Hold 7 in one hour."

His eyes widened. "All that within an hour, Sir?"

"Yes, so best you stop wasting time. Run! Go! Hurry!"

As the Ensign sprinted away, I looked back up to Haite. There was no way he, or MATHR, could have heard my whispered instructions to Ensign Plorinne. But that didn't mean he wouldn't be able to track him throughout the ship.

When the giant Varapin spoke, his grating voice thundered within the compartment, "Do not test my patience, Captain! You have lost . . . but you have been offered a means to save your crew from certain death. As we speak, the *Hamilton's* shields have been lowered and your weaponry taken off-line. Hundreds of Grish troops are en route within transport vessels . . . soon to land within your unsecured flight bay. Again, you have lost."

There was a commotion at the back of the Bridge. I spun around to see Doc Viv running – gasping for breath. Chasing her, a mere three strides behind, was one of the HealthBay surgery robots – a Cutter Bot. One of his articulating appendages had been fitted with a spinning and loud whining bone saw. It was extended outward, ready to fillet anyone that came into contact with it. The bot's upper torso was splattered with blood. Two more Cutter Bots appeared, also wielding bone saws. Viv ran past me, putting the Captain's Mount between herself and her pursuers.

"That thing killed two of my med techs, then came after me! Quintos . . . all the ship's bots have gone fucking crazy!"

Three more bots entered the Bridge – all three came to a stop just out of range of striking distance.

Haite really has taken complete control. My eyes were drawn to the CIC, where they locked onto the seven-foot-tall ChronoBot now coming our way. His face display was a lifeless pitch black. That and his demeanor was all *off.* Hacking Hardy's AI, or more likely, hacking LuMan's AI, would have been no small feat. With Hardy now fully under the Varapin's influence, we were all truly screwed. This was game over.

Haite said, "This vessel has more robots than it does crewmembers. HealthBay bots, as you can see, many maintenance bots, security bots that are well-armed, and even an indestructible combat-ready ChronoBot. So please, Captain. Dispense with any thoughts of resistance . . . resistance will be futile."

Hardy had come to a stop several paces away – standing rigid and unmoving.

I said, "How do I know you'll keep your end of the bargain, Haite? How do I know a fleet of Rage Class Landers wouldn't soon be deployed to Unero, your Varapin ghouls coming to suck the lives from everyone on that world?

"My patience has reached its limit. Believe me or do not believe me, but if you wish to avoid violence . . . avoid the death of your crew, decide now. I suggest you hand over the Thine scientist without any further turmoil."

The high-pitch whirling racket of the combined three bone saws was making my head pound. Just thinking was becoming difficult. It seemed as though this was, in fact, a checkmate situation. Thinking things couldn't get any worse; I heard the gentle voice of the Thine scientist right next to me.

"Captain Quintos? You requested my presence here?"

Dismayed, I wondered how Coogong had managed to enter onto the Bridge, walk past the three Cutter Bots, and join me here, unaccosted.

Haite said, "Excellent . . . a good first step."

"First step?" I said.

"Yes, bringing the Thine scientist here . . . as a good faith offering to me."

XO Pristy cleared her throat. I looked her way and saw that she was doing something strange with her eyes. She kept glancing to her right. Obviously, she wanted me to look at something. I looked where she was gesturing and only saw Hardy still standing there like a statue. Ready to pay her no mind, I saw it. Hardy. The idiot robot's face display had altered his appearance once more. I also heard it. The soft pinging sounds as a little white prompt was being bounced from side to side. Hardy was playing Video Pong. This was becoming an issue. The more serious, even life-threatening, a situation becomes, the less Hardy seemed to act appropriately. I honestly wondered if there were burgeoning, worsening mental issues with this robot.

I said, "Just to make sure . . . you are not under this asshole's control, is that right Hardy?"

The ChronoBot raised up an arm while making a single-finger flipping-the-bird salute toward the towering Varapin. Hardy said, "Sure, for an uncomfortable few minutes both

LuMan and I were under the Varapin's influence . . . even a bit stymied for a while . . . but hey, we got over it."

In the blink of an eye, the ChronoBot extended out both of his arms in front of himself. In unison, access panels opened, and chrome weapon barrels snapped up and into place – one on each of his mechanical forearms. Mini canons came alive, firing bright plasma bolts into the three Cutter Bots – catapulting their flailing forms up and backward. All three crashed down onto the deck. On their backs, immobile, multiple blackened craters continued to smolder into the air.

Haite Caheil discounted this latest development with the wave of a clawed hand. "Too little too late, Captain. As we speak, heavily armed, Grish transport vessels are poised to land upon your vessel's outer hull. The incursion will soon commence –"

I cut him off. "Two questions, Hardy. First, can you take back control of MATHR?"

"In a word, No. Although Science Officer Derrota certainly hasn't given up."

I thought about that. "Okay, second . . . how much of MATHR's essential functionality can you administer, take on, on your own?"

"You mean . . . as if she were no longer operational? You do know she handles everything . . . drive power distribution, internal environmental functions . . . breathable atmosphere regulation, not to mention GravLifts . . . hell, all the flushing toilets!"

"What about *Hamilton's* navigation system? Her weapons systems? Shields? Can you take back control of those systems?"

"Yes, to navigation. Give me an hour. The others . . . *that* would take a bit more time."

"How much time do we have before the first of those Grish transports arrive?" XO Pristy asked. "Tactical is pretty much being locked out," she added.

"About an hour-and-a-half, at their current rate of progress," Hardy said.

I looked up to Haite Caheil, who had become noticeably quiet. Locking eyes with the Varapin, I said, "Do it, Hardy . . . start shutting down MATHR. Do it now. And as your first priority . . . remove this backstabbing bastard from my Halo-Display."

Chapter 28

It took a full hour to get everyone assembled within aft Hold 7. Elevated, I stood upon several stacked crates and looked out to more than three hundred concerned faces looking back at me.

Heavily armed, the Army/US CAPRI contingent and Marine forces had taken up positions along the back bulkhead of the compartment. I saw Sergeant Max and his team standing several paces away from the others. Twinwon and those remaining of his Pleidian crew stood together, and Captain Wallace Ryder, along with his limited number of Arrow pilots, gathered closer into the middle of the hold. HealthBay personnel, surgeons and MedTechs, stood wearing their multi-colored scrubs – while Doc Viv was absent. She had insisted someone needed to watch over the unconscious Captain Tannock. But with so many Cutter and other bots still on the loose, I was more than a little uneasy about that. The rest of *Hamilton's* crew stood shoulder to shoulder, distributed throughout the hold. Coogong and the two other Thine scientists were right below me. I wanted them close by. They held the answers that Haite was most desperate for. I was armed with a holstered tagger, and what none of the scientists were cognizant of was that I would not hesitate to kill one, or all of them, if necessary. Nothing was more important than keeping secure US Space-Navy's strategic secrets. Namely – our new PE-2 transporter designs.

Missing here was my Bridge crew, who were still manning their stations. Hardy was keeping sentry there while taking on more and more of MATHR's functions as they became available. Prior to me leaving the ChronoBot there at the Bridge entrance, Hardy made it clear he did not like his new responsibilities – so every time an onboard toilet was being used, an animation played on his face display showing fast swirling water accompanied by gurgling toilet flushing sounds.

Loud, intermittent clanging was coming from outside the hold's large metal hatchway. Everyone was on edge. The onboard bots still were under Haite's control, and eight crewmembers had been killed while attempting to reach the hold. Currently, Chief Mattis and his limited security forces were out there attempting to keep the killer robots, if not at bay, at least distracted.

I cleared my throat and said, "You know why we're here." I looked about the stark, expansive compartment. "*Hamilton* has been compromised. Although we are taking steps to rid the ship of enemy influences and eavesdropping, that is yet to be guaranteed. But this hold is secure, and we can talk freely here."

"Is it true Grish transports are coming? Will be landing on

the ship's hull?" a crewmember I recognized from Mess Food Services asked.

Before I could answer, Wanda, from the back bulkhead, arms crossed over her ample chest, yelled out, "Yeah . . . what's with the damn shields? Shouldn't getting those back up be a top priority?"

"Priority over what?" I asked. "Breathable atmosphere? Gravitation generators? Weapons systems? Look, we're doing the best we can. Hardy has taken on many of the ship's AI functions . . . all the ones he can. Together with Science Officer Derrota, they will bring back MATHR's functionality just as soon as the various systems become available. I assure you; shields are of the highest priority for them . . . along with weapon's systems. As for those Grish transports, yes, they are coming. And we need to be ready. Captain Ryder, you'll be rotating deployed Arrows immediately after leaving here. I've been assured your crafts onboard communications have not been infiltrated, and steps have been taken to keep them secure."

I noted just how few, maybe several dozen, pilots Ryder had standing there alongside him. "I know your resources are limited, Ryder, do your best . . . take out as many of those incoming transports as possible. We're all counting on you. In fact, best you head out of here now."

Ryder and his team started for the hatch. Halfway there, he turned and said, "I'll have an Arrow fueled and ready for you in the bay, Galvin. If it comes to that, you want to lend a hand." The hatch door opened, and Ryder filed out after his pilots. Sounds of the distant tagger and shredder gunfire came in through the opening. The hatch slammed shut with an echoing metallic *Clang!*

I continued, "Until secure shipwide communications can be restored, we'll be in a world of hurt. On a three-mile-long dreadnought, one with thousands of passageways and compartments, that's a big problem. So, I need a team of message runners. And not any of your military personnel, you will have your hands full defending the ship from what I expect to be multiple breach incursions. And those of you assigned to weapons systems or any other key stations; you're not available to be a runner."

Still, hands shot up from all around the hold; LaSalle and most of his Shipwide Maintenance crew, a number of Twinwon's people, and at least forty others.

"Good. But if you're not in shape, can't run long distances without keeling over, you'll be manning any one of the intermediary message hub stations we'll be setting up around the ship. Talk to SWM LaSalle here for further instructions and where you'll be assigned. Talk to Ensign Plorinne here about being a runner."

A soldier from a group at the back of the hold took a step forward. I recognized the five of them there, Bob, Garrett, Alex, Troy, and Cash. Cash, who still exhibited injuries, such as bruising around the eyes sustained within the gym courtesy Wanda, offering each of them an epic beatdown none of them would soon forget.

"Is it true that this onslaught could have as many as a thousand piglets busting in . . . maybe more?"

Grip, from the opposite side of the hold, yelled over, "I'm sure you still have time to call your mommies if you and your CAPRI princesses are scared."

Cash shot Grip the bird, "Bite me, jarhead."

"Listen up! Quiet!" I yelled over the beginnings of a full-on mouthing off session. I looked over to the CAPRI grunts, "Yes . . . expect a major invasion. In all likelihood, they will outnumber us by many . . . and, most likely, will be better armed. This was not intended to be a combat mission. With that said, what the piglets have in the way of superior numbers and advanced weaponry, we have better training. The Grish will be attempting a siege of the *USS Hamilton,* coming onto our ship uninvited. I don't know about you, but that rubs me wrong. That makes me angry as hell."

My eyes leveled on Colonel Drake Bonell. The older man was standing ramrod straight, and he too looked angry.

"Colonel, we will be fighting for survival . . . for our very lives. Tell me your teams are ready. Tell me this fine ship will not end up in the hands of that horde of squealing piglets."

A crooked smile appeared on his lined face. "Captain, as I understand things, the Grish forces know our numbers . . . are fully aware this ship is gravely disabled."

I nodded – *it was the truth.*

"That, Captain Quintos, is our advantage. Army, CAPRI, Marines, and your onboard security forces have trained on this vessel for months now. We know every inch of her, and we know how to defend her. At least until you can bring back those critical systems you were talking about. So yes, Captain . . . we're ready. And if we have to . . . we'll die protecting what is ours."

I let his words sink in. He knew as well as I did that many, or most, or hell, maybe all of us, would die onboard this old dreadnought today.

I discharged the meeting – everyone knew where to go, what their jobs were. I motioned that Sergeant Max and crew to stay behind. This caught Colonel Bonell's attention; he clearly was not pleased.

I stepped down from the stacked crates and waited while the last of the stragglers exited the hold. Max, Wanda, Grip, Ham, and Hock – each had relaxed expressions while the three Thine scientists looked anything but relaxed. I still was not sure where the missing design plans were for the PE-2 transporter device were being stored. Although, I knew MATHR did not have them. The truth was, I didn't want to know. In all likelihood, if I survived and was captured, I would be one of the first to be tortured. So, what I did not know, I could not divulge.

Max said, "You do know, we do not actually report to you, sir . . . there are protocols for –"

"I don't give a rat's ass about protocol right now, Max. If the Colonel isn't used to the way I do things by now, he's in for a rude awakening. I trust you . . . all of you, to serve the greater good of the *USS Hamilton*. But if you prefer, I can talk to Colonel Bonell –"

"Just spill the beans, Cap . . . what do you want us to do?" Wanda said.

I didn't answer right away, instead, looking at each of them – including Coogong and his two Thine colleagues. "There was one question that nobody asked me."

Oddly, it was Ham, not one I'd pegged as a deep thinker, who volunteered the answer. "Why . . . why are the Grish so set on boarding us? Why not just blow this ship into space dust?"

"That's right, Ham. That would be my question."

"So? Why?" Wanda asked.

"Each of you recently had the opportunity to transport down to Unero via that PE-2 transporter device."

"And back up again!" Ham added, reconfirming he really wasn't a deep thinker.

"Well, that *capability* is unique . . . no other world, no other civilization, at least in this part of the galaxy, can do something that. The military implications for an opponent that holds this technology . . . well, they're beyond words."

"And, as of right now . . . that's us," Grip said.

"That's us. That's only us."

"Maybe we should just self-destruct the ship," Hock said with a shrug.

"Oh, I guarantee, we've contemplated doing just that. But this technology could well alter the course of the war. It needs to get back to US Space-Navy Fleet Command. Which, being so secret, only EUNF U.S. Space-Navy's Executive Five Star Fleet Admiral, Cyprian Block, even knows about."

"Okay, we get it . . . the tech is super important. What do you want from us?" Sergeant Max asked.

I gestured to Coogong and his cohorts. "These three Thine scientists here know more about this technology than probably anyone, anywhere." It occurred to me there was one more, Sir Louis de Broglie, who could be included in that group. And right now, I had no idea where he was. I continued, "Keeping them safe may be tantamount to mankind's survival, not to mention the survival of the alliance. I want you to stay with them . . . protect them with your lives."

Chapter 29

We had made the Bridge/CIC compartment as secure areas as we could. Everyone was armed with a tagger and shredder long guns were propped and leaning against consoles within easy reach. The Thine scientists, along with the PE-2 device, were back within my adjoining Captain's Ready Room. Max and his team were maintaining continued patrols nearby, mostly out within Whale's Alley, while Hardy, moving considerably slower and with less agility due to the zettaflops of floating-point calculations currently being required of him. His AI capacity being stretched to the limits, he had become uncharacteristically quiet as he paced back and forth at the rear of the Bridge. With one exception, the incessant toilet flushing. What had been mildly humorous hours earlier was now beyond annoying.

"Ten miles out, Captain," XO Pristy said, unnecessarily.

I, too, was watching the steady advance of the Grish transport vessels on the Halo-Display. Not having a runner of our own within the Bridge, I yelled out, "Stephan! Talk to me . . . we need shields!"

It was a few moments before my rumpled looking science officer strode into view. He looked tired and irritated at being disturbed. "All I can say is we're getting close, well, or maybe closer, Galvin. I, for one, do not know *Jopshoin*, the Varapin programming language Haite has intermixed in with our own code. What he's done is ingenious, like cascading firewalls, one after another, keeping us from accessing the areas within MATHR's programming we need to reach."

"Sorry to disturb . . . keep at it. Let me know if there's anything I can do to help."

Derrota nodded, but before disappearing back into the CIC, he glanced over to the still pacing Hardy. "You can tell that ChronoBot to stop with the incessant toilet flushing . . . it's driving all of us fucking crazy."

Nervous laughter swept over the Bridge. One rarely heard Derrota curse, so hearing him now do so was not only funny to me but the others on the Bridge as well.

I said, "Believe me . . . I've tried. But I think it calms him . . . we'll just have to put up with it, for the time being."

"Captain!" the XO called out. "Frist of the enemy transports is landing."

The Grish transport vessel, now seeing it up close, was puke-green color – oblong and bulbous. Almost organic looking. There were no view portals, and the hull of the vessel was streaked with corrosion and what looked like rust.

"What a piece of shit," Crewmember Grimes said from the helm station.

I estimated the thing was big, maybe seventy-five yards long and half of that wide. Previously hidden landing struts were now lowering down from the transport's hull – a moment later, I heard the distant sound of something metal clanging against metal. The craft had touched down. I knew the muffled, high-pitched, whining noises that followed were drilling clasps being secured into *Hamilton's* hull.

Pristy looked up, "God . . . they're close. Like right on top of us."

Crewmember John Chen, seated at Comms and with mostly nothing to do, said, "Unlike ours, their sensors are fully operational. They know right where the Bridge is . . . where everyone on board is."

Within minutes, eight more transports had lowered onto the dreadnought's hull – each at strategically key locations. The Engineering and Propulsion Department, the Environmental Conditioning department, and right outside of Flight Bay, to name a few. Since propulsion was no longer under our own control – all we could do is watch as these leech-like parasites adhered themselves to our hull.

I looked to the expanse of black space beyond; under my breath, I said, "Okay Ryder . . . now would be a good time . . ."

As if on cue, the first of the bright red Arrow fighters came into view. I suspected it would be Captain Wallace Ryder himself, who'd be making this first flyby. The plan was to go ahead and wait for the transports to clamp onto *Hamilton's* hull. A sitting target was far better than one that could take evasive action.

Suddenly bright green plasma bolts streamed from beneath the Arrow's wings while the Grish transport's shield's flared to life during the assault. There was limited return fire; an invasion transport vessel was not much of a warship. From what I remember, from past combat experience fighting the Grish, the shields on these smaller vessels were tuff – nearly impregnable – at least for a while. But as supply power resources became stretched, they overheated and, if not shut down, could cause the vessel to explode. But as the other Arrows now began their own sorties, a constant weapons fire onslaught, we were still a good ways away from that happening. Ryder's pilots would tirelessly continue their attack until the inevitable happened – that the Grish fleet deployed their own deep space fighters. Truth was, I was surprised that hadn't happened yet.

I stood and joined Pristy at her tactical station. That first of the transports to land had now deployed a kind of cowling tube, which undoubtedly contained a plasma cutting machine that will, over time, bore through the various layers of hardened hull plating. Not long after that, holes wide enough for Grish shoulders to pass through would allow enemy entry into the ship. If the Grish kept to their past playbook, they would deploy a number of armed bots first in order to fend off any awaiting forces.

"It's the waiting that's hard," Chen said, staring at his idle Comms board.

I didn't comment.

Pristy sat back in her seat, looking defeated. "And here they come . . ." she said.

I'd just seen them too. Grish fighters.

"There must be over two hundred, maybe three," Grimes said.

"Try four hundred and six," Pristy shot back, not hiding her anger.

I stood, staring at the display. I tried to think of a time I'd been in a worse pickle than this. I couldn't think of one. My eyes fell upon Gail Pristy; her blonde hair had fallen forward in such a way as to hide much of her face. But could tell she wasn't looking at the Halo-Display or her control board; instead, her gaze was downcast. Her lips were moving as she soundlessly spoke, or maybe she was praying.

My heart sank, seeing her like this. Her being so uncharacteristically dispirited. I tried to think of something encouraging or even funny to say. Nothing came to mind. At that moment, she looked so small and vulnerable. Everything about her was petite. I watched as a tear tracked down the side of her small, upturned nose.

"Are you praying?" I asked in a voice only she would hear.

Without looking up to me, she shook her head and said, "No."

After several moments she looked up and said, "I'm singing."

My breath caught. I had always known Gail Pristy was very attractive. I did everything I could to leave things at that in my head. Hell, even though I was not a stickler for rules, there were rules of conduct that should not, could not, be tested. Hell, she was my second onboard this ship. There was no one I counted on more than this uniquely competent Space-Navy officer. Professionalism was essential within the confines of a warship's bridge. But seeing her now, with those large, glistening with tears, blue eyes staring back at me – I wavered. Her beauty simply took my breath away. And at that moment, she saw my reaction to her. *Crap!* It was almost imperceptible – a slight upward tug at the corners of her lips into the beginnings of a smile.

Shit!

"It's a song my mother used to sing to me as a small child . . . you know, like when I would wake up from a bad dream." She started to sing, her soft voice little more than a whisper. *"We're going on a lion hunt. We're going on a lion hunt. I've got my binoculars. I've got my binoculars. I'm not scared. I'm not scared . . .*

I pulled my eyes away from hers. *Damn it. This can't be happening.*

The battle stations klaxon, which I'd purposely had lowered the volume down on recently, suddenly blared at least fifty octaves louder.

XO Pristy was back tapping at her tactical board. The Halo-Display became a flurry of wild activity. As the Arrows altered their attention from the transports to the incoming Grish fighters, my hands tightened into white-knuckled fists. A space battle this oh-so- powerful dreadnought would be totally incapable of taking part in. The Halo-Display flashed bright and then flashed bright again.

"Two Arrows . . . just eviscerated," Pristy said.

I spun around looking for Hardy. He had stopped his interminable pacing and was now staring up at the Halo-Display.

"Tell me something, anything, good. That you have a clue how to give me my ship back!"

Hardy's face display remained black and lifeless. He swayed slightly from side to side. I wondered if this was becoming far too much for him. A lone ChronoBot was taking on the complex, mind-numbing functionality of an entire US Space-navy dreadnought. He looked as though he might topple over at any moment. He began his pacing again; only this time, he was singing. *We're going on a lion hunt. We're going on a lion hunt. I've got my binoculars. I've got my binoculars. I'm not scared. I'm not scared . . ."*

Fucking robot.

Just then, Ensign Plorinne ran onto the Bridge, out of breath and gasping. "Captain! They've breached the hull . . . their pouring into the ship! Hundreds of them."

Chapter 30

The piglets came at us with a fierce ferocity no one had expected. Apparently, each transport carried close to five hundred of what would be the equivalent to our US Marines. Sitting at the Captain's Mount, I heard the weapon's fire coming in from Whale's Alley. I grabbed a shredder and hustled over to the entrance to the Bridge. A virtual wall of short, stout combatants dressed in helmeted, light tan, combat suits, all armed with short-barreled energy weapons of some kind, were making their way forward. Max and his team, each having strategically positioned themselves crouched behind portable battling constructs, or PBC's, basically four-foot-tall crates on wheels, slathered with multiple layers of SmartCoat. There was a hell of a lot more PBC's out there in Whale's Alley than we had Marines to utilize.

"Hold your fire," Max barked.

Looking at the approaching piglets filled me with dread. Just five top-notch US Marines against so many. But this same scenario was undoubtedly either taking place – or would soon be taking place – all over the ship. I glanced back into the Bridge and the closed hatch-door leading into my ready room. I'd spoken to Coogong earlier, and he'd agreed – if the Bridge and subsequently the ready room is breached, he was to destroy the PE-2 transporter device. The thing was ready to blow with the triggering of a remote transmitter. What Coogong and the other two scientists didn't know was that there were enough explosives strapped to the thing to vaporize the entire compartment and everyone in it. The knowledge in those scientist's heads could not fall into enemy hands. I suspect Coogong knew as much but figured it best to leave such things unsaid.

"Fire!" came Max's order.

Each of the Marines stood, took aim, and fired. Plasma bolts tore into the front line of piglets, now just two hundred feet away. As Grish bodies toppled over, others stepped over them, or on them, while returning fire. I raised my shredder, took aim, and fired. I picked off three, four, then five piglets. Enemy plasma fire peppered the bulkhead just inches to my left, prompting me to hunker down. *That was way too close.*

I caught Wanda's eye in between her taking out handfuls of piglets at a time. She was smiling – hell, they all were smiling – enjoying themselves – even though this was the end. This was Custards last stand, and none of us had long to wait before we would be overrun.

The piglets were fifty feet away, and close enough I could see their beady little eyes and snorting snouts. Wanda had to yell over the weapon's fire to Max, "You think now's a good time?"

Ham, who was doing a magnificent job picking off one Grish combatant after another, said, "Aw, come on, a few more seconds . . . it's like shooting fish in a tub."

"That's *barrel*, not *tub*, you moron," his brother, Hock, admonished.

Max fingered something on his belt.

Whale's Alley, the deck, the adjacent bulkheads, shook as no less than ten big, previously hidden, mounted plasma cannons were now firing from each of those other PBC's. Compared to the sounds of shredder fire, these big guns gave off a thunderous amount of noise.

My jaw dropped open as I watched the enemy being cut down. My exhilaration at seeing our side not only going on the offensive but obliterating the enemy – was soon cut short. I was sickened by what could only be considered a total massacre. Hundreds upon hundreds of little piglet bodies were being transformed into screaming, flailing balls of fire. And just as suddenly as it had all started, it was quiet again. Not one of the attacking piglets had survived.

As the acrid smell of burnt flesh wafted forward, Wanda stood taller, taking in a deep breath. "God . . . how I love the smell of cooked bacon in the morning."

It was then that I turned, knelt down, and threw up at the base of the nearest bulkhead.

I was under no illusion that this was but one minor victory within a greater battle we could not win. And there were other small wins soon to follow.

Derrota and his team had managed to take back control of certain ship functions. For one, *Hamilton's* robots were no longer being controlled by Haite. Unfortunately, more than half of them had been destroyed – but yeah, having them back was a welcome bit of good news. At the present moment, a dozen SWM bots were clearing Whale's Alley of the dead – transporting the charred Grish bodies to a below main deck airlock.

No longer did we have to use our exhausted runners to communicate with one another within the ship. Hardy had been the one to get that bit of technology operational again for us. Currently, new TAC-Bands were being distributed to crewmembers – all having been pulled from stock and reprogrammed to utilize a more secure means of transmission. Colonel Drake Bonell and I were communicating as often as every twenty minutes or so. As a Colonel, he and I were both 06 level officers. But me being a Space-Navy Captain – and the skipper here on *Hamilton*, I outranked him. Older and far more experienced with the kind of in-ship fighting we were experiencing, I was giving him tactical control in that regard. It had been his idea to employ the use of hidden, transportable PBC's to hold off the incursions. Incursions that was ongoing, although, from what the Colonel relayed, we were holding our own. Thus far, we had lost twenty-seven Army and thirteen Marines.

Back sitting upon the Captain's Mount, I had two main concerns. The first was for Hardy. He was no longer pacing back and forth at the rear of the Bridge. In fact, he wasn't even on his feet. He had found a recessed cubbyhole within the CIC and was seated there, motionless. From what little I could get from the ChronoBot, Hardy was pretty much being kept to the background, while LuMan was dealing with keeping *Hamilton's* primary systems operating. But it was all too much for him. As a combat ChronoBot, it had not been designed for this. I wondered just how long it would be before the robot would reach its breaking point. *What then?*

My second major concern was for our few remaining Arrow pilots who were now stranded farther out in deep space. By the hundreds, the Grish fighters had swarmed around *Hamilton* – forcing the six remaining Arrows to back off to positions several hundred miles away. The pilots had exhausted their primary oxygen supplies and were well into emergency allocations. Both Captain Wallace Ryder and Lieutenant Akari James were among those stranded.

I hailed Ryder on my new TAC-Band. "Talk to me, J-Dog."

J-Dog was Ryder's call sign – short for Junk Yard Dog – a moniker he had earned more times than I could remember. Captain Wallace Ryder was typically laidback and easy going. That is until he's seated within an Arrow's cockpit in a combat situation. At that point, he becomes someone else completely – vicious, unyielding, and downright mean – a junkyard dog.

"Go for J-Dog. Over."

"How are your levels?" I asked, referring to levels of remaining breathable air. Over."

I heard him cluck his tongue. "I have eight minutes

and thirty-three seconds left. . . Ballbuster, has about twelve minutes. Over."

"Roger that," I said. Look, it's time. I'm going to transport you and your team back –"

"Negative, Brigs."

On multiple occasions as a young pilot, I'd spent time in one ship's brig or another for not following direct orders to drop pursuit of an enemy fighter craft – *to RTB* – *return to base.* The moniker, *Brigs,* had stuck after one of my three or four-day stints behind bars.

Even though I wasn't out there with him, I appreciated his use of my call sign. "What, you want to play the martyr . . . call it quits out there in the deep black? Over."

"Hell no! Sure, we're loyal to the cause and all that, but come on . . . no, we've had time to think. I want you to transport replacement environ-tanks. We can swap them out by hand. We can still be of use out here. Over."

"Transport the tanks into those six respective, extremely compact, cockpit areas. Over."

"Affirmative. And by the way . . . I'm down to seven minutes and change now . . . Over."

I thought about what Ryder was asking me to do. *Was it even possible?* Jumping out from the Captain's Mount, I sprinted for my ready room. Entering the compartment, the first thing I noticed was that Coogong's stick-figure legs were protruding out from beneath the PE-2's control console – like seeing the bottom half of a mechanic working beneath a HoverCar. There was a myriad of parts, gizmos, strewn about the deck nearby. The other two Thine scientists were kneeling down by Coogong's legs. Startled faces within oversized helmets looked up at me.

"What the hell are you doing? Who gave you permission to work on this device!?"

From beneath the console, I heard Coogong's friendly voice. "Is that you, Captain Quintos?"

Knowing time was quickly running out for my six Arrow pilots, I got right to the point. "How long before you can get this thing operational again?"

Coogong's stick arms revealed themselves from beneath the console. He said, "Please . . . pull me out." His two cohorts grabbed a hand each and pulled – sliding the rest of Coogong into view. Lying on his back, holding some kind of tool in one hand, he said, "You have need of the PE-2 transporter, Captain?"

"Yes! I need to transport replacement environ-tanks into off-ship Arrow fighters. We only have a few minutes."

I stared at the parts lying upon the deck – realization was setting in. There was no way I was going to save Ryder – save any of his team.

Coogong must have read my defeated expression. "These parts have already been substituted with others, my good Captain . . . please do not fret. Do you have the replacement environ-tanks with you?"

"With me?" I shook my head. I didn't even know where tanks like that would be stored. No doubt within a parts depot compartment off the flight bay somewhere. In all the excitement, I'd failed to consider this one, most important, component, necessary to save them.

"Coogong., we need to transport the pilots out of those Arrows. Get up . . . I'm talking like right now!"

Coogong got to his spindly legs and began working on the control board.

My TAC-Band began to vibrate.

"I'm working on it!" I barked to Ryder.

"I take it you can't get replacement tanks in time. Over."

"No. We're working on bringing you back into *Hamilton*, one at a time."

"Can you transport our Arrows . . . with us in them? Over."

"What? Are you crazy? Arrows are big . . . complex –"

Coogong had turned to look at me. His expression could best be described as thoughtful, or maybe, speculating.

"Wait . . . Coogong, is that even possible? Transporting an entire Arrows with humans inside them?"

Although it took Coogong several seconds to answer, it felt like hours. He said, "It would be pushing the limits of the device." He gestured to the part lying about the deck. "But with our most recent upgrades . . . yes, I believe it is possible." His face went sour. "Ah . . . but finding available memory clusters within *Hamilton* is the issue. MATHR has yet to –"

"I'm down to about a minute of breathable air . . . just saying," Ryder's voice said from my TAC-Band.

"Where else can we utilize enough memory on this ship?" I said, sounding desperate.

"On this ship?" He shook his head.

"And Hardy?"

All three Thine shook their heads. The ChronoBot had already taken on far more than he could handle.

The hatch door slid open behind me. Hardy stood there, teetering, head lulling to one side.

"You were listening to us?" I said.

"Um . . . yeah."

I waited, getting more impatient by the second. "Well?"

He said, his words coming out as a mumble, "Coogong said . . . on this ship."

"What do you mean?" Hardy was here wasting my time. He was obviosity borderline incoherent.

He said, "MATHR's virtual memory is still, mostly, inaccessible . . . and there is not enough free memory within my own AI construct . . ."

"Thank you, Hardy, but we already knew all that!"

His head lulled. One of his legs began to tremble. He half-heartedly raised one of his mechanical hands to gesture to the PE-2. "There's adequate memory within any one of the Grish warships . . . plenty."

Ryder had gone quiet. Undoubtedly, he would be gasping for air by now.

The ChronoBot continued, "The bad news . . . we'd have to transport the Arrows into the same respective Grish ship where we access their memory banks."

I wanted to ask how he was even able to access those ships. When had he and Derrota reestablished that level of communications?

"I like it! Coogong said, now tapping at his console. "I see what Hardy has done . . . has established a stealth micro-worm-hole laser transmission link to one of the Grish vessels. I can see . . . can access a virtual layout of one Grish ship in particular –"

"Damn it, Coogong! We're out of time. Transport those Arrows! Do it now!"

"It will have to be one at a time."

"Fine . . . put them into their flight bay!"

I heard Ryder's gasps, but also a laugh. His voice was little more than a whisper. "This should be fun."

My eyes were locked onto Coogong – what was taking him so long?"

"Just tell me they have a similar breathable atmosphere . . . over." Ryder gasped.

"Very similar," Coogong said.

"Good luck J-Dog . . . I suggest you go in weapons ready."

Coogong made one final definitive tap at his control board. "Captain Ryder's Arrow has been successfully transported . . . I am now proceeding to transport the others . . . now that I have the process figured out, it should go somewhat faster."

Behind, a loud clattering noise of metal hitting metal caused me to nearly jump out of my skin. I spun around to see Hardy lying in a heap on the deck.

Chapter 31

I gave Hardy a cursory check and determined he was still among the living. His blackened faceplate afforded a tiny, cartoonish looking snail – which was slowly traversing, making a slime track, from one side of his face display to the other. *Relieved.* Sure, he was down, but not out – at least not totally. I left him where he lay.

Entering the Bridge, the forward Halo-Display provided a live view from what I guessed was J-Dog's Arrow fighter. It was a split-screen feed, one feed showing the inside of the Grish warship's flight bay, the other, a wide-angle showing J-Dog, just now starting to perk up, sitting there within his Arrow's cockpit.

Standing, XO Pristy approached the Halo-Display. She pointed, "The other five Arrows . . . you can see them, two there and three farther off there."

I heard the crackle of an open comms channel. J-Dog's voice sounded weak but very much alive. "Damn it!"

"Ryder . . . J-Dog? What is it? Over."

"And here I was, all ready to go out with a bang . . . but not before taking out a few Grish assets."

Looking at the feed, I saw what he was referring to. No real spacecraft there to mention – no fighters throttling up for rapid deployment into space. None of the excitement, the craziness which occurs within a busy flight bay – like fighter crafts on deck with loud engines whirling while being refueled, or a myriad of flight crews rushing from one place to another. Ryder was right; this was a little anticlimactic. All six of the Arrows had raised their canopies to allow fresh air into their cockpits and replenish atmosphere tanks.

That particular warship does not carry fighters. That's the *Gorgazine* . . . used more for fleet support. Onboard sensors will have detected your abrupt arrival J-Dog . . ."

"Best the lot of you get the hell out of that hold . . . and as soon as possible. Over," I said.

Roger that Captain . . . but that may be easier said than done. Seems you found us a bay without actual bay doors."

Pristy and I exchanged a quick look. I could almost read her mind and the simple *oops*, she was thinking.

I said, "Well . . . we transported you in there, I'm sure we can –" There was a gentle tapping on my right shoulder. It was Coogong.

"Very sorry to disturb, good Captain."

"Coogong . . . what is it?"

"A problem. It is only temporary, I assure you."

"What . . . I'm actually busy here, Coogong. Can we discuss this later?"

"It is the PE-2 device. It is what you would call, down."

"Down? What do you mean down? We just used it." I gestured to the Halo-Display and the six Arrow fighters.

"Thangrong Crystals is the problem. Once overheated, it seems they get cloudy and no longer diffract light properly. I am hoping that once they have cooled, the PE-2 device will be fully operational again." Coogong smiled as if we were discussing something no more relevant than a passing rain cloud.

"Can't we just replace them? These Than . . . "

"Thangrong Crystals."

"These Crystals. Substitute in new ones?"

"Oh no . . . that would not be possible. They are effectively non-existent in the known universe. The ones we are using now came from Sir Louis de Broglie's original two Port Entangler devices. We are using all of them for our PE-2."

I sent Coogong back to my ready room to find a way to get the PE-2 working again, fast.

Loud weapons fire made me jump – quickly, I realized the racket was coming from the Halo-Display. All six Arrows were firing toward two of the crew entrance ways into their bay, which was more of a hold than a bay – since there wasn't bay access to the space. For the time being, J-Dog, Ballbuster, and the others looked to be holding their own. I had other things to worry about.

About to take a seat at the Captain's Mount, I saw that Hardy was no longer lying there at the entrance to the ready room. I caught a flash of movement on the other side of the Bridge; Hardy was running into the CIC. *Running?*

Heading off toward the CIC, I said, XO, you have the Captain's Mount. Tell Ryder to sit tight and to try to avoid bringing any more attention to himself."

She laughed. "I have the Captain's Mount. And I'll let him know." Pristy said, taking the seat.

I caught up to Hardy, where he was standing before a bewildered-looking Derrota and several of his team. Mid conversation, Hardy said, "I can't guarantee the link will go unnoticed for long."

Joining them, I said, "Talk to me . . . how is it you're not still lying in a heap back there?"

Derrota said, "Hardy's off-loaded some of *Hamilton's* system processes . . . big memory allocations, over to that Grish vessel."

I was already shaking my head, "That's a major, dangerous, security risk, Hardy. You should have spoken to me first."

Hardy said, "Cap, there's a whole lot that MATHR takes on that is neither proprietary nor high security. It's just function- ality and data. Necessary at the moment, not long-term. Like which water supply reservoir should be used for above-average use showers and toilets on Deck 5 and 6. Yes, MATHR, more accurately of late, me, needs this information short term while ship functions are occurring, but we don't need to save that data. Unless you want to track Chief Frank Mintz's afternoon craps. Look, Cap, I'm utilizing that stealth micro-wormhole laser transmission link I established to offload all non-essential function commands along with the short-term memory alloca- tions required."

"And what about Haite? He's not aware of what you're doing? Won't be able to use that same stealth data link to make further data breach incursions into *Hamilton*?"

Derrota said, "As of late, we've been making excellent progress in that regard. It took us a while to decode that Varapin programming . . . bypass all those firewalls he installed within MATHR's base operating code."

"So, I have my ship back, Stephan?"

"Not yet. We're going system by system. It's not enough to exercise the Varapin's intricate cybernetics . . . we must install our own firewalls, ones even more robust than those Haite had installed. Thanks to LuMan's utilization of –"

"Stephan! Just tell me when I'll have shields and weapons back under my control!"

Derrota looked momentarily flustered by the rebuke. Thinking, he looked to Hardy. "Well, shields within the hour . . . weapons, maybe twenty minutes after that."

"And propulsion?" I asked.

The science officer suddenly looked abashed, "Actually . . . we may have propulsion back online already. According to Craig, ship reactors were showing signs of life over an hour ago."

He was referring to Craig Porter, Chief of Propulsion and Engineering. "And you didn't think it pertinent to inform the Bridge?"

Hardy came to Derrota's rescue, "We've had a lot of false starts, Cap. LuMan's AI has – and still is – being used as a testbed for code enacting simulations. But Stephan's correct; you do have your ship's drives back online."

"Jump springs? We can manufacture a jump wormhole?"

"You can jump to your little heart's desire," Hardy said.

"The big question is, how aware is Haite of our progress?"

"Last check, he had twelve hundred intrusion points into MATHR. Every few minutes, a new one pops up. Oh, the Varapin pilot is fully aware of what we are doing and has become more and more aggressive trying to reestablish control."

"And?" I said.

"And nothing," Hardy replied indignantly. "He is being stopped, cut off at the pass at every attempt. Those intrusion points are becoming dead ends for him. But we've also enacted our own reactive programming . . . so with every attempt Haite now tries to make into MATHR, we virtually counterattack right back into the Grish fleet's network. Haite's so busy, so distracted, that he's missed detecting our own stealth comms connection." Proud of himself, Hardy displayed his spinning pinwheel in a vivid rainbow of colors.

"So, now you've unburdened yourself, your memory, of those trivial ship-wide functions. Are you working on restoring MATHR to her previous full glory? No offense, but major ship systems do require her oversight. Don't forget, it wasn't that long ago, overburdened, you dropped to the deck like a bag of hammers.

Seated at the station next to Derrota, one of his young techs punched a fist into the air, "Yes!"

Self-conscious of his outburst, he looked somewhat abashed.

I said, "What . . .?" I caught sight of the embroidered name on the breast of his uniform. Crewmember Colby Wise. "Mr. Wise . . . what is it?"

He looked at an equally young tech seated next to him, where the two exchanged a triumphant smile. I half expected them to high-five each other. It was clear; these two were amongst Derrota's most competent team. Those who were systematically expunging Haite's pernicious hacking of MATHR. Attempting to hide his enthusiasm, Crewmember Wise said, "Captain, you now have both short- and long-range sensors capability . . . back under Bridge control."

"Good job, Crewmember Wise. Both of you . . . excellent work."

The two techs beamed. Then, just as quickly, they were back at work – their faces concentrating on their displays.

I placed a hand on Derrota's shoulder. "And thank you, Stephan. An hour ago, I was certain we were just treading water . . . waiting for the inevitable end. Boarding parties no longer fended off . . . the Grish would inevitably infiltrate the entire ship. But you've given us a fighting chance. Thank you." I looked up to Hardy. "You did pretty good too . . . not bad."

Even the two techs glanced up for that.

I laughed, seeing Hardy's non-expression. "Okay, bad joke . . . we all owe you a world of gratitude. Thank you, Hardy . . . truly."

Derrota said, "Yeah . . . but you do realize we still have an entire Grish fleet out there. Even if she were at one hundred percent, which she is not, *Hamilton* would be no match for eighteen warships – not to mention the thousands of Grish fighter craft. It may be time to jump away. Perhaps to fight another day again when we're better equipped."

Both Hardy and I stared at Derrota.

Derrota nodded. "Did I just say that? Really bad idea. And yes, I know we can't let even one of those piglet ships leave this system."

I rubbed at the stubble on my chin. "Or . . . transmit out of this system what they've learned of our transporter technology," I added. I let out a breath. "This is bigger than us. We prevail or die trying."

Back at the Captain's Mount, I contacted Colonel Drake Bonell. "Colonel, how about an updated sit report on ship breaches."

Now that MATHR's sensors were operational again, I had a good idea of where things stood but wanted to hear from the colonel directly.

"They keep coming, and we keep fending them off," he said, but sounding defeated.

"But that's a good thing, isn't it?"

"They're adjusting their attack methods, Captain. They've learned certain weaknesses and exploited them."

This was the first I've heard of this. "But we're holding them at bay," I said.

"No, Captain, we're not. As of ten minutes ago, they're

holding us at bay." His voice had turned angry – his frustration evident. He continued, "Two Grish transport ships hit us with a staggered attack. While we were dealing with one incursion, another incursion snuck in behind us and is holding a section of the ship."

Shit! "What deck . . . what department?"

"Deck 10 . . . the piglets have taken HealthBay, Captain. Taken hostages. When you hailed me, I was discussing options with my team leaders."

Doc Viv. Was she one of the hostages? Of course, she was. Undoubtedly, she's been there in the operating room. There would be no shortage of battle-injuries; it would be all medical staff on duty.

The colonel was talking to me. ". . . piglets sent out a messenger. One of the patients came out from HealthBay's entrance. She held up there and said the Grish are willing to make a trade. Said the ship's captain, you will know exactly what they want."

The colonel's voice trailed off.

"What happened?"

His voice went cold, all inflections gone, "We called for her to run . . . to run for safety. Her eyes showed her uncertainty. Her fear. She ran for us, a line of PBC's, where we were hunkered behind."

I waited for him to continue, but he didn't.

I said, "They shot her. Shot her in the back."

The colonel cleared his voice, "Yeah . . . that they did, Captain. That they did."

"What's next?"

"How many Grish are in there?"

"Hold on . . ."

My mind raced, waiting for him to come back on the line. How many of my crew would be sacrificed with an offensive into HealthBay? Would one of those lost be Viv?"

"It's a small band, Captain. Seems your ship sensors are back online . . . you could have found this out on your own. Thirty-five armed piglets."

I said, "Colonel, I want you to hold up making a run at HealthBay."

"That's not your call, son. You and I have talked about this . . . this falls under my authority, not yours."

"I know that!" I snapped back. I let out a breath and tried to sound less confronting. "Look, your way, hostages will die. I'm hoping to avoid that."

"Use that transporter thing? The same that got us into this mess in the first place? I say maybe we should just give them the damn thing . . . be done with it."

I let him think a moment or two about what he'd just said.

"Okay, fine. Maybe that is a moronic idea. God knows we don't want to make it any easier for our enemies to board our warships."

"I want to personally talk to the commander of that team."

"To the piglets?"

"Maybe they're willing to negotiate. Let them know we're willing to sacrifice the hostages . . . that they too will be heading off to their own pig-heaven."

"Call their bluff, huh?"

"It's worth a try."

"Unless they just shoot you two steps into HealthBay."

There was that . . .

Chapter 32

The GravLift took mere seconds to descend from Deck 13 to Deck 10. Max and his team rode with me; the five of them looked peeved. Having told them my plan, they hadn't held back telling me just how hair-brained a scheme I was contemplating.

Exiting the lift, my TAC-Band vibrated. I glanced at my wrist. I said, "XO?"

"Captain . . . we're moving dangerously close to the NorPliet Sector . . . and that Grish Comms Hub. Even though we've pretty much been space-drifting, we've been moving along at a good clip."

I'd been reluctant to fire up *Hamilton's* big drives. Sure, our reactors were operational, but I hadn't been ready to convey to Haite that we were, in fact, fully capable of dashing off – or jumping away. There would be little reason for the Varapin pilot to hold back a full-on attack. He wanted the transporter tech; destroying *Hamilton* would be the last resort. "Talk to Chief Porter . . . see if he can bring just one drive on-line while mimicking engine troubles . . . we need to change course, but we don't want to give the impression we can go anywhere all that fast."

"Copy that, Captain. I'm on it . . . consider it done. You have enough on your mind rescuing your . . . rescuing Viv." The connection cut abruptly.

Pristy hadn't been subtle. I was sure, in her mind, I was risking everything and everyone to rescue one person, Major Vivian Leigh, above everyone else. *Was it jealousy?* I shrugged. Or was it simply Pristy acting irrationally due to the same relentless high stress that the rest of us were experiencing right now?

I felt a low rumble vibration coming up through the deck plates – good, one of *Hamilton's* drives was indeed coming to life.

Up ahead were eight strategically placed PBC partitions and no less than thirty hunkered down CAPRI soldiers. I wondered why there were no Marines or even some of Chief Mattis's ship security forces here but then remembered this was but one incursion of multiple Grish forces that had breached *Hamilton*.

"Hold up, Captain," Wanda said from behind. "Put this on." She came close, and I felt her attached something to the belt's tagger holster.

"What is that?"

She shook her head. "It should go unnoticed. It's your combat training projector."

She saw my bewilderment. "Your three combat avatars .

. . I've configured them for battle-assist mode. They can't fire weapons, nothing lethal like that, but they can fight."

I just stared at her, "You want me to take Larry, Moe, and Curly, in there with me?"

"You put it like that, it seems ridiculous," she said, understanding the Three Stooges reference. "Just take the damn thing anyway. Okay?"

I shouldered the small pack, but my mind was already contemplating what I was going to say to the Grish combatants. And if that didn't work, I did have a backup plan. Kind of – I'd left Hardy in my ready room standing atop the PE-2's platform. Coogong had been encouraged; the crystals looked to be regaining a little of their clarity. But I couldn't count on Hardy transporting in at the last minute, like some kind of superhero. For now, I'd have to hope my poker face would convince those little fuckers that they had no choice if they wanted to survive other than making a deal with me.

Colonel Bonell tore himself away from his makeshift post where he'd been barking off orders to a husky CAPRI sergeant, still maneuvering one last portable barricade into position. Seeing my approach, his overgrown silver brows pulled together. "This is a damn fool idea, Captain."

I said, "I'm open to other suggestions . . . one's that don't include risking the lives of HealthBay hostages."

"There's always risk in battle, son. Those hostages you're so intent on rescuing, all of them signed up for this. They're military . . . not civilian. A captain risking his life, recklessly, could very well cause more deaths . . . if we're going to get out of this mess, don't you think you'll be needed on the Bridge?"

Bonell had made an excellent point, and I'd made the same argument to myself pretty much non-stop since I'd stepped out from the GravLift. But no. I wasn't willing to sacrifice those HealthBay crewmembers – to sacrifice Viv. I said, "You may be right, Colonel, but I've made my decision. You'll be able to listen in via my TAC-Band. If things go south . . . if I need your help, I'll say a code word. How about that?"

"I think you and I both know, by the time you are saying any kind of silly code word, it'll be too late. The piglets will have pulled your ticket."

"Mickey Mouse."

Again, the colonel's bushy brows bunched together.

"My code. I'll say Mickey Mouse if I need you to storm into HealthBay. And yes, by then, it'll probably be too late for me."

I entered HealthBay with my hands raised. It occurred to me that the raising of one's hands may not mean the same thing to the Grish. It may mean "your sister's a whore," or any number of things totally unrelated to "I'm here to talk, not make war."

It was then, in my peripheral vision, I saw two illusory forms on my left and one on my right. Mostly invisible, but I could make them out – their outlines were like distorted, always-moving waves of heat in the air. My combat avatars – I hadn't realized Wanda had activated them prior to me entering HealthBay. During my time training with them, I'd come to notice them while in their respective stealth modes. Just one more issue to worry about, if I could see them, would the Grish be able to, as well?

The double-wide HealthBay hatch doors slid open, and I stepped into the ship's medical facility. Seven combatant piglets, weapons raised and pointed at my head, stood in a line before me. Not one of them was taller than five feet; most, closer to four feet tall. *I guess my raised hands don't mean their sisters are whores.*

"Hold your fire. I have something you want . . . I'm here to talk. Who among you is your commanding officer?"

Taking a quick glance around HealthBay, I noticed several beds within one dedicated area of the compartment was occupied. There, Fleet Commander Twinwon laid unconscious with a jumble of tubes attached to various parts of his anatomy. Obviously, he'd been among those caught within the crossfire of one of the piglet incursions. *Shit!* I thought of Empress and inwardly chastised myself for not taking better care of the Pleidian commander. Hell, it was her concern for his and his crew's welfare that *Hamilton* had been deployed in the first place.

"I am," came a squealy voice off to my left.

I saw him alter his approach from loping on all fours to walking upright on his back legs. He was one of the taller Grish I'd seen, maybe five one or two. Behind this combat helmet's faceplate, his beady black eyes assessed me.

He squealed something unintelligible, as my aural implants then translated. "Captain Quintos . . . I had not expected you would come yourself. Humans are not known for their bravery . . . in fact, we have a term, a nickname, for your kind."

"Is that right? Tell me. What do you call us?"

"We call you *Spooffies* . . . which is a tall, lanky, animal back on my homeworld . . . one that trembles and shits itself at the slightest provocation."

I had to laugh at the characterization.

He continued, "Now, I am well aware of the human characterization of the Grish. The association of one of Earth's most prevalent livestock breeds. Pigs."

"Piglets," I said, offering an apologetic shrug.

He came to a stop three paces in front of me. "I am Sub-Capitaine Gwan Ho Myn."

I had yet to see even one of the HealthBay crewmembers alive or otherwise. Previous scans of this area of the ship had assured me there weren't casualties, but that was close to an hour ago."

"Sub-Capitaine Gwan Ho Myn, my crew? I take it they have not been harmed?"

He didn't answer my question. Instead, he asked one himself. "The Varapin would like to know –"

"You mean that back-stabbing, duplicitous, ghoul, Haite Caheil, is that the Varapin you speak of?" I couldn't read the piglet's expression behind his faceplate, but if his hesitation had any meaning, I'd certainly pressed a button.

"I would not recommend besmirching Admiral Haite Caheil's good name, Captain."

"Admiral is it now? And can I take it he is listening to our conversation . . . as we now speak."

"Captain, it is no accident my forces and I are here. Have infiltrated this particular department at this precise time. In fact, it was under the Admiral's explicit direction we take this medical facility without violence. I'm told you have a special relationship with the HealthBay's chief surgeon, no?"

No longer was I interested in continuing this back-and-forth banter.

He said, "Come now, Captain. You came here to negotiate, yes? To mediate an agreement?"

"Take me to my crewmembers? I want them released."

"You are in no position to make demands, Captain Quintos. To turn one of your own phrases, you do not hold any of the cards for that."

"No. You're wrong. I hold one very . . . very, important card. Transporter technology. And that bony ghoul fuck very much it needs it in order to return to Devastin . . . to petition the Counsel of Nine for his redemption."

Suddenly, a light flashed from Sub-Capitaine Gwan Ho Myn's wrist. On his left arm, he was wearing the Grish equivalent of a TAC-and. A cone of blue-tinted light rose within the space in front of the Sub-Capitaine. At almost his full height, there stood, or better put, there hovered, Haite Caheil. This was not Grish, but the more advanced Varapin technology. Haite's three-dimensional presence was incredibly real looking, and I could almost feel the wicked chill coming off his hooded black robes.

The Varapin pilot, now fleet admiral, said, "You have made some accurate assumptions, Galvin. And I commend your science officer, as well as your ridiculous robot, at effectively extricating my code from your ship's AI. All not unexpected."

"It's over, Haite. Time for you to –"

"To what? Surrender? For my Grish fleet to concede to the great US Space-Navy?"

I let his own words stand.

"The assumptions you have made may have been true, at one time . . . that I would be so desperate to regain favor with the Counsel of Nine, that I would risk everything, including my life, to bring them your Port Entangler technology. But things have evolved over the last few days, Galvin. While you were concentrating all your attention on extricating my firewalls from *Hamilton's* AI, I was hard at work building my own Quantum Entanglement transporter device. Yes, there were holes, missing design elements, from those build specifications I'd previously pilfered from MATHR. But now, with the help of Sir Broglie . . . I am on the verge of –"

"Did you say Sir Broglie . . . Sir Louis de Broglie?"

"I did."

"How is that possible? He is here. Onboard *Hamilton*."

My aural implants crackled. I inwardly cringed at hearing Hardy's voice, "About that, Cap . . . Broglie is currently not onboard *Hamilton*. As it turns out, all these multiple piglet incursions, evidently the Grish have had other, ulterior, motives. Which was to grab that nutty professor."

"Do not look so crestfallen, Galvin," Haite said in his

typical condescending tone. "Sir Broglie may not have seemed to know the necessary intricacies of the technology, those necessary to fill in the missing blanks. But I assure you, he is far more intelligent than you have given him credit for."

Hardy said, Captain . . . there's a problem –"

I cut the ChronoBot off. "So, Haite . . . you don't actually have a working Port Entangler. Am I correct about that?"

"No. But I have a scientist now onboard my ship who is familiar enough with the latest technology incorporated by the three Thine scientists. I am certain of that."

Hardy was still trying to get my attention, but I continued talking over him. "Good luck, Haite, you don't have the Thine scientists, you don't have Hardy, and no, Broglie won't be able to connect the dots. I'm calling your bluff."

"You are partially correct, Galvin . . . but I do have the other scientist that does have that information. And she can most absolutely, connect the dots."

I went silent, looking over the Sub-Capitaine's shoulder, down the passageway leading to the surgery center.

Hardy said, "I've been trying to tell you, Cap. They took Doc Viv . . . took her out that same transport craft cowling tube they'd come in through. The transport ship is preparing to move out . . . I'm sorry, Captain."

The projected virtual Varapin continued to stare at me, probably waiting for some kind of an unhinged response on my part. But I wasn't going to give that to him – although inside, I was seeing nothing but red and was picturing my hands wrapped around that hooded fiend's boney neck. It took all of my willpower to slow my breathing and keep a bemused smile on my lips.

"What now, Haite? You apparently have everything you need. So, what's stopping you from destroying my ship?"

"Galvin, I can live with humanity along with your allies having this technology. Unlike you, I believe this technology should be shared amongst all contenders, including Varapin and Grish. Think of it as similar to your own world's admonitions that come with enemies all having civilization-threatening weapons of mutual destruction. No one dares to use them . . . it makes no logic."

"So, you expect me to what? Just let you leave with Major Leigh?"

"Yes. And let me tell you why. First, I know that dreadnought of yours as well as anyone. I have studied her strengths and faults like few others. And right now, she is undermanned and by no means capable of thwarting an attack by my fleet of eighteen warships. Second, I am offering you a kind gesture."

"A kind gesture?"

"Yes, for you and your crew, the opportunity to live . . . to survive this day. For that ship of yours to go undamaged. I have not forgotten you provided me a safe haven for a time. Do not throw away an opportunity to live to fight again – another day. I promise, if Doctor Leigh agrees to assist us over the coming days, she will be returned to you unharmed. But you will not attempt a rescue. You will not utilize that PE-2 device to transport onto any of my ships. Do so, and I will destroy *Hamilton* without hesitation. And as soon as I'm finished with Doctor Leigh, she will be killed."

Chapter 33

I needed to get to that Transport ship before it disengaged from *Hamilton's* hull.

But I was unarmed – no match for the five piglets still pointing their weapons at my head.

As quickly as Haite Caheil had previously appeared, he vanished. The Sub-Capitaine signaled something toward his team and turned to leave.

Under my breath, I said, "Hardy?"

The ChronoBot answered right away, "I need another thirty seconds . . . the crystals are clearing."

If I made a move, any kind of move, I was as good as dead. And there was no way the military forces out there in passage-way would be able to reach me here in time.

The Sub-Capitaine had almost reached the entrance into

the surgery center. I turned to face the five Grish, who themselves were now moving, following after their commander.

It was now or never. Under my breath, I said aloud, "Drole, Shred-Ma, Chi . . . engage the enemy."

There was a translucent blur of movement – like phantom warriors, the three had leaped forward and were assailing the Grish. Could I see the combat avatar's specific series of near-invisible kicks and punches? Not so much. But I knew these avatars had been programmed to utilize the same fighting techniques that I'd recently been training with, including that Thai Kickboxing, Tang Soo Do, Kung Fu, and Krav Maga. All of a sudden, the five Grish combatants were being knocked about, unable to reciprocate in kind. Spinning and jerking, flailing, it looked as if an army of crazed ghosts had descended upon them. One of the Grish soldiers, having suddenly doubled over from a gut punch, jerked over backward, falling victim to an exquisitely placed follow-up knee to the front of his helmet.

It was then that I, too, jumped into the fray. Eying one wildly swinging around a weapon, I got both of my hands upon its muzzle. I gripped it tight and yanked the weapon hard to my right side. I felt the weapon come loose in his hands, and without missing a beat, I reversed that momentum, driving the stock right back into the combatant's exposed gut. He doubled over and retched. Then, I saw something splatter inside of his helmet. Sensing there was someone close behind me, I stepped back, raised a tucked-in-tight leg, and let loose with a formidable Tang Soo Do back kick that Wanda would have been proud of. Something snapped, broke, at the heel of my boot. Only now did I turn my head to see. The piglet had taken the kick to the back of his neck. His *now-broken* neck.

In the excitement, I'd forgotten to mention the secret Mickey Mouse code phrase, but fortunately, Max and crew were now charging into HealthBay. Ham was the first to fire his shredder.

I spun toward the surgery center. *Crap!* Sub-Capitaine Gwan Ho Myn was gone, the hatch-door leading into the surgery center in the process of sliding closed. As I sprinted down the passageway, I heard a whole lot more shredder fire come alive behind me. As I approached, the hatch-door slid open. Still holding the piglet energy weapon, I tried to force my index finger into the weapon's trigger guard – it was no use; piglets have much smaller fingers than humans. Bursting into the surgery center, a woman screamed. A man yelled. In a tight huddled together group, there was over a dozen HealthBay staff. There were several bodies splayed out on the deck – not everyone here had survived this particular incursion. The one person I did not see was Doc Viv.

Desperate, frightened faces stared back at me. "Where is she? Where's Major Leigh?" I yelled.

Wide-eyed, no one seemed able to answer.

"Where!" I repeated.

Finally, one of the med-techs pointed, then several others followed suit.

One of Viv's surgeons I recognized said, "There!" They went out there!"

At the far other side of the compartment, high up on the

ceiling, there was a circular opening with charred and black-ened edges. If there had been a ladder or some other kind of method that the Grish had used to ascend, it was gone now.

Behind me, Hock, Ham, and Wanda ran into the surgery center. They looked at me with questioning eyes. I pointed to the opening that was easily twelve feet above our heads. "They escaped through that. Can you get up in there?"

They moved with well-practiced precision. Hock hurried over and stood right below the opening. A moment later, Wanda, while slinging her shredder, ran right at him. She jumped, and Hock grabbed her at her hips. Transferring that forward momentum directly upward, he thrust her overhead. Like a rocket, Wanda's body shot up and disappeared into the opening. Next, Ham was on the move. This time, Hock had interlaced his fingers, making a foothold for his brother at down low at knee-level. Ham reached his brother with a leap, and, like Wanda before him, he was propelled upward toward the opening – Hock let out a deafening painful sounding grunt – the lifting the Ham's substantial girth was no small feat.

Max and Grip joined me at my side and were looking up toward the opening. I said, "The piglets?"

Grip said, "On their way to hog heaven."

Soon, noises were coming from above. Finally, Wanda stuck her head down through the opening. She didn't look happy. "We were too late. Found the inside access to their cowling tube hatchway. Fortunately, they'd closed it. Beyond is open space. We heard the transport craft's lift thrusters coming alive . . . then the craft taking off from *Hamilton's* hull."

Startled, I heard a familiar *thunking* sound behind me. There, Hardy, block by block, the ChronoBot was taking form. In full attack mode, all of his energy cannons were deployed from their hidden compartments. As the last block at his head, transported into place, he raised his weaponized arms and quickly looked about the compartment.

Wanda, grabbing Ham's thick forearm, was being lowered down. Released five feet from the deck, she suddenly dropped down into a crouch. "Oh, look who's late to the party."

My TAC-Band vibrated, and I saw it was XO Pristy. She didn't wait,

"Captain! Sensors tell us fleets preparing to jump!"

This can't be happening. My mind raced. *How do I stop them?* I looked at Hardy. "Are they preparing to jump individually, or using a primary jump ship, as we typically do?"

It took Hardy a quick moment to make the determination. "One ship . . . a heavy super-max battleship."

"Tell me we have weapons . . . any kind of weapons back online."

Hardy said, "We're close, but no, not yet."

I closed my eyes. We had mere seconds to do something. *Think!* I opened my eyes. "The transporter . . . it's obviously working."

Hardy held up one of his mechanical hands and teetered it back and forth, "Sort of, kinda."

"Well, it'll have to be good enough," I said. "Tell me you can talk to Coogong there in my ready room.'

"I can."

"Tell him to lock onto and transport Ryder's five Arrows back into open space. Put them where they can do the absolute most damage to that Heavy Apex Battleship. Wait! Better yet, where they can do the most damage to that Heavy's jumping capability. Can you do that?"

The ChronoBot' s face display had dissolved into the familiar pudgy, balding, John Hardy. Eyes looking up and to the side, he was mimicking a thoughtful characterization.

"Hardy!"

He looked at me. "You do remember . . . transporting those Arrows last time, that it pretty much fucktipated the PE-2."

"Do it anyway . . . Tell Coogong to do it!"

By the time I reached the Bridge, Captain Ryder's six Arrows were in full view in open space on the Halo-Display. Clearly, the PE-2 had worked, had transported the six Arrows. Already, each fighter's energy cannons were fully engaged and streaming their continuous plasma pulses – fiery blast eruptions flashing, flashing, flashing, as the battleship's shields ignited momentarily.

Before this fleet could jump, they'd had to recall all of their fighters. That had taken a bit of time. The Arrow pilots were fortunate in that regard and could concentrate their attention on their target. But a number of the big battleship's guns were firing now, blazing energy bolts at the dodging and spinning fighters. Thus far, the Arrows seem to be concentrating all their attention on one mid-section area of the warship.

XO Pristy said, "There . . . two decks down beneath their

hull . . . that's the ship's equivalent of our CIC. Where they do their jump calculations."

"Not exactly the kind of easy, vulnerable spot I was hoping for. Surprised they haven't jumped anyway, already."

"Agreed," she said. "Ryder's pilots are hammering a single target location, hoping to make a small breach in that warship's shields. Both Captain Ryder's and Lieutenant Akari James' Arrows carry a handful of smart missiles. Fusion tipped . . . we think maybe . . . they could penetrate to that level."

Suddenly, one of the dodging and weaving Arrows exploded in a great ball of fire – which was quickly extinguished within the vacuous void of space. I closed my eyes, relieved that the pilot wasn't Ryder or James but also saddened that any one of my pilots had been killed. As I'd had to do too often in this war, I'd be writing to a mother, father, or maybe a sister or brother, that they had lost a dear family member – a loved one who had died in battle – a hero. There again, we were not supposed to be here. This was not a sanctioned mission. No, that poor pilot's death would be explained as the result of an unfortunate, terrible training accident.

I cleared my mind and said, "That Heavy's active defenses are nothing to sneeze at, XO. Any of those Arrow smart missiles will undoubtedly be picked off the moment they're deployed."

I was tempted to open a channel to Ryder, but right now, he needed all of his attention focused on just staying alive. Like angry, swarming bees, the remaining five Arrows, however unlikely, seemed to have increased their onslaught, their rapid-fire attack on that one vulnerable section of the battleship.

"Why don't they jump? The piglet fleet." Derrota said at my side. I hadn't noticed him there.

"You sound like you want them to jump," I said irritably, not taking my eyes off the display. "You know they have Viv . . . she's on one of those –"

Pristy interjected, "She's on that same ship . . . that Apex-Class Heavy Battleship. And according to Hardy, so is the Varapin. It is the fleet's command ship, after all."

But Derrota was right, I thought. Why haven't they jumped yet? Get away from these pesky Arrows, not to mention *Hamilton,* which hopefully, is poised to come back alive soon. Which reminded me, "Shouldn't you be working on MATHR . . . we desperately need her back online, Stephan."

Chapter 34

Grish Apex-Class Heavy Battleship God's Thunder, Central Bridge Area

Major Vivian Leigh - three hours later

Once within the Grish warship, Doc Viv was pushed and sometimes prodded at the barrel of an energy weapon. Clearly, her Grish captors needed her to move faster, to hurry it up. The ship was so different than that of *Hamilton*. Everything was scaled down in size – cramped – narrow passageways were painted with a dull pea-soup green color, and the metal decking was an open grate affair. By the looks of things, she suspected Piglets, those not wearing combat suits, simply defecated wherever they happened to be at the time, like primitive animals running in the wild. The smell here was awful, but why shouldn't it be? This ship quite literally was a pigsty.

She was taken to a kind of makeshift laboratory, one with

the same surrounding pea-green painted bulkheads. Here, there were several Grish scientists milling around. In the middle of the compartment, she could only assume this was their version of a Port Entangler device. Upon this larger, elliptically shaped pedestal were four conjoined circles – currently, all four were softly glowing a dull yellow. *They'd be able to transport four individuals . . .*

And there he was, Sir Louis de Broglie. *That traitor!* The fact that he was speaking with the scientists, making over-dramatic gestures with his hands, only confirmed that assumption. The Frenchman offered her a disinterested glance her way before continuing on with his conversation. Didn't he realize he was spilling top-secret engineering specifications to the enemy? It infuriated her.

"You need to shut up, Broglie! These guys are not your friends . . . they do not have Earth's, humanities', best interest at heart!"

Her outburst hadn't even warranted another glance from him. It was several minutes before Broglie gestured for her to be brought over.

Broglie and the three piglet scientists he'd been speaking with now turned their attention to her.

"I can't believe you're even talking to these shits," she scolded again.

Sir Broglie waved away her admonishment as if it was a pesky fly. His French accent seemed even more pronounced than usual, "Science must elevate above all tribal squabbles,

Major Leigh. No. There is no place for politics in the pursuit of scientific truth and wisdom."

She already knew the 20th Century scientist was an ass from prior dealings with him onboard *Hamilton,* but she had not anticipated he was this level of deplorable.

He continued, "You were a part of the team involved with constructing the new PE-2 device. I have to admit; you contributed sound scientific advice, Major. Your understanding of quantum and particle mechanics, not to mention a more advanced laser-based conveyor of matter." He looked to the Grish scientists, "But keep in mind, the PE-2 would not exist if not for my own highly advanced technological breakthroughs with my original two entangler units . . . units, I should add, *her* people had stolen from me."

She just looked at him with raised brows. The blowhard knew perfectly well; nobody stole anything from him. Probably, via his own fumbling, he'd transported himself into a virtual memory state for close to two centuries. And those highly advanced technological breakthroughs he was bragging about had come from an alien being, who had most likely been stranded on Earth at the time. Only days ago, had Coogong unraveled the actual science behind that alien's complex circuit board technology. She knew some of it, but certainly not enough to duplicate a working prototype here.

She glanced over to the glowing pedestal, which did seem to be, at least somewhat, operational. "Wait. You've you gotten it to work? You've tested it?" Viv asked, trepidation in her voice.

"But of course," Sir Broglie said, gesturing to a Grish

combat helmet lying upon a lab bench across the room. "You should have seen the delight on their little faces when that helmet materialized across the room. I cannot, of course, take all the credit . . . with the specifications brought to them by Haite Caheil, they were very close."

This is bad, beyond bad. "Then why do you need me?" she said.

The three Grish scientists exchanged a concerned look with Sir Broglie. He gestured for her to follow him, providing her with a better vantage point to see into an adjacent compartment – an extension of the laboratory. There, on that same open grated deck, were six heaping mounds of red and pinkish goo. A putrid deathly smell wafted toward her. She made a disgusted face. These were six failed attempts at transporting Grish test subjects. "Transporting organic material is not the same as transporting things . . ." she said.

For the first time, one of the Grish scientists spoke to her directly, "You will tell us how to fix this issue. We know it is a particle entanglement issue . . . perhaps that organics are much less stable."

She thought about the issue and thought she actually *did* know what might be wrong. It had to do with particle spatial proximity. With their own tests, they discovered there can be abstract correlation paradoxical effects. In the quantum world, particles aren't static – they move, they spin around. At the time of transport, particle spin needs to be coerced into a total zero state. Even that Grish helmet sitting on that lab bench, which looked to be just fine, she surmised, actually wasn't.

Perhaps because of its non-organic elements, it had, *somehow*, still remained in one piece. She suspected, giving the thing a good tap would make it crumble like a dried-out sandcastle at the beach.

"Nope . . . I have no idea how to help you with this." She looked to the three scientists, "Did he tell you about all the help he had . . . the alien technology provided to him? Technology *only found* on the original circuit boards. No, you will never get this to work." She strode over to the same lab bench with the piglet helmet sitting atop it. She gave one of the table legs a little kick with the toe of her shoe. The helmet crumbled into several large chunks. She kicked the table again, even harder, and this time the helmet disintegrated completely.

The Grish scientists gasped. They turned to look at Sir Broglie, who, in turn, blanched – now speechless.

With a tilt of her head toward the Grish transporter device, she said, "That's a piece of junk in there . . . it'll never work." She smirked at Sir Broglie, "*Pfft*, good job, Frenchie."

The indignation she saw on the physicist's face was almost worth what came next. One of the combatants who'd taken her hostage lifted the muzzle of his weapon.

No, they wouldn't actually shoot her – would they? She saw a bright flash and then darkness.

* * *

Viv awoke with her head pounding and with a bad metallic taste in her mouth. *At least I'm not dead – not yet anyway.*

Breathing in, a pinpoint burring pain in her chest made her wince. That must be where they'd shot her – some kind of stun energy bolt most likely. *Oh God . . .* Realization was setting in. They were probably going to kill her. She inwardly chided herself for being so stupid. Why hadn't she told Sir Broglie she'd help him. Stall for time. But no, she had to get all righteous and make a fool of the man, not to mention, make her presence here on this ship totally irrelevant!

She heard voices. Only now did she blink her eyes open and look about her surroundings. She was seated upon a too small for humans, uncomfortable, metal chair high up within the Grish warship's Bridge. Her bound hands were unconsciously twisting and wringing upon her lap. At the center of the dark and low-ceilinged compartment, she watched a 3D display as Arrow fighters attacking the Grish vessel's mid-section. To her, it seemed a desperate, impossible kind of last-ditch effort by *Hamilton* pilots. Arrow fighters were going up against an entire Grish fleet. *But what else can they do?* She was well aware *Hamilton*, hulking and massive, sitting there immobile off in the distance – a totally ineffectual dreadnought. She shook her head, letting out a controlled breath.

She sat there for several minutes taking stock of her situation – not to mention her life. How there had been no shortage of this kind of life and death situation – and not just for her, but the entire *Hamilton* crew. Was it because of the ties the vessel had with the Pleidians, the Empress? That the ship was owned by Quintos and wasn't actually a US Space-Navy on-the-books asset. That the Pleidians have instilled an unspoken obligation, manipulating Quintos to do things that weren't in the US Space-Navy's, or Earth's, for that matter, best interest? *I shouldn't be sitting here.* Talk about going beyond the call of duty – *duty to whom?* And this fiasco. Here again, the crew of *Hamilton, me,* being thrown into just one more ill-conceived mission – if you could even call it that. Her mind turned back to Quintos. How several months back, he'd gotten himself into a heap of trouble. This time facing a court-martial for events, actions that she wasn't convinced he should have been charged for. *Honestly,* the guy's like a shit storm magnet. There again, he *had* fired on that US Space-Navy Corvette warship . . . the *USS Brave,* with supposedly several remaining Bridge crew still alive. The captain had done what he felt he had to do. Who am I to judge?

She raised her bound hands and wiped at the scrape on her left cheek. Her hand came away with a smear of blood. The well-orchestrated capture within HealthBay had happened so fast. Grabbing a scalpel off a nearby tray, she'd been prepared to fight them off, to die before letting the Grish combat team take her. But that was before they had started killing her staff – a young doctor and a med-tech – both executed without a second thought. She looked up to her right. Her guard. He'd removed his combat helmet. The piglet who'd been in charge of her kidnapping, now keeping guard, Sub-Capitaine Gwan Ho Myn – somehow, someday, if she survived this, she was going to kill that fucking squealy bastard.

She transferred her attention back to her surroundings. Elliptically shaped, the Bridge was configured as four rings of curved consoles upon descending levels or steps. And there at the bottom lowest level, like an illuminated stage, was the central 3D display – where Arrows zoomed in and out of view as they fruitlessly fired their plasma cannons upon this ship. She heard and sometimes felt as subtle vibrations coming up from the deck, the continuing energy strikes.

She suddenly sat up taller – there he was. She watched as Haite Caheil's dark form loomed tall above those sitting behind the nearest row of console stations. Their up-lit piglet faces looked mesmerized, like small children leery of being reprimanded. *They're afraid to speak . . . afraid to even move.* She watched the Varapin as he began to move back and forth and back and forth again – ominously hovering, pacing, his dark robes fluttering inches above the surface of the platform.

She jumped in her seat, startled by a sudden commotion below her.

"Jump this fleet, jump this fleet now, Fleet Commander Conch!" Haite's scratchy voice was beyond grating when he spoke in normal tones; when he yelled, as he was doing now, it was like a dagger to the spine.

Unseen until now, the chubby Fleet Commander Conch waddled out on all fours from behind the towering display, then stood up upon stubby back legs. He glanced up at the ensuing attack by Arrow fighters and then back to the self-appointed Varapin leader. "Apologies . . . um . . . yes, yes, we will commence our manufactured wormhole jump momentarily, Admiral. There is a small issue of a stealth micro-wormhole laser transmission . . . a temporary annoyance really, I assure you. *God's Thunder's* AI is being influenced . . . seems to be locking out our ability to initialize necessary jump protocols."

"Errr . . . that irreverent ChronoBot!" Haite grumbled. "So many opportunities to destroy that bothersome robot postponed over these past few months. And once again, I have underestimated his capacity to cause mayhem." Haite made a kind of hissing noise as he hovered higher into the air, moving up over the top of several lower-level Bridge stations. "Move! Get away from there!" he screeched – prompting three upward staring Bridge crew to jump and scamper away. Haite lowered himself, gliding in behind one of the vacated stations, where he began tapping at the control panel.

Viv wondered if Haite, with his superior technological capabilities, how long it would take him to close down that micro wormhole link. Maybe there's something I can do, she thought. Perhaps a distraction. Even a few moments could make a difference for Quintos to pull another rabbit out of his hat. She let out a breath – she was doing it again – *thinking about him*. God, the man was irritating. Didn't he know his knack for getting himself in trouble carries over to those around him – those that care about him? *Do I care about him?* She thought about the young XO . . . Gail Pristy. How she'd surprised her – confronted her. Viv had been checking on the unconscious Captain Tannock when she realized she wasn't alone within that small HealthBay patient room. Gail must have been there prior to her entering. Arms crossed over her chest, she was leaning back against the bulkhead nearest the foot of the bed.

"Oh! You startled me, Gail . . . you been here long?" Viv asked.

She shook her head, not taking her eyes off the sleeping captain.

"Well, I'll leave you to your visit . . ."

Before Viv could turn to leave, Pristy said, "I need to know something."

Viv hesitated, looked at her, then glanced back to Tannock.

"No, not about him . . . about Galvin."

"Captain Quintos?"

Pristy made a *let's get real here,* kind of expression. "You're not interested in him . . . not really, Viv. But you do enjoy stringing him along, don't you?"

Viv stared back at the XO blank-faced for several long beats, not liking the young XO's accusatory tone. "What I do or don't do, in my personal life, is none of your business, Gail. Who the hell do you think you are, second-guessing my motives?" Then the realization hit. Viv said, "You're in love with him."

Pristy raised her chin as if in defiance of the statement. "I'm leaving *Hamilton* . . . this is my final deployment aboard this ship. What I feel is immaterial . . . because I'm moving on with my life. I'm just saying Galvin deserves better. Better than you . . . better than someone who gets her kicks out of stringing men along. I see the influence you have over men, Viv . . . it's all a game to you . . . it's a game that only you win, leaving a trail of broken hearts behind. All I'm asking is you not do that with Galvin. That you find it within yourself to let him be . . . let this one go. He's different. And he's broken in so many ways. Do you really want to destroy him?"

Viv was ready to tell the young officer to get the hell out of her HealthBay, but the woman was already leaving. Infuriated and momentarily tongue-tied, Viv seethed with anger. *The gall!* Who the hell did this little pixie of a woman think she was? Opening her mouth to speak, she realized the young XO was already out of the room.

Was what she said true? Viv shook her head unconsciously. Had she done that? Strung men along knowing the influence she'd had over them? She didn't think so. Sure, she'd had had that one-nighter with Wallace Ryder, a big mistake. And yes, he still had feelings for her; she knew that. And there had been that one encounter with Quintos . . . there in the Japanese hot springs. The corners of her mouth curled up thinking about that. She was fairly certain he didn't know that was her. Sure, he may suspect . . . *But do I string men along? Is it a game I play?* No. If I were a man, my actions wouldn't be questioned like this. Who was she to judge me? What was true is that Gail is in love with Quintos, and, for some reason, she's jealous of me. There's nothing to be jealous of – *or is there?*

She'd been looking at her feet, lost in concentration when she sensed his all too close presence. The Varapin had a distinct, musky smell about him, and that smell was here, close, permeating the air around her now. She looked up to see Haite Caheil was looming above her, his black robes close enough to reach out and touch.

A skeletal hand, black as obsidian, shot forward and was

tightening around her upper arm. "Ow! That hurts!" she blurted. Yanked to her feet, she was being forced, more like dragged, down the central metal staircase – down toward the stage-like Bridge platform. Haite, hovering, was keeping her upright as the soles of her feet barely scuffed the top surface of the stairs. She tried to pull her arm free from his grasp, but the Varapin was too strong. Reaching the bottom of the stairs, she was dragged up onto the central platform. Abruptly released, she fell back upon a surrounding metal railing, which caught her in the lower back, and she cried out in pain.

Fleet Commander Conch sent a nervous glance her way. The nostrils on his pig-like snout flared several times in succession.

She realized the feed for display was not showing the attack by the five Arrow fighters. Instead, she was now seeing *Hamilton's* Bridge from an elevated perspective. Standing there – and looking more than a little apprehensive – was XO Pristy, Stephan Derrota, and Captain Galvin Quintos.

She said, "Hey there," raising a hand, offering a tentative wave to her fellow shipmates.

Viv hadn't noticed that Sub-Capitaine Gwan Ho Myn had joined them on the platform. A knife blade was suddenly at her throat. Going still, she didn't breathe; she didn't so much as blink her eyes. She felt the first trickle of blood now making its way down the front of her neck. She was going to die right here, right now. Her throat cut – and witnessed by the only family she had left in this world – her shipmates.

Chapter 35

USS Hamilton

Pleidian Weonan Fringe Frontier Space

Captain Galvin Quintos

"Stop!" I yelled, reaching a hand up toward the Halo-Display and taking a step forward. I looked into Haite Caheil's eyes, hoping to see some semblance of empathy there. But no, those two cold dark orbs were just as black and lifeless as they'd always been. Expecting any kind of humanity from someone so inhuman would be futile. And in that instant, I knew that showing any kind of weakness to this creature would be counterproductive.

I wondered if I'd made the right decision, using the PE-2 to send out the Arrow Fleet instead of transporting Viv from the Grish shuttle back to *Hamilton.* Truth was, I knew the device was teetering on the brink of failure; a choice had to be made. It was simple; our chances for survival – for all of us – depended on the Arrows' success.

"Come on . . . don't do it, Haite. You have nothing to lose and everything to gain by negotiating with me. We can work this out. So, you'll get everything you want . . . I promise."

"So, you are now willing to hear my conditions? Hmm. I seriously doubt that, Galvin. No. Perhaps I should allow Sub-Capitaine Gwan Ho Myn to prove just how serious I am. You need to understand; there is nothing left for you to negotiate with. Sure, you have that colossal ship, but it is without shields and without weapons. It is virtually dead in space, no? Add to that a small and ineffectual crew that will be incapable of thwarting our many incursions. It may take some time, but time is on our side. Face the inevitability of it, Galvin . . . you have lost . . . you are finished."

With a casual bony claw gesture, The Varapin gave the go-ahead for the Sub-Capitaine to cut Viv's throat. She struggled, and her eyes went wide as the edge of the blade bit into one section of her throat – blood starting to pool upon the flat surface of the knife. She'd been cut, how deep, I wasn't certain.

What Haite was not aware of was the one-way conversation currently going on within my aural implants – Hardy's distracting voice giving me updates on the PE-2 device's slow progression towards full functionality. It was those damn cloudy crystals again. That last transport of pilots and Arrows out into space – once again, bringing down the device.

"Coogong is taking another look," Hardy said. "All I can

313

see right now are those skinny stick legs of his sticking out from beneath the console. Best you keep that dark reaper there, talking for a few more minutes."

I wanted to scream that we didn't have a few more minutes – *we didn't have a few more seconds!*

Moisture was welling up in Viv's eyes. Blinking, tears began to stream down her cheeks.

"Haite! Stop! Come get the damn thing . . . come get the PE-2 . . . hell, take the three Thine scientists too! But if you kill Vivian, I promise you . . . I'll self-destruct this ship which will destroy any Grish vessel in close proximity . . . such as one particularly close Apex-Class Heavy Battleship. So best you take that knife away from her neck . . . do it now."

Viv, paralyzed with fear, didn't so much as twitch.

Haite silently conveyed, somehow, to the Sub-Capitaine for him to bring the knife away from Viv's throat. Immediately she brought her bound hands up in an attempt to staunch the flow of blood. The threat had been a bit of drama; the cut didn't seem to be all that deep.

But the Varapin continued to look down at her, his jaws now involuntarily gaping open like a gasping fish finding itself stranded out of water. I read his mind; she was as good as dead, anyway – why not just suck the life-force out of her first?

Oh God, no . . .

The temptation was too much for the Varapin. He certainly wasn't buying my threat to self-destruct *Hamilton*. A stupid threat, since the process is an elaborate one and takes far too long – which he, of course, would know.

He suddenly reached for her, taking hold of her ponytail in one clawed hand while forcing her head back, so she was looking directly up into those dead eyes of his.

Terrified, she cried out, "Please . . . no . . . stop!"

More blood began streaming down from the open slit on her throat.

Then I heard it. A click within my aural implants followed by Hardy's way too loud voice. "I think Coogong just gave me a thumbs up . . . but to be honest, it's hard to tell with those twigs for fingers –"

It occurred to Hardy; he wasn't tapped into the feed from the Grish Battleship. He wasn't aware of just how dire a situation this was. "Shut up, Hardy! Transport Doc Viv into HealthBay! Do it now! Hurry!"

In front of me, XO Pristy stood up. "Oh no, this can't be happening. No, no, no . . ."

To my left, Derrota lowered his head and began mumbling something – I think it was a Hindu prayer.

Haite Caheil's bone-white open jaws were now just inches from Viv's mouth. She had closed her eyes – her face becoming lax. It was as if she'd fallen into a deep sleep. *She looks so young – so vulnerable.*

Thunk!

The first of Viv's transported segments was gone. *Thunk! Thunk! Thunk!*

Haite Caheil looked up, his concentration broken as Viv proceeded to vanish right before his eyes. Within moments, his claws held nothing more than empty air.

At the moment, I couldn't worry if Viv had been successfully transported into HealthBay or not.

The comms channel into the Grish battleship's Bridge went black. The feed showing our still-attacking Arrow fighters resumed – filling the Halo-Display.

"There's only four," I said.

The XO was back seated at her station, "We lost another Arrow, Captain."

"Recall them," I said.

I heard her talking over her comms in low tones to Ryder. She turned to face me. "Ryder says they still haven't completed their objective. That fleet can jump away at any moment."

"Tell him to abandon the objective and return to flight bay immediately."

She did as told.

I turned to Derrota, "How much of *Hamilton* is currently back under our control? What primary systems are still compromised?"

He stared back at me, suddenly looking alarmed. "Oh, crap. It's why I came over here in the first place . . . it was to tell you. I got so caught up with seeing Viv –"

"Stephan . . . just tell me."

"With the exception on cloaking capability, all of it . . . shields, propulsion, even weapons should be accessible. So, I believe you have your ship back, Galvin."

Pristy, tapping away at her board, was nodding, "I can confirm that; I'm initializing shields and weapons systems as we speak. Chief Potter says Propulsion is fully operational if you want to call up a jump wormhole."

I took in the new feed that showed a wide view of the Grish fleet. What I really needed was to cloak this dreadnought. I said, "How long, Stephan . . . before we can disappear?"

"At least an hour," Derrota said.

I rubbed at the stubble on my chin, which was becoming a nervous habit. There was nothing keeping them from jumping away. I was fairly sure they have enough of the transporter technology specifications already, that in a relatively short amount of time, they could figure things out. Haite Caheil had won. Under my breath, I said, "So why haven't you jumped, asshole? What are you waiting for?"

XO Pristy spun around to face me again but this time looking annoyed, "Why haven't *we* jumped?"

I didn't answer her.

Others within the Bridge had stopped what they were doing and were also now looking at me.

Derrota said, "Galvin . . . we cannot beat them. *Hamilton* could not —would not – prevail over an entire Grish fleet. Eighteen against one."

I continued to stare at the display, "Why haven't they jumped?"

"Does it matter?"

"We can't let them leave with that technology. We've talked about this, Stephan."

"But it's already happened. We lost this one, my friend. It's time we jump – come back to fight another day."

My eyes locked onto the Grish Apex-Class Heavy Battleship – the same ship Haite Caheil was on, undoubtedly within that vessel's Bridge and perhaps, in turn, looking back at *Hamilton* at this very moment.

"I know what he's thinking."

"Who? The Varapin?"

"He's thinking the same thing I am."

"And what is that?" Derrota said.

"That he no longer is willing to share this technology with the enemy. It's just too big of a strategic advantage. No . . . the one who controls this transporter capability alone, will win this war."

Pristy's voice was soft, non-confronting, "Captain . . . we don't have the crew, the people, to man the onboard weaponry."

"We have Marines, CAPRI soldiers, and our onboard security forces . . ."

I cut myself short, remembering our fighting ranks were still actively fending off Grish boarding parties. At this very moment, there were multiple Grish transports clamped onto the hull of *Hamilton*.

She was still talking, "And remember Captain; this is a 60-year-old vessel. Sure, she's been upgraded, automated, but –"

"How short are we . . . how many of our big guns would go unmanned?"

She looked away, thinking for a moment. "Maybe three hundred guns would be a rough count. Even our big automated Phazon Pulsar cannons require crew personnel to man turret enclosures. And crew to supervise our munitions stores within armories. Rail spikes don't load themselves."

I turned to Derrota, "How many bots were left operational after the Grish incursions?"

"Derrota exchanged a quick look with Pristy. I knew what they were thinking; *how do we convince him he's not thinking clearly? That he's delusional even contemplating any of this.*

"Stephan?" I said.

"Um, maybe half if you include the medical cutters, the SWM bots . . . and we have a number of Hold Runners still in crates. In total, four hundred, maybe."

"Hold Runners?"

"Strengthened robots for heavy lifting . . . mainly used when were docked . . . like at space-port. Restocking supplies, removing waste canteens . . . the kind of automated work that requires more brawn than intelligence."

"But all of the bots on board, have an AI . . . can think, even if its rudimentary. And can be programmed on the fly."

"Of course," Derrota said, making a *that's obvious* expression.

"Can you upload, say, a programming package used for our weapons manning bots into an SWM or one of those Hold Runner bots?"

Derrota pursed his lips, thinking. "Yeah, I guess. They may be a bit clumsy. Some bots have claws; others have five finger digits. Some have two legs; others have four or treads . . . but they're all intuitive enough to figure things like that out . . . how to make adjustments, but again, they'd be clumsy for a while."

"Go, Stephan . . . get them activated and reprogrammed. You'll need to assign them specific weapons post-work duties."

Derrota took in a breath looking overwhelmed by the task at hand. He hurried off toward the CIC. He stopped and spun toward me. "I could use Hardy's help with this."

"Take him."

He still didn't move off, "Stall them, stall the Grish, Galvin. I'll need some time."

Pristy said, "Captain, it's not like that fleet is going to just wait around until we're ready to make a move. I'm kind of surprised they're still here."

Actually, so was I. I saw that Chen, relieving Gomez, had taken a seat at the Comms Station. "Crewmember Chen open a channel to the *God's of War.*"

"Aye, Sir. Channel's established, Captain."

Haite Caheil's ugly face filled the Halo-Display. "Ah, Galvin."

"Haite . . . I just wanted to say goodbye. We'll be jumping out of the system momentarily. So, I wanted to offer up my sympathies. You certainly gave it a good try. Hey, I know, losing is not easy."

"You think I have lost in this scenario of yours? No . . . I possess what is important. The clear winner here is me."

"Uh-huh, that's fine," I said, looking bemused.

"What . . . you find that amusing?"

"No. Well, yes, kind of. I was just thinking about what it will be like for you. You know, when you address the Counsel of Nine. You'll be all dressed up in your brand-new black robes, all excited for your little presentation where you tell them you have acquired this amazing, wonderful, new kind of transporter technology. A technology that is almost working . . . it's super close to being operational. And look, without a doubt, they'll see the strategic advantage the Varapin will gain, wielding this amazing capability. You'll be a hero, Caheil. You will have redeemed yourself in their eyes; I have no doubt about that."

The Varapin raised his chin, knowing there was more to come.

"But . . . certainly, they'll be concerned the thing isn't fully operational yet . . . that you've brought them a kind of work in progress. And then, of course, they'll want to know who else has this amazing technology, right? Who else has this capability . . . to transport matter from one distant location to another in mere moments? And that's the rub, right? They'll be curious why you jumped your appropriated Grish fleet away. That you had the opportunity to destroy that one vessel that not only shares this technology but had a functional working version of it. But hey, Haite, if you want to think you've won, came out ahead here, that's fine. Anyway, we're fully operational, time to leave." Smiling, I gave him a casual two-fingered salute before gesturing Chen to cut the connection.

All eyes were on me. The silence within the Bridge was absolute.

"Great. By pulling his chain like that, you pretty much just guaranteed the destruction of *Hamilton*, Captain," XO Pristy said. "Unless we jump, like right now, this second."

Crewmember Chen, who rarely spoke out of turn, said, "Nah, XO . . . what the Captain just did was deliver up an epic bitch slap to that Varapin shit head. Reminded him there can be only one survivor here . . . that it's them or us."

Crewman Grimes at the Helm station said, "Wait. We're not jumping . . . are we, Captain?"

Overhead, MATHR abruptly announced:

INCOMING MISSILES!
INCOMING MISSILES!
INCOMING MISSILES!

Chapter 36

"**D**ivert auxiliary power to port side shields! XO, tell me what's coming at us!"

"Smart missiles, seven fusion tipped warheads from the *Gods of War*. The rest of the fleet is on the move and jockeying into an attack formation."

"Deploy sensor drones . . . as many as we've got. I want to see every angle of this battle. Fire at will, XO. Needless to say, I want *Gods of War* taken out of the equation first."

"Aye, Captain," Pristy said.

On the Halo-Display, *so many Grish warships*, contrasting bright white against the backdrop of inky blackness and flickering starlight; it was an impressive sight. That and it was discouraging – no, it was daunting. *We can't win this battle, one against eighteen. So, how do I even the odds a little?* I thought about that. *I need a couple of those warships to change sides. Is that even possible?*

Ensign Plorinne, out of breath, was at my side. Hands on

knees, the Symbio-Poth swallowed hard, "Captain . . . Marine Colonel Bonell reports that Grish incursion parties have all been neutralized."

"Excellent news, Ensign. But I'm a little busy here. You could have just TAC-Banded me the report."

"Um, yes, Sir. The Colonel said you're not answering your hails."

I glanced at my TAC-Band and saw that I'd missed multiple hails from the Colonel, one from Doc Viv, good to see she was still alive and indeed onboard, Captain Wallace Ryder, and several others.

The Ensign continued, "Anyway, the Colonel said he's deploying his Marines throughout the ship to assist with manning various weapons posts. Science Officer Derrota had apparently made the request."

As if on cue, a fast-moving, odd-looking matt-black robot sprinted past the Captain's Mount. Like a bat out of hell, the thing didn't slow, didn't let up. Not until it ran face-first into the forward bulkhead. The loud clang of metal hitting metal had all of us jumping from our seats. The robot was now on the deck – legs and arms spasming.

From the CIC, Derrota stuck his head out from around the corner, "That's what a Hold-Runner looks like."

Ignoring the distraction, I said, "What about the CAPRI ranks? Did the Colonel deploy them to weapons posts?"

Ensign Plorinne shook his head, "Not that I know of, Sir. I think they're on mop-up duty; there's a slew of dead Grish lying about, as well as some of our own fallen."

Keeping my eyes on the Halo-Display and the battle at hand, I said, "Here's what I want you to do. Find Sergeant Max and tell him I have a mission for him and his team. Tell him he'll need to collect as many of the CAPRI soldiers and what few Marines he can spare. Round them up. Have them convene within Whales Alley, here, outside of the Bridge. Go, what are you waiting for, Ensign!"

Four brilliant white flashes, one right after another, filled the display.

Pristy said, "Our rail cannons took out four of those smart missiles. They detonated on impact . . . but three are still inbound and headed for our bow."

"Redistribute power to forward shields to compensate," I said, knowing full well she would have done so already.

Currently, *Hamilton* was deploying massive numbers of her own nuclear as well as fusion tipped smart missiles. I watched as hundreds of bright blue tongues, trailing burner exhausts, all headed away at thousands of miles per hour – missiles locked onto enemy warship targets with catastrophic destruction on their limited AI minds.

"XO . . ."

Pristy shot me a scolding look over her shoulder. With her thin brows bunched, she said, "What? Christ, I'm busy here!"

Boy, she was getting cheeky lately. "Pick two Grish assets you wish were on our side. Two others than the *Gods of War.*"

"What? Why?"

I got up from the Captain's Mount. With hands on hips,

I began to pace. I said, "Humor me . . . pick two. Then stop firing on those two."

I checked my TAC-Band, forty-five minutes before we'd be able to cloak ourselves. I had to yell above the above overhead alarm, "MATHR, ask my science officer to get in here."

Jarring, consecutive impacts shook *Hamilton* to the point I had to reach out for the Captain's Mount armrest to keep from falling.

"Shields at 95% and holding," Pristy said.

Our first volley of smart missiles had started to find their distant targets – more bright white flashes momentarily distorting the Halo-Display.

Pristy yelled over her shoulder, "The *Breath of Guile* and *We Mock the Winds* . . . the two Grish warships you asked for. They're an A-Class Destroyer and another Heavy Apex Battleship. I'm diverting already deployed smart missiles away from those two assets. But keep in mind, they, like the rest of the fleet, are still firing on us! I can't even count the number of inbound missiles headed our way right now."

Both Hardy and Derrota showed up at my side. Hardy said, "Eighty-seven . . . inbound missiles are currently locked on to *Hamilton*."

Derrota said, looking to Hardy, "Look, it's still another forty minutes, Galvin. As you know, with a battle like this, my teams needed to support Tactical."

"Yeah . . . copy that," Pristy said as she continued to tap away at her board.

I looked to Hardy, who had returned to using his colorful

pinwheel animation for his face display. "So, you're working on that . . . getting our Cloaking capabilities back online?"

"That's a big 10-4, Rubber Ducky . . . I'm on it. FYI, I don't need to be sitting at a CIC console to reverse engineer malevolent Varapin code. The wonders of modern-day background processing."

I put a hand on Derrota's shoulder and looked at him and then Hardy, "What can you two tell me about taking remote command of a Grish warship. I'm talking navigation, weaponry . . . the whole kit and kaboodle. Perhaps using that same micro wormhole laser link, you used earlier to disrupt —"

INCOMING MISSILES!
INCOMING MISSILES!
INCOMING MISSILES!!

Pristy yelled, "Nine fusion tipped warheads! Hold on to something!"

Hamilton shook for close to a full minute.

"Damage report!?"

"Um . . . we have an open to space breaches on Decks 2, 4, 24, and 33. What we don't have are emergency crews to deploy to those areas."

I said, "Close the Vac-Gates on all affected Decks." Turning to Chen at Comms, I said, "Contact Chief Mattis, see if he has any security people, he can deploy to those damaged areas, tell

him he should call on SWM LaSalle . . . he may have maintenance personnel that can assist him. And let Doc Viv know, she
should expect a new influx of injuries."

I brought my attention back to Derrota and Hardy and
tried to remember what it was I had just asked one of them.

"The answer is no," Hardy said. "You were asking if we can
take remote control of a Grish warship using a micro wormhole laser link. No. One would have to physically get on board,
perhaps an invasion team, such as what the Grish attempted
here on *Hamilton*. Which, of course, we are in no position to
attempt."

"Hardy, could you pilot a Grish warship . . . do you have
that know-how in your memory banks?"

"The short answer, yes," Hardy said.

Talking more to myself than anyone else, I said, "Who else
on board this ship could captain a Grish warship . . . besides
anyone who's here on this Bridge . . . like me or the XO? Fleet
Commander Twinwon would have been the easy choice, but
he was still recovering from multiple plasma fire wounds in
HealthBay."

XO Pristy said, "Captain Ryder certainly could handle
that."

Chen said, "Nope, heard he's recovering in HealthBay.
Apparently, his Arrow's cockpit was penetrated by a stray
plasma bolt. He's ok, but not in any kind of condition to go on
an assault mission."

Ensign Plorinne had entered the Bridge and was hovering
nearby. "They're all there, Max and his team, a few Marines,

and a bunch of the CAPRI pricks – oops, sorry. They're out within Whale's Alley, sir."

"Excellent, good job, Ensign," I said.

"Uh, Captain?" Plorinne said, "I have a suggestion. Someone who could pilot a Grish warship?"

I shook my head, "Thank you, Ensign, but I'm looking for seasoned pilots, not to mention an officer that knows battle tactics, knows the ins and outs of command."

"No, I didn't mean me. That would be ridiculous. I'm talking about Captain Tannock."

Right off, I wanted to tell the young Pleidian Ensign his suggestion was ridiculous. *But was it?*

I said to the Helm station, "Keep us on the move, Crewmember Grimes. Keep us in the fight, but be smart about it . . . tactical maneuvering, no sense making it easy for the enemy. XO, you have the Bridge."

Pristy shot me a desperate look.

"I'll be right outside in the passageway . . . and I'll be right back. Derrota, Hardy, you're with me. Ensign Plorinne go ask Doc Viv to wake up Tannock. And yes, I know she'll have a problem with that. Tell her it's life or death . . . the survival of *Hamilton* and her crew depends on it."

The ship shook again, "Aft shields down to 83%," she said as we moved away.

Out in Whale's Alley I saw, Max's squad, along with a band of other Marines I didn't recognize, and no less than thirty of the cocky-looking CAPRI soldiers. The Marines were outfitted in white combat suits, while the CAPRI squad wore light grey. All were armed with shredders.

"Listen up, everyone. We're going to be evening the odds; amend that, we're going to be bettering our odds." I looked to the CAPRI's and Marines, mostly men, but there were women within the ranks as well. "We have a squad leader here?" I asked

One of the soldiers in light grey straitened his shoulders and offered up a casual wave of one hand. "That would be me, Sergeant Major Cash Lipton," came the familiar, haughty voice. I saw that his cohorts Bob, Garrett, Alex, and Troy, were among the other CAPRI combatants here.

"From this point on, you'll all be under the command of Sergeant Max Dryer."

"Absolutely not . . . I'm a Sergeant Major, he's a Master Sergeant . . . I outrank the Mofo jarhead."

"This bullshit stops now! There's no time for any rivalry or dissent. If you haven't noticed, we're under attack. Marines are running point on this mission . . . you go along with that, or I call Chief Mattis, and you can spend what little time any of us have left still breathing, in the brig. Take it from me, those *jarheads* have excellent prior experience boarding and commandeering an enemy vessel."

"Is that what we're doing," Wanda asked. "Nobody's told us shit. This is first we've heard of it."

Three people were hurrying their way towards us within Whale's Alley: Ensign Plorinne, Doc Viv, and kept upright holding an elbow between them, a quasi-coherent-looking Captain Eli Tannock.

"Good, I'll only have to say this once," I said.

Viv, still wearing her bloodied scrubs, had a bandage at the base of her throat – blood had seeped through, leaving a rust-colored stain. She radiated furious anger. "What the hell, Quintos! This man is in no shape to do anything but lay in a hospital bed! Bringing him out of unconsciousness so quickly is dangerous!"

Tannock was blinking his eyes, and I could tell he was trying to make sense of what was going on around him.

"Desperate times desperate measures, Viv," I said, taking a step closer to Tannock. I said, "Let go of him; let's see if he can stand on his own."

Doc Viv huffed but did as I asked, as did the Ensign. Tannock wavered but stayed upright.

"What, exactly, is going on here, Captain Quintos? The last thing I remember was . . . I was on the Bridge . . ."

"Listen to me carefully, Captain. Everyone listen up. *Hamilton* is in grave danger. We are greatly outgunned, over-matched, one against eighteen Grish warships. I believe we can, somewhat even the odds, by commandeering two of the enemy ships, The *Breath of Guile* and *We Mock the Winds* . . . an A-Class Destroyer and a Heavy Apex Battleship, respectively."

I placed a hand on Tannock's shoulder, staring intently into his still unfocussed eyes. "Captain, I need you to skipper that Grish, A-Class Destroyer."

His forehead furrowed as he tried to make sense of what I was asking. "Captain a Grish vessel?"

"Can . . . you. . . do . . . that?" I asked definitively.

He swallowed and looked over to Doc Viv. Nodding, he said, "I'll need coffee. But yeah, I can do that . . . I know the Grish A-Class Destroyer . . ."

Viv did not look happy but was no longer giving me the death glare.

"Ensign, didn't you hear? Get this man a coffee!" Grip said.

"Hardy, the Heavy Apex Battleship, uh, the *Breath of Guile* . . . will be yours and yours alone to take. Tell me you can't handle that, and I'll come up with another solution."

A Superman S symbol appeared on his face display. "Nah, I got this. You going to use the transporter thing to get me onboard? Just so you know, there are 362 piglets scurrying around on that vessel."

"Is that a problem?"

"No. I'll infiltrate the ship; once there, I can interface directly with the ship's AI. I'll take command of all shipwide systems and begin neutralizing the crew. At that point, I'll be ready to commence attack on the Grish fleet."

"Good, we'll need to coordinate that attack before you go all —"

"Hog wild?" Hardy introjected. To emphasize his point, he rapidly deployed his battle-bot weaponry in unison: chrome weapon barrels burst from previously hidden compartments, swivel-mounted shoulder energy cannons along with similar thigh-mounted pulsar cannons, as well as his de facto — one on each mechanical forearm _ two more big chrome canons, all within a blink of an eye — snapping into place — an ensemble of highly lethal-looking weaponry. Sometimes it was hard to take Hardy seriously, with all of his antics and goofery. But seeing him now, like this, I remembered that this was one badass ChronoBot. A feeling I could tell was shared by the others standing around us.

I pulled my attention away. Plorinne was handing Tannock his coffee. I said, "The A-Class Destroyer, *We Mock the Winds* . . . Tannock, that will be your ship."

He nodded, looking slightly more coherent.

Hamilton shook violently as another wave of enemy warheads detonated upon *Hamilton's* shields. From behind me, deep within the Bridge, I heard Pristy yell, "Shields down to 69%!"

Hardy said, "The Grish destroyer has a crew of 289."

I looked to Max, "That means you'll be outnumbered by . . ."

Hardy said, "254."

"254," I repeated. Your teams, I'm sure, will be good, but they won't be that good."

Derrota said, "I've been thinking about that, Galvin. I may have an idea."

All eyes went to the Science Officer.

"That destroyer utilizes centralized environmental conditioning. There's a high-gravity ozone filtration system, along with an atmospheric equalization distributor —"

"Stephan! We're on a timetable here," I said.

"Galvin . . . we can transport in, right there next to that atmospheric equalization distributor, a kind of poison bomb."

I thought about that. Yes, the teams will be wearing their

sealed helmeted combat suits. But sometimes, suits get battle damaged. "We won't want to kill our own teams, Stephan . . . all it would take is a cracked faceplate."

Wanda said, "A chance we'll have to take."

"Piglets are deathly allergic to citric acid."

"You mean like lemons?" Hock asked.

"That's right."

"Like oranges?" Ham asked.

Ignoring the idiot twin, Derrota said, "Once the lemon balm is in place and triggered, it'll take a good ten to fifteen minutes for the rest of the ship's ventilation ducts to start spewing the poising."

I looked at Max. "You have little time to come up with an assault plan. Your primary objective will be getting Captain Tannock there and onto the destroyer's bridge, where he can go to work."

"I don't have time for this . . . HealthBay is filling up, and we're undermanned. Try not to get us all killed," Quintos," Doc Viv said, now hurrying off down Whale's Alley.

Chapter 37

A brilliant white explosion filled the Halo-Display and those few of us manning *Hamilton's* Bridge cheered with short-lived excitement. Until now, there'd been no revising of that eighteen to one odds. It was now seventeen to one, with that nearly vaporized Grish Frigate no longer detectable up on the display. This was a different kind of space battle than I was used to. All assets were keeping their distance from one another, by many hundreds of miles – making the use of energy weapons, namely our Phazon Pulsar weapons and our big rail cannons – far less effective. Thus, this battle was about the relatively slow back and forth volleying of smart missiles. In time, as reserves of missile resources diminished for all concerned, close-quarters warfare would follow. But until then, I welcomed the extra time this afforded us to prepare.

At the back of the Bridge, our impending invasion squads were moving equipment and weaponry into my ready room, where Hardy, Derrota, and the three Thine scientists, were prepping the PE-2 transporter for use. We were five minutes out for the assault onto the *Breath of Guile* and *We Mock the Winds*.

Shields holding at 45%, Captain," Pristy said.

The display was literally filled with ordinance indicators along with associated meta-tag descriptions of each. Also, in varying colors and shades were the calculated trajectory paths of all missile assets. Chen had moved to the secondary Tactical station next to Pristy, "Looks like we may have a runner! Grish Light Cruiser is throttling up and heading out of the system."

"Was wondering when that was going to happen," I said. "Haite will want those transporter design specs transmitted away for safekeeping."

Chen made a face, "If that was the case, that cruiser's heading off in the wrong direction. The closest Grish Comms Hub is still in the NorPliet Sector . . . that ship's heading away from there."

"Interesting," I said, smiling. *Haite, you sly dog, is it that you no longer want to share your newly acquired technology? Perhaps figure you'll keep the spoils of war for your own future ambitions?*

"Tactical, let's show that Light Cruiser that nobody's leaving this fight early."

"Copy that, Captain," Chen said. "Five missiles . . . fusion tipped warheads, reestablishing targeting coordinates. Okay, all five are currently locked onto that vessel."

We watched in relative silence as the five closest missile signatures had changed course on the Halo-Display. It would be close, as the Light Cruiser, too, was now picking up speed and soon would be gone from the fight. I briefly wondered where the Varapin pilot was sending that cruiser off to, if not make a communications transmission. Here in the frontier, we were literally light-years from anything or anyone.

Four consecutive flashes filled the screen.

"Four hits, one miss," Chen said. "One Grish Light Cruiser turned to space dust."

XO Pristy glanced back. "Down to our last hundred smart missiles, Captain. I imagine the Grish are scraping the barrel for missiles as well."

This battle was about to get a whole lot more intense. "Let's not exhaust everything we have . . . hold fifty back for a rainy day, XO."

"Aye, Captain."

My TAC-Band vibrated, and I saw that it was Captain Wallace Ryder.

"Ryder? Heard you got nailed pretty bad. Was planning on coming to see you as soon as things eased up a little."

He looked angry. "Tannock? Seriously? You're sending that old, befuddled fart bag out on a mission . . . to skipper a Grish warship?"

My longtime friend sported a bandage on his upper right shoulder, but he looked fine other than that. "You would have been my first choice, Ryder . . . but you had to go and get yourself shot."

"I'm fine. There's no reason –"

"Save it. Decision's made, and we're executing in about two minutes. Heal up, Ryder; there'll be plenty of opportunities to play the hero in coming days."

"Days? Bullshit . . . you and I both know, this will all be over, one way or another, today."

I smiled and cut the connection.

I briefly wondered if Ryder was right. Would Tannock be up for the task? Befuddled old fart bag or not, he'd have to be.

From the right side of the Bridge came Derrota's voice, "Galvin, we're ready."

I hurried over to the entrance to my ready room and was taken aback by the frenzied commotion going on within. I'd always considered this compartment overly spacious until this minute. Close to forty men and women were readying for the mission at hand - a mission that had far larger implications than just winning this battle today. This was truly a would-be-winner-takes-all for turning the tides of this war. I still believed the military that held this technology could – no – *would* prevail as the preeminent spacial superpower in the region.

Thanks to Hardy, who had established new cloaked micro wormhole links to each of the remaining Grish warships, everyone would be transmitting live feeds via their combat suit helmet cams. *Hamilton's* Bridge would remain engaged with decision-making. Because this would be an off-ship offensive, Marine Colonel Drake Bonell would be on the Bridge with me and commanding both the Marine and CAPRI ranks. Even Max and his team were technically under Bonell's direction, but he typically gave them more leeway to take direction from me – time would tell, though. As for Hardy and Tannock, they were under my command.

My TAC-Band vibrated. It was Pristy. "Go ahead, XO."

"As expected, the fleet is moving in, tightening up."

"Copy that. I'll be back in there in a couple of minutes."

I'd been watching Derrota pulling shoebox-sized metal canisters down from a now depleted stack, placing them onto the PE-2's pedestal. Coogong, manning the transporter's console, in turn, and one-by-one, was sending the citric acid poison off to the various warships.

Coogong said, "I am positioning these into the intake jetways for each atmospheric equalization distributor. That was the last of them, sixteen in all."

I'd only planned on using this stuff on the two warships we were infiltrating; poisoning *all* the vessels was ingenious. Sure, a good number of Grish crews would manage to get themselves safely into space or environ suits, but many, if not most, would not.

Offering up a crooked smile, I said, "Well done, Coogong."

I looked about the compartment and saw that everyone was standing idle. They were ready. I debated whether to give a short motivational speech and decided against that. Best to treat this mission like any other and don't bring attention to the fact that most if not all of them would not be returning back to *Hamilton*. This was going to be a last-ditch Hail Mary endeavor; we all knew that.

I said, "Derrota, go ahead . . . activate the canisters."

Hardy took up his position on the PE-2's pedestal. He looked lethal with his exposed armaments, and for once, was not making light of the moment by projecting something stupid on his face display.

I stepped close and looked up at the ChronoBot. "Be careful what you shoot at; remember, that Heavy Battleship has to remain functional after you have your fun."

Hardy looked down at me. "This'll be a walk in the park, Cap." With that, his face display went from black to an animation of a man walking in a park with a dog – a dog that proceeded to squat and take a crap.

I turned my attention to Captain Tannock; the only one here I had serious doubts was up to the task at hand. "Captain. You know your mission?"

He looked surprisingly alert and cognizant. "I take command of the A-Class Destroyer, *We Mock the Winds*, and on your directives, engage the enemy. Look, Captain Quintos, I was commanding fleet battles while you were still popping pimples and making fart jokes back in junior high school . . . so don't worry about me. I'll do my part. You worry about *Hamilton*; I still may want that command back someday."

I made eye contact with Sergeant Max and each of his squad members. They would be protecting Tannock and getting him safely onto that destroyer's Bridge.

"Go ahead, Coogong, transport Hardy . . . time to get this party started."

Instead of the painfully slow, block segment by block segment, transport, Hardy disappeared in a swirling flash of blue light.

Derrota said, smiling, "Our Thine scientists have been busy. Only this morning were they ready to test this new, improved, molecular energetics, transport process."

I watched as three, not one, of the armed CAPRI soldiers stepped onto the pedestal. Three Marines stepped up, ready to be the next group. I looked at Derrota questioningly.

"Another recent upgrade. Again, it's been tested. Three at a time will transport . . . far more efficient, yes?"

I heard Pristy in my aural implants, "Captain . . . Hardy's feed is live. And we're taking plasma fire from four piglet ships."

"On my way . . ."

Chapter 38

Taking my seat on the Bridge, I saw that Pristy and Chen were now busy engaging no less than eleven enemy warships that had moved into close-range battle configurations. Other independent video feeds were popping into view, too, as my key assault team leaders transported onto *Breath of Guile,* which was Hardy's feed, and on *We Mock the Winds,* feeds from Sergeant Max, and CAPRI squad leader, Sergeant Major Cash Lipton. One more feed popped into view, that from Captain Tannock.

With the teams all transported, both Derrota and Marine Colonel Bonell joined me at the Captain's Mount. The Colonel was already in contact with his team leaders, his voice a constant monotone that I tried to ignore.

Derrota did a double-take looking at the primary Halo-Display. "Is it my imagination, or is the Grish fleet . . . floundering?"

Pristy answered for me, "Not your imagination. Right now, the piglets are starting to smell lemons. I imagine any crewmembers that haven't keeled over are running for available environment suit."

"And we're taking full advantage of that distraction," Chen added.

Hamilton's Phazon Pulsar cannons were firing from all areas of the ship. Bright green energy pulses streaking across the divide in between *Hamilton* and Grish vessels, while their return fire had slowed to a trickle.

Pristy said, "Shields back up to 83% and holding, Captain."

My attention was on the multiple assault feeds. Hardy, who had transported into a *Breath of Guile's* mid-ship passageway, was currently making his way to the vessel's primary barracks area. There would have been no sense dropping him into the Bridge if he'd have to spend all his time there fending off one attack after another. From what I saw from Hardy's POV camera, many of the Grish crew had, in fact, gotten themselves suited up into environment suits in time to face off with him. Clunking forward, Hardy's two mechanical arms suddenly rose up into view as plasma bolts tore into anyone, *and anything*, standing in his way. Return weapons fire seemed to be coming at Hardy from both in front of him and behind him, which I assumed were being addressed by those big shoulder mount spinning turret cannons of his. It occurred to me now that as badass of a ChronoBot Hardy was, he may not be as impregnable, indestructible, of a warrior robot as necessary to take on an entire warship of defending crewmembers. The video feed was becoming jerkier and jerkier as both energy fire and projectile fire – I was seeing some kind of small-arms rail rifles in use by the enemy – Hardy was already having a hard time staying up on his feet. From the feed's perspective, all we could really see were his extended arms out in front of him, and both were now showing hundreds of individual blackened scorch marks. Hardy suddenly turned a corner and slowed. Up ahead, the Grish had set up several barricades, not all that dissimilar to our own PBC's. No less than twenty helmeted piglet heads – along with the barrels of their weapons – were in view along the tops of those barricades.

"Why has he stopped?" Derrota said.

"I don't know, maybe he's catching his breath," I said, knowing full well that wasn't it. What I did know was that the last thing Hardy needed right now was me distracting him with stupid questions.

I turned my attention to the *We Mock the Winds*. It took me a second to get my virtual bearings between Max's feed and Tannock's. Max, out in front of the team, which had encircled Tannock, seemed to be making good progress forward, toward the Bridge. Tannock, surrounded by the five Marines, was keeping up – that and keeping his head down. The one other feed – that of Sergeant Major Cash leading his CAPRI and Marine units – showed they had stumbled into an all-out battle of epic proportions. Weapons fire was coming from everywhere. Suddenly, Cash dove for cover. The earlier droning monotone from Marine Colonel Bonell next to me was now a sporadic cacophony of loud directive shouts.

XO Pristy slammed a fist down onto her board, "Crap!"

The entire Grish fleet had tightened up around *Hamilton*.

"Talk to me, XO; what's the issue?"

"I'm sorry . . . should have caught this earlier." She pointed up to the other Heavy Apex Battleship, *God's Thunder*. See how it's holding back? Hasn't joined in with the in-close fight?"

I'd been keeping an eye on Haite Caheil's command ship all along. But Pristy was right. *God's Thunder* was staying farther back and out of the fight.

"I've tasked MATHR with keeping track of the expenditures of enemy smart missiles. So, we'll know what we'll be up against as the battle progresses."

She turned around and looked at me. "I must have missed it before. But that ship, Haite's ship, has not depleted any of its smart missiles. MATHR's estimate . . . she's carrying about 400 nuclear warhead-tipped missiles."

"We've got fifty of our own —"

"Look at the Grish fleet's configuration, Captain.

I saw it. The enemy fleet was all around us and bunched in far closer than any standard command structure would have typically initiated. But it had been an ingenious move on the part of Haite. Because any smart missiles we would deploy, while initially getting up to speed, would now provide far easier targeting by any one of those in close Grish vessels.

"So not only can we not get to his warship, but he's also stockpiled an ample supply of missiles he'll be able to finish off this already heavily damaged dreadnought."

Pristy didn't answer but instead returned her attention to her tactical board.

Derrota was speaking with one of his young technicians

nearby, while the Colonel's voice had returned to a droning monotone. I wasn't seeing the same level of weapons fire coming from Sergeant Major Cash and his CAPRI ranks.

* * *

Hardy's relationship with his inner LuMan was not as much of a relationship as some onboard *Hamilton*, such as the Captain, assumed there to be. It was more like that of an owner of an old automobile or hover-car and its driver. Sure, for Hardy, there was, after a year's time, a kind of loyalty built up – *a kind of we're in this together* kind of bond. But LuMan was all AI with little – if any – real personality. Hardy spoke to his inner ChronoBot AI, as one would speak to a computer, not as a friend. Hardy had once been mildly curious if LuMan had any kind of emotional sub-routines built into his mental constructs but never cared enough to breach the subject. But now, standing within a narrow passageway's recess, with plasma fire streaming past him from both sides, he wondered if LuMan would miss him. Because right now, at this very moment, Hardy was having serious doubts that he would survive the next five minutes. But there again, neither would LuMan, which made the thought, the point, mute.

Hardy's internal power plant was not inexhaustible. Sure, he didn't need to plug in at the end of the day to recharge or anything like that – but in times such as these, where he was utilizing virtually all of his weaponry for extended periods of time, he needed interludes of inaction. During these moments, he, through LuMan, furthered their connection with the *Breath of Guile's* central AI. According to the ship's schematics, he was less than one hundred feet from his intended destination, the ship's barracks. He should be on the Bridge by now, but there again, as the old adage goes, *no plan survives contact with the enemy.*

Hardy checked his internal readings and measurements. On average, he was operating at fifty percent effectiveness. There were 182 active Grish life signs onboard this ship. Over 110 had died of Citric Acid poisoning, and another 75 had been killed by him. *That's it? A measly 75?* The barricades down the passageway, with all those little piglet heads peeking out over them, were his next primary obstacle. He rechecked the ship's central AI – *there has to be a way to expedite things here.* And there it was. Hardy had to resist the impulse to enact fireworks upon his face display. As it turns out, while the piglets are not all that terrible when it comes to defending their ship against incursion by a ChronoBot, they do have one fear that goes beyond rational, as indicated by the many, many, often desperate sounding, shipwide maintenance service requests. Interesting . . . As it turned out, the piglets loathed *slothmorts.* As far as Hardy could surmise from the onboard logs, slothmorts were indeed a kind of insectile being, one that looked to be a cross between an Earthlike extra-large cockroach and a Pleidian insect called RuFu-Cip – which looked a hell of a lot like a little, hairy, monkey. Three-inch tall hairy cockroach-monkey things that yipped and bit. He called up an illustrated rendition of the things – an exoskeletal hardened shell, six bug legs, an actual tail, and a chimp-like, highly-expressive face. Hardy could understand the disgust the Grish felt for the things. The comingling of insect and mammalian physiologies was just wrong. In any event, this ship was infested with the little things. They liked to hide in dark places, crevices, hidey-holes, all over the ship. *Slothmorts* loved to snack on the rubber-like material used for ship's wiring and communications conduits. And here was the kicker, the Grish had come up with an amazing means to deal with the cockroach-monkeys. Apparently, they were attracted to a certain combination of guttural whining sounds – the *slothmorts* mating song. Drives the little bastards crazy, makes them come running like a dinner bell's been rung. The Grish use this methodology to periodically herd the creepy crawlies into an awaiting airlock – whereby they would then spew out into deep dark space. This periodic eradication process does not kill off all the varmints, they breed like no one's business, but it's at least somewhat effective.

Hardy checked his readings. He was operating at 80%. That would have to do. Not unlike a ventriloquist, ChronoBots had an uncanny ability to 'throw' their voices. And right now, Hardy began to do just that. He started by making just whispers of a sound, those guttural whining sound the *slothmorts* supposedly react to – supposedly, with such vigor. With all the crossfire of plasma fire going on, he doubted they could be heard. He increased the audible decibel levels accordingly. *Nothing happened.* Perhaps, here on board the *Breath of Guile*, they'd instigated a recent cleanse to a nearby airlock. Maybe there weren't enough of the little fuckers to – Huh! Never mind. There's one now. A tiny creature, indeed, cockroach and monkey-like at the same time, stopped within the passageway and was now looking up at him, beyond creepy. Hardy raised his left arm several inches and shot the *slothmort*. Vaporized into a puff of black smoke, Hardy suddenly had to push himself back farther into his little nook as the passageway decking before him had become filled, brimming, with the scurrying little beasts. Hardy continued to *throw* his mating call song to the approximate passageway positions of the Grish combatants at both ends. All sounds of weapons fire stopped, supplanted by the sounds of yelling and screaming piglets. Several Grish combatants ran by with *slothmorts* clinging to them.

92% operating levels – time to kick some piglet ass . . .

Chapter 39

Mesmerized, I watched Hardy's video feed – seeing some kind of small, hideous creature on the deck in front of him, which he proceeded to zap into smoke. The Grish were apparently frightened and running for their lives, seemingly more frightened of the tiny creatures than a rampaging ChronoBot. The good news was, Hardy was back in the fight and, apparently, headed for the ship's barracks.

As for the incursion onto *We Mock the Winds*, the CAPRI and Marines ranks were not faring nearly so well. The original thirty combatants had been reduced to twenty in several serious close-quarters confrontations. The good news was that their high-intensity altercations had drawn the attention away from Max's team, with Captain Tannock, who'd been steadily making their way forward within smaller, less utilized passageways. Periodically, one or even several piglets were caught off guard, whereby Max or one of his team dispatched them quickly and quietly.

"Midship shields are faltering . . . Zone E, Deck 5 and 6 just took a direct plasma blast that almost penetrated all the way through the ship," Pristy said.

"Survivors?"

"I don't see how. There's no one to check on them. As it is, we're losing what limited crew we have."

Utilizing my own projected armrest display, I did a quick run-through of *Hamilton's* operating weaponry. Less than half of her Phazon Pulsar Cannons were active now, while only ten percent of her big Rail Cannons were active. Too few crew and/ or bots to man them. For the tenth time in so many minutes, I considered just jumping the ship away – perhaps several thousand clicks to give us some breathing room. But what then? Leave the enemy fleet to make their way to that Grish Comms Hub within the NorPliet Sector? No, we needed to finish this, somehow. I leaned back in my seat. *Gods of War,* Haite's Apex Heavy, lurked out there at the far edge of the battle. Clearly, the Varapin pilot would have jumped away himself if he'd wanted to share his newly acquired technology. So, we had that in common.

My XO said, "Looks like Max's crew is approaching the Bridge."

* * *

Wanda, fast walking to Tannock's right, had a hand on the older man's elbow to coax him along faster. The rest of the team moved with their shredders held high and tight to their cheeks, sighting down their weapon barrels, ready to pull triggers at the slightest movement up ahead. Periodically, they passed beneath high-mounted security cameras. Hardy's micro wormhole laser link connections had supposedly dealt with these and all other onboard security measures, but she still had the impulse to fire several energy bolts into them.

Max, taking point out front, suddenly lifted a fist into the air. The team stopped, staying perfectly quiet within the passageway. Max looked back and found Wanda's eyes. With a knife-hand gesture, he signaled for her to hurry ahead and reconnoiter what was around the next bend. She moved fast, her boots making zero noise upon the deck plates. Easing up to the corner bulkhead, she stole a quick peek. Pulling back, she signaled back to Max with hand signals – three armed guards, this was the entrance to the Bridge.

Max signaled back, asking her if she could dispatch the guards herself or if she needed more help. Her signal back to him was the middle finger of her right hand.

Stealing another peek around the corner, she saw that the guards were overly relaxed and jabber jawing. Every so often, one turned to look to see what was going on within the Bridge, which cause the other two to mimic his actions. *Idiots.* She waited for the next opportunity and moved with both stealth and speed. She unsheathed the combat knife on her belt as she approached. All three piglets were standing, blocking the entrance with their stout little bodies, deep in conversation about something. She dragged the blade of her knife across the neck of the closest guard and was already stabbing the middle guard before the first had crumpled to the deck. She buried the blade to the hilt in his back, having to guess where the creature's heart was located. Apparently, she'd guessed correctly because he too went down to the deck, never knowing what hit him. The last piglet standing was swinging around and raising his weapon – was opening his mouth to yell out – to warn those within the Bridge. But Wanda was faster. She drove the blade of her knife upward, pinning the piglet's lower jaw shut – like driving a nail upward to secure a flapping trap door. She had to catch his wide-eyed lifeless body and eased it down to the deck. As she dragged each of the three out of the way, the rest of the team approached from down the passageway. Wanda retook her place next to Tannock, and Max maintained his position at point. On Max's three-finger count, they rushed into the Bridge.

About one quarter the size of *Hamilton's*, the compartment was jam-packed with little piglets sitting at multiple consoles. Heads turned, and squeals erupted as they made their way into the Bridge. Wanda had known what to expect here; she, like the rest of the team, had reviewed the layout of the ship in detail beforehand. Grish ships had rising staggered steps or layers to their Bridge compartments, which had a lower-level platform where the main display was located and where the ship's captain typically stood beneath overhead spotlights, like some kind of stage actor. They had entered at the lowest level of the Bridge, and before them, there in the middle of the compartment was the ship's piglet captain. And like everyone else here, he was stymied, paralyzed, at the site of the intruding combat force. Before the captain could bark off one command, Max put a plasma bolt into his forehead.

Wanda gave Captain Tannock two quick pats on his shoulder, "Batter up Captain . . . it's your show now."

Tannock hesitated for a moment, then made his way onto the platform. Behind him, the main display showed the raging space battle, the *USS Hamilton* at the center of things. Wanda chewed the inside of her lip, nervous and waiting for Tannock to say something. This was a crucial moment. Although it was theoretically possible, Tannock could pilot this destroyer on his own; it would be much easier with those crewmembers sitting within this Bridge. *Say something, old man . . .*

He cleared his throat and said, "Who here wants to live to see their families again? Who here wants to avoid being shoved out the closest airlock while still alive and kicking?"

Now that's a rousing way to start a presentation, Wanda thought. She and Grip exchanged a look. He made an *I'm impressed* expression.

One Bridge crew junior officer, who was down close to the platform, timidly raised a hand in the air. Soon, others followed suit. Within twenty seconds, not a soul had opted for the being dragged to the closest airlock, while alive and kicking option. Go figure. Tannock began issuing orders, starting with the retargeting of all weapons upon the three closest Grish warships. Did the Grish Bridge crew move on those orders right away? Certainly not. That was to be expected. Wanda aimed her shredder up high to one particular piglet sitting behind a console on the top level. He sat there looking back at her – the whites of his eyes expanding wide in fear. She fired off two energy bolts into the piglet's head. His body flopped over – his head thumped down onto the control board in front of him.

Immediately, Captain Tannock found his new Bridge crew more amenable to taking his orders. Wanda watched on the main display as *We Mock the Winds* began firing on three Grish warships simultaneously.

Wanda, Ham, Hock, Grip, and Max each took one of the Bridge levels and paced back and forth before the captive bride crew. None of the piglets made eye contact. Wanda noticed several had urinated themselves, and she had to step over moistened deck plates. Listening to the open command channel, she heard Marine Colonel Bonell confirm that the CAPRI and Marines teams had indeed either secured or killed all remaining Grish combatants onboard. The ship was theirs.

*   *   *

At last, some good news, I thought. The Halo-Display was zoomed in on *We Mock the Winds,* as it continued to maneuverer around while firing on those closest of Grish assets. Tannock was in command. Inwardly, I wondered how long he'd be able to keep things together.

Derrota said, "Those Apex Heavy Battleships are substantial warships. Unlike *Hamilton*, all her weaponry is automated." As if to highlight Derrota's point, the closest of the vessels to that battleship was taking a terrible beating from thick, bright scarlet-colored, energy beams. Seeing that it was a Frigate, labeled as such by meta-tag information on the Halo-display, that smaller vessel, at key hull locations, began to spew debris along with atmosphere out into space. The aft propulsion section of the frigate flared bright, and then the entire ship, a thousand tiny porthole windows, suddenly went dark. Like a bloated whale, the crippled ship slowly began to flip over – drifting lifeless within the ensuing space battle.

Chapter 40

The odds had improved, slightly, now it was just one against fifteen. Unfortunately, operating *Hamilton* with such a limited crew would be unsustainable. Creeping into my psyche was the unavoidable realization that the end for *Hamilton*, along with those of us left on board, was imminent. I turned, there was a commotion at the back of the Bridge. To my surprise, Fleet Commander Twinwon was standing there, although he was not looking to be at the pinnacle of health. Slightly hunched, clearly in pain, I saw copious amounts of sprayed-on AugmentFlesh peeking out from the top of his uniform caller. Filing in behind him, were other, still on two feet, Pleidians. These were all that was left of his fleet – I counted twenty-three.

I hefted myself out of the Captain's Mount and headed toward the gathering. I staggered like a drunk sailor, as *Hamilton* shook as constant weapons fire struck the dreadnought from virtually every angle. More had joined the fray. Captain Ryder, Lieutenant Akari James, and fifteen other Arrow pilots pushed their way onto the Bridge. Looking beyond the pilots, more crewmembers were accumulating out in Whale's Alley. I saw craggy-faced Bay Chief Frank Mintz along with what must have been most of his flight bay squad – no less than thirty men and women. And finally, Chief of Security Mattis, along with his remaining security team, about fifteen, hurried to join the party.

Together, Twinwon and Ryder took a step forward. Ryder said, "There we were, lying in our beds feeling like shit –"

". . . And looking like shit," Akari James added.

Ignoring her, Ryder continued, "I got to talking to Twinwon across from me there in HealthBay. We figured we could feel like shit just as easy being useful as we can doing nothing. I made some calls and, well, here we are. I figure there's close to eighty of us here . . . any chance you need a little help manning a few of those big guns? It's not like we'd be loading artillery shells . . . you need people manning the individual weapon's booths, right? The control boards. I think we can handle that."

"Screw that, I can load artillery shells," Akari James said, bringing her arm up and flexing her bicep.

"This isn't World War II, Lieutenant; we use rail spikes, not artillery shells," one of the other Arrow pilots said, laughing.

Ryder offered up a crooked smile.

I stared at my longtime friend, dismayed. I could have kissed him right then and there. "Well, Ryder, I just might have a few open positions for you all. Thank you . . . thank all of you."

I spotted Ensign Plorinne. "Ensign, how about you

coordinate with the XO to assign these crewmembers weapon's posts. They'll need brass tacks instructions."

Aye, Captain, I'm on it."

By the time I was back seated at my own post, I saw that little had changed on the battlefront.

Pristy said, her hands working her board and not looking back at me, "You know, putting that many untrained crews on our big guns may be more trouble than it's worth. It's not as if I don't have my hands full as it is."

"Let's hope they surprise us," I said.

She shrugged; the tension was getting to her.

Keeping an eye on Hardy's video feed, I'd become aware the ChronoBot had slowed his progress substantially – was moving with an obvious tilt to port, and he had an odd gait to his walk – maybe a limp? Only one of his forearm plasma cannons was working. That and he seemed to be spending more and more time taking cover than trudging forward, taking the offense, which would be typical. I found myself having to look away from the feed. I felt sick; my friend was being obliterated right before my eyes – each Grish plasma bolt quickening his demise. I was tempted, again, to talk to him. Maybe offer up some words of encouragement. But no. Hardy wouldn't want that – not now, not like this. He would succeed or he wouldn't – and do so all on his own. Or. . .

Marine Colonel Bonell had drifted over to the far-right side of the Bridge. Standing there with his arms crossed over his chest, he was still barking off orders to his troops. According to the colonel's last Sit Rep, his CAPRI and Marines were now doing final mop-up on Captain Tannock's Heavy Battleship, *We Mock the Winds.*

I gestured to get the colonel's attention. He kept on talking, via his TAC-Band, acting as if he hadn't noticed me.

I looked at the Helm station. "Crewman Grimes, you've mirrored Comms onto your station?"

"That I have, sir."

"Can you break into the colonel's comms?"

"Easy-peasy, Captain."

"Do so."

I watched as the Colonel, looking annoyed, abruptly began tapping on his TAC-Band. Once again, I signaled to him.

He stormed over, a locomotive spewing steam. "What is it, Captain? I'm in the middle of –"

"I need a favor. And I need it now, fast."

"What?"

"I'm pulling Sergeant Max and his squad. I'd like you to replace his team with several of your CAPRI or Marines on the Bridge."

"Absolutely not!"

Hamilton not only shook but audibly groaned as repeated weapons strikes struck the ship somewhere close to the Bridge. The Colonel wavered on his feet, and I had to reach an arm out to steady the man. Angered, he tore his arm free from my grasp.

"You can't just abscond with my people willy-nilly. I told you, you'll need to adhere to proper protocol . . . Remember, I out-rank you when it comes to off-ship operations. And it just so happens, my people are busy."

I leaned over closer to him, smiling, and said, "Coronel, do you take me for a man that would offer up idle threats?"

He made a face, "I don't know, and I don't care."

"Let me be as frank as possible. Ultimately, I am in charge of who and when anyone is transported back onboard *Hamilton*. I assure you, those CAPRI shits of yours will be the very last people brought back onboard. I've noticed the *We Mock the Winds* has been taking a beating. Be a shame, when the time comes, I couldn't get those good men and women out of there in time."

"You wouldn't."

I sat back in my seat and stared at the Halo-Display, looking as calm as a man taking a Sunday drive around the neighborhood.

"Fine, but your actions are getting reported up the line of command. This won't be the end of it."

I chuckled at that. Hell, I was already court-martialed; add the charges to the fucking list. The colonel stomped away, huffing.

"Crewmember Grimes, please connect me to Sergeant Max."

A feed opened up on the display, and his face appeared via his inside helmet cam. "Captain?"

I proceeded to tell Max that he and his squad were about to be transported from *We Mock the Winds* over to *Breath of Guile* and that Hardy was in trouble and needed his help. That he had two minutes to coordinate with Sergeant Major Cash Lipton, for replacements there on that Bridge. After closing the connection, I looked for Derrota. I remembered; he'd been called back into the CIC. I got up and headed for my ready room. Hopefully, Coogong was there and not taking a potty break. The hatch-door slid open as I approached. The compartment was far less bustling than the last time I'd been in here. The three Thine scientists were working on the PE-2, which immediately made me nervous.

"Coogong? Damn it . . . tell me you're not screwing with the PE-2 . . . tell me that the thing is still operational."

Within his oversized looking helmet, Coogong's friendly worm face smiled broadly back at me. The alien was impossible to be mad at. Having reprimanded him, I felt instantly guilty and regretted my words.

"Captain! Good news, we have added six more interface junction connections."

"I don't know what that means."

"Like this pedestal . . . we can add six more just like, all operating in parallel."

"Okay . . . but do you have to work on the thing while we're in the midst of an operation?"

"Oh, nothing we are doing could possibly affect the primary operation of the PE-2 . . . that would be impossible."

"Whatever. I need you to transport Sergeant Max and his squad over to the *Breath of Guile*. Locate Hardy and put them right there next to him."

"So, you need to do a remote transport, from one ship to another."

"Yes, right now, Coogong."

The three Thine scientists all looked at each other. The silence in the compartment was ear-shattering. "Coogong!"

"I'm sorry, um, well . . . that may be a bit of a problem. Yes, I could bring individuals from any of those vessels back here to *Hamilton*, but transporting from another ship to another ship?"

Coogong must have seen the murder in my eyes because he raised his stick finger hand out in front of him. "I only need five minutes. Maybe ten. A few reconnections are all that will be needed."

I left my ready room before I did something I'd regret, like tearing the Thine scientist apart with my bare hands.

Stepping back onto the Bridge, there was yelling, everyone was up on their feet. XO Pristy, a hand to her mouth, turned to look at me. She pointed to the Halo-Display. There, in ultra-high 3D resolution, I witnessed what looked to be a massive aft chunk of *Hamilton,* now drifting free – a thousand sparks flashed upon torn apart power lines. That section of the ship included the dreadnought's flight bay. As if to empathize the awful destruction, no less than 500, mostly bright-red, Arrow fighters were floating out into space.

Pristy, seated back at her station, zoomed in on the sheered away section of the ship. Sure enough, the bay was mostly gone. A few craft were visible, teetering on the remaining ragged edge of the bay deck. One such craft was the old Hub Gunther; it's forward landing strut hanging precariously over the edge into open space.

I reached the Captain's Mount feeling surprisingly calm. I'd heard about this . . . that feeling one gets when they've reached the end of the line. That acceptance of the inevitable, bringing clarity and appeasement to a situation that nothing less than an act of God could rectify.

Chapter 41

I took in the dynamic battle scene on the display. Two more Grish warships were drifting, rudderless – lights out – *thirteen to one.*

Max and team were now on the *Breath of Guile,* and from what I was witnessing, a firefight was ensuing that was impossible to make heads or tails out of. Max's feed was a jumble of quick spins and then a dive for cover as plasma fire zipped past him. I saw a glimpse of Ham (or maybe it was Hock) take a hit on the shoulder, which flared and quickly flamed out; the big man didn't lose a step as he returned fire.

A square of snowy static had taken the place of Hardy's previous video feed. I didn't want to even think about the repercussions of that. If Hardy was no longer capable of piloting that vessel, Max and his team were fighting in vain.

The overhead lights flickered, and then half of them remained off, putting *Hamilton's* Bridge into partial darkness.

PRIMARY POWER COUPLINGS HAVE
BEEN DAMAGED

"Somebody let MATHR know we got the message!" I yelled to no one in particular. Both she and the battle station's klaxon went silent. That was fine; there was no one onboard unaware of our battle stations situation.

The temperature within the Bridge had elevated by at least thirty degrees in the last few minutes, and I didn't know if that was related to the power couplings situation or something else. Both Pristy and Chen were taking off their uniform jackets – perspiration making their wet shirts nearly transparent. My eyes were drawn to Pristy's turned away back, her moistened skin tones showing through the thin fabric. Her lithe form stirred something in me, which of course was totally inappropriate – this was a cataclysmic moment in time, and here I was, gawking? As she stood there talking to Chen, she turned her upper torso just so that I could see the curve of her small breast. She wasn't wearing a bra, and I could see the contrast of the darker pink of her nipples – her eyes suddenly caught mine and held there. *Shit!* A second shared moment between us, when there shouldn't have ever been a first. But denying the truth was becoming more and more impossible for me. At that particular moment, all I wanted to do is take her in my arms, pull her in close, and kiss her.

"Captain! We've got a real problem," Derrota said as he was making his way back from the CIC. "The ship's operating with less than half her power conduits still functional, and those that *are* working, are quickly overheating."

"I guess that explains the rise in temperature in here," I said. I thought I heard a quiet snort from Pristy, now seated back at her station, but maybe it was my imagination. She said, "Propulsion just went down, Captain . . . we're not going anywhere for a while."

Derrota continued, "The problem, Galvin, is we'll lose those few over-taxed, overheating, conduits we have left if we don't start shutting down major systems. Shields are already fluctuating, as indicated by that massive chunk of the ship floating away into space, but it's our big Phazon Pulsars drawing the most power right now."

The lights were indeed now rhythmically dimming in unison to the sounds of distant firings of our energy cannons.

"Well, we need our shields, and we certainly need our Phazons, Stephan."

There have been few occasions I've ever witnessed Stephan Derrota actually losing his cool, his temper. This was one of those times, "Damnit, Galvin . . . this ship is on the verge of going dark. And it won't be just lights out for *Hamilton*; it'll be lights out for the crew as well!"

So, how do I want to go out? I asked myself. As a three-mile-long dreadnought, rudderless and darkened, powerless to fend off her inevitable destruction? Or . . . go out in a blaze of glory? It was time I accepted the inevitable. We, no, *I've* been beaten. This is where the fat lady starts to sing. I could feel the sideways glances from the Bridge crew.

Maybe I could begin transporting what was left of the crew over to Tannock's ship. No. Too little time and nobody would go, anyway. *I wouldn't.* I stared at the Halo-Display. *Huh . . . that's interesting.* The *Breath of Guile,* Hardy's ship, and *We Mock the Winds,* Tannock's, had moved closer to each other. Guns blazing, now both Grish warships were firing on the enemy.

Pop!

Hardy's display feed jumped into life. I held my breath, not sure if what I was seeing was actually real. Sure enough, it was.

"Hardy's on the Bridge . . . he's on the fucking Grish ship's Bridge!" Grimes said from the Helm station. "Sorry," he said, looking around nervously.

"No, that's quite all right, Crewman . . . he's fucking on the Bridge, and that's something to curse about," I said.

XO Pristy said, "That's good and bad . . . look at the rest of the fleet. They're converging in on those two. Concentrating all their weapon's fire on them."

"Can you discern —"

"Condition of their shields?" She said, cutting me off. "Uh, looks like both are in big trouble . . . they have mere minutes, if that, before shields go offline." She shot a glance back at me, anticipating further orders. She said, "Why are you smiling, Captain?"

"Because . . . our Varapin friend just made his first, crucial, mistake. He still thinks he can take *Hamilton,* along with her secrets, as a prize of battle. He knows we're not going anywhere fast, and subsequently, we're not taking much in the way of enemy fire."

Derrota and the Colonel, to the left and right of me, respectively, asked, "What mistake?" at the same time.

I stood up and looked at Derrota, "You told me Grish warships, their weaponry is far more automated than that of *Hamilton*. "Patch me into the command channel for both ships; I need to talk to both Tannock and Hardy, like right now. And patch in my ready room, as well."

Crewman Grimes did as told, and immediately the Bridge filled with the sounds of distant weapons fire along with the mayhem noises one would expect from two fully battle engaged warships.

Hardy's Boston accented, way-too-loud voice seemed to bounce off the surrounding bulkheads. "Good afternoon, Captain! How may I be of service to you today?"

"No time for being a smartass. Do as I say and don't argue."

"Roger that."

"Get that Battleship's weaponry on full auto and prepare to be transported off ship. Do it now. Captain Tannock, I assume you heard my orders for Hardy. Same for you, weapons on full auto, and prepare for transport."

It was several beats before Tannock responded. "Bring me back last, Captain . . . this A-Class Destroyer is far less automated than you might think."

"Coogong, I'm assuming you heard my orders. And if I find out that PE-2 isn't fully functional, I'm going to . . ." I couldn't bring myself to threaten the kindhearted Thine scientist. "Just start transporting my people, okay?"

"Yes, Captain. Hardy is already back onboard and headed your way."

I felt his heavy stride upon the Bridge's deck plates. Several people behind me audibly gasped. I turned to see something almost unrecognizable. Hardy, walking with a gimping limp, and tilting to one side, was a blackened, charred mess. As he approached, I heard straining servo motors whining. His face display was too cratered and marred for there to be any of his typical goofball animations.

"Crewmember John Hardy, reporting for duty, Captain!" he bellowed. He came to a listing stop on the other side of Marine Colonel Bonell.

Amazed the ChronoBot was still standing on two feet, I pointed to him. "Does all that . . . hurt?"

"A little," he said.

"Maybe you should go lie down. Before you fall down."

"No. I'm good," he said.

"Captain, I have an incoming hail for you," Grimes said. "It's not coming from the *Breath of Guile*, or *We Mock the Winds*. It's coming from *God's of War*."

"Haite Caheil," I said, my fists already starting to clench. Has he come to glower at his victory?"

"Um . . . No, sir . . . it's Sir Louis de Broglie. He's using an encrypted channel."

I looked to Derrota with raised brows. "Would he even

know how to do that? Gain access to an encrypted comms channel?"

"He's incredibly smart."

"That and he's an ass," Hardy added.

"Put him up on the Halo-Display."

The French scientist form came into view. He was in a darkened compartment and looked to be hiding. Leaning closer in over a console, his face took up the entire display. "Captain . . . Captain Quintos, ah . . . good, there you are. I am ready to be transported off this miserable ship."

"Oh, you are, are you?"

"Yes, as soon as possible, please."

"I'll think about it. Don't call back; you'll only piss me off more." I signaled for Grimes to cut the connection.

Pristy said, "Coogong's brought Max's team back onboard from *Breath of Guile,* and the last of our Marines and CAPRI teams from *We Mock the Winds* are transporting now. All except Captain Tannock. Apparently, he wishes to stay on board that ship . . . to the end."

I thought about that for a moment. I didn't blame him. He knew his career was over. This would be a way for him to go out with dignity. I nodded. "His choice. Send a message to his TAC-Band . . . Thank you, Sir, for your faithful service to the US Space-Navy and, specifically, the *USS Hamilton.* Godspeed." I waited for her to send the message; she was using her own TAC-Band to do so. Once sent, she nodded at me. "Message, received, Captain."

We watched as Tannock's warship began to move.

"Where the hell's he going?" I asked.

Within the next minute, the destination was clear; he was heading for the Varapin's warship, which was still hanging back at the far fringe of the battle. *Smart.* Enemy fire increased as brilliant scarlet streaks of plasma crisscrossed open space. But *We Mock the Winds* was already beginning to break apart – hull fragments shedding, flaking off like dried pieces of skin.

"Come on, Tannock . . . you're almost there," I said, taking a step closer to the Halo-Display. Everyone was on their feet now. Everyone was cheering for the brave captain to make this one last, *perfect* sacrifice. "Just a little closer and you be right on top of her!"

Pristy said, "*God's of War* is powering up!"

Feeling my heart drop in my chest, I watched as Haite's ship began to move away.

The Halo-Display flashed into distorted bright white. Tannock's ship, *We Mock the Winds,* had blown up. I wasn't sure if it was caused by nearby Grish weapons fire, or it being self-destructed by Tannock himself. It didn't matter. The Bridge went quiet, the loss of one of our own weighing heavily on all. What was clear, though, was that *God's of War* was no longer speeding away. She'd been damaged.

I, and then the rest of the Bridge crew, including Hardy, saluted the Captain's sacrifice.

"Hardy, your sensors operational enough to detect the level of damage to that ship?"

The damaged ChronoBot teetered his head from side to

side. "Propulsion is most definitely offline. Still, a good many lifeforms, including one Varapin asshole, left breathing."

I let out a breath. "MATHR . . . shipwide announcement." She replied, her voice booming from above.

GO AHEAD, CAPTAIN

"All crew personnel . . . those manning Rail Cannons and Phazon Pulsar Turrets . . . abandon your posts. Move fast, people. We need you all to man *Hamilton's* portside Broadsides. I repeat, man the portside Broadside Cannons. If you're unfamiliar with how to operate those big guns, find someone who can. Some of the remaining bots will help. Talk to each other. Work together. You have ten minutes to get situated. Move it!"

Immediately, I heard my voice echoing in from Whale's Alley and beyond. I put a hand on Derrota's shoulder, "Happy? I've done what you asked . . . no more energy weapons heating up our power conduits. Now I suggest you and everyone else on this Bridge start talking to those taking positions at our Broadside turret booths . . . I need all twelve guns, fully operational. That means bowlers need to be loaded and primed."

I knew ten minutes would be a pipe dream. Bowlers were massive. Big bots were used to move them from nearby armories. And like immense bowling balls, each had strategically placed circular finger-like holes all around their circumference.

These holes were the dispersal channels for white-hot magnesium scatter frags – which effectively weakened enemy hull-armor plating a nanosecond just prior to impact. Sure, this was old (relatively speaking) technology, but who says just because something's old that it's not still remarkably effective?

The next ten minutes passed like ten hours.

Chapter 42

"Captain, reports have nine of our port side Broadsides manned and operational," Chen said.

Before I could answer, XO Pristy, next to him, said, "Not good enough . . . Captain said all twelve. Keep at it, Chen."

Chen looked at me and then back to her.

"You heard her, Crewman." I said, "All twelve."

I realized my right foot was nervously gyrating up and down like a jackhammer, and I had to will myself to calm down. The Grish fleet, less preoccupied now by one, instead of two, defector warships, had begun to separate – which was the complete opposite of what I needed to happen. That and *Hamilton* was taking weapons fire again, albeit it was half-hearted. Clearly, Haite had given the order that *Hamilton* was not to be destroyed.

"Eleven Broadsides ready to go with locked on targets. The twelfth . . . well, it's imminent," Chen said, looking pleased with himself.

The deserted and on-autopilot A-Class Destroyer, which

had been firing pretty much non-stop, suddenly blew up. *And what a convenient distraction.* "Fire! Fire Broadsides!" I yelled. I stood there with a fist in the air and waited. Nothing happened.

Pristy, glancing back and suppressing a smirk, said, "Gun crews are not quite up to speed yet . . . give it a second."

. . . And then the big guns began to thunder. *BOOM! BOOM! BOOM! BOOM!* The deck plates beneath my feet shook and rattled with each HoverCar sized bowler blasting away. The Halo-Display became a dazzling cacophony of sparkling tracer trails, a 4th of July extravaganza display like nothing I'd ever witnessed.

The Bridge crew started making *Oooohs* and *Ahaaas,* and Marine Colonel Drake Bonell commented with an "Oh my God . . ."

The first big bowler came into contact with the closest warship target, and that's when the real fireworks began. The resulting explosion was both chilling and exhilarating at the same time. Unlike the previous bright white vaporizing kind of explosions, this was far more satisfying. Almost as bright, but there was an actual short-lived associated massive fireball. Add to that, the ship didn't just disintegrate; it fragmented. Big, ragged chunks of the vessel were propelled outward at tremendous speeds. And just one or two seconds later, the second and then the third Grish warship blew apart in fantastic, dramatic fashion.

"Holy shit . . ." Grimes said.

"Mother of God," Chen said.

All the while, *Hamilton's* Broadsides continued to fire, *BOOM! BOOM! BOOM! BOOM!*

One by one, the Grish fleet was being eviscerated. A modern-day blitzkrieg that nothing could withstand. For another five long minutes, the big guns continued to fire.

"Hold fire!" I ordered over the ensuing racket.

The sound of the big guns went quiet. The rumble beneath my feet settled. The Halo-Display depicted a spatial landscape of near-total desolation. I say *near-total* because there was but one Grish vessel, seemingly, still in one piece amongst the wide swath of ruined and fragmented warships. There within a literal fog of debris and expelled frozen bodies, I saw it. That one ship, having stayed at the far reaches of the battle, was the other Heavy Apex Battleship. It was Haite Caheil's ship.

"Give the order, and we'll finish her off," Pristy said. "Although, I'm picking up substantial radiation spikes. Seems the ship's reactor is overheating . . . going critical and ready to blow is my guess."

I said, "Fuck," under my breath. I just remembered the incoming communication from Sir Louis de Broglie. The little weasel was still on board that ship.

About to ask Coogong to attempt to lock onto and transport the French scientist back onto *Hamilton*, Chen suddenly leaned forward over his board. "What is that?" he said.

Pristy assessed what Chen was referring to. "Captain . . . we're picking up on some strange telemetry, or . . . *something*, from that same Heavy," she said, furrowing her brow. She continued to tap at Chen's board. "Oh no . . ."

"What? What's that *oh no*, about, XO?" I asked.

"Those are, well . . . I think those are transporter signals. But they're different than what the PE-2 puts out."

INTRUSION ALERT
INTRUSION ALERT

I looked to Hardy; he'd be the first to know if there was another incursion onto *Hamilton*. But Hardy was no longer standing there – he was splayed out, face down on the deck.

"Hardy?"

He attempted, unsuccessfully, to raise a mechanical arm. I heard his muffled voice, "I'm ok. I'm good."

Blue flashes, one right after another, were coming in from Whale's Alley in rapid succession. I closed my eyes. *Will this frickin' day ever end?* The sounds of heavy weapons fire pulled me back into the moment.

Looking at his tablet, Derrota said, "Oh my . . . the Heavy's crew, the piglets . . . they're transporting onto multiple Deck locations. All over *Hamilton*!"

I headed toward the entrance to the Bridge. Over my shoulder, I yelled, "You have the Captain's Mount, XO!"

I stopped short at the threshold out of the Bridge. Looking out into Whale's Alley, I saw Max and Wanda had taken cover, their shredders blazing plasma bolts down the length of the passageway. The recently returned CAPRI and Marine teams were farther aft, utilizing the PBC's left behind from the last incursion. As we looked to be already outnumbered three to one, I watched in horror as more Grish combatants were being transported onto my ship. *How? How could this be happening?* I answered my own question. The Varapin had figured out how to make their own version of a PE-2 to work. Viv had said they were very close. Over the subsequent hours, they must have made excellent headway. And now, the enemy was pouring into the ship, like a pirate invasion – one, with our limited crew, that will be impossible to fend off.

Three plasma bolt impacts flared upon the bulkhead SmartCoat near my head; reflexively, I ducked down. *That was way too close.*

It was then that I saw him. An armed piglet had transported in not ten feet away from me. And he saw me too, still ducked down at the entrance to the Bridge. I was armed, a holstered tagger at my belt, but it may as well have been a hundred miles away – no way would I be able to draw and shoot before being shot. Speaking of which, now looking at the muzzle of his energy weapon, *why hasn't he fired?* And why does the piglet have three arms – one of which was protruding out the middle of his chest?

The Grish combatant was pulling the trigger, alright. I could see his little finger tightening over and over again. The problem was, it was the finger on the wrong hand, on the wrong arm – the arm protruding from his chest. Only now did I notice the other weird *anomalies* the poor bastard had incurred from an obviously flawed transportation. One of his piglet ears was dab smack in the middle of his forehead, and he had two snout noses. His eyes seemed to be in the right place, but the guy was clearly a clusterfuck of incongruous body parts. That and he was having a hard time breathing. Huffing and puffing, he looked down, only now realizing he had three arms. A combination of fear and disgust looked back at me. The circus had truly come to town.

"Sorry man . . . can't help you." I stood up, pulled my tagger, and shot him. Twice.

Stepping over the dead piglet, I took another, more appraising look at the combat scene going on before me. Yes, we were outnumbered by a lot. But the Grish combatants were not doing so well. More and more of them were discovering what the piglet I just killed had discovered. That their bodies had been mutated, fucktipated, via that last transport. It's not easy to continue the good fight, realizing your arm, or leg, or your dick, for that matter, is in the wrong place. More than a little distracting, it's a major life-altering event. It was easy to tell; the piglet's hearts just weren't in the fight right now.

I spotted Ham, Hock, and Grip, hunched and moving forward – taking the fight to the enemy. I knew it was dangerous to do so, but I chanced to have a glimmer of hope. Could it be? *That we just might survive this day, after all?*

My TAC-Band was vibrating. It had been for some time now. I saw that it was my favorite Thine scientist. "Go ahead, Coogong."

"Yes, Captain Quintos. I have been contacted by the Earth

human you call Broglie. He would like to be transported back onto *Hamilton* via the PE-2 device."

I had to smile. Good thing he didn't opt for the Varapin's means of transport travel. "Yeah, go ahead and bring him back onboard."

I turned to reenter the Bridge and froze. An odd thought occurred to me. As far as I knew, Haite Caheil had not yet transported onto *Hamilton*. *Oh no . . .*

Chapter 43

I ran to my ready room, had to pause as the hatch-door slid to one side, and then rushed in with my tagger drawn and raised. Coogong was at the controls with the other two standing behind him.

"Stop!"

All three scientists, startled, looked over to me. "Captain Quintos?" Coogong said.

"Don't initiate that transport . . . not until we know who'll exactly be coming over."

"But Captain, we already know . . . the transport process has been completed."

I looked about the compartment, not seeing anyone else other than the four of us.

Coogong said, "They asked to be transported to Deck 10."

"They? Who the hell are *they*?"

"Why, it's Sir Louis de Broglie, of course. Oh, and one other . . ."

I didn't wait for his further explanation. In three running strides, I leaped onto the PE-2's pedestal. "Transport me into HealthBay . . . do it, hurry!"

I materialized within the hospital section of HealthBay. As with the Bridge, only half of the overhead lighting was working, making the space dim and dreary looking. From what I could see, about half of the beds were occupied, slow-turning, skinless, with their internal organs in full view; patient avatars hovered over their beds. There was a constant, high-pitched sound coming from each bed station – heart monitor alarms. The patients were all dead.

I nearly tripped over a body splayed out on the deck. I had to lean down and flip him over onto his back to see who it was. It was Sir Louis de Broglie. I reached down to feel for a pulse at his neck but stopped when the French physicist's eyes suddenly blinked open. I saw recognition in his stare.

"Captain Quintos . . . why are you . . . where am –"

"Where's Haite Caheil? Where's the Varapin?"

He blinked several more times and reached a hand up to his head. His fingers came away bloody.

"Where is he?!" I repeated.

Broglie pointed down the passageway leading into the Surgery Center.

Heading toward the passageway, I came closer to two of the occupied beds. Now, in the semi-darkness, I could see the patient's upper torsos were somewhat elevated, and their faces a ghastly shade of milky grey. Their jaws were agape, their eyes wide in a kind of terrified death glare. The Varapin had been feeding here onboard *Hamilton* – something he hadn't resorted to previously.

As I moved down the passageway, I had to skirt three dead bodies, each wearing light pink scrubs. Checking each, I found that their life force had been sucked from wide-open jaws. I was relieved to find Doc Viv was not among them.

I made a mad dash for the Surgery Center entrance at the end of the passageway. I could see that the double doors were open. Beyond, total darkness awaited.

Stepping inside the surgery center, my eyes adjusted further to the darkness. Only various medical devices: tiny power indicator lights, another hovering avatar somewhere across the space, the green hue was coming off a CutterBot's visual sensor band. That and the unmistakable aqua blue radiance coming off an active TAC-Band. I don't know how I knew, but I knew that it belonged to Viv. She was there, but it was too dark to see her face.

"Are you okay, Viv? Talk to me . . ."

I heard her sniff. I heard nervous inhalations of rapid breaths. Her voice was little more than a whisper, "Don't come any closer, Quintos . . . he has me."

I tried to make out their forms in the gloom. Yes, I could make Viv out now, but not Haite. The ghoul's black robes obscured his presence. And then I saw the whiteness of his exposed jaws.

His scratchy, hideous voice was beyond chilling, "I was so

hoping it would be you. Captain Quintos . . . coming to the rescue of the poor damsel in distress."

"Let her go, Haite. I'm the one you want, right? Tormenting Viv serves no further purpose."

"Oh, but she does. You're so predictable. The two women in your life . . . you do know . . . they are your greatest weakness, Captain. It's that all too human heart of yours . . . it has made you weak . . . vulnerable. And the reason you will do exactly as I say.

I heard a soft tap – and a bulkhead mounted light came on. The Varapin certainly was dramatic; I had to give him that. Haite was seated upon one of the beds, his long robes cascading down off the side. Doc Viv was on her back, her head on his lap. Her ponytail grasped tightly within the clutches of one boney black claw. Her chin was slightly elevated, forcing her mouth to open. The visual provided no doubt what he was ready to do to her.

"Hold on, Haite . . . you hurt her, and you lose all your bargaining power."

Viv said, "You can't bargain with him. Shoot him."

The Varapin's expressions were always tough to read, with that mostly obsidian black skull of a face of his. But I had the feeling, right now, he was smiling.

"One quick tug and twist of my left hand and this woman dies. So, tell me, Captain . . . is she the love of your life. Or is it the other one . . . the one you try so hard not to look at on the Bridge . . . Pristy, isn't it? Do you think the crew of this ship are oblivious to the situation? The truth is, if you think about it, I will be doing you a favor. Make your decision making easier by removing one of these women from the equation." He tightened his grip on her ponytail, causing her lips to open wider.

"What do you want? Just tell me! Look . . . I can assure you safe transport off *Hamilton*.

His eyes, two small pea-sized orbs, stared back at me. "I honestly find it hard to comprehend how you do it."

"Do what?"

"Bumble your way to success. You're not particularly intelligent, human. You have little command experience . . . so how is it you rise to the occasion, time and time again? A fleet of eighteen Grish warships against a lone, undermanned, dreadnought. The outcome should have been simple." He shook his head in frustration.

Viv was trying to say something – I could see the tendons in her neck flexing. It came out as a whispered croak, "He . . . no longer. . . hovers."

I didn't know what that meant.

Haite Caheil continued, "I will take you up on your offer. With other stipulations."

"What other stipulations?"

"First, you will have the PE-2 device moved to the cargo area of your Hub Gunther vessel. And yes, I know that vessel remains, still intact, within what is left of your destroyed flight bay. Second, the three Thine scientists will be escorted to that craft, also to be secured into the cargo area."

"Anything else?"

"You will allow me safe passage onto the vessel and allow the Gunther to leave local space unaccosted. Oh, and I will be taking the Doctor here along with me, just to ensure my safe passage. I will return her to you at a later date if all my conditions are met to my satisfaction."

"Don't . . . do . . . it." Viv croaked, her eyes going wider with the strain of talking.

I just stared at the wretched alien wondering how far I would go to keep this woman alive. Would I give up Space-Navy's most prized new secret technology? Was Haite Caheil right? Was I in love with her? And maybe with Pristy as well? Fuck it; there was no way I would let this monster leave this ship – there had to be a way out of this. What had Viv meant, *He . . . no longer. . . hovers.*

"Time to decide her fate, Captain. Will she live or die?"

I knew what she meant now. Somehow, maybe during the transport process, the Varapin had lost his ability to hover. Just looking at him now, actually sitting when he most typically would be hovering, proved the point. He had lost one of his most dominant physical advantages. I had to do something and do something now. *But what?*

I actually felt the answer come to me more than I thought it – a small, consistent pressure poking me at the small of my back. The little box Wanda had clipped onto my belt. And within that box, when activated, were none other than Drole, Shred-Ma, and Chi. I nodded to Haite, acting as if, sure, I would comply with his demands. I said, "Initialize Combat Avatars . . . Attack!"

Nothing happened other than Haite Caheil tensing, forcing Viv's head back even farther and causing a desperate moan to escape her mouth. The Varapin relaxed some, seeing there actually was no imminent danger. "You are a fool, human, and I am tired at your – "

The first invisible punch hit him at the right side of his head. Not sure if it had been Moe, or Shred-Ma, making that strike. So surprised was he, he loosened his grip on Viv's ponytail. She jerked herself free and dropped to the deck gasping for breath.

"Get out of here!" I yelled to her while raising my tagger and pulling the trigger. Three plasma bolts struck Haite, two in the shoulder and one in the chest. Not bad shooting, considering I hadn't had time to aim.

In a blur of motion, I saw Viv, crouching low and scurrying away on all fours. And at the same time, I saw the Varapin leap towards me, arms outstretched – his incoming bony claws coming for my neck. And in that brief Nano-second of time, Wanda's profound words came to me.

"Look, Quintos . . . you're never going to be a great fighter. Hell, you're just not all that big and strong. And you're not particularly intuitive or smart, either. Sorry, it's just a fact. And there's just not going to be enough time for you to learn the various martial arts disciplines . . . so I'm going to teach you to fight as ruthless and dirty as humanly possible. We'll start by practicing these ten offensive attacks. Using Grip as a test dummy, she proceeded to show me. First miming the actions in slow motion, then, faster, actually making physical contact with Grip, who took the abuse, but clearly nor liking it. She demonstrated each dirty fighting attack:

1. Open Palm Ear Slaps

2. Head Butt to Nose
3. Vicious Carotid Neck Bite
4. Spinning Elbow to Face
5. Hammer Punch to Face
6. Pull and Squeeze the Gonads
7. Repeated Eye Jab with Knife Fingers
8. Fishhook Fingers to Mouth
9. Repeated Groin Stomps
10. Grab an Arm and Side Kick into Ribs

"Look, Quintos," she said, as Grip attempted to recover from the abuse, "You must be as vicious and ravenous as a rabid dog . . . do you hear me? You do not give up . . . you do not ever fucking give up."

Over time, I had continued to learn more martial arts techniques above and beyond those ten go-to moves. But at this particular Nano-second of time, I would be hard-pressed to react with anything other than these well-practiced reactions.

I was spared Haite's death-lurch for my neck by Moe's delivering an incredible jumping front kick, landing the blow to the Varapin's lower jaw. I didn't hesitate, adding a number 4, the spinning elbow to the face. I felt something crack and crunch. Spinning away from him, I saw Haite's lower jaw was now somewhat askew.

With incredible speed, the alien was upon me. Boney claws taking hold of me, ripping, tearing, at my shoulders – he lifted me up and tossing me like a rag doll some twenty feet across to the far side of the Surgery Center. It was just by chance I landed upon a hospital bed with a patient lying upon it. A dead patient, thanks to another of Haite's previous feedings. But the limp body had broken my fall, just the same. Barely able to extricate myself from floppy dead limbs, I saw Haite was already coming for me.

I took a punch to the cheek that brought tears to my eyes, not to mention flashing stars. Before I could collect my wits, I felt his claws, first left then right, swipe across my chest – causing my flesh to tear – to rip open. I felt a virtual waterfall of blood streaming down my torso. The agony was paralyzing and like nothing I had ever experienced. Wanda's words came to me once more. *"You must be as vicious and ravenous as a rabid dog . . . do you hear me? You do not give up . . . you do not ever fucking give up."*

I blinked away the moisture in my eyes. Gasping for breath, all I was positioned for was a *number 1.* With open cupped hands, I gave it everything I had – I whacked my palms onto both sides of the ghoul's head. *Smack!* I'd assumed Varapin anatomy was similar to that of human's – that he had an ear positioned there at each side of his ugly head. The screech that bellowed from Haite Caheil's crooked jaws was both frightening and satisfying at the same time. Being so supremely buffeted, two gargantuan smacks that Wanda would have been proud of, the Varapin was now bent over, reaching for his obviously blown out eardrums. Although a number *6, Pull and Squeeze the Gonads,* would have been most gratifying, I seriously doubted he had a set of big balls hiding there beneath those flowing robes of his. I settle for a number *10 – Grab an*

Arm and Side Kick into Ribs. I snatched up one of those skeletal wrists of his, one still planted to the side of his head and yanked it in toward me. That move coincided with me delivering an epic side kick to the side of his torso – perhaps his ribs, if he had any of those in there. But, there again, according to the sounds of bones *snapping,* yup, he indeed had ribs.

I stepped away to catch my breath. Staggering, I clutched a hand to my bloodied chest and regretted doing so, reigniting a lightning strike of more pain.

Like three distorted waves of heat signatures rising off hot pavement, I saw my invisible combat avatars moving in. It looked to be a Tang Soo Do spinning heel kick to the head, but it was hard to tell in the dim light and the whole being-invisible thing. What I do know, the whack Haite Caheil's noggin, was a good one. The other two avatars, not to be outdone, pounced.

I was honestly tempted to call a halt to what would be a beat down of epic proportions but didn't. I let Drole, Shred-Ma, and Chi have their fun. That, and I was feeling a tad light-headed. Wavering on my feet, it was lights out – I dropped like a sack of hammers.

* * *

I woke up sometime later beneath the covers of a hospital bed. I swallowed and grimaced. *Ouch!* I felt AugmentFlesh tight across my chest wounds. I felt her presence then. She was sitting next to me on the side of the bed – the warmth of her body pressed up against me. Gentle fingers moved a few strands of hair off my forehead.

"You really are an idiot, Quintos . . . you know that, right?"

I opened my eyes to see concern looking down at me. Slowly, Viv shook her head. "He almost killed you. The blood loss should have –"

I cut her off, "Well, I guess it's a good thing I was already here in HealthBay, and I had a somewhat adequate surgeon nearby."

She didn't even attempt a quip back. I could see there were raw emotions there in her eyes, brewing just below the surface.

Changing the subject, I said, "The ship? The crew? The Varapin?"

She shrugged, "A lot has happened while you've been napping. You've been out for six days. Let's start with the Varapin. He is alive and recovering from his multiple injuries within the ship's brig. He will be dealt with by high command, I'm told. As for your ship . . . Chief Porter managed to get propulsion back online, allowing us two large jumps toward home before the jump coils blew. After that, your XO managed to get an encrypted communique to one very busy Admiral Cyprian Block at US Space-Navy Space Command. The situation was explained to him, whereby he's ordered this operation to remain top secret. Officers and crew alike are to never, ever, to speak of what happened there within deep Frontier Space. The USS Javelin, a Space Carrier, has been deployed to intersect with us. Give us a tow. It'll be a few days before that happens . . . give you a tad more time for you to recover."

"Recover enough to return to my jail cell, I said.

She smiled and looked like she wanted to say something more. Again, emotions were close to the surface with her. It was a side of her I hadn't seen before. A softer side. Her next words were just above a whisper, "Thank you for saving my life, Galvin." She leaned down and kissed me on the lips.

She never calls me by my first name.

She stood up suddenly and put on a smile. "I have other patients to attend to. You've got a few visitors waiting if you're up for it. You're XO, for one." She held my gaze for a long moment before heading off.

Things were getting complicated.

Epilogue

There had been little time to lie about in a HealthBay bed recovering. I still had a poor excuse for a ship to skipper – and the remnants of a crew to attend to.

While waiting to intersect with the *USS Javelin,* I toured, with SWM Crewman LaSalle at my side, *Hamilton's* many battle-torn damaged areas. Deck by Deck – Zone by Zone, we walked the crippled ship, mostly in silence. The beating the dreadnought had withstood, at the hands of the Grish fleet, was beyond catastrophic. It wasn't long before realization set in, this ship, *my ship,* was far beyond repair. She would be decommissioned – towed off to some deep-space salvage port, where piece by piece, she would be sold off for scrap. As much as my chest still hurt from Haite Caheil's attack, it was my heart that was most affected. The feelings of loss were almost too much – A ship I had come to love, and too many dead crewmembers having given the ultimate sacrifice. I thought about Captain Tannock's last heroic and selfless moments. He went out on his own terms—what more could a space Captain ask for?

Before the crew would leave the *USS Hamilton* for the last time, I took time to meet with each and every one of them. For some, it was a few minutes of laughing and reminiscing with good friends like Chief Aron Porter, Captain Wallace Ryder, and Stephan Derrota. In the end, though, it was bittersweet. Goodbyes, such as these, are often symbolic milestones in our lives – the end of one chapter and the beginning of something new. But the hardest goodbyes were the three people in my life I cared for most: my XO, Gail Pristy, Doc Viv, and the all-too-human ChronoBot. My true affection for these individuals was unique to each of them. So, I had decided not to say goodbye, but *so long* . . . who knows, maybe our military careers or even personal lives would cross paths again at some point.

Once the *USS Javelin* arrived, everyone, the entire crew, was quickly taken aboard. *Hamilton* was no longer deemed safe. With *Hamilton's* hatch door secured and latched with a loud, definitive, *Clang!* I suddenly found it hard to swallow—hard to breathe. Standing at the airlock's observation window, it wasn't long before the *Javelin's* big thrusters flared to life, and moments later, the Space Carrier was rocketing away. Soon, the warship's white exhaust flame was indecipherable from the other bright points of light within deep space. I waved half-heartedly, wondering if either Gail Pristy or maybe Vivian Leigh was standing at a similar window looking back this way.

But I wasn't completely alone. Left behind with me was what was left of Hardy. His prone girth was currently being supported by a straining overtaxed hover cart. With my hand resting upon a blackened and cratered arm, I pushed him along the passageway. I spoke to him as if he were conscious. Sure, Derrota had assured me, the robot was completely deactivated, but still, a part of me hoped he could hear me.

"I hear you're going to get the full hero's treatment, Hardy. Get all those blackened plasma craters buffed out. And we'll get LuMan's bio-AI processor serviced, along with any hardware issues needing work. I did notice you were walking with a limp there at the end and that you listed to one side a bit. Yeah, so, all that will get fixed . . . get you back in proper form, buddy . . . like new." I stared at the heap of blackened metal and wondered if he really could be repaired. Or, like *Hamilton*, was he too, too far gone to be repaired and destined for the scrap heap? Not if I had anything to say about it.

MATHR announced that another vessel was just now coming up along on *Hamilton's* starboard side, and hull clamps were being engaged. We arrived in time to see the Hatch door being opened. Beyond, an attached jetway was visible. It was the Pleidian Weonan freighter, *Titangig*, which sounded similar enough to the iconic *Titanic*, to make me nervous. I let out a long breath – our ride was here.

Within several minutes, a couple of Pleidian crewmembers dressed in helmeted white environ suits were coming down the jetway and had entered *Hamilton*. Both offered me the Pleidian Weonan version of a salute and proceeded to maneuver Hardy's hovercart around and pushed it back onto the jetway. I waved to the ChronoBot as he disappeared into the other ship.

Realizing it would take some time for *Hamilton* to be configured for being towed out of the system, I headed forward, meandering down one oppressively silent passageway after another. So deep in thought, reminiscing my time upon these decks, within these bulkheads, I was surprised at having already reached the Bridge. Striding forward, I took in the unoccupied space—it seemed so much larger now. I took a seat upon the Captain's Mount and sat there in the eerie quiet. The dreadnought's propulsion system and most of the ship's other major systems had been taken offline.

My TAC-Band vibrated—it was the Captain of the *Titangig.*

"Captain Quintos, I am Captain Panroll Fithe. We will be departing within the next few minutes. When you are ready, please come aboard."

I extricated myself from the Captain's Mount and headed for the Bridge's exit. I stopped and took one last look around the Bridge. I said, "MATHR . . . it has been an honor serving with you."

THE HONOR HAS BEEN MINE, SIR. GODSPEED CAPTAIN QUINTOS

Two Days Later . . .

We arrived within Pleidian space with little to no fanfare. Here, I was quickly offloaded onto another Pleidian vessel, this one a non-descript Frigate called the *Lorr Racken.* We parted ways with the *Titangig* and *Hamilton,* both destined for some distant Pleidian spaceport. Soon, the *Lorr Racken* was making fast progress toward Earth. Upon arriving at my small, albeit clean, quarters, I found neatly folded bright orange prison overalls lying upon my bunk, and the reality of my situation hit me like a punch to the nose. Although there had been no orders requiring me to do so, I kept primarily to my quarters for the remainder of the voyage—a voyage back to Earth, where I'd be facing a court-martial for the murder of multiple US Space-Navy crewmembers.

I was awakened by my vibrating TAC-Band on the third night at precisely 0300 hours. I was given thirty minutes to get dressed and be ready to debark. When the knock came at my door, I stood and tried to clear my mind of what was to come. Undoubtedly there'd be a court-martial conviction. I'd heard nothing more from Admiral Cyprian Block about my case. A bad sign. Sure, he'd said he would try to help - to do what he could to influence the Judge Advocate General proceedings. To stress, there had been special circumstances . . . that this had not been a cut-and-dry situation. As I now walked aft down a narrow passageway, between my two-armed Pleidian guards, I felt, for the first time, humiliation. *Shit!* This was really happening. My career as a US Space-Navy Captain was over.

I was expecting to be taken to the ship's flight bay where we'd be loaded onto a jump shuttle—from there, flown down to the surface. Instead, I was hustled off to a different mid-ship compartment. And by the looks of things, it was a clean-room type area. All kinds of high-tech gear was about - active 3D displays hovered at various workstations, and the people here all wore long white lab coats. Up ahead, surrounded by a number of scientists, I recognized one specific piece of equipment—it was the PE-2 device from *Hamilton*.

One of the scientists turned around as we approached. I was surprised to see it was none other than Coogong. Within his helmet, his Thine worm-like features beamed with delight at seeing me. "Captain Quintos . . . I am so very happy to see you again." He brought his stick finger hands up in a kind of welcoming greeting.

"Coogong . . . uh, how did you get here? Get on board this ship?" I then noticed his two Thine colleagues were here amongst other Pleidian scientists.

"It has been a whirlwind of activity. Took several rush-jumps and then getting the PE-2 transferred here, onto the *Lorr Racken* . . . well, it has been a challenge."

"Okay . . . so, what exactly is happening here?"

"Up, up . . . we're on a tight schedule, Captain," Coogong said, ushering me up onto the PE-2's glowing pedestal.

"Where am I going, Coogong?"

The three Thine stood behind the connected console; all were busy tapping away at the control board. Whatever was happening, it was happening now. "Are you sure this thing is working . . . you've tested it since moving it here, right?"

Coogong looked up from what he was doing, "Tested? No . . . no time, Captain. They are coming for you as we speak. You are due in court." He tapped at his control board once more, and in a sudden flash of blue light, and I was gone.

And in an identical bright flash of blue light, I found

myself standing within my CCU Norfolk Naval Station detention cell. Three walls of cold hard cement and one wall of metal bars surrounded me. I was back in the brig. And there, sitting on my bunk reading a book, was . . . *me.*

My Galvin Quintos Symbio-Poth looked up, clearly startled by my abrupt appearance, and smiled. "You sure like to cut things close . . . like right down to the wire, man."

He sounded just like me. "Down to the wire?" I said.

In the distance, a metal gate clanged and rolled open. Footfalls echoed. Murmured voices signaled their imminent approach.

My Galvin Quintos Symbio-Poth stood up, looked down to the bunk, and then around the confined space. He shrugged, "I guess that's it, then."

Before I could say anything, the Symbio-Poth began to melt. It was as if his body was made of soft clay and placed beneath a downpour of water. His flesh, his hair, his internal organs – even his skeleton – had been turned to gelatinous gooey puddle on the floor within seconds. Even his orange overalls were indecipherable from the rest of the messy slop.

Admiral Cyprian Block and two other officers approached from down the hall. I recognized the other two as being my JAG attorneys. Coming to a halt on the other side of the bars, he looked me over, his bushy brows knitted together questioningly. Then he noticed the congealed mess on the floor.

"Captain Quintos?"

"Admiral."

"Everything . . . in order here?"

I took his question to really mean, *did I accomplish my mission as instructed.* "Yes, sir . . . everything is fine."

The Admiral gestured with his chin toward the gate. "Open it up, Lieutenant."

I said, "I need to change . . . should be wearing my uniform before I go before the Trial Judiciary. I'm pretty sure the Chief Trial Judge won't appreciate my prison garb."

The metal gate rolled open on complaining metal wheels. Block waved fingers, "Come on. Out. . . . and watch your step."

Admiral Block made another subtle gesture, and the two JAGs moved off in front of us. "I expect a full sit report by the end of the day, today. Leave nothing out."

"I take it you've talked to XO Pristy . . . that you know—"

"Yes, yes, I've already received her sit report. It seems you go through dreadnoughts like most officers go through changes of underwear."

There wasn't much I could say to that, so I said nothing.

"You'll be happy to hear; you've been cleared of all charges. In fact, your conduct was found to be exemplary. I wouldn't be surprised if you were awarded another damn medal." He stopped, waved the others to continue on, and turned to me. "I'm sorry, Galvin. I'd put you into an unwinnable situation. Captain Tannock was a fine officer . . . but, hearing how he died, the final sacrifice he'd made, well perhaps it was for the best."

"Yes, sir. He died with honor."

"Unfortunately, he will never be recognized for his sacrifice, nor any of the others that died on that mission. A mission that never took place."

"And the loss of the *USS Hamilton*?"

"Yes, a little more difficult to hide something like that. But, there again, the vessel was a loaner."

"From me."

The Admiral smiled, making an exasperated expression. "Yeah, sorry about that. Has got to sting . . . a loss like that."

"Sting?"

Again, the Admiral smiled. "But hey, you got your freedom back. That's got to account for something, right?"

All I could do is nod as we continued on through the indistinguishable maze of concrete hallways.

It was two full hours before I was officially signed out, dressed into my Captain's uniform, and walked outside by Admiral Block.

Together we stood beneath the mid-day Virginia sun. "Galvin, you need to take some time for yourself. You've been through a lot."

"The war's not letting up, sir. I'm ready for my next assignment – if there's a ship available. Doesn't have to be anything special . . . a Frigate, maybe a Gun Ship, or Destroyer?"

"I'm sorry, Galvin. I have nothing for you. Not right now."

A shiny black military HoverCar arrived, as if on cue. "My ride," he said.

He saluted, and I offered my best salute back. As he turned to leave, I said, "What am I supposed to do now, Admiral?"

He was already hustling over to an open car door. Over his shoulder, he said, "Wait there for a spell."

The door slammed shut, and the military HoverCar sped off. *Wait here for a spell? Seriously?*

After being transported several times by now, I knew that familiar *feeling*, kind of a sickening mental blur, the moment it started to occur. In a bright flash of blue light, I disappeared from the entrance of CCU Norfolk Naval Station. What I didn't expect to happen was then reappearing and transporting over and over again, no less than six times, each at different locations. First onto US Space-Navy warship, then a space station (one I briefly recognized as Colby Cross Space Station), then a prison barge, another warship, this time a Pleidian vessel, and finally, a Pleidian space-port I recognized as Stoiling Build Base.

It took several moments for the vertigo and nausea to recede. A one jump destination transport was bad enough. Six was awful. *And how was doing that even possible?*

Glancing around, I was standing within a deserted ultra-new-looking Passenger's Arrival Concourse. Stoiling Build Base was newly built and, last I'd heard, was yet to open for business. In actuality, this was a Pleidian ship-building mega space station.

I wasn't surprised to see who was here, awaiting my arrival. Empress Shawlee Tee was wearing a long robe comprised of multiple layers of sheer light blue fabric. Today, she was wearing a crown of what looked to be made of hundreds of glistening diamonds. She glowed blue, as all Pleidians did, but for some reason, she always seemed to glow the brightest amongst her people.

She squealed with delight at seeing me and ran to me. Arms open wide. "I love you, Galvin Quintos . . . I love you, I love you, I love you!"

She flew into my arms and nearly bowled us both over.

"Do you know what you did? Do you have any idea how remarkable that was?!"

"I'm glad you're happy, Empress—"

She stopped me with a serious look, and I said, "Sorry, I mean, Shawlee."

You brought Twinwon back to me. The love of my life . . . the future father of my children."

Before I could say anything, she continued, "And the price was high . . . I know that, Galvin. I'm so, so sorry. It was selfish of me. Pushing you to take on that operation. I do that . . . put great demands on the people I care about most. And you're not even Pleidian Weonan."

Looking at me, she took my hands in hers, "I am also aware that your – nor your crew's – bravery can ever be acknowledged by your military. Because this was what you would call a *black ops mission*, yes?"

"That's about the size of it. It's fine, what we accomplished . . ."

Shawlee cut in, "Was simply amazing. The rescuing Twinwon, but also defeating that horrid Varapin, Haite Caheil. Not to mention an entire Grist fleet, how was that even possible. Galvin? Oh, and you kept the Transporter technology out of enemy hands . . ."

"Shawlee, you didn't have to bring me here to thank me.

And you've done more than your share for me, as well. My time spent upon *Hamilton* will always be very special to me."

"A ship I put in harm's way. A ship beyond repair, I'm afraid. Although, I have had my best shipbuilders make an evaluation, just in case." She shook her head, "It saddens me to say, it cannot be repaired."

I knew as much, but it stung to hear the words just the same.

"Come, let me show you something." She took my hand and led me to the closest floor to ceiling window. What I saw beyond took my breath away. This was a ship-building space hub like nothing I've ever encountered. For miles in both directions, warship after warship, all in various stages of completion, were being built.

"There must be over a hundred ships being constructed here," I said.

"More than that, Galvin. Twice that many. Heavy Cruisers and Star Cruisers, Great Battleships too." She looked at me, her expression as serious as I'd ever seen her. "Any of them, you name it, it's yours. My gift to you."

I let out a long breath and shook my head. "No, Shawlee. I appreciate the gesture. The kindness you offer. But—"

"Okay, okay . . . I knew you would say that. Forget about these stupid ships. Come with me. Hurry, this way . . ."

She still had my hand in hers as she dragged me all the way across to the other side of the concourse to another ceiling to floor observation window. As many ships being constructed on the other side, it was mirrored here as well. I gazed out and shook my head – *so many warships.*

"No, you're looking the wrong way. With her hands on my shoulders, she physically turned my body to face the opposite direction to see the ships being built that way. But ships weren't being built in that direction. I simply stared, slack-jawed.

She said, "A little birdy told me that when the *USS Hamilton* was originally commissioned, she was one of three."

"Was that little birdy named LaSalle?" I asked.

She nodded, an impish smile on her lips.

"At the time, all three dreadnoughts were of unparalleled military prowess. *USS Hamilton, the USS Adams* and the *USS Jefferson*," I said, looking at the two immense dreadnoughts.

"I've got the budget to refurbish one of them . . .. which one do you want, Galvin?"

My eyes locked onto the *USS Jefferson*. It was run down and in need of refurbishing's, but I had to admit . . . she was a fine-looking ship.

The End

Thank you for reading **USS Hamilton – Broadsides** book three in this series. If you enjoyed this book, PLEASE leave a review on Amazon.com—it really helps!

To be notified the moment the next and all future books are released, please join my mailing list. I hate spam and will never, ever share your information. Jump to this link to sign up:

http://eepurl.com/bs7M9r

Acknowledgements

First and foremost, I am grateful to the fans of my writing and their ongoing support for all my books. I'd like to thank my wife, Kim—she's my rock and is a crucial, loving component of my publishing business. I'd like to thank my mother, Lura Genz, for her tireless work as my first-phase creative editor and a staunch cheerleader of my writing. I'd also like to thank Sarah Mayor for her fine work editing the manuscript as well. Others who provided fantastic support include Lura and James Fischer and Stuart Church.

Made in the USA
Middletown, DE
14 December 2021

55924225R00243